MW01132504

ISLANDS OF DEATH
ISLANDS OF VICTORY

By

John Bailey

To Brian & Judy
Thank you so much.
Semper Fi.
John Bailey - 6-8-18

ISBN: 0-7596-8046-9

This book is printed on acid free paper.

1stBooks - rev. 04/02/02

AUTHORS DEDICATION

This book is dedicated to Naomi, my long suffering and understanding wife of fifty-five years, and to my two lovely daughters, Joan and Brenda who have been so much help and an inspiration. To my two strong sons John and Steven, to Mom and Dad whose prayers sustained and brought me home. And to all the others who have been so supportive.

But most of all it is dedicated to those who never came back.

NAOMI'S DEDICATION

The real heroes lay on far away islands
White crosses mark their resting place
They gave all for family and country
And paid the price for you and me
We owe them a debt of gratitude
That we all might be free

CONTENTS

1. Slaughter Of The Innocent 1

2. In The Beginning 6

3. Training Camps 10

4. Outbound 19

5. Noumea 23

6. One Average Day 26

7. The Gang 30

8. Gookville 32

9. Idle Hands 35

10. Australia 39

11. New Guinea 47

12. New Britain I 52

13. New Britain II 67

14. Pavuvu I 78

15. Pavuvu II 86

16. The Hunger 91

17. One Night 112

18. Hot Lips Brown 117

19. Return To Pavuvu 119

20. Malaria 128

21. Mail Call 132

22. Preparations 138

23. To Okinawa 142

24. L—Love Day 154

25. First Days 161

26.	The Kamikaze	164
27.	The Woman	174
28.	The Old Man	177
29.	The Little Kids	180
30.	Ramah	183
31.	Naha	185
32.	The Ridges And Valleys	192
33.	Too Young To Die	201
34.	Premonitions	204
35.	The Valley Of Death	206
36.	No Greater Love	213
37.	Shuri's Shadow	215
38.	The Coward	225
39.	Screaming	227
40.	Angel Of Mercy	231
41.	Deep Dark Pits	232
42.	The Cave	233
43.	The Light	238
44.	Awake	243
45.	The Search	244
46.	First Glimpse	246
47.	Guardian Angel	250
48.	The Touch	254
49.	The Night Winds	258
50.	The River Of Life	261
51.	Teaching-Learning-Trusting	266
52.	Kim Li	271

53. The Footprint 274

54. The Rescue 277

55. The Hulk 282

56. The Weapon 287

57. Searching 294

58. The Murder 298

59. Peace 302

60. The Final Surrender 306

61. The Soldier 311

62. Going Home 313

63. Conclusion 324

64. Unit Citations 325

65. Postlude 329

66. The Wounds That Don't Show 331

67. Post Script 333

SLAUGHTER OF THE INNOCENT

Where does a story start? Is there ever a beginning, or for that matter, an ending? Stories, like life, have no point in time one could call a beginning. Have not all things been leading up to them since before the beginning of time? Will they cease just because the teller has returned to the dust? Does that stop them from ever having been?

Peleliu, Palau, kind of rolled off young Ted Alexander's tongue, but who had ever heard of such a place? Was it just a name some one in operations had made up? No, it was a real enough spot, one of the tiny Caroline Islands. To Ted it sounded more like a place of peace and solitude, a place to vacation, instead of a place to wage war.

It was a tiny dot of land in the Mid Pacific, only about two miles wide and five miles long. The importance the Japanese and Americans placed on Peleliu far exceeded its size.

The Japanese had constructed an airstrip on the small plot of level ground that the island contained. The American Naval planners thought it was needed to protect the Armies advance into the Philippines. Little did anyone dream of the fortifications and preparations the Japs had made for holding it.

Briefings aboard the transports carrying the Marines to the invasion said it would be another Tarawa, short and fierce. Forty-eight bloody hours should secure the island. In seventy-two hours the Marines would be back aboard ship, heading for the island of monotony, Pavuvu, Russel Islands.

Ted thought someone in the high command must have failed to inform the Japs of the timetable for they had other ideas concerning this island.

For days the small convoy steamed toward Peleliu and each day Ted sat in on briefings. Every regiment, every company, every platoon, and every squad had its assigned landing point. Beach White One, Beach White Two, Beach Orange One, Beach Orange Two, and Beach Orange Three, it all sounded so simple, so routine, so easy.

The big guns of the Americans battleships, cruisers, and destroyers were to knock out "all" of the Japanese gun emplacements. All the Marines had to do was go in and mop up what was left of the Japanese soldiers.

In again, out again, no more rotting in the jungles for months like in New Guinea, and New Britain. Everyone knows the human body can take most anything for a short period of time.

The Marines had been aboard one of the crowded troop transports for two weeks, practicing landings, eating the slop dished up, sleeping on the broiling hot steel decks, waiting, waiting, waiting. On the night before an invasion sleep seldom came easy, if at all. Ted knew that many were going to pay the price this day, and his number just possibly might come up.

The little convoy of troop transports anchored several miles off shore, well out of range of any gun emplacements that could be left on Peleliu.

Ted was up on deck in the early morning, before real daylight. He could hear the reports of the firing of the Navies big guns; see the flames leap from the guns of the old battleships as they laid down broadsides on the island's defenses. He could see the smoke boiling up from the island's interior and the runs of the aircraft that were bombing, and strafing the beaches. It didn't look like a pleasant place to be going into.

The first glimpse of Peleliu struck fear in the young men's minds as they prepared to attack

Ted donned a full combat pack and weapons. Over the side and down the cargo nets, into the bouncing Higgins boats, which would take him in closer to the island.

Transfer into the slow, awkward, amphibious tractors to cross the treacherous coral reef that encircled Peleliu. Navy Frogmen were to have blown passageways through the coral reef to allow the amphibious tractors to reach the various beaches.

To Ted it all sounded so simple so easy. Good old Yankee ingenuity, with the strength and resources of the greatest nation in the world to back him up. "No more targets," the navy war ships had reported. "A piece of cake."

The big guns fell silent, the planes of the air support withdrew, and the amtracs headed for the reef. How agonizingly slow they crawled, yet their motors were revved up to full R.P.M.'s, straining to get every ounce of power available. There was a taste of fear on the air. Where were the passages for the amtrac to go through? At high tide Ted could see nothing but huge breakers crashing on the reefs. The amtracs crawl up on the reefs, get stuck, try to back off, and flounder around in the breakers. Find another likely looking place, and try time, after time to cross. Many were stuck permanently, or roll over and spill the occupants into the water where they were slashed to pieces on the razor sharp coral, or drowned with all their equipment on. With super human efforts, some of the drivers managed to get their vehicles over the reef and into the lagoon beyond.

The splashes started slowly, but soon the Japs shells were exploding all around, and their mortar fire was devastating. Ted found out later that the Japs big guns were mounted on railroad tracks, concealed in caves with the reef pinpointed for accuracy. When the ships guns stopped firing the Japanese rolled their guns out and started firing at the landing craft.

Amtracs all up and down the reef were burning, great plumes of black smoke was everywhere. All around Marines were in the water, struggling to stay afloat with all their gear on. Others were floating around, some face up, and some face down, their life preservers of no more benefit to them.

A few men had found footing and were advancing on the beach. The amtrac in which Ted was riding slowly crawled up on the reef. Grinding and scraping it stood on end, surely it was going to tip over. A big wave, a mighty lurch, and miraculously, it cleared the reef and had entered the "calm (with big shells and mortar rounds exploding all around) lagoon," between the beach and the reef.

They passed a Marine struggling in the water and ask if he needed help. His eyes stared and rolled and he shook his head no. Afterwards, Ted realized he was merely trying to decide whether to try to keep going, or to just give up, let the water flow over him, and give him that eternal rest.

A little closer in and they have passed under the Japs big guns fire, but now smaller splashes started landing all around. Over the roar of the amtrac motors Ted could hear the swish, swish, swish of the mortar shells as they came sailing in. The smell of death and of cordite was heavy on the air.

Dozens and dozens of amtracs were seen blazing up and down the line when Ted had the courage to peek around. Had anyone made it to shore? What was surely waiting when they hit that beach? Little splashes of machine gun fire were already kicking up puffs of water all around and many were pinging off the shell of the amtrac.

What happened? Ted would never know, probably an explosive on one of the submerged obstacles the Japs had so liberally placed all around the lagoon. One second they are grinding along in the amtrac, and the next they are in the water. This is not the time to worry about what has hit them. With the help of two taller Marines (bless them) Ted was able to struggle in close enough to the beach to stand up in the water, even though it was neck deep. He was still a long quarter of a mile or more out. There was splashes all around, and in the ranks, many Marines were going down.

There was no place to hide in the ocean. Hang on to that rifle; he was going to need it, if he ever got ashore. About ten yards in front of Ted, a Marine, or Corpsman, was suddenly without a head. It just disappeared, and he slowly sank into the water.

The water was no longer blue; it was turning red and brownish. It takes a lot of young men's blood to turn the ocean red. On and on, one more step, men were falling all around. Was there no way to get out of this water? Would the slaughter never end?

Ted wondered if life was worth struggling for, or would it be better to do as the lone swimmer probably did, just give it all up and surrender to the ocean? Self-preservation was too strong, so the will to live sustained Ted to keep placing one weary foot in front of the other, as inch by inch the land grew nearer.

Then Ted dared to look at the beach. All over there was black smoke from the amtracs and small Higgins boats that were burning. Most of them were in the water, but some had managed to get up on the sand. So some of them had made it that far at least. But what of the Marines who were in them?

A new sound was heard as Ted approached the beach. In addition to the swish, swish, swish, of the mortars, the machinegun and rifle fire were picking up. The extremely fast chatter of the Japs light nambu machine-guns, and the more reassuring sounds of the slower Marine's machineguns and rifle fire answering as best they could.

There were little splashes all around. How could they possibly miss? As Ted and the Marines slowly emerged from the water their vulnerable upper torsos were exposed, making an even larger target. The Jap machineguns were taking a terrible toll. Like a giant hay-mowing machine, they were reaping their grisly harvest. Every second was a lifetime as Ted advanced into the slaughter, knowing that at any moment his time might be up, and he would sink down into the red waters as so many others were doing.

All around now, there were dead Marines floating in the water, some were face up, some face down, some have no face at all. Their bodies were rolling and tumbling in the surf, bouncing back and forth as the tide lapped in and out. It was necessary to step on, over, or around them to gain the sanctuary of dry ground. But even on the dry ground there was hardly a foot of soil, which did not contain the body of a dead or wounded Marine. The Japs were extracting a fearful toll.

Finally, finding hard packed sand on which to place a foot, Ted, totally exhausted, both physically and mentally, flopped down behind a burning amtrac. With mortars, grenades, and bullets raining all around, he felt a moment of "complete safety," but only for a tiny, fleeting moment.

Was this then the glorious war Ted had been fearful would end before he became a part of it?

With so many brave young men dying all around was this already broiling hot sand to be his final resting-place, also?

How had he come to be in this abominable situation? In that fleeting moment the past flashed through his mind. He must go back to the beginning to sort it out.

IN THE BEGINNING

In the beginning was innocence, in innocence was faith, and in faith was trust. It was that kind of a world, then. Oh, everyone knew there were good guys and bad guys. There were Cowboys, then there were Indians. It was quite a shock to learn that just maybe, the Indians were the Good Guys.

Children grew up being taught they could trust adults like their schoolteacher, doctor, aunts, and uncles, as though they were above reproach. The leaders of the nation were doing their best (or so it was thought) to fashion a government "of the People, by the People and for the People."

It was perfectly all right to be "shrewd" in one's dealings, to be a slick trader, but it was never all right to be dishonest.

This was the atmosphere in which young Ted Alexander and millions of others grew up. Times were tough; the Great Depression was upon the land. Virtually no one in the working class had much more than enough to eat, many didn't even have that. But what they had was shared with family, friends and neighbors. Anyone who came to the door asking for food was fed if there was a crumb of bread in the house to feed him with.

Born Ted Alexander, on May 31, 1925, to loving and God-fearing parents. Ted's first nine years were spent on farms in the remotest parts of the Missouri Ozarks. There was no electricity, running water, or in-door plumbing.

He was the fifth of eight children, two girls and six boys. There was always someone to play with, or someone to fight with, depending on his personal mood at the time.

His dad was a Master Blacksmith. He could make or repair anything made of steel or iron. Though short of stature, he had great muscular arms from wielding the large hammers to fashion wagon rims, plowshares, shoeing the horses and mules. He was a very loving dad, could sing lullabies or wield the razor strop depending on which was needed. He was also a strong "Man of God." His faith ran deep, and his prayers were fervent. He was fiercely proud of his family.

Ted's mama was a tiny thing, barely five feet tall. She controlled her brood with a song, love, and a smile. Her arms were always open, waiting for a hug from the various grandchildren. She never complained of her lot or the burden of rearing so many children. When food and money were scarce, her reply would always be, "God will provide!" and He always did.

Ted could not remember seeing a doctor before moving to California. His wounds were treated with iodine or kerosene. His coughs were treated with alum and honey. A stone bruise on the heel was treated with a cow manure poultice to draw it to a head.

His dad ran a blacksmith shop in town, two small grocery stores, a tiny one pump service station, a cafe, a church, a mill to grind corn, and not much more. The older boys worked the various farms where the family lived, milking ten or twelve cows, raising hogs and chickens to help bolster the family's income. Ted was just old enough to carry in water from the well, wood for the cook stove, and to help milk the cows.

His days were full with school, fishing the small streams, or hunting squirrels and rabbits in the woods. It was a good life.

The depression took its toll. The bank went broke and his parents lost their life's savings, a tidy sum of four hundred dollars. The government bought all the cows in the county for three to eight dollars each. Pigs brought fifty cents apiece.

Ted's parents loaded their eight children and everything they owned in an old Chevrolet and joined the "dust bowl" exodus for California.

There was migrant work to be had in California, picking peaches, plums, apricots and cotton. The whole family would work and all the money was pooled, hamburger was seven cents a pound, sausage was a nickel, store-bought bread was a nickel a loaf, or three for a dime. God did provide!

After attending several grade schools a year during the migrant years, Ted attended only one high school, the Union High School in Santa Paula, California.

As the nation geared up for war in the late thirties and early forties there was work for everyone. Ted worked every weekend and all summer on a small lemon ranch. He was making twenty-five cents an hour by this time. On this sum he had money to buy a 1927 Model A Ford Roadster with a rumble seat. He felt like a very worldly young man touring around the county, in his car.

Ted had a passion for roller-skating, in a roller rink or on the sidewalks of the town. There were milk shakes, cherry cokes, and hamburgers at the drive-in restaurants. Sumptuous Thanksgiving and Christmas dinners,

Saturday night "hamburger fries" with the whole family present. There were church services to attend, and Sunday dinners for any and all who were able to visit, company and family alike. There was a closeness, a "feeling," they were a family. The children, the in-laws, and the grandchildren all functioned as one unit.

There were friends, then there were girl friends. Ted never lacked for companionship. "You can touch me here, and here, but not here," the girls would say. It was that kind of a world, then. His old Model A Ford (Ted had painted it jet black with a paintbrush) never lacked for occupants.

In January of 1941, when he was fifteen, Ted came Under Conviction and was shortly "Saved by the Grace of God." A commitment he never, ever, regretted.

Life was full, and life was good. There was prosperity and money (meager though it may have been) flowing throughout the land. There were the rumors of war, and of the country's involvement in it. Hitler was ravaging Europe and the Japanese were becoming ever more aggressive in the Pacific. Daily and nightly the old Model A cruised the streets and back roads of the county, often burning kerosene for gasoline had become rationed.

On Sunday December 7, 1941, Ted was working on a lemon ranch, irrigating the orchard. As with every other person in America he could take you to the exact spot where he was sitting when he heard the shocking news.

The Japs were attacking Pearl Harbor, wherever that might be. It was a very large world then. Ted had no concept of where the far distant countries lay, much less of the remote islands of the Pacific. Oh yes, everyone had heard of Hawaii, but few knew where it lay in relation to California. A certain fear permeated everyone. What was war? What did the future hold for Ted and his family? Only time would tell!

Overnight the world had changed, everything was just the same, and yet everything was different. There was urgency in life that had not existed before. It was as though life itself had been speeded up. Ted at sixteen, a small five-foot-five country lad, was hurled into this whirlwind of a period.

Ration boards were set up, draft boards were in full swing, and people were volunteering and marching off to war. America was receiving defeat after defeat in the Pacific. The Japs were overrunning everything in their path.

At seventeen, Ted joined all the other fiercely patriotic, loyal, proud Americans wanting to fight for their country. He began to pester his dad to sign the all-important papers so he could join the Navy and go to war, whatever that might be. Late one evening in December of 1942, Ted talked his daddy into signing the papers and they marched off to a notary public. His daddy proclaimed, "It feels just like I am signing your death warrant."

If Ted and the other young men had known what lay ahead, would they have been so gung ho to go? If they had not gone, would there be a United States of America today, or would it be the United States of Germany or the United States of Japan?

The period of innocence had ended.

They left home boys

TRAINING CAMPS

In the first week of January 1943, seventeen-year old Ted Alexander joined millions of other young men going to the training camps. America had already been in the war for a year and many of the naive young volunteers were afraid it might be over before they got to be a part of this "great adventure."

Ted was sent to the San Diego Naval Training Center, Company 43-15 for his term of boot camp, which, at that time, was a period of some twelve weeks.

Haircuts! One's locks were sheared off and everyone looked like peeled onions. It wasn't hard to tell a new recruit for his head was shiny white where it had once been protected by hair.

Clothing issue was a great adventure in itself. Now Ted was really in the Navy. Sea bag, hammock, mattress, and every piece of clothing and equipment he was to need for a long, long time. What a thrill to try on the gleaming white uniforms, and the dress blue, heavy wool uniforms. Pee coats to underwear; it was all there; just waiting to be tried on.

Ted was very fortunate for most of his clothes fit him in a reasonable manner. All the clothes were issued in a larger size than the young men actually wore for they were expected to gain some weight, even with the vigorous regimen of training that was coming up. Name stencils had been issued with the clothing and everyone had to stencil his name on every last piece of clothing and equipment he was issued. Exact instructions were given on where to place the name on each item, caps here, and shorts there, socks just so.

Ted learned to fold each item for packing into the sea bag. The sea bag bulged, and if everything wasn't folded and stored just right it would not all fit inside.

Inspection, Ted had to learn to place each item on his cot in an exact location with the name folded out so the inspecting officer could read it. Heaven help the poor recruit who was slow to learn; or who tried to hide some dirty clothing among his clean ones.

Shots, shots, and more shots, there was no end to the shots that were given. Most every week the company was marched into the infirmary for more shots all around.

Reveille, in the wee small hours of the dark morning it sounded. Up and shave, (Ted was one of the few unlucky enough to have to shave every morning) shower, and do the morning duties. Dress in the "Uniform of the Day," make up his bunk, clean the barracks, then out to muster, and it was still dark. March in company formation to the parade ground and form up with all the other companies waiting to be called to morning chow. It was cold and miserable and often wet at this time of the year. The young men usually stood in formation for an hour or so waiting their company's turn, and it was still dark. Oh how that extra hour of rest would have been cherished in the early dawn.

Finally, one's turn came and they marched off to the chow lines to wait some more. The only salvation was that the chow was always worth waiting for. The Navy fed sumptuously by the standards Ted was used to in civilian life. Scrambled eggs, bacon or ham, hash browns, fruit, plenty of butter and bread, or possibly French Toast with huge slices of baked ham. One day it might be Navy beans with all the trimmings or it might be S— on a Shingle, (chipped beef in gravy, on toast). Ted never found a meal he didn't enjoy. Lunch and dinner were great feasts, also. Plenty of potatoes, meat, and vegetables, along with fresh baked bread and desserts that were often fresh baked fruit or cream pies. It took a lot of food to fill up and maintain the healthy young bodies.

Exercises and close-order drill, Navy style, not Marine Corps style. He only had a wooden rifle to practice with but everyone learned to march in step and to do the Manual of Arms. Every available minute was filled with classes on seamanship, knot tying, rowing, Rocks and Shoals (Navy regulations), weapons firing, and Naval guns firing.

The first three weeks were quarantine time. No one could get leave or even go to the movies at night. But then everyone was too tired to do anything but get a hot shower and drop off to sleep if they didn't have guard duty to pull.

After the quarantine period and the month of training, everyone eagerly looked forward to his first liberty. What a thrill it would be to go into town, show off their uniform to the girls, and see the sights, after only seeing sailors for so long.

San Diego, a large city to Ted, held many attractions but girls wasn't one of them, at least "available girls," also, one didn't show off their uniform. There seemed to be more service men in San Diego than there were in the camps. Army, Marine, and Navy personnel literally jammed the sidewalks. One had to elbow their way around and many, many fights started from a little too vigorous an elbowing. The MPs and SPs were almost as numerous as the troops. One little infraction and they grabbed the offender and hauled him off in the paddy wagon. Pound the pavement from one end of the street to the other. Many of the bars, stores, and cafes had signs proclaiming, "No Servicemen or Dogs Allowed." That did wonders for one's morale. It was kind of a relief to get back to camp (home) after an afternoon and evening in San Diego.

Shortly before boot camp ended, Ted's parents made the trip down to see him. It took them the whole weekend to get there and back on the busses, some hundred-and-fifty miles. Since Ted did not have liberty that weekend, they got to spend only two hours together and this at the visitor's center.

Boot camp finally ended and with it went the designated A/S (apprentice seaman) after Ted's name. He was now a Seaman 2nd Class, (S2c) and ready for assignment. Many of his classmates were sent to ships and stations all around the world to serve or to continue they're training in some field or other. Ted was assigned to Hospital Corps School in Balboa Park, San Diego, California. How lucky could he get???

The food was good and the hours were reasonable compared to boot camp. Mostly it was study and study, cram and cram for tests. About the only formality was the muster after morning chow, then it was straight into the classrooms where many of the classes were taught by nurses or doctors. The Hospital Apprentices (HA2C) were expected to learn in six or eight weeks what a nurse had to learn in two years during peacetime. It was extremely interesting study for a little country boy. Name all the bones in the body, two hundred and six, if memory serves well. Many proclaimed there were two hundred and seven when the healthy young men awoke in the early mornings. There was classes in administering medication, bandaging, giving shots, the organs and muscles of the body and what medication to give for a particular illness or injury, suturing, pharmacy, and how to fill a prescription. What does one do for bedsores? Prevent them, then they won't need treating. It seemed there was no end to the knowledge that was being imparted to the young minds.

Probably the best thing about the Corps School was its location; it bordered the San Diego Zoo. Big, spreading trees overhung the fence separating the school from the zoo. It was a simple matter to climb over the fence, go out the zoo gate and into town, and then return by the same route if one got back before the zoo closed at ten p.m. There was no charge for servicemen to enter the zoo, about the only thing that didn't leach off of the troops stationed in the San Diego area.

Ted's old Model A Ford Roadster had been left at home and his daddy had written him a letter (undated) telling him that if he could come home to sign the papers, he had the car sold. Since a different officer had the duty most every weekend Ted used this same letter to get weekend passes to go home several times while he was in the school. Here, he could show off his uniform, and swagger down the lone, four-block-long Main Street.

During this period of time any young man who joined the service in his senior year of high school was awarded his diploma of graduation at the time his class would have graduated. It just so happened that Hospital Corps School ended a couple of days before Ted's class at home was to graduate. Ted talked to the officer in charge and was given the option of a few days leave to attend his high school graduation, then back to the San Diego Naval Hospital for duty, or of going to the Mare Island Naval Hospital near San Francisco. Ted had had enough of San Diego, he opted for San Francisco; the farthest away from home he had ever been.

Mare Island and San Francisco were paradise compared to San Diego, or anywhere else for that matter. The classes continued and were augmented by ward duty for practical experience. Taking blood pressure, temperature and pulse became second nature. Giving shots, bandaging, medications, sitting in on autopsies and operations was common.

Ted was assigned to a "mental observation" ward. Mostly these people seemed to Ted to be just mean and shiftless. They were able to take care of their own needs and were allowed to go and come pretty much at their pleasure. There was absolutely nothing for Ted to do except "observe."

Liberty was granted anytime that one was not on duty. All Ted needed was a clean uniform and a quarter to share the taxi fare into Vallejo, and then the world was his oyster.

Vallejo, Richmond, Oakland and San Francisco were booming with the shipyards, docks, training camps, etc. The whole area was just the reverse of San Diego. The civilians had a motto, "No serviceman waits more than five minutes for a ride when hitchhiking." They were all true to their motto. One might sit on another person's lap or scrunch in between, but the people cared and took care of "their servicemen."

Young Ladies (and the great majority of them expected to be, and most were treated as such) without number it seemed, and they were definitely available. Most all these young ladies worked in the shipyards or other defense jobs and had a ready supply of money. They would gladly slip one a five or a ten to pay for a dinner or other treats or for amusements. Few of them had cars or gas to burn, but there was a great bus, train, street and cable car system once one reached Richmond. Servicemen rode free on nearly all the transportation in the bay area, or else one would pay his dime, then just keep getting transfers to go anywhere he wanted to go. The young ladies of Richmond wined and dined the troops and invited them home for home-cooked meals with their families.

San Francisco was the serviceman's paradise. A serviceman could spend weeks there and not be out a penny. There were the USO Clubs, the Pepsi Cola Club, YMCA, and all sorts of clubs and lounges for one to eat, sleep, and relax in, and it was all free. Every afternoon and night there were fantastic USO shows with big name bands or entertainers. There was music, dancing, food, and pretty hostesses. One only had to ask, and often not even that, to get free tickets to almost any attraction.

There were huge bulletin boards on which people had posted invitations for servicemen to spend the weekends in their homes. Many even offered to pay the bus or train fare if there was any. About the only time servicemen paid for anything in San Francisco was if they went to one of the large cafes or nightclubs for dinner, and then the girls virtually always footed the bill. Ted usually went home with a few extra dollars in his pocket to start the next night's liberty with.

The mental ward was a nightmare, but for Ted it didn't last too long. After spending most of the nights on liberty, and having nothing to do on the ward, he developed the habit of crawling into an empty hospital bed and sleeping the day away. This was great until they held inspection one day and the Officer of the Day wanted to know where the Corpsman was who was supposed to be on duty there in the ward. Ted was summarily posted to the galley to wash dishes.

**Ted and his tailored Bell Bottomed Uniform of Salt-Water Gaberdine
- Each leg was larger around than the waist**

At first this was a great blow to his ego, but it soon turned out to be the biggest blessing he ever received. There was a huge dish washing machine in the galley and all Ted had to do was guide the trays of dirty dishes into it. The nurses in the diet kitchen determined they were going to fatten Ted up so they made him great trays of rich food. He ate steaks and chops and chicken and roasts and desserts without end. The best food he was ever to receive, before or after. There were two of the Corpsmen to operate the dishwasher, even though there was little for even one to do. Soon Ted and the other fellow decided there was no reason for both to be on duty at the same time. They would alternate; every other day one or the other was off. This meant that after dinner one of them had two whole nights and a whole day to do as they pleased, the other one did the dishes for the next three meals; then they had their turn. Fantastic Duty!!! It was no wonder Ted and millions of other servicemen learned to love San Francisco.

All too soon this beautiful paradise came to an end. One morning Ted came on duty and everyone was asking where in the world he had been. He had been put in charge of a group that was being transferred to Field Medical Training with the Fleet Marine Force, in San Diego. Their detail left in only an hour or two, there was no time to call or see the "Girls" to say good bye.

Ted had thought he was joining the Navy to keep out of the infantry and here he was, virtually in the Marine Corps. One of the first transactions at Camp Elliott was the total change of uniforms. They were issued all new Marine Corps uniforms, khaki, and dress green wool uniforms, ties, caps, underclothes, boondockers and dress shoes. They were also issued a real rifle and a gas mask. This should have been the tip-off that they were no longer just Corpsmen in the Navy. All of their Navy gear, uniforms, sea bag, hammock, mattress, etc., was packed up and sent home. They were to sever nearly all connections with the Navy, except the Marine Corps is a branch of the Navy.

Navy boot camp had been a picnic compared to the rigorous training regimen that commenced the very first day. The large company of Corpsmen who had been assembled only thought they were in great physical condition.

It was reveille before the break of dawn, calisthenics before chow, which was still very adequate but not quite the same quality as in the Navy. Morning classes in field medicine, combat dressings, bullet and fragment wounds, burns, broken limbs, sanitation and mosquito control were held.

Right after noon chow the real training started. Close-order drill, double time, forward march, to the rear march, right shoulder arms, left shoulder arms, right oblique, left oblique, halts. Present arms, parade rest, inspection arms, over and over and over and over until it became second nature.

During all this close-order drill the real torture was dished out on the rocky parade ground or on the gravely blacktop. "Hit the Deck" still reverberates in Ted's ears. Hit the deck, hit the deck, and hit the deck, over and over and over. His elbows and knees was almost a bloody pulp, so sore he could hardly stand to touch them. The rocks, gravel and dirt were embedded in each person's forehead, belly, arms and legs, until after a few weeks they became toughened to the torture. They really learned to hit the deck from the standing, walking or running position. The Marines and Corpsmen were harangued with the epithet, "You are tough, you are a Marine." Inspections, inspections, inspections.

There was a story that made the rounds. During inspection, an officer stopped in front of a private and hit him across the face with his swagger stick. He asked, "Did that hurt?" The private answered, "No Sir." Officer: "Why?" Private: "Because I am a Marine, I am tough, Sir." At the next stop the officer struck a private across the chest with the same dialogue ensuing. The officer proceeded until he came to a private with a "thing" protruding about a foot out between his legs. The officer raised his swagger stick and hit it with all his might and then asked; "Did that hurt?" The private answered, "No Sir." The officer asked, "Why didn't it hurt?" The private answered, "Because it belongs to the man behind me, Sir."

After a couple of weeks of classes and close-order drill came the real field training, hikes into the hills and valleys; hot, dusty, and miserable. Practice bandaging "wounded" with various types of wounds. Carry, drag, or roll a wounded person off a hill, often with a real live rattle snake buzzing in one's ears. Hug the ground, real rifle bullets barely miss one's tail when they are prone. Some are really wounded, a couple killed. Machine-guns chatter, grenades explode on the perimeter, and explosive charges hurl dirt and rocks into the air. There would be a five to ten mile hike back to camp in the blistering east wind and heat of summer. Many passed out from sheer exhaustion and from the heat.

Back at camp and there would be hours on the rifle range. Standing position, sitting position, prone position, over and over and over, the rifle butt would dig into Ted's shoulder or bounce him several inches backwards. Finally the Corpsmen mastered the rifles. They could disassemble and reassemble them in pitch darkness. Clean, clean, clean. At the end of the interminable day they would boil their rifle barrels out in huge vats of boiling water. Clean, dry and oil them up for inspection the next morning. Heaven help the poor marine that had a speck of dirt or rust on his rifle. Over and over it was proclaimed, "Your rifle is your very best friend." When, or before taps sounded, the young men fell into their bunks, exhausted.

Saturdays were barracks and clothing inspection day. After inspection was shot time. The Corpsmen literally gave thousands of shots to them selves and to the Marines stationed there. Saturday afternoon and Sunday was liberty day but no one could leave the base until all the shots were given. Besides, San Diego wasn't the best place to make liberty, especially to the Old Salts who had made liberty in San Francisco. Many opted to just stay in the barracks and rest, write letters, read, or play cards.

The close-order drills became a snap, the ten-mile hikes were like a stroll in the park; the rifle range no longer intimidated the troops. Field Med. Training was drawing to a close. The Corpsmen were becoming tough, they were becoming "Marines."

OUTBOUND

Boarded USS Mormachawk

On a late fall day in 1943, Ted Alexander sailed from the port of San Diego, California. It was up early, wait for chow, wait for trucks to haul them from Camp Elliott, the Marine training base, to the waterfront. Wait for hours to go aboard the troop transport tied up at the dock. Wait to be assigned a bunk, wait, wait, and wait. Wait in line to get a meal ticket, for what, he never knew. Certainly no one was going to stand in line three hours for seconds, to eat the slop they served on that scow.

Ted Alexander was assigned a bunk deep in a stifling, hot, smelly hold. The bunks were stacked one on top of the other with little more than a foot between. If one turned on their side they bumped the person above.

So bad were the conditions in the hold that many Marines, Ted amongst them, opted to stay on the open top steel decks, where, after sundown it was at least cool enough to sleep. The filth and stench became almost unbearable in the holds after the first day or two. Most everyone had been seasick, had heaved all over everything and everyone else. Actually, Ted was to find that it smelled like a perfume factory compared to what he would later encounter.

Ted, along with the other Corpsmen and Marines, entered into this new adventure with great enthusiasm. Being strong of mind and body from the weeks of training, regular hours, and good nourishing food, they were ready to conquer the world. They even halfway believed the epithets hurled at them in the training camps. *"You are tough, You are a Marine!"*

The ship weighed anchor in the late afternoon and sailed out of the harbor. Great adventure. For a little country boy on his first time away from home, it was a monumental step into the unknown.

Ted was afraid he would be seasick, like so many of the other fellows who were already hanging over the rails, but as the hours wore on into the night he became more confident. Maybe he would be spared after all.

The coastline receded into nothingness as the ship sailed away. Finally, only one light remained to mark the shores of home; then it disappeared too. Possibly it dawned on Ted at this time, that he was going away to war, and all the preparations were not just a game.

About midnight, Ted went down into that stifling hold and spent his only night of an eighteen-day trip in that abominable place. The creaks and groans of a liberty ship, plowing through the waters at fourteen to sixteen knots is something awesome.

Early in the morning, up on deck, hundreds of Marines and sailors were hanging over the rails letting everything fly. Being down wind, or hanging over one of the decks below meant that one was going to get sprayed good.

Ted was feeling great. Oh boy, no sign of seasickness. He got in the chow line with some friends and began the slow crawl up, over, down, and around the decks to reach the door to the mess hall. Some three hours later, his turn finally came to step through the door for a much anticipated "breakfast."

He never made it inside. One foot went through, the hot stifling, smelly air hit him in the face. Instantly, he was headed for the rail to join the others, now two and three deep all along.

All day long he retched and retched. Oh for a drink of water, but they had painted the inside of the water tanks on that tub. The water tasted of paint thinner, or kerosene or some such. Ted had a canteen of water with his pack and one of his friends brought it up on deck for him. For the next six days and nights, this was his only sustenance. He lay in the scupper, near the bow of the ship, too sick to roll himself over the side, and there was no one else about with enough strength to push him overboard.

Much of the time, and especially at night, the waves were coming over the bow and kept Ted and the others constantly wet with salt water. He was hoping one of the big waves would wash him on overboard. No such luck!

After six days, he had a need to go to the "head." (Toilet) Weak beyond description, he struggled into one of the heads. They were just long, open troughs, with seats placed side by side, and salt water flowing through them. As Ted sat on one his head was always hanging over the trough in front of him. As the bow of the ship rose and fell with the ocean swells, the water, paper, and feces would float to one end of the trough, and then immediately reverse it's self and go the other way. "Great for seasickness."

As aforesaid, the water on board was almost unfit for human consumption. (But then, no one during the war ever considered that Marines or Soldiers were human.) There were only two drinking fountains for the several thousand troops aboard. Armed guards were placed on these to keep the lines moving and to let no one fill a canteen.

It was at a U.S.O. stage show in San Diego, sponsored by the Coca Cola Co. At the end of the show a beautiful young lady appeared on stage and said. Quote. "Remember, any place in this whole world that you go, when you step off that ship, a bottle of ice cold Coca Cola will be waiting for you". Unquote!

The remainder of that eighteen days and nights without seeing a speck of land, and only one other ship which passed far away; Ted dreamed constantly of the bottle of ice cold Coca Cola, which was waiting for him. In a spot he knew not where, because his destination was only a number, not a name.

Finally, on the eighteenth day of the journey, on a bright sunny morning they sailed into sight of a beautiful green island. Palm trees swaying along a lovely sandy beach. A more beautiful sight has seldom been seen. After sailing almost completely around, and Ted was sure, threading a mined channel, they entered the harbor at Noumea, New Caledonia.

All around the harbor were the masts of ships sticking up out of the water. They were French ships, which they had scuttled to keep the Americans from getting them, some friends. New Caledonia was a French possession.

Ted's mind worried not about that beautiful island, the sandy beaches, or the scuttled ships. It had only room enough for the bottle of ice cold Coca Cola that was waiting. He was on the first boat headed for the pier, his mouth watering, he could hardly wait; he could almost taste it.

No Coca-Cola, it was Ted's greatest disappointment of the whole war, but at least it helped prepare him for the many that would come.

New Caledonia was an adventure beyond imagination for Ted and his friends. From the great disappointment of the docks they boarded some rickety old busses, and headed for their camp.

They threaded their way through the streets of quaint, foreign looking houses. Mansions where the High Ranking French Officials had or did live, where the high up Officers of the U.S now lived. Past shacks, swarms of funny looking people, and all manner of strange sights. Sights which had only been glimpsed in the movies, but that one never in their wildest dreams ever expected to see in person.

Ted's disappointment soon faded. Out through the countryside with fields, grass huts, South Sea Island Natives, and finally into a tent camp. What a day! They had arrived at a Marine replacement battalion.

Replacement centers are probably the sorriest places a group of young men can end up in, be it in the states, or overseas, there is very little to do and little discipline. Just wait, and wait, and wait, to see where they will be assigned. Wait to see what fate has decreed for one's future. Muster in the A.M. to see whose names are called to be shipped out, then hang around camp for the rest of the day. Restless young men soon find ways to get out of camp and start to explore.

Ted couldn't really say this replacement center was guarded, or secure. There was a sentry at the gate leading into camp, but the rest of the perimeter was just open. No fences, no nothing, but a single strand of rusty barbed wire in a few places. A gold embossed invitation for a group of curious, bold, daring, mischievous, young Marines to wander away and explore everything within their realm. There was much within their realm to explore.

The war still seemed to be a million miles away, an adventure happening to someone else. The young, innocent Marines thought they wanted to be a part of it, but for now the replacement battalion was home.

NOUMEA

NEW CALEDONIA

If you have ever read or seen "The Adventures of Marco Polo" you have some idea of the attraction of the city of Noumea, New Caledonia on the young marines. Most were away from home and the states for the first time. Little seventeen and eighteen year olds, who thought they were grown up? Little country boys, or small town lads, who had seldom if ever been out of the counties they were born in. Cocky, proud, fiercely patriotic, Americans, knowing everything, and yet knowing nothing of the real world.

Noumea had strange people, strange sights, and strange shops, a melting pot of many peoples and races, but above all, a place to go. It was a place of excitement for curious young minds.

Each evening, trucks ran from the replacement camp in to town to take those with passes, then they returned around eleven o'clock. If one missed the truck, it was a very long fifteen to eighteen mile hike, through the dark, strange countryside back to camp. There was no place to stay in town, and the M.P.s swept up any unfortunate enough to be left on the streets after a certain hour.

Ted and Sam Schissler, and some other friends had made liberty in Noumea a few times. After they had browsed the shops, walked the streets, and had an "Ice Cream" at the lone soda fountain, there wasn't much to do for the ones too young, or too innocent, to visit the bars.

The streets were jammed with Soldiers, Sailors, and Marines. After a trip to one of the numerous bars they were usually ready to fight anyone who had on a different uniform to the one they were wearing.

One night five Soldiers confronted Ted and Sam and another "Friend" on a side street, by a little park. It seemed the sidewalk wasn't wide enough for all to pass abreast at the same time. Neither side would give way. What better excuse could one find for a fight?

Now five Soldiers to three Marines (or Navy Corpsmen in Marine uniforms) was never, ever, considered bad odds, so the fight was on in real earnest. Fists and boots were flying from every direction. Sam and Ted quickly found out it was only two against five, which was not good odds at all. Especially when one of the two was a puny little devil like Ted.

Fortunately, the cry of M.P.'s went up just in the nick of time and everyone scattered. Ted came out of the fracas with just a black eye, a big fat lip, and a crooked tooth.

When Sammy and Ted confronted their "Friend" back at camp the next day, he said that he had "Gone to get help." Scratch one friend!!!

Ted had struck up an acquaintance with a young French girl who worked in a soda fountain. Though he spent hours, and multitudes of Francs, for this was the currency they were paid in and they conversed freely, she would never go out with him.

Her daddy had told her, or so she said, that service men only wanted to go out with her for one thing. Ted could never convince her that he only wanted to walk her home. He finally found out she lived in the rear of the same building, and didn't even have to go outside to get home. At least Ted devoured lots of "Icy Cream" which was their name for ice cream, and it kept him off the streets.

One of the major attractions of Noumea, but one, which never attracted Ted or his friends, was the "Pink House." This was a house of prostitution, run by the Army, for servicemen. There were supposed to be five girls there, all from different countries, Australia, New Zealand and some of the various Islands. It was also said the charge for "visiting" at the Pink House was seven dollars American. Supposedly each of the countries received a dollar, the Army got a dollar, and the girl got a dollar. There were always five long lines of men outside waiting for their turn.

Oh Yes, the large old house was painted pink, hence "Pink House." Should this shock some, it should be well remembered that the Army had several houses of Prostitution right here in the good old U.S.A.

About half way between camp and town was a little roadside cafe. Some enterprising farmer had turned his home into an eating establishment. Here Ted could get most any kind of a home cooked meal of really good food, for a very reasonable price.

It was rumored that their food came from the camps round about. If so, it was marvelous what they could do with it, when the camps served only slop. Possibly they were getting the food which the camps were supposed to get.

Along with a nice steak, or roast beef dinner was one of Ted's favorite foods, fresh cucumbers and onions, sliced in a light vinegar and spice solution.

24

On New Caledonia all the troops were paid in French currency and it was a marvel what a wad of bills one would receive for a few dollars pay. The "Francs" didn't go very far, but then no one cared for there was nothing else they were good for. It seemed none of the Marines ever considered the French currency, or later the Australian currency they were paid in, as being real money, only play money.

The first Australian soldier Ted ever met was there in Noumea. While waiting at the truck (bus) stop, for a ride back to camp, this very drunk Aussie came up to Ted and wanted his help. When Ted finally made out what he was saying in his "funny English" it was. "I say Yank, You see that bloody M.P. (the one directing traffic) over there. You hold him while I —— him and I will hold him while you —— him." He was dead serious too. Fortunately, the truck came before Ted had to fight the Aussie, also.

Of such was Noumea.

ONE AVERAGE DAY

NEW CALEDONIA

It was a beautiful clear sunny day, like one can only find in the South Sea Islands. Bright and clear, with the whitest of white cumulus clouds floating along in the bluest of blue skies.

Now Sam and Ted, having some way ducked out of a day at the firing range decided it would be a good day to go to town. They had never spent a whole day in Noumea, only evenings and nights.

Even without passes, it was no problem to get off the base, as the old barbed wire fence was almost non existent. Then too, no one really cared. If one got picked up in Noumea, it was his own tough luck.

Out on the road, within a couple of minutes, a jeep came by and stopped. A full Colonel was driving. He said, "Do you fellows have passes." Sam and Ted said "Yes Sir" but made no effort to produce what they didn't have.

The Colonel said "O.K. hop in" and away they went, with a cold trickle of sweat running down their backs. The Colonel dropped them off near a little park, where Ted and Sam had had a confrontation with some Army fellows a few nights previously.

Noumea was a completely different place in the daytime. Whereas by night it was crowded with service personnel, by day it was crowded with civilians of many nationalities. The stores and shops were bustling, and every shop was open, not just the souvenir shops, as at night.

There were many "high class" stores along the streets. Shops with clothing of all descriptions, from sarongs to formal wear. Silk shops, with every conceivable color of bolts of silk, basket shops, food stores, souvenir nooks, they were all there.

Ted and Sam came onto a Barbershop and Bathhouse. They decided to indulge, as neither had shaved that morning, and hot showers were hard to come by at camp. Ted sat down in the barber chair and asked for a shave.

There were three French barbers in this shop and they got into a lively discussion, or argument about something or other, jabbering away in their own tongue. The one who was supposed to be shaving Ted was yelling and waving his arms around like mad. Ted was scared to death he was going to get his throat cut, for the barber never once looked at him, while all the time he was flailing away with the long straight edged razor. It was a real relief to get out of that chair, all in one piece.

An old, fat lady gave each of them a bar of soapy smelling soap, and herded each of them into a shower stall. There they stayed and soaked, and soaked, until the whole bar of soap was gone. The old, fat lady, waddled by every once in a while as if trying to hurry them out, but there was no way they were going to leave as long as the hot water and soap held out.

After lunch in a quaint little side street cafe, Sam and Ted were idling against a storefront, when a kinky little Second Lieutenant in the army came by. He eyed the Marines and went on past, then turned and came back by. Ted and Sam didn't budge, so he stopped and proceeded to read them out for not saluting him. It just so happened that the store had an awning out, and Ted told him, "In the Marines one is not supposed to salute when under cover." (true, but meaning inside a building). The shave tail dropped his head and said "Oh" backed up and saluted. He stalked off with the determined look that he was going to look that one up in the regulation book.

While Ted and Sam were loafing on a corner there was suddenly a great commotion from the opposite side of the street. Two Javanese (or some Oriental type) gals were yelling, and screaming at each other. The fight got serious, and the next thing you know they were rolling in the gutter, scratching, and kicking, yelling and screaming insults. Their hair, which had been rolled neatly in a "bun" on the back of their heads, was soon loose. It would almost touch the sidewalk when they stood up.

Each time one would start to walk away the other would start screaming, and cussing, and grab the other one by the hair and sling her around and slam her to the ground. If you didn't see it, you could never imagine what a battle it was. First one passer by, then another would get into the argument and egg one of them on. All this in a screeching oriental tongue, which Ted could only interpret, as his imagination dictated.

The fight went on for half an hour or more before they finally parted company and went their separate ways. Screaming insults from as far away as they could see each other.

Occasionally, big Cadillac limousines, with sharp military chauffeurs would pass by. Inside would be a Diplomat, a General, or an Admiral, out seeing the sights in style. There was also big Chevies and Caddies carrying smartly dressed "ladies" these were rumored to be mistresses of the Admirals and Generals. Let the lowly GIs go to the "Pink House."

Although New Caledonia was owned by the French, it was a melting pot for the whole South Pacific. There were people of many nationalities, each in their own peculiar style of dress. Each section of town had it's own ethnic group, from mansions on the hills, to the run down buildings on the waterfront.

Near the waterfront, Sam and Ted came upon a Navy "Small Stores" store. For some unknown they decided they had worn Marine uniforms long enough and wanted some Navy clothes to change back into. For a handful of francs they each purchased a set of blue jeans, a shirt, and a white cap. Not daring to wear same on the street they had them wrapped in brown paper to carry back to camp.

After seven or eight hours of pounding the pavement, Ted and Sam had taken in most of the sights in Noumea. They decided to head for home and made their way out of town, and onto the road to hitch hike back to camp.

They stopped at a little country cafe for dinner, as they knew what chow would be in camp. Roast mutton, dripping with cold grease, and dehydrated carrots and potatoes. It was virtually the same thing every day of the week.

They enjoyed a fried steak dinner, with real mashed potatoes, gravy, and green beans, and this was followed by real chocolate cake.

About the only thing, which was not, available at the little cafe was fresh milk. (The only fresh milk Ted was to enjoy in the two long years was at a brief stop in Australia.)

Back at camp, Sam and Ted changed into their new Navy clothes, and were the envy of the whole camp. Small stores were being issued at a warehouse, quite some distance from the bivouac area, that evening. In the Marines, clothing was issued free of charge, any time it was available. Whereas in the Navy they gave you a clothing allowance, in cash, to purchase the clothing you needed. Now the Corpsmen, attached to the Marines, enjoyed the best of both systems. The Navy continued to give them a clothing allowance, and they got their clothing free of charge from the Marine supply depots.

Several of the Corpsmen were going over to the warehouse, about a mile from the bivouac area, to get needed items. Ted and Sam decided to join them, as much for the stroll, as for the couple of pair of socks they needed. The line of people waiting to draw clothing was tremendously long. The Corpsmen were debating on whether to get in it for the few things they needed. A Master Sergeant stepped up to Sam and Ted (still wearing their Navy Jeans) and said, "Are you the two who were ship wrecked," Not wanting to be put on report for being out of uniform, they said, "Yeah, I guess so." The Sergeant said, "Come with me." Sam and Ted just knew they had done it again, but followed along for there was no way to duck out this time.

The sergeant took them to the front of the line and said to the Marine behind the counter. "These men were shipwrecked, the only clothes they have is what the Navy gave them, and they have on. Give them complete outfits of everything."

Now Ted and Sam were between a rock and a hard place, so with mutual eye consent, they just kept their mouths shut. They were issued several pairs of khaki pants, shirts, hats, and shoes, under clothes, socks, and even new blankets. Not really knowing what to do with all of it, they gathered it up, quickly disappeared in the swampy brush, and back to their tent. Ted often wondered what happened to the poor devils that were actually shipwrecked when they showed up to get their clothes.

Ted and Sam gave their Navy clothes away, and never wore them again for fear of being recognized by the Master Sergeant who had befriended them.

A trip to an old, old movie, in the pouring rain, and a stroll past the "Belle's" grass but, ended what was more or less an "average" day on New Caledonia, for two mischievous young men.

THE GANG

NEW CALEDONIA

There was never a dull moment in the tent where Ted and all his close friends lived. They had talked, bluffed, cajoled, or what ever was necessary, to get their own gang into one single tent, instead of being scattered throughout the replacement camp, as they had been assigned.

They were a group of fun loving, mischievous, rascals who never, ever, backed down from a dare, or missed an opportunity to get into any kind of trouble or excitement that was going around. They were always giving the guys in the tents surrounding theirs a hard time and those guys in return would try to get even.

One night after time for lights out, they were all laughing and joking and yelling around. Well, the Marine on guard duty just happened to come by and he tried to quiet them down. They gave him such a hard time that he said he was going to get the Captain of the Guard.

The fellows in the tent next door had heard, and "The Gang" heard them laughing about how they were in for it this time.

Sam Schissler and Ted decided to have some fun. They put on their helmets, slung a rifle over their shoulders and slipped out the rear of their tent, coming around from the opposite direction. When they were in front of the tent next door, in a disguised voice, Ted said, "In here Captain, this is the tent here," then Sam and Ted barged in. The fellows in that tent started trying to explain that it wasn't them but that bunch "next door." Sam ordered them all out of bed and out into the Company Street. About this time Ted started laughing and they recognized him, so the battle of words was on.

Sam and Ted beat a hasty retreat, and had just reached the street when the real Captain of the guard, and the guard came up. The Captain wanted to know what Ted and Sam were up to. They told him they were just coming off guard duty and were trying to quiet that bunch down before they went to bed. The Captain said, "O.K. go ahead." Since all the noise was now coming from the neighbors tent, the Captain and the guard barged in there to be met by a barrage of boots and foul language.

Every one of them was put on "Report" and spent a week on a work party. They never quite forgave Ted and Sam for that one, but then, one needed something to liven up the days and nights in the replacement battalions.

One morning Ted woke up to a black sky. The winds were picking up something fierce. The word was passed that they were in for a hurricane, and to tie everything down real tight.

Everyone went around and tightened their tent ropes, put their tent flaps down and crawled inside. As the winds increased and the rains started, Ted, Sam, Willis T. and some of the others decided they might best anchor their tent some more.

Searching around they could find nothing to tie it down with except the ropes on the other tents. They cut all but the corner ropes on the tent's surrounding theirs and secured the ropes to their own tent.

It wasn't very long before all the other tents were on the ground in the mud. All those guys spent a miserable day and night huddled under flopping wet canvas.

The next day the Gangs was the only tent standing and when the neighbors found all the extra ropes on it; they told them they only took their ropes "after" the tent's had blown down.

Do you know, most of them believed it, or was too chicken to say anything since the Gang had quite a viscous reputation.

That hurricane blew down all the mess halls, tents, storage buildings, etc. but as far as Ted could tell it never even took a single blade of grass off of the Native huts.

The gang would sit in their tent playing cards, and each of them would lay a big knife or a forty-five pistol by his hand. They would scream and yell, and raise all kinds of cain with each other. Yelling, if you cheat again I will carve you wide open. Or if you do that again I will blow your head off, all in fun with not the slightest bit of malice intended.

There was a great big Marine (six-foot plus, 250 pounds) that always wanted to play with them, but he would never, ever, come inside their tent. He would sit on the outside, under the raised flap, and play from there, always losing good-naturedly. (More than a year later, as Ted lay in a fox hole, bandaging his wound the big Marine said, "Do you know why I would never come into your tent to play cards on New Caledonia?" Ted said, "No, why?" He said, "Because I was afraid of you!" What a thought; when you he was laying there bleeding and possibly about to die.)

If it could be thought of, "The Gang" was going to give it a try.

GOOKVILLE

NEW CALEDONIA

Across the road from the Marines Replacement Battalion Center was a real Native Village. Back about a quarter of a mile off the main road, in a grove of huge towering, spreading trees, and on the banks of a small stream. Each family or group had a small plot of ground on which they built their large grass houses. Each plot was enclosed by a sort of log rail fence.

It was really amazing how the natives could take a few polls, tie them together with reeds, and cover them with bundles of grass, and them never leak a drop. It is even more amazing how these grass huts can go through the very worst hurricanes, and lose not so much as a blade of grass, while the best engineered buildings of the Americans go sailing off into the wild blue yonder.

The Natives in this village were real friendly and nice, just the opposite of the village in back of the camp, and beyond the coconut groves.

Young Ted Alexander and his friends had soon explored every "street" in this village and had become pretty well acquainted with several of the families living there in. New Caledonia, having been a French colony, most of the Natives spoke French, and had some French Nuns and probably a Priest, living amongst them.

Two of Ted's friends were from the Cajun Country of Louisiana and spoke fluent French, so their problem of communication was solved. Ted and his friends spent most early evenings wandering up and down through the village, visiting with various groups.

They found the Native women very eager to do their laundry. They would drop off the bags of laundry one night and pick it up the next. Even though the Natives wore very few clothes, mostly loincloths for the men and skirts for the women, they always did a marvelous job on the young Marines clothes. The clothes would come back immaculate, folded to perfection, and the exact number of pieces as turned in. Also their prices were very reasonable. Not one of them ever tried to take advantage of any of the Marines.

One of the prime diversions of Ted and his friends was wandering around Gookville after the evening movie in camp. There were fires in all the yards, which served to light up the "streets" as well as provide the light for the villagers.

Each hut seemed to hold dozens of people, children, chickens, dogs and pigs. Visiting different families was a pleasant diversion, but the greatest pleasure was strolling by the hut that sheltered "The Belle of Gookville," She was a very lovely young Native girl who wore only a skirt hanging around her waist. Her slim, shapely body, and bare pointed breasts were a sight for the young Marines to behold. It would be a gross under statement to say they lingered long, and went very slowly, by the fence that surrounded her grass hut. Virtually always, this shapely young maiden found some excuse to stroll out of the hut and tantalize the onlookers, although she never ever let on that she saw them.

Virtually all the camps in the pacific that were not in actual combat had an evening movie. The movie was always outdoors and it's total refinements was a crude "screen," a small shack for the projector, and coconut logs, placed in a semicircle for the troops to sit on. These logs were quite often placed on a hill or rise so you had a pretty good view if not a soft seat.

Rain was such a common thing, and came up out of nowhere so fast, that a poncho was a must to take to the movie. But Ted was never sure whether one got wetter from the rain torrents, or from the perspiration, if he put the poncho on, for the rains were seldom cold, just wet.

The films were mostly old, black and white, and they would break several times during a showing, prompting everyone to yell, and curse, and otherwise heckle the projectionist. It was a rare treat when a fresh batch of "old films" would arrive on an island, as one sometimes had seen the same films ten or twelve times, at various periods and places. On most of the "uninhabited" islands the evening movies were the only diversions in an otherwise dull and monotonous life. One went to the movie regardless of how many times they had seen it, even if just the night before.

Every one saved their best and cleanest pair of faded dungarees to wear to the movies, in fact they often folded and placed them under their blanket, or mattress (if they were fortunate enough to have one) and slept on them, so as to press them. It was about the only measure of pride in their personal appearance they had left.

The only thing unique about the movie at New Caledonia was the old Native who always squatted on top of the hill, in back of the rows of logs, to watch all the westerns.

His name was Joe, and he always wore an old pistol strapped on his hip. Very unusual, as none of the Natives ever carried any weapons, except for spears or machetes. Ted and his friends got well acquainted with Old Joe, as he spoke pretty good English. Joe's one great ambition in life was to go to America and be a cowboy, so naturally, he became known as Cowboy Joe. He would spend hours quizzing the Marines about the American west, and cowboys, and the Marines would expound on how wild it was, and then cite last night's Cowboy and Indian film as proof. Old Joe's eyes would really lite up when they would tell him the Cowboys really needed him to help them out.

One evening as Ted and his friends were loafing by the fence that enclosed the "Belles" yard, who should come along but old Cowboy Joe. The young Marines teasingly asked him if he could fix it up for them to get a little "loving" from the Belle of Gookville. He uttered his usual statement "OK" and headed up the path leading to her door. After a few moments of wild jabbering and waving of arms, everyone except the young maiden started trotting away from the grass hut. Joe turned around and waved, and yelled. "OK."

The lot fell on Ted to be the first to test this new adventure, and with a fluttering heart he headed up the path. Afraid to go ahead, but more afraid of being called a chicken to back out.

Just as Ted stepped through the "door" into the dark gloom of the hut, he glanced back at the road and saw ALL of his friends running away like mad. They had chickened out. Ted took off in the opposite direction and hid out for awhile.

For days and days, Ted's friends quizzed him about his "experience" inside that grass hut, but all Ted ever did was smile at them, or say, "wouldn't you like to know."

Ted's esteem rose several degrees amongst his friends when a few days later he got a dose of the crabs, (body lice) and had a horrible time getting rid of them, but that is another story.

Oh yes, all the Natives of the South Pacific were referred to as Gooks, thus Gookville.

IDLE HANDS

NEW CALEDONIA

The food in the enlisted men's mess at the Replacement Center was horrible. In the mornings it was sloppy, soggy, dehydrated eggs (this was the early days of dehydration), a few strips of greasy bacon, and black coffee. Ted didn't even drink coffee.

The evening meal (no lunch) was virtually the same thing every day. Mutton, baked in huge pans, and floating in its own grease. A spoon full of dehydrated potatoes, and a big spoon full of dehydrated carrots. Now this same slop was served day in and day out, seven days a week.

In a Marine Replacement Battalion there was seldom many routine duties, or regular authority due to the fact that so many were constantly coming and going. Ted was surprised one day when his company was ordered out to the rifle range for weapons firing. They were to march to the firing range, which was a few miles distance from the camp. This activity didn't readily appeal to his group. After muster they slipped off, and hid out until all the others had marched out of camp, then they returned to their tent to sack out.

No doubt all would have been well and they would never have been found out except they got into a very loud argument over a card game. This brought the corporal of the guard to see what was going on. He reported them to the Captain and the Captain put them all on mess duty at the officer's mess hall.

At first this seemed a severe blow to the Gang's ego, and their freedom, but they soon found out the officers got special food in addition to the food from the regular mess. It was their duty to fry them up some pork chops or steaks, besides bringing up the slop from the enlisted men's mess.

Sanitary conditions on New Caledonia (and all the other islands as well) at that time were very poor. The Marines were only allowed one shower a week. The Gang went to the O.D. (Officer of The Day) and convinced him that the medical rules stated that each person on mess duty must shower at least once each day. They secured an "open" pass to the showers that were always guarded by an armed Marine. They enjoyed showers every day for the rest of their stay on New Caledonia.

It only took the Gang one meal to decide that meat was too good for the officers; and that most of it should go into their own stomachs. All was well as long as they only filched a few chops or steaks.

Everything went well until they got greedy and decided to feed the officers peanut butter one night and keep the whole case of pork chops to cook for themselves. That evening after a nice cool shower, a trip to the outdoor movie, and a stroll through "Gookville" to catch a glimpse of the "Belle of Gookville" they decided to cook their pork chops.

They had failed to anticipate what the odor of frying pork chops could do to a hungry camp. Just as they sat down to eat, several officers came in to see why they had had to eat peanut butter, when the Gang was eating pork chops. Also, a group of Marines had gathered to see what the tantalizing smell was and wanted their share, also.

For no good reason at all that ended the Gang's stay in the Officers Mess. Two days scrubbing the black greasy pots and pans in the regular mess hall had gone by when the Gang decided there must be an easier way to clean the stuff. The next day they rolled up a fifty gallon drum of gasoline to wash all the pots and pans in. Worked great: except that night no one could eat any of the food for the taste of gasoline.

The Captain got real mad and kicked them out of the mess hall. He said they had better not come before him again. Ted didn't know just what he meant by that.

To insure that no more problems were created in camp, the Captain, who was furious, said they would be shoveling sand for the rest of their days in his camp. This was to be a seven day a week task as he wasn't taking any chances on them having Saturdays and Sundays off.

Each morning after muster they were to load into an old dump truck for a trip to the beach. They would shovel sand into the truck, the driver would move over about fifty feet and dump it, then they had to shovel it back in again. Off for a mid day break, then back to the old sand pile until night. Not too many shovels full of sand were being pitched after the first morning. What worse could the Captain dream up: and who was to know how hard they were working but the truck driver, and he wouldn't dare tell.

The second day shoveling sand was Sunday, and this group of young men was to learn that possibly "shoveling sand" wasn't such bad duty after all, especially on Sunday.

It seems this was the beach where all the women and young Native girls (no kids) from a nearby village came each Sunday to bathe and swim. What a sight, as thirty or so women came marching across the sandy beach, dropped their sarongs onto the sand, and went laughing and giggling into the surf.

Now this was just too much of a temptation for the young men to endure. Quickly stripping to their skivvies, all, including the truck driver, joined a group of squealing naked, young ladies in the surf.

French not being too necessary, but helpful, it wasn't long before, two by two, the laughing and squealing was heading for the brush surrounding a very large coconut plantation, some fifty yards away.

Just as the first groups were reaching the fringes of the brush, an Army truck came flying onto the beach. Out poured a whole load of M.P's. They started off in hot pursuit of the skivvie clad young men, who retrieved their clothes, but didn't have time to put them on.

The M.P's were probably more interested in rounding up the young girls than catching Marines in bare feet and skivvies. They were soon outdistanced as the chase progressed through the coconut plantation, and across the swamps that the Corpsmen had traversed many times before.

Back in camp, scratched, cut, bruised, and sore feet, the Corpsmen waited the rest of the evening for the Captain to come for them with armed guards. The brig here was said to be a particularly viscous place, as were all the Marine brigs. It was a great relief when muster was over on Monday morning, the dump truck pulled up, and they hopped aboard.

Now shoveling sand was for the birds, so Ted and Sam determined to get out of it. The best way out of work in the service is a "no duty" or a "light duty" chit from a Doctor or from a Corpsman. If one is willing to do a little acting, or can conjure up a little temperature, these are easy enough to procure. After the noon break they went to sick bay, which was operated by permanent Navy personnel and not by the transients. Sam checked in with a "sprained" back, and Ted went in holding a very sore, (supposedly) sprained wrist.

The Doctor on duty checked Ted's wrist. Each time he squeezed or bent it, Ted oh'd or ouched, or winced. The Doctor determined that the "unhurt" wrist wasn't broken, and gave Ted some liniment to rub it with.

Ted, having a case of the "crabs," decided to get help for them too, so he asked the Doctor about it. The Doctor sent him into the next room, where a Corpsman was to spray him with campho-phenique.

Ted dropped his pants and was told to hold his "privates" up. Now, forgetting that his hands were covered with strong liniment, he obeyed. Ted soon found out what a "turpentined" cat must feel like. Him and Sam both got "no duty" chits and that ended their sand shoveling details, but not their Sunday strolls to the beach.

AUSTRALIA

Boarded USS Orizaba

Orders finally came for Ted and his friends to board ship, and leave New Caledonia. This transfer was a very welcome thing at the time. Had they of known what was waiting for them, it is very doubtful they would have been so anxious to leave this "Island Paradise."

No doubt it was fortunate that orders came when they did, for it is certain Ted and his friends would have wound up in serious trouble. You can only leave healthy young men so long with idle hands and feet, before they will make excitement happen. These young men had created more than their share of it already.

Boarding trucks, they reversed their incoming route, and wound their way through the hills of Noumea, and down to the harbor. They embarked on a troop transport, (a liberty ship) for a destination they knew not, for destinations were never given out to the troops. Only mysterious numbers or code names, and without the code books these meant nothing to the average Marine, Sailor, or Soldier.

Ted was now a seasoned traveler and knew what to expect when going aboard ship. Quickly selecting a bunk on which to stow his sea bag, pack, and rifle, he was soon back on deck, to watch the "getting under way preparations" and taking in the comings and goings of the busy harbor.

In a short time the ship was threading its way through the minefield surrounding the harbor entrance. It was soon on the high seas, with New Caledonia fading in the distance.

The Liberty Ships used as troop transports all had very similar accommodations and characteristics. The bunks were stacked four or five high, with only room between rows to squeeze through when turned side ways. The holds were all stifling hot with almost non-existent ventilation. They soon became almost untenable from the body odors of perspiration, and the smells of vomit from persons being seasick. It was a very undesirable place to be.

Each group of buddies, ranging from three or four, to six or eight, usually, more or less staked out a section of the above decks for their own private little area. Not that one stayed in the same spot all the time, but this was the place they always migrated back to. Some of the gang usually occupied the space, or else some other group, having a much less desirable position, would move in and occupy it.

If one had not found a place in the shade, which they seldom did, then the tops of the holds were always the next most desirable place. They were covered with wood, with canvas over the wood for weather proofing. (Much softer than the steel decks for sleeping and sitting.) The open steel decks were the last choice. The heat from the tropical sun soon had them hot as a broiler, but even this was preferable to being below decks in the stifling, smelly holds.

It always seemed to take from two to four hours, both morning, and evening, to wind one's way several times around the ship in the chow lines. Although very monotonous, this at least served to occupy a great deal of the steaming hot daylight hours. The worst part of a chow line was that it seemed to always wind by the ship's officer's mess. Ted could look through the portholes and see the officers seated at tables covered with immaculate white cloths. Negro or Filipino mess stewards were serving the officers food on fine china in white uniforms. It was very discouraging, as Ted was going to wind down into a steaming hot, stinking, mess hall, and be served slop on a metal tray. The thought of them having big tall glasses of iced drinks, and him having a mug of warm, powdered lemon drink, or hot coffee, didn't sit too well.

There was always card games, poker, pinochle, hearts, or cribbage, going on from one end of the ship to the other. One could wander around, and around, and watch, or join in a game, for participants were constantly coming and going. As soon as one person got up, another took his place. In this fashion the games never seemed to end, but seldom had the same participants for more than a short time.

A rainsquall was always a welcome thing, for even though one would get drenched, it brought the only coolness of the day or night. It helped reduce the blistering heat, from the steel decks for a short time. By late afternoon these decks would be so hot one could hardly stand on them. Everyone was just drifting from fore to aft, or from one deck to the other trying to find a little relief. Every time Ted found a place to sit down, some sailor, or officer, would come by and say, "You can't sit there Mac." Ted would mumble a few choice curse words, behind their backs, give them the "finger," then get up and amble on to find another spot. In these ways, the long dreary days finally draw to a close. With the coming of evening everyone began to group up again, and spend some time just talking amongst themselves: passing along the latest scuttlebutt gleaned from the days wanderings.

With the coming of night, the ships would blow their stacks. This would send big clouds of black smoke and soot into the air. This was never permitted during full daylight, as the smoke could have been seen from a great distance by any lurking Japanese submarines or ships. It was always done just at dark, every day.

Following the blowing of the stacks, the ships P.A. system always blared out. "Now Hear This." "All Hands, Darken Ship." "The Smoking Lamp is Out Above Decks." The lights were dimmed in the holds; or else red lights came on in place of the regular ones. Huge double sets of black out curtains were pulled across the hatchways and the ship became a different world. Of necessity, all games and most activity came to a halt above decks. Everyone began to pair off. Best buddy with best buddy.

The favorite spot now was at the rail, where one could feel the slight breeze, and watch the phosphorescent glows as the ship plowed a path through the water. There was a wide band of white froth spreading out from the bow that went trailing off into nothingness, as it was left far astern.

The Paravanes (mine catchers) running out on either side of the bow, on cables, leave their own wake, like a porpoise running along beside, and just under the water. There was a different view from every angle. On moon light nights, the ship seemed to be just a little dark blob, on a huge sea of light.

As the hours dragged on, the crowds thinned out along the rails. Now it is just oneself and their buddy, with a little private nook all their own. Now one can pour out their innermost thoughts and feelings, with the complete confidence that it will never be repeated, or one can listen to the confessions of the soul of their friend. It is a time of reverence, of confidentiality, a time when one is at peace with one's self.

Finally, it is time to seek out the gang again, be it on the hatch cover, or on the steel deck. Here they curl up without a pillow, blanket, or other comfort. They go to sleep for a few fitful hours of rest before the blazing sun comes up over the horizon, and the ships P.A. blares out. "Now All Hands," "Secure From Darken Ship," "The Smoking Lamp is Lit Above Decks." The routine starts all over again, and is about as predictable as the tides, or of day and night. The never ending chow lines, the blistering heat, the monotony of it all, will this journey never end?

Some two weeks later Ted awoke one morning to a new sense of excitement which was coursing through the ship. Word had spread that they were near Australia, and were going to land there. Everyone sought for a vantagepoint in the bow of the ship, for all were anxious to spot some sign of land. In all this time of sailing they had not seen one ship, or island. It was like one could sail on forever, and not get anywhere at all.

Finally, a great cheer went up, for on the top of a swell, land had been sighted. This land begins to grow, and grow, until Ted could see the outline in both directions. A great smooth expanse of the greenest green grass you can imagine. Then a lighthouse came into view, a white tower with a bright red tiled roof.

There was a narrow passage through this sea of green grass. All at once the harbor opens up, wider and wider, until it was as if the ship had entered into another ocean, so huge was this Inland Sea.

About half an hour after entering this harbor, they met an American Submarine. It was cruising on the surface, outbound, with a broom tied to its periscope. The sign of a clean sweep on it's last patrol.

After hours of sailing in this Inland Sea the harbor began to narrow until Ted could see the rolling green land on both sides again. Shortly, it narrowed until it was more like a large river, then all at once the hills rose up and houses began to appear. It was the most beautiful sight Ted was ever to see. As the ship neared the houses people began appearing on their porches and balconies, or hanging out the windows. From virtually every house, as far as the eye could see, people were waving white sheets, and white towels, and colored cloths, until it was one great sea of movement. There could never have been a greater welcome, or a more touching moment.

The people of Brisbane appreciated the Marines, even if the people in San Diego didn't. Even though the Japs were in New Guinea, right on Australia's doorstep, and they had a right to welcome help, it was a welcome Ted would never ever forget. Somebody cared!

All the houses looked so clean and bright, and could have been "Any City, U.S.A." but this was Australia, down under, and a half a world away from home. At that time the world was still a big place.

The P.A. system blared out. "Now Hear This," "All Marines will pack a combat pack, and prepare to take their sea bags ashore." "There will be No Liberty granted." Moans, groans, disappointment, you can only imagine.

A short time later the ship slid into a dock beside rows of huge warehouses. Australian Stevedores tied the ship up, and a gangplank was slid into place.

What does one put into a "Combat Pack?" The green recruit tries to put everything he owns in it, whereas the veteran has learned to travel light. Ted, like all the other replacements, tried to put in many personal items such as pictures, a New Testament, writing materials and shaving lotion. The only real necessities for combat are few; Rifle, Ammo Belt, Canteen, Poncho, and Dry socks. Virtually every other item he takes is a luxury. A luxury he cannot afford, when struggling through the swampy, muddy, jungles of the South Pacific.

In a short time, Ted and his friend Sam had hoisted their sea bags on their shoulders and were making their way up the companionways. There was a steady stream of Marines and Corpsmen going up and down the gangplank, and they joined the slow procession, down to the docks, and into the warehouse.

Such huge stacks of sea bags were in the warehouse that they seemed without number. Ted and Sam deposited their bags on a high stack, little realizing they would not see them again until long after the war was over, and they had been home for some years.

Now returning aboard ship, when a whole new continent lay out there, just waiting to be explored, seemed such a waste. Ted and Sam decided to look around just a little bit, for they knew the ship couldn't sail for an hour or two at best, and might even be tied up there for days.

Ducking behind the stacks of sea bags, they found a door leading to the outside, away from the ship. An older Australian man who was very friendly guarded the door. He talked such funny "English" that it was hard to understand what he was saying.

The Australian workers were all older men, for the young ones were all in the service. Most were in Africa, or India, and almost none were left to guard the home shores, or to "entertain" the lovely young ladies. Maybe this was the reason for the warm welcome. They took a Tea Break nearly every hour. They would brew their tea on a little stove. The guard said tea should never be brewed in a metal pot.

Ted and Sam had been told that a pack of cigarettes was worth its weight in gold in Australia. Though neither of them smoked, at this time, they had brought along several packs, "just in case." They offered the guard or watchman a pack if he would let them out the door. He took the cigarettes and never hesitated. He only admonished them to "Watch out for The Bloody M.P.s as they are all over the streets."

What a thrill it was to set foot on Australian soil, and just anticipating taking a few minutes stroll down a side street, they set off.

Not far from the docks they came across a little store, that was much like our "old" neighborhood stores. Here they were able to buy milk for the first time since leaving the states. Ted couldn't believe how many bottles they consumed. Had they of known there wouldn't be more for the next two years, they would no doubt have consumed even more.

A lovely young lady and an older woman ran the store, probably her Aunt or Mother. Sam and Ted talked with them for quite some time before two quite "thirtish" "ladies" came in, one obviously pregnant. These "ladies" offered to show the two Marines some of the city, if they would only go with them. By this time it was getting dark. Ted and Sam knew they should be getting back aboard ship, but the offer was just too tempting. After not talking to a "white girl" for so long, (It only seemed long then. Two years later, without speaking to another white girl, it was long.)

It was a great thrill to carry the meager bag of groceries, and walk down the streets, with a woman's arm around Ted's waist, and his around hers. (Part way at least.)

It was only a couple of blocks to the ladies "flat" and Ted and Sam quickly learned that unlike American girls, Australian girls were very uninhibited. Shortly there after the two young Marines made an excuse to leave the "ladies," and the flat, and struck off for town on their own.

There were few people on the streets, but the ones who were, were so very friendly. It was only a few short blocks before Sammy and Ted had struck up an acquaintance with two non-thirtish, and definitely non-pregnantish, young ladies. They were all strolling towards a "Pub" when the inevitable happened.

A Jeep, with two M.P.s passed and eyeballed the two out of uniform Marines. The Jeep started making a fast U-turn at the next corner. Ted and Sam knew they were in big trouble, but first they had to be caught. They took off on a dead run, around the corner, down an alley, through back yards. Dogs were barking and snapping at their heels. People were yelling and pursuing them, over fences, through yards, around houses, more alleys, and more streets.

Some how they managed to elude all their pursuers, and miraculously, dash into the same little store they had started from.

The young lady wanted to know what the trouble was. They told her, "The Bloody M.P.s were after them". She immediately took them into their living quarters and hid them out in the bedroom, saying she would return soon.

Shortly, there was the sound of heavy boots on the wooden floors, gruff voices of inquiry, then silence, but how to get back to the ship again.

This time Mama came in and said they were going to close the store for the night and would be back shortly; and sure enough they were. Ted liked the young lady, and the older one struck up with Sam, who was a great deal taller, and looked older than Ted.

As seemed the custom, tea was soon brewing in the kitchen. Tea and sweet cakes were soon served on lovely china, which Ted was afraid might break, it looked, and felt so fragile. When tea was over, baths were offered, and it is certain the two young men needed them, like bad, after the weeks aboard ship with no baths at all.

Hot baths and a home cooked meal, what a luxury after the months of cold water or no showers and the greasy slop served in the replacement battalions mess hall.

Some hours later, the ladies said it would probably be safe out now, but they would motor the Marines back to the dock, just to be sure. It was a good thing they were so generous and thoughtful. (It was only much, much later that Ted realized they had probably used most of their petrol allotment.) When they pulled up to the dock, the ship was no longer there, and a new watchman was on the gate.

They shoot soldiers for desertion in time of war, and this fact flooded Ted and Sam's mind. After much entreaty it was learned the ship was at another dock for refueling, and it was on the other side of the harbor.

The ladies inquired directions to the new dock from the watchman. Soon they were motoring Ted and Sam along in their vintage small car, to the new location.

Relief! You will never know what a beautiful sight the old P.A. U.S.S. Orizaba was, when they pulled up beside another dock, and there she was, with smelly fuel lines over the side.

Hasty good byes were said. Sam and Ted got back aboard without incident. It was no problem to get aboard, for who would want to stow away on a ship headed for the combat zone.

It was only a couple of hours before the ship sailed away, bearing the two young Marines. But the memory of a "Night in Brisbane," and, of a lovely young lady, who knew how to send a young man off to war, would linger long.

Map of the Pacific battle area - The Japanese had overran most of the islands in their initial onslaut

NEW GUINEA

Ted was back aboard ship and the mood had changed. No longer was it sort of a holiday atmosphere. Seems everyone realized at the same time that they were really going to war. Those combat packs, the sense of urgency, the whole tempo had changed. That brief interlude on the Australian continent was at an end before it had hardly begun.

It was a silent bunch of young Marines who stood at the rails and watched as the ship slipped its berth and backed away from the Brisbane docks. How those huge propellers stir up a muddy froth as they bite into the water, trying to get the big chunk of pig iron moving. The decks vibrate, and the whole ship shudders, and shakes, as it starts to move, then the whole process is repeated as it shifts from reverse to forward.

Inch, by precious inch, it slides away, and soon is clear of all obstacles. It never ceased to amaze Ted that so many tons of steel and cargo could bob along on top of the water, when every time he got in the water, he went straight to the bottom.

Back down the channel and out into that huge open bay, but this time the narrow passage was not an inviting sight. It was a rather lonesome, forlorn sight for tensions was still mounting. Everyone knew that for many of the Marines the chance to see this beautiful harbor would probably never come again.

Even the ocean and the sky seemed to pick up the somber mood. The ocean became angry, with huge, rough, rolling swells. The skies turned sullen, gray, and drizzly, as if even the Gods were sad.

Aboard U.S.S. Orizaba

A few days later Ted stood by the rail watching as the coast of New Guinea came into sight and the ship pulled into Milne Bay and dropped anchor. A few days later they sailed to Goodenough Island, then on to Oro Bay New Guinea. The shoreline became outlined against the dark skies. It was a deep, dark green with huge towering trees, the most forbidding, and abominable looking place Ted had ever seen.

No docks or gangplanks here, it was over the rails of the swaying ship. Down the cargo nets, suspended over the side, into the bouncing higgins boats, for the journey to shore. No big wide sandy beaches here either.

The ocean went right up and onto the land. Shrubbery and mangrove swamps came right out into the ocean currents, for such they seemed rather than the big, rolling breakers, that crash upon sandy beaches everywhere.

It seemed that no more fearsome or un-godly place could ever be found than New Guinea, but then, Ted had not yet been to New Britain. Deep, dark, wet, and the most depressing atmosphere one could ever dream of.

From out of the trees and swamps came the most heinous screeches and screams of the birds and animals that infested the place. A most unnerving experience, especially for a raw recruit who had never seen combat.

There was still Japs around, and more struggling over the towering mountains, and through the dense forests to reach this area. Jap snipers were still taking a few pot shots at the troops, and there were still roving Jap patrols scouting the area. This fact, or rumor, was not taken lightly by the "green men," as they trooped through the wet, soggy, overgrown coconut groves.

Ted looked for a Jap behind every tree, and was constantly glancing over his shoulder to be sure one wasn't sneaking up from the rear. The fear of the unknown is often worse than facing the actual event.

Rain!!! If you haven't seen New Guinea, or New Britain rain, you really haven't seen rain; you have seen only showers. There was over four hundred (400) inches (33 feet) of rain a year on New Guinea, and it seemed it could get half that much in any five-minute period. The rain literally came down in solid sheets and it flowed across the land like huge rivers.

There was a crude sort of camp set up at one end of a large coconut grove. The reason the camps were always in coconut groves was that they were the only semi-cleared areas. Usually the only flat ground on any of the South Pacific islands. Proctor and Gamble and Lever Brothers owned most of the groves. It was said that every time a coconut tree was cut down, or destroyed by bombs or shelling, our government had to pay them x number of dollars.

The tents were barely standing upright, and everything inside was wet and soggy. Ted was to learn that these sagging tents were near palaces compared to lying out in the open rain, or wallowing in a foxhole full of mud and water. This was only a staging area, for the real combat was on New Britain.

If one dared set their shoes on the ground by their soggy cots at night they would soon be gone. Every time a rainsquall came over, and they came over often, the water would run through the tents near a foot deep. Everything in it's path would be swept away. At most any given hour at night Ted could reach out his hand and pat the water that was flowing through his tent.

Needless to say one was always wet, a thing that was not unusual anywhere in the Pacific Islands. But New Guineas rain was real soggy, a deep, dark wet that just penetrated through and through.

All of the Marines and even the Corpsmen for once were set to working parties. They were loading L.S.T.s. (Landing Ships Tank.) "Specially built small ships for transporting tanks, and trucks, and heavy equipment, and infantry to the battle fronts." Or L.C.T.s. (Landing Craft Infantry) both could go right up onto the beaches and drop a front ramp so the vehicles or troops could wade, or drive ashore. They were preparing for the run to New Britain. They would take valuable cargo, and fresh troops, to the Marines who were locked in mortal combat with the Japs who held the island.

The few trucks that were available were loaded and put aboard the L.S.T.s, but most of the supplies had to be carried on one's shoulders. This was the very early stages of the war, and very little of the necessities were available. Virtually none of the equipment to move it had reached the front yet.

There was plenty of ships and aircraft to deliver daily loads of sea foods, meats, fine pastries, fine wines and liquor or women, from all over the U.S. and Europe, to McArthur and his staff, who were living in mansions in Australia. There was no ships or aircraft available to deliver food, or ammunition, to the Marines who were fighting for their lives in the front lines. Such was the fortunes of war.

The first battles with the Japanese were really pretty much hand to hand, compared to the later battles, when there was virtually an unlimited supply of ships, and guns, and material to overwhelm them with. Also, the First Marine Division was removed from McArthur's command and put under Admiral Nimitz and the Navy. They could control much of their own destiny, without the stupidity, and incompetence, that came from McArthur and his staff.

The final end was always the same however. It was eyeball, to eyeball with the Japs for the Marines. The percentages were a little better when there was a surplus of ammunition, gas to burn, water to drink, bull dozers to pull the trucks and guns through the mud. For now it was hoist a crate on the shoulder, wade through the surf and stack it in the cavernous hold. Return and get another one and repeat the process, or gang around a truck or jeep and almost physically move it through the soppy mud, and up the L.S.T. ramp.

It was four hours on, and two hours off, four hours on, and two hours off around the clock, until the ship was loaded and moved. There might be a slight respite before the next L.S.T. nosed into the beach, and the routine would start all over again.

The terrain and the atmosphere were such on New Guinea that even during the few times when Ted and his friends were off duty, they never ventured far away from the tents, or loading area. Occasionally, Ted would see one of the wildest, fiercest looking Natives flitting through the edges of the coconut plantation. All these Natives were either totally naked or wore only a sort of loin cloth, the men had bones through their slit ears and noses. They either carried a spear, a club, or a hatchet. The women were similarly attired, or un-attired. They were always bare-breasted and usually completely naked, also, a sight that amused the young Marines to no end. If there were any burdens to be born, the women were the ones who carried them. Always they walked in single file with the man in the lead, and the women and an occasional child following.

These Natives were as different from the natives on New Caledonia as a drug store Indian is from a wild one. Many of these natives were real cannibals, and were seeing their first white man. The New Guinea natives were one of, if not the last people, to come out of the dark ages.

Ted would always wonder if it was right to try and "civilize" these people. They had no jobs, they danced and sang, and ate when there was food. When the food supply ran out they moved to a more abundant area. They fought their enemies, and celebrated with their friends or families. For the most part, they lived a life of ease, and died at a young age. Who could ask for anything more?

Once Ted stepped away from the beach area the huge towering trees and vines blotted out the sunshine and light. Everything was in semi darkness, wet, soggy, and very forbidding. Every few minutes there would be a piercing, screeching sound from the birds and animals in the jungles, but they were seldom seen for the density of the foliage.

Sometimes they sounded exactly like humans screaming, and who was to say they weren't.

Three or four days after landing on New Guineas shore, when the L.S.T.s were loaded, orders were issued to get your gear and fall in on the beach. Muster was held, and each person was assigned to one of the three L.S.T.s. They were issued "extra" ammo clips for their weapons and sent aboard.

There were no fond memories left on New Guineas shores. There was no desire to stay just a little longer. Everywhere in the pacific was called "Jungle" in the press, but New Guinea, and New Britain really earned the name. The huge towering rainforests, the mangrove swamps, the endless rain, the screeching and screaming were left behind, with no regrets.

Surely it could be very little worse, fighting Japs on New Britain, for such was Ted's destination, than rotting in New Guinea.

Some months later there was a bulletin read at muster informing all hands that anyone, who had been in New Guinea at any time between a certain date, and a certain date, was authorized to wear a battle star on their Asiatic-Pacific combat ribbon. Big deal! This was the way McArthur got most of his medals. He would wait until the fighting was all over, fly in, get his picture taken, and collect his credits for the medals, then fly back to his wife, kids and servants.

The Natives and animals were welcome to New Guinea.

NEW BRITAIN I

Embarked on U.S.S. L.S.T. Patsy #245

Aboard the LST's (Landing Ship Tank) the mood of the troops had taken another turn. Now, instead of the fearful apprehension that had invaded the ship when it left Australia, the mood had changed to one of quiet, more of speculation, or of relief. They were finally coming to a climax of what they had been training for since the very first minute of entering the service.

The old Army-Navy game of hurry-up-and-wait was about over, for this was the last wait. Everyone knew that the time of reckoning was at hand. "Who would be the living, and who would be the dead? Who would be the Hero and who would be the Coward?" "Please Lord, let it not be the coward!" For who can say which heart will faint at any given time.

The Good Book says something like, "One excelleth today and another tomorrow," So much of ones destiny is controlled by chance. What one would do one second would probably be totally different in the mere twinkling of an eye's time.

It has been said, "There are no Atheists in fox holes." There seemed to be no atheists aboard those LST's for virtually everyone, in his own way, was asking his God to give him the strength, and the courage, to face what ever might lie ahead. "Please lord, let it not be the Coward."

An LST is much like a big barrel that has been flattened on the topside. There is a huge, cavernous hold in which the front hinges down to make a landing or loading ramp. Tanks and trucks can be driven on or off the ship by way of this ramp. Even fully loaded they draw very little water. They can run right up on the beach to load or unload thus requiring no transfer of troops or material to other vessels for landing.

On either side are several very narrow compartments with bunks for the crew, and for some of the troops. In the stern is a small galley, mess hall, lounge combination, and the engines and officers quarters. Everything is extremely compact, or crowded, to say the least.

Topside the Control Tower is in the stern and a large flat cargo deck is forward: with tie downs for the vehicles which are brought topside by an elevator from the lower hold.

Virtually every inch of the decks, topside, and below, were covered with vehicles of various descriptions. Sandwiched between, around, under, and over, was the loose cargo, crates, boxes, gas and oil drums, water drums, and cargo of all shapes and description. The LST's were the "work horses" or infantry of the navy. Shipping was in such short supply at this time that every available inch of space was taken advantage of.

The troops lounged, slept, and for the most part ate on any flat spot they could find, on top of trucks, on the hoods, on top of crates or barrels. Underneath trucks was the most desirable spot for it was in the shade, and somewhat out of the rain. The very limited sleeping and eating quarters below decks were so crowded and stifling that one could hardly walk through them, much less sleep there, even if they drew a bunk.

Aboard any ship, a life jacket became what the rifle was on land. One's best friend, and constant companion. The life jacket was never out of one's hands, or off of one's back, usually over one's shoulder. It was a pillow at night, a nuisance by day, hot, bulky, and just a real headache to keep up with. It was a rule aboard "ALL" ships that everyone has one in their possession at all times. You just better not get caught without one.

Before the LST's could back off the beach, General Quarters, Condition Red, was sounded. Japanese planes were in the vicinity.

Due to the fact there were Jap patrol boats, destroyers, or planes, constantly patrolling the New Guinea, New Britain strait's, and surrounding waters, General Quarters was seldom completely off. Sometimes it was General Quarters, Condition Yellow, which meant they could stand by, or nap, near their guns, instead of manning the guns and being ready to fire instantly.

The LST's were very vulnerable. They were slow and fat, lightly armed, and really just "sitting ducks" for any enemy planes or ships. Early mornings were the most dangerous times, for planes could come out of the sun and be diving before they were seen.

The LST's sailing's were timed so as to arrive at their destinations shortly after daylight. This was to take advantage of the darkness for protection against Japanese planes during their final approach.

The days were weary and draggy aboard the LST's. They seemed to be sitting still, so slow did they progress, and one could hardly see a wake. There was nothing to do but play cards or "gossip." There was no room to stroll around, or to do calisthenics, or to exercise. One was lucky to find a spot just large enough to lie down in to sleep. Meals were of necessity, very limited; the final breakfast long before daylight, was a real treat for the cooks had did there best with what was available. They served bacon, dehydrated potatoes, dehydrated eggs, and coffee. Always there was plenty of coffee. This would be the final meal for some of the troops on board.

The dawn came, bright, clear, and warm. There was their destination, Borgan Bay, Cape Glouster, New Britain. Lying there as calm as a sheet of glass, the ocean ran right up to the jungles edge. (Another deep, dark, impenetrable, green.) No coconut groves here, there were just mangrove swamps and rain forests, rising up to the sky as far as Ted could see.

As the ships drew closer to land, the boom, boom, boom of big guns could be heard, coming from somewhere within that green blob. It was impossible to see, or tell exactly where they were coming from, or from whose guns. As it was to turn out, they were from both, the Marines and the Japs.

The ships had been at General Quarters all night and with the coming of dawn, they went on G.Q. condition Red. The troops, having received an early wake up call, and an early breakfast, gathered their possessions and weapons. Checked for live rounds of ammunition in their rifles, and made ready for what ever it was they were going to face.

The word came blaring over the P.A. system. "Now Hear This," "Now all troops, stand by with your gear, be ready to disembark as soon as the ship touches land."

Just before the ships reached the surf, Ted could see people on the beach. A "Beach Master" with signal flags, guiding the LST's to the proper spot to land.

The G.Q. siren blared again, and the P.A. system announced; "Now all hands, stand by to repel air attack." "Now all troops, stand by to hit the beach and disperse."

The sounds of machine gun and rifle fire could now be heard coming from under that green umbrella.

Down in the hold, the drivers were revving up their engines, getting ready to off load as soon as the ramp touched down. The smoke and fumes was stifling. The troops amassed in the hold, ready to swarm ashore, were choking, gasping for breath.

There was a scraping, a shuddering, the ramp dropped and almost instantly, everything, and everyone was in motion. Full speed ahead, through the surf, and sand, and mud, and up under the great canopy of trees.

There was the sound of an airplane and the ships antiaircraft guns opened up. Streams of tracers flowed forth; black puffs appear in the bright blue sky. The plane dived and dropped some bombs that exploded in the water, just aft of the LST's. The black puffs of exploding shells followed it, as it crawled away. Not one speck of activity had stopped. The unloading was going on just as if nothing had happened. "Welcome to New Britain," the Man said.

The big guns were still booming, and the little guns were still talking to each other. Just a little "skirmish," the Man said. "Not to worry," he says, "The Japs are maybe two or three hundred yards away." Nervous glances keep trying to penetrate the dark gloom under the rain forest.

Stand by for roll call, and assignment, the Man said, but don't bunch up. When I call your name step forward, and stay with the group you are assigned to.

He yelled so and so, Able Co. 1st. Marines, So and so, Baker Co. 5th. Marines, So and so, Charley Co. 1st. Battalion 7th. Marines, etc., etc. "Alexander, Ted," G.R.S. 1St. Service Battalion; so the fickle-finger-of-fate had made her choice, and one's destiny was sealed, just like that.

Five or six Corpsmen were assigned to G.R.S. and not one of them did Ted know, but what in the world was G.R.S. Not one of them had ever heard of such a thing, much less know what it was.

"Graves Registration Section," the Man said. But what was that? This was something they hadn't taught in Hospital Corps School or in Field Medical School either. "Just stand by and you will find out soon enough," the Man said. Ted didn't like the sound of his voice.

It seemed that no two buddies went to the same outfit, but such was the service. One day you were the best of friends, and the next you were separated and became almost total strangers. Everyone frantically tried to get the name of the outfit his friends were assigned to. "No transfers, no changes," the Man said. "The Man" is God.

Soon people started coming for the different groups, a sergeant here, a corporal there. They would troop off, only to disappear after a few yards, as if the jungles had just swallowed them up. Some got aboard trucks and crawled away, but Ted's group just waited and waited.

After some time the Man went and talked to a truck driver who was hauling supplies from the beach. After much talking, pointing, and gesturing, he told them to get aboard and the driver would drop them off, for he was going within a mile or two of their outfit; he thought.

They got aboard the truck and out onto the road. Was that really a road? It looked more like a long twisting, skinny, mud hole. The huge trees towered overhead until Ted couldn't see the sky. The truck bobbed and weaved, trying to miss the worst of the mud holes, and the biggest stumps. Brush and vines dragged the sides and the truck never got out of low gear, in the low range. Occasionally the "road" would pass close by the ocean and one could see the sky and the blue water.

There was a scattering of bivouacs along the way. A few jungle hammocks strung between trees. Shelter halves set up on the wet, soggy, brushy ground. People were trying in vain to dry a pair or two of wet socks on a bush or a wet blanket draped over a vine. There were unshaved, wild-eyed, sparsely-dressed Marines, slopping around in the mud and water. All these sights would become familiar signs of a near combat area to Ted before he left the South Pacific.

The new men were so frightened of the jungles they imagined there was a Jap behind every tree. Rifles were always at the ready. It was a miracle that someone wasn't hurt or killed on that trip.

It was really no surprise that the green troops should be apprehensive. Up to this time, the Japs had been portrayed as invincible, almost supermen. During the first months of the war they had swept the Pacific clean of almost all opposition.

The newspapers, the newsreels, and all forms of the news media had pictured them as the greatest jungle fighters of all time. Their fierce reputations of barbarism were well known. They took few prisoners, and the ones they took were worse off than if they were already dead.

It took some real soul searching to go up against a foe of that magnitude. Until the enemy was actually engaged, it was no wonder there were more than a few faint hearts. Once you squeeze a trigger everything changes. One's imagination is usually stronger than the actuality.

After some two hours and a distance of possibly five miles the truck ground to a halt. The driver pointed up the first "side road" they crossed, he said G.R.S. was up there, he thought.

After much entreaty he relented and agreed to take the replacements all the way to their new "Home." The side road was just a mere trail, only wide enough for the truck to squeeze through. It wasn't cut up by mud holes quite as bad as the main road, for Ted was to learn that it had only been dozed out a few days before.

Shortly, the jungle opened up, and all at once they came out above the rain forest into a field of Kuni Grass. The road was just as muddy, but there was the sky and sunshine. The deep, dark, wet jungle was left behind. This seemed to be another world, not as forbidding, even though events were to prove there were more Japs here than in the deep jungle at this time.

Finally, after a year in the service, and bouncing around from training camp, to training camp, to replacement centers, Ted had a permanent address. The location would change many times, and to many islands, but the address would remain the same. Graves Registration Section, 1St. Service Battalion, 1St. Marine Division. Fleet Post Office, San Francisco, California. A Division he could be proud to serve.

There were two rows of tents, perhaps a dozen in all. They were all set up with the "wall flaps" stretched out wide. This not only gave a great deal more room, but the main object was to allow for ventilation. The humidity and heat made this method of erecting tents almost a necessity. There was absolutely no privacy, but the wide open canopy furnished shade in the daytime, and kept one reasonably dry during the tropical downpours which came several times a day and night. From six to eight people were usually assigned to each tent. One's cot was one's own private kingdom, to have and to hold.

Ted and the other new men were logged in, introduced around, assigned a tent, and within an hour, they had found out what G.R.S. stood for. Sure enough, it wasn't pleasant.

So people do die in war, and some one has to gather them, or the parts of them, off the battlefield, identify and bury the remains. Ted's job, along with the other Corpsmen, would be to render first aid to the sick or wounded and to "identify" the dead.

There was a large contingent of Marines to do the physical labor, such as Stretcher-bearers, Gravediggers, Truck drivers, and Cooks. Mostly they were privates, with a scattering of private's first class, three corporals, one sergeant, and one master sergeant.

The commanding officer was a First Lieutenant. Also a Gunnery Sergeant (A Marine who had come up through the ranks and the lowest rank of a "Commissioned Officer," but the most respected) as second in command. The man in charge of the eight Corpsmen was Eugene Van Horn, a Chief Pharmacist Mate.

There was a room dug into the side of a hill, with a tarp stretched over it. This served as a "Morgue." It rained so much on New Britain that it was almost impossible to do the paperwork required out in the open, as was practiced in later campaigns. Poles had been set in the ground to form racks on which to set the stretchers bearing the bodies. They were set at about waist level. This made it very convenient, and sped up the work considerably.

As soon as Ted would finish with the fingerprinting and other ID work, two Marines would bear the body away and put another in its place. This would go on from morning until night.

The camp and cemetery had just been moved to this location from the lower ground along the beach. It was so wet in the low lands, and the jungle that the bodies that were buried would float right up out of the ground.

The Marines were in the process of digging up, and moving the bodies that had been buried earlier, to this new location. The stench from weeks old bodies was so stifling that it was hard to breathe. Ted could only sympathize with the poor Marines had to dig them up and rebury them here.

It was hard to imagine how there could have been more water at the old location. The newly dug graves filled with water as fast as they were dug. A large Marine stood on the shoulders, and one on the legs of each body when they were placed in the graves; to hold them down until the dirt could be shoveled back in, and packed down. "This would be a very poor place to get killed."

"Come Ye Back A Hero, or Come Ye Not Back Home." Somewhere, Ted had read these words, and one night, shortly before leaving the states, a young lady had whispered in his ear, "Come Back A Hero." It would be hard to become a Hero in G.R.S. But Ted was to learn that the Real Heroes were planted there in the ground, with a big Marine standing on their chest and legs to hold them down.

Cape Gloucester was on the southern tip of New Britain. On the northern tip was Rabaul, a huge Japanese Navy Base and Airstrip, from which they could attack, and control much of the South Pacific and Northern Australia. They had hacked out a small airstrip there on the cape. This was the purpose of the Marines assault; to deny them this forward base to attack New Guinea, and the shipping in these waters. It would also provide the Navy with a forward base for fighter planes to help protect its bombers and to help neutralize Rabaul, one of the bastions of Japanese power in the South Pacific.

Several times a day Jap planes came over and harassed the troops by bombing and strafing. These were mostly "strays" or singles as the Navy kept the air base at Rabaul pretty well shot up and under control.

The big harasser was "Washing Machine Charley." So dubbed from the sound of the aircraft's motors. It had a peculiarly loud clunking noise, and could be identified from the other planes. Every night, and usually two or three times a night, Washing Machine Charley came over. He would circle and circle, to just keep everyone awake, (which was no doubt his purpose) and nerves a little on edge, for one never knew when he would drop his "eggs." Sometimes he would drop them shortly after arriving, and sometimes it would be an hour or two after. There would be a short respite while he went back to Rabaul to re-arm, then, the battle of nerves would start all over again.

Several times there were three to six Jap planes that would come over at the same time. There was no cruising around now, they found a target and dropped their bombs. One found what ever cover was available and buried deep when these came over. Occasionally a few rounds of anti-aircraft shells would be fired, but at this time the Marines had no huge batteries of anti-aircraft guns and search lights, as they would have later in the war.

About a quarter of a mile from camp was a fair sized stream that flowed clear and swift at this point. The Marines and Corpsmen would occasionally go over there to bathe; trying to rub off "some" of the filth and stench. There were big black leaches in this stream, as in most waters in the pacific. It was necessary to check each other over when they came out of the stream. Otherwise, one would find a big fat (with his blood) leach on his body some time later. It was amazing how these things (usually several) could latch on to a person, suck their blood out, and him not even feel it, then there would be nasty, festering sores later.

The kuni grass (tall scraggly stuff, maybe three to five feet tall) fields held a variety of life; three of which were of particular interest. The first and foremost was the Japs. The airstrip and cemetery were somewhat close together which always seemed to be the case. The Japs never liked to give up an airport, or any other ground they possessed for that matter.

The most interesting thing that lived in the Kuni grass was the Wallabies; they were little miniature kangaroos. They would hop around nibbling the grass with the little joey's (Babies) in their pouches. (Quite amusing to watch.)

The third, and most deadly of all the inhabitants was the rats. They were covered with fleas that transmitted a deadly plague called "Typhus." Quite a number of Marines died with the Typhus Fever before a vaccine could be brought from the states, and all hands were inoculated. This was the most painful of all the vaccines the troops were ever inoculated with, and they were given shots for virtually everything. It was so painful that the instant the needle entered the arm, one would grab the arm and hold tight or try to squeeze out some of the pain. It took a good deal of time for the pain to subside and the arm was usually sore for a few days.

Everything burnable, weeds, grass, trash, brush, etc. was burned. As much of the rats habitat as possible was cleaned up, so, with the vaccine and the protective measures, the plague was finally brought under control.

It was a practice in the First Marine Division, that a G.R.S. Corpsman should accompany the "line companies" (the front line troops who did ninety nine percent of the actual fighting, their only real job) into combat. This was done to help identify the dead.

All information pertaining to the dead person was "supposed" to be logged in, including the area in which they were found, the company or squad that occupied the area. Their name if it could be procured from other squad members. All this information was helpful if no fingerprints were to be had from the corpse.

The theory was probably sound but in practice it seldom worked, and was something else. First and foremost, ones job was to try and stay alive and to eliminate Japs. The next most pressing need was to help the wounded so they would have a better chance of survival. Only later was any thought given to the dead, for they were already beyond help. However, this practice was useful when there was total "basket cases." At any rate, this accounted for the G.R.S. Corpsmen often being in the forward combat zones and with the line companies.

Twenty-seven (27) days and nights it had been raining with almost no let up. Water literally flowed over all the terrain, and stood inches deep on all the flat ground. Everything was soaking wet. Shoes and boots were saturated. Socks were never dry, only less wet. Billfolds and anything made of leather molded, rotted, and came to pieces in a few days. A leather watchband would rot in a couple of weeks. Ted had sent home for several, which would not arrive until after he left New Britain.

Only the very rugged Marine "boondockers" (shoes) seemed to hold up, but if one scraped the mud off, and washed them, they would soon turn green from the mold that would attack them.

The only way to even partially dry clothes or socks was to sleep on them. Even this never completely dried them and they were very damp when put on, but a few minutes later they would be sopping wet anyway. Either from the rain or from perspiration, if one put a poncho over the top of their clothes. At least in G.R.S. there were tents to sleep under. In the forward lines there was absolutely nothing but a poncho or shelter-half, or nothing at all if one was in the front lines at the time.

Even One's blanket was wet, almost like when clothes come out of a washer, before they are put into the dryer. Rain, rain, rain, wet, wet, wet, mud, mud, mud. Was there no end to the rain? It literally penetrated to the bone, men, material, and equipment. Everything was totally saturated. Would it never stop? But the fighting and dying went on, taking its toll of Japs and Marines alike.

After Ted's arrival on New Britain, the Marines completed the moving of the bodies from the old cemetery. A portion of the stench had been washed away by the rains when Ted got his first taste of combat.

Finally, scuttlebutt filtered down that one more big push could break the Japs backbone on Cape Gloucester. Preparations were made for the big assault on the Japs headquarters and supply dumps. Ted was assigned to accompany a unit on this assault.

Early one morning the platoon Ted was to accompany loaded on trucks, half-tracks, and jeeps. They proceeded down, or up an inland route, and were brought forward, where it was hoped they would be able to complete an encirclement of the Jap positions.

They followed a narrow road, or trail, through the open fields that skirted the upper side of the deep rain forest. Shortly the open fields gave out, and the forests started closing in.

As they drew nearer the front the sounds of the Marines heavy artillery were heard booming their voices over the tops of the trees. They were bombarding the Japanese positions in preparation for the assault that was already beginning to take place. Soon, Ted could hear the sounds of machine guns chattering, and of grenades and mortars exploding.

The trucks ground to a halt and everyone off-loaded and formed up into platoons and squads. Instructions were given out as to the direction and order of March for each squad to take. "Keep in contact with the unit on your left," the Man said.

The lines of infantrymen began to string out, then peel off into the deep, dark jungle. First were the riflemen and the automatic weapons people. (Thompson submachine guns, BAR's Browning Automatic Rifles, and Thirty caliber machine guns.) Following closely were more riflemen with boxes of rifle and machine gun ammo, then the heavier stuff, boxes of grenades and mortar shells, and mortar tubes. (Launchers)

Each and every one trained first and foremost as a rifleman, even to the Corpsmen, who were mingled throughout the squads. Their primary purpose was to care for the wounded, but first it was imperative to kill any Japs before they kill them. In the First Marine Division, regardless of rank or position achieved, one never escaped the periodic training on the rifle range.

The squad Ted accompanied was with the second, or support group, that followed close behind the assault squads. They peeled off and headed into the dark rain forest and were soon swallowed up by the vines, and roots, and undergrowth. Huge, towering trees beyond description reached for the sky and obliterated all traces of the bright sun, which was shining as they left the trucks. Their massive root systems started way up on the trunks and spread out, reaching for the swamps below.

Each huge tree base was a mass of honeycomb like, dark caves, that one could imagine, and often did hide Jap snipers or machine gunners. These had to be cleared out, or bypassed as the troops advanced. If bypassed, they would take their toll, but be engaged by the units following close behind.

A few steps behind the person in front and he was completely out of sight of everyone else. One second a person is with a lot of people, the next second he can be totally alone. Lost, with not one person in sight, and without the slightest sound of anyone moving around. It would be easy for panic to set in as this deep, dark, slimy, rainforest swamp closed in on every side. Even a Jap might be a welcome sight at this point.

Ted slogged on through the knee-to-waist deep water and slime, tripping over roots and vines, through ferns and lush undergrowth. Visions of snakes, alligators, and such flit through his mind.

The crackle of small arms fire draws Ted back to the present. The Japs forward lines had been reached and the resistance was starting to pick up over a wide area. A few yards farther and Ted struggled up, out of the slimy swamp, and started up a slight incline. The trees were just as big, and the undergrowth was just as lush, but he was on somewhat solid ground and had come up with other Marines. Not the squad he had started with, but who would be choosy. Any human being was welcome.

The whine or smack of a Jap rifle bullet is heard. The call of Corpsman, Corpsman, the Jap snipers have scored again. There was a flurry of Marine rifle and automatic weapons fire the Marines had spotted another sniper; who had tied himself away up in the branches of a huge towering tree. A few more yards and if one looked closely, they might see the riddled body of the sniper hanging in the tree. His blood was still dripping down to nourish the growth below. His body would soon disappear, devoured by the myriad of parasites and insects that swarmed in this tropical jungle setting.

A few more yards and it was no longer scattered fire. All at once it was machine gun, mortar, grenade, and light artillery fire, coming in, as well as going out. The ground began to rise upwards and the huge trees were a welcome bulk to hide behind. They had found the Japs, or maybe even worse, the Japs had found them. What was Ted's first reaction? He never knew. It wasn't fear, for fear itself had died back there in the swamps when Ted had found himself all alone in that vast deluge of nothingness. He would be afraid, and scared, many times afterward, but the fear of death itself would never come again until near the end of the war. He was then "considering" staying over for one more campaign, in China. A "still small voice" whispered in his ear. "Go home now, or you will never go home."

The Marines were probing to find a weak spot in the Japs lines, but none was to be found. In fact, they held the strong points, the high ground, and it was well defended.

Soon the gloom became deeper, and word was passed along to dig in for the night, for night was fast approaching. Where in the world had the whole day gone?

How could one dig in the massive root system of the jungle floor? No one could, but they found what protection they could, for everyone knew it would be a long, wet night. Ted found a downed tree trunk and scooped out a hole as best he could. He had a fairly open field of fire before him and would not have to crawl out in the face of the Japs to cut one, as so many of the Marines were having to do. All hands were part of the front lines this night.

Darkness descended upon the jungle and more rain came, although it was hard to tell when it was raining, and when it was only dripping from the great canopy of trees for they was dripping almost constantly, and one was always wet.

Total darkness came swiftly, and it was impossible to see one's hand before their eyes. How could one possibly see a Jap if he came right at him?

Japanese voices could then be heard up on the mountain. Sometimes loud screeching voices, sometimes just jabbering. What were they up to? Everyone knew they were coming, just where, and when, was the question.

Firing broke out on both sides of Ted and he quickly joined in, squeezing off his "first" rounds of fire, in a real, live war. There was fleeting glimpses of shadows out front. Grenades exploding everywhere, rifle and machine gun fire lit up and rended the night. It was only afterwards that Ted realized the Good Lord had rolled the clouds back and a bright moon had penetrated the forest just enough to allow the fleeting shadows to be seen. Another minute or two and the Marines lines would have been overran by the Japs.

The clouds closed in, and the rains began again in earnest. Throughout the long night many firefights broke out up and down the line but none came as close to Ted as the first.

Occasionally everything would go completely quiet, no birds or animals screeching, no gunfire, no voices, just total silence. At times like this one might wonder if everyone else were dead. Was he the only one left alive? Had everyone else pulled back and left him stranded all alone? It was real eerie to be just totally alone. At least when there was firing Ted knew there was still others left alive. Sometimes, it was a comfort when firing broke out all around, but not right in front!

The night drags on, and on, and on. How many hours can one night have? Ted never closed his eyes that entire night. He squeezed off many clips of carbine ammunition, some at real shadows, and some at only imagined ones. When morning finally came there were dead Japs not fifteen feet in front of his position, as well as all up and down the line. Ted procured his first Jap flag from the nearest one. He never knew for sure if it was his bullets, or some one else's that had ended that Japs career. They didn't look so invincible in death.

Where as at night one felt all alone with the breaking of dawn Marines were coming out of the wood work and were all around. Jokes, laughter, everyone was just glad to be alive to greet the new day. There would be plenty of work for the G.R.S. Corpsmen this morning. The stretcher-bearers were busy removing the dead Marines and Corpsmen from the battlefield.

A hasty breakfast of K rations. One's morning "duties" done, and the attack was again in full swing. The Japs were throwing everything they had down that hillside for this was their last bastion, and if it fell, so did they.

All morning long the battle became fiercer and fiercer. Everything the Marines could bring to bear would concentrate on a Jap machine gun nest, or log bunker. Inch, by precious inch, they crept up until a squirt of fire from a flame-thrower would end the chatter of the Japs machine gun, and the crack, crack, of the rifles. Then it would be move up to the next one, and it would start all over again, fiercer yet, if possible. Jap dead were strewn all over the mountain, but the Marines paid a heavy toll for that hillside real estate.

The sounds of battle could be heard from far off when everything would go quiet for a spell. The Japs were being pressed from all sides, not just this one.

By afternoon the skirmishes were getting fewer, but fiercer, if possible. The Japs were being pressed in, and were becoming desperate.

Nightfall came again and word was passed to dig in for another night. Try to get some rest, for tomorrow they hoped to take hill number so and so, which was to be later known as "Aogori." The Japs last stronghold on Cape Gloucester.

Ted paired up with a Marine for the night, no more alone if possible. They agreed to take turns sleeping but this was an agreement that would never be kept.

With the coming of night, the Japs became totally fanatical. They came screaming, Banzai-Banzai, hurling grenades and firing their rifles. The Marines answered with their own machine guns, grenades and rifles. Virtually everyone was squeezing off rounds as fast as they could. No flares were overhead here to light up the night. It was just fire at any flash, or shadow, or sound; then hope, and pray.

A couple of hours after "complete darkness" the young Marine sharing Ted's hole was hit by a bullet or a grenade fragment. It was impossible to tell which in the murkiness, but his shoulder was badly mangled.

It was some time before Ted was able to quit firing and attend to his wound. When the Jap charge finally fizzled out Ted put sulfa-powder on the wound and did his best to stop the bleeding with a dressing, but he had no morphine left for his pain. This was Ted's first experience in combat and he had not yet learned to carry a large supply of morphine syringes and extra bandages in his I.D. pouch. Ted was able to get some stretcher bearers to take the wounded Marine to the rear, but never knew if he survived or not.

How many charges the Japs made that night Ted never knew; they went on continually. The next morning the ground in front of the lines was covered with Jap bodies. Some grenades were tossed amongst them to be sure there were no fakers in there midst. Jap flags or souvenirs were the last thing on anyone's mind that morning. The price had been too high.

The resistance had dwindled to a few isolated pockets. Evidently the Japs had expended their manpower in the night. Later that afternoon only scattered shots could occasionally be heard.

Late that evening the remnants of Ted's unit was relieved and made their way back through the swamp, and back "home."

The morning and the evening were the third day and second night without rest, but sleep did not come fast, or easy, that night.

NEW BRITAIN II

Shortly after the attack on Aogori, the Japs having lost their main supply base, their airfield, and having been soundly mauled, started a withdrawal from Cape Gloucester. In fact it was to be more of an escape than a withdrawal. Since being thoroughly defeated at Midway Island the Japanese fleet made no attempt to rescue the remaining soldiers on New Britain.

Only by seeing, and hardly then, can one imagine the New Britain terrain. Along the coast, there was huge mangrove swamps with great towering trees, layers upon layers of roots, like tentacles, starting far up on the trees and reaching down into the water and slime, to draw up its sustenance. Small skinny trees, reaching up for the roof some hundreds of feet above, with tropical growth and vines everywhere. One could see only a few feet in any direction. The sun never penetrated the great dome of foliage. In this deep jungle it was always a wet soggy twilight, like a deep shade. No breath of air moved and the steamy stickiness just penetrated everything.

Inland only a few dozens of yards and the mountains rose up reaching for the sky, they too were covered with the same lush growth and towering trees. They were cut with deep ravines and canyons. Large streams poured down out of the mountains, spread out into the lowland mangrove swamps, and finally seeped on out into the ocean.

The only "road" was the crude one aforementioned that the Marines had dozed out along their perimeter. It ran from Borgan Bay to the vicinity of the airport.

The only route of escape for the Japs was a very crude trail hacked out of the swamps and forests along the coast. It was probably near two hundred miles through this terrain that they would have to slog before they got to their beleaguered comrades at Rabaul. It would be a totally impossible trip over the mountains. However, the Marines did make a wide sweep through the mountains and destroyed a few small units of Japanese who were in scattered bivouacs there.

Getting wind of the Japanese withdrawal, the Marines loaded a battalion of troops in landing craft and leapfrogged eighty miles up the coast to intercept the Japs as they came through.

Two G.R.S. Corpsmen were attached to this force and landed with them at Iboki Plantation. This coconut grove had been hacked out of the jungle. Being the only clearing for miles, it was used as a supply base by the Japs.

The Marines (with the loss of several lives) quickly took the plantation and the surrounding area, and destroyed the few remaining supplies there. They encamped in the coconut grove which was also the trail head for which the Japs who had "escaped" Borgan Bay were struggling towards. The trap was set and there would be no escape.

A few days later, Leeds and Franklin, for such were the Corpsmen's names returned to G.R.S. headquarters saying there was nothing left for them to do at Iboki Plantation. The Lieutenant was furious that they would return without being ordered to do so. He immediately dispatched Ted and Chuck Lassell to take their place.

Now eighty miles in a Higgins boat is a mighty long ride, but Ted and Chuck finally arrived at Iboki Plantation. This was a rather pleasant place after being at Borgan Bay. They could stroll through the coconut grove, pick through the scattered Jap supplies, or swim in the warm ocean and lay on the lovely sandy beach. There was a sandy beach here, for the coconut grove was on ground a foot or two higher than high tide. The mangrove swamps ended below and started above the plantation. They also surrounded it, and if one left the coconut plantation they were back in the swamps and jungles.

There was an unbelievable amount and variety of Marine life that inhabited the coral reef, which was only fifteen or twenty feet out in the ocean and was only about knee deep at this point. Ted found tiny octopuses, little seahorses, small, colored fish and snails or large shellfish beyond description. Every time he would pick up a hunk of coral it would yield some new marvel. In a different time-span, and different circumstances, he could have stayed there forever and just become a "beachcomber." This mini stretch of beach was truly a paradise after the filth and stench, the mud, and slime, of the Cape Gloucester jungles. Beautiful clear blue water, and bright warm sunshine, one could even be dry here, at least part of the time.

Just beyond the very narrow sandy beach the brush and tangle of the jungle took over and formed a "border" to the coconut grove. In this willow like brush, or growth, Ted and Chuck found a little shack. It was probably a coast watchers shack; it was just tall enough to stand up in at the center. There were two wooden bunks, one on either side, with a narrow passage between. It was open at both ends and afforded a perfect view of the ocean, and of the coconut grove. It was snug and dry inside. The first really dry place Ted had seen on the whole of New Britain. Ted and Chuck immediately put their combat packs and their G.R.S. gear inside, and appropriated the place for their very own little domain.

It was a miracle that some officers hadn't appropriated it, but then, Colonel Chester Puller was their Commanding Officer, so that accounted for it not being occupied.

Now Colonel Puller was a GI Marine. If you could have a sample of blood from him and checked it, you would find his red and white corpuscles wore Marine corps insignias on their caps and uniforms. They wouldn't dare be caught without either. Colonel Puller, it was said, had vowed to come home with a "Congressional Medal of Honor," (no matter how many lives it cost.)

The Colonel was later to become Commandant of the whole Marine corps, but for now, everything was strictly going according to the book. In the field, and here at Iboki, no officer ever got one bite of food until all the enlisted men had theirs first. Colonel Puller "demanded" that "His" First Marine Regiment be the toughest and best-trained troops in the whole corps. Col. Puller who wouldn't even let his men sleep on a thin, hard, GI mattress, even in rest camp, for fear they would go soft.

Col. Puller, who, when he spoke, every one jumped or squatted. Col. Puller, who would walk out between "His Men" and the Japs, and stop and talk to the lowest private on the front lines. Who would call his men by name and tell them he was scared too, but the lines had to be held at any cost. Col. Puller, whom his men hated, loved, and died for. Over all a rugged, mean little S.O.B. who could out hike and out fight any one in the whole Marine corps.

The first Jap prisoners Ted had ever seen were here at Iboki. They were kept in a chicken or pigpen, about ten feet square. There was nothing to shelter them from the rains but a couple of pieces of corrugated tin. The chicken wire was about four feet high and covered the top.

The four miserable wretches inside couldn't have stood straight up, even if they been able to stand. They were so emaciated that every last bone in their filthy bodies stood out sharp and plain. They were so starved, and weak, and sick from malaria that they hardly resembled humans.

When the American/Japanese interpreter would go into their pen to take them out for some reason or other, he would kick and slap them around viscously. It was said that this was the way the Japs treated "all" their own enlisted men, whether sick or well.

The poor wretches disappeared after a few days. Ted never knew if they were taken out and put out of their misery or if they were sent away for medical treatment and to a prisoner of war camp. At that time one didn't ask too many questions. They were only Japs anyway, not real people.

Japs were never considered humans, and dead Japs were never "buried" or any attempt at identification made. They were just bulldozed under. No markers were ever placed over them, whether in ones, or in hundreds.

Every day patrols were sent out to intercept the Japs who had survived and were straggling along the trace of a road leading up from Borgan Bay. Ted and Chuck often accompanied one of these patrols out in the pouring rain, and mud, and goop. On New Britain rain and mud just became a way of life. When it rained everything just went on as if nothing were happening.

These patrols were all very similar. They either went down the "road," or out around the back of the plantation. The men strung out and sloshed through the water and mud; around dead Jap bodies and soon, they were wet and muddy as the ground itself.

The Japs were on starvation rations before leaving Borgan Bay, and the only food rations they had, had to be carried on their backs. After two, three, four weeks of struggling against the elements, they were nothing but staggering skeletons. Many, if not most, had been wounded in the battles that raged around Cape Gloucester. Not having medicines, food, or shelter, many perished along the trail. The ones who had made it this far were either plodding along the trail, or lying in the mud beside the road. The very last drop, of their very "Being" drained from their emaciated bodies. More defeated by the elements than by the Marines.

Several times Ted was to see, what to the Marines was a familiar sight. For a brief instant, he would see the body of the plodding, skeletal, Japanese soldier come alive. The glimmer of hope that they had made it would shine in their eyes. Then, total dejection as they realized these were Marines and not their people at all. The long struggle had been for nothing. They would either hold the grenade or lay upon it in the mud.

Their bodies seemed to explode as the grenade detonated. So this was the fierce, indomitable, jungle fighters one had feared so much!

If there was any slightest doubt of the Jap being dead, a Marine would make sure with a well placed shot through the head. You were just as dead if a dying Jap pulled the pin on another grenade as you approached, as you were if he stood up and squeezed the trigger while looking you right in the eye.

One day while out "exploring" a long distance below camp, Ted and Chuck spotted a Jap who was in a little better condition than the ones they had formerly seen on the trails. Having no rifle, he reached for the usual grenade at his belt. Ted and Chuck, being somewhat closer to a live Jap than they liked, waited with pointed carbines for the explosion. The Jap started bringing his arm back as if to hurl the grenade. Both Chuck and Ted squeezed off four or five rounds each into the miserable creature. The grenade exploded as he crumpled to the ground.

There was no slightest question of his being dead but they waited a few minutes for any further detonations of grenades that he might have been carrying, then they proceeded to check him out.

A few coins in his pockets, and a "Thousand Stitch Belt" around his waist seemed to be the only things he had left. No doubt he had thrown away every thing else to lighten his load in an attempt at survival. Ted took the "Thousand Stitch Belt" as a souvenir which he later sent home. The only problem was, he had failed to launder it immediately, and it bore a stench that would never come out. Ted sent it home and his folks almost vomited when they opened the box. It really smelled like roses, compared to the "real" smells of war.

About a third of the way back to camp Ted and Chuck met a squad of Marines, double-timing it down the trail from which they had just came. They didn't stop to inquire, but just kept barreling it on down the muddy trail. It was only after the Marines came slogging back into camp a couple of hours later that Ted and Chuck realized they had been dispatched out to help in what had probably sounded like a real fire fight back in camp. Colonel Puller and the Lieutenant in charge of the detail were very cool to the Corpsmen after this episode. One can only imagine what the GI Colonel thought of two lowly Corpsmen assuming the roll of Marines. Everyone to his own trade and that trade respected.

This incident probably accounted for some of the Colonels wrath when a few days later Ted did a very stupid thing. What with all the rain and mud and slime it was really murder to keep a rifle clean, and in working order. Every Marine and Corpsman had learned to disassemble, clean, and reassemble virtually every infantry weapon in pitch-blackness. Taking care of one's weapon was the number one priority. It came before eating, or sleeping, or anything else whatsoever. One can survive without food or water for a long time, but one didn't survive long without a weapon in good working order.

One day, having nothing better to do, Chuck and Ted decided to give their carbines a thorough cleaning. Somehow Ted managed to get the bolt and firing pin assembly apart. A project he had never before attempted and one that some tools were needed for. After a long and arduous struggle the firing pin was finally secured back in the bolt, and the rifle (never ever say gun) was reassembled. Many a Marine in boot camp walked the barracks guard post all night with his "rifle" slung over his shoulder and his penis in his hand, repeating over and over. "This is my rifle, this is my gun. This is my fighting, this is my fun." They never ever said gun again, when they meant rifle.

Chuck said, "There is no way that thing will ever work again," but Ted was sure it would. There was a one star General encamped just inside the coconut grove, right back of Chuck and Ted's little shack. He was a kindly old "gentleman" who was totally out of place in a war. He would often come by and stop to talk and visit with the two Corpsmen. He was particularly interested in the Marine samples they brought up out of the coral in the ocean. This "Old" fellow must have had someone higher up that didn't like his looks. Who had shipped him out just to get rid of him, for there was not the slightest doubt that in spite of being out ranked by the General, Col. Puller was in complete charge there at Iboki Plantation.

Thinking (or not thinking) that the General was out of his tent, Ted took aim at the steel pin sticking out the top of the tent and squeezed off three quick shots. The General was in his tent, and was quite disturbed by someone shooting up his tent pole. The General came flying out the door, then came over to talk to the Corpsmen. Ted explained to him what had happened. He said, "just don't let it happen again" then he turned around and went back to his tent.

Before the General hardly got back to his tent, up ran a Lieutenant and four armed Marines. They "escorted" Ted back to Colonel Pullers headquarters, and the Colonel was furious. He ordered Ted to start helping some natives who were digging a drainage ditch around his headquarters building. This had no doubt been the plantation manager's home for it had several rooms and a wide veranda circling all.

The natives were using maddocs and machetes trying to cut through the masses of coconut roots, but they were making very little headway. Occasionally, they would get a little loose material and Ted would get a part of a shovel full to toss out.

The Colonel watched awhile with disfavor then ordered the Corpsmen to get their gear and catch the "night boat" back to Borgan Bay. Guess he didn't think Ted was working hard enough or else he reconsidered, and decided it was even below the dignity of a Corpsman/Marine to work with the natives.

He also ordered a Deck Court Martial for firing a rifle within camp limits. It was barely O.K. with the Colonel for a Corpsman to shoot at a Jap, but never at a Generals tent.

Just at dark the armed guards hustled the two Corpsmen aboard a stripped down PT boat. It's only other passengers were a load of Colored Marines. At this time Colored People were only used as laborers, and not as combatants. Colored's and Whites were just not mixed, so it was surprising to be put on board with them, not that Ted had anything against Colored People, it just wasn't done.

With more than a little fear of being thrown overboard in the darkness the two Corpsmen kept their weapons at the ready. They also chose a spot where they couldn't be surrounded. It was really pathetic how little one knew, and understood, of the different races at that time.

Total darkness engulfed the little boat before it was hardly away from the shore. Steering only by a compass and by dead reckoning, the PT boat started its way on the eighty-mile journey. The boat ran straight out to sea for quite some time. It was necessary to stay well off shore to clear the reefs and shoals that skirted the island. Though battered and mauled, the Japanese still could mount air attacks on craft that were caught out in the daylight. Their patrol boats still dominated the seas in this area. Some two hours later, while running at slow speed the sounds of heavy motors was heard. This could only be a Jap destroyer or patrol boat, for no American ship was to be in these waters this night. There were absolutely no lights on the PT boat and everyone was cautioned again against lighting a cigarette or smoking.

The sounds grew louder, and louder. The skipper was poised to crank the PT boat wide open when the sound of the motors seemed to recede a little. He eased the boat towards land to take advantage of the shallow draft and the darkness of the background. For a long time it was touch and go. The motor noise would get louder, then fainter, then louder, and then fainter. Evidently, the heavily laden PT boat had been glimpsed, or heard, by the Japanese patrol boat at some point, for they seemed to be seeking it out. Having only one machine gun, mounted aft, the PT boat would be no match for a heavily armed patrol boat.

The PT boat was just creeping along, keeping its motor noise to a whisper. The dim outline of the island could occasionally be seen. All at once, white, foamy breakers could be seen in nearly all directions. The boat was within the reefs, in pitch-blackness. A flashlight was procured from below decks. One of the crew, along with Ted and Chuck, laid out flat and hung over the bow, with the flashlight pointed straight down, trying to spot the treacherous coral reefs, before they tore the bottom out of the boat.

It was port, port, port, scrape, back off and ease around. Again, port, port, port/ no, no, starboard, starboard. STOP, STOP, back off, back off. How many times the crunching of coral was heard? How close was land? A block, a mile, two miles, ten miles, no one knew. Finally the boat cleared the reefs and was back in deep water.

The sounds of the patrol boat were gone, but were they in front, or in back of it? Still the skipper dared not bend on much speed, for who knew where the next reef or small island would lay.

Finally, the dawn began to break, and it was a happy bunch that had lived to see the daylight again. Better to take one's chances with a Jap plane than to wander through the reefs at night.

At last Cape Gloucester, then Borgan Bay were in sight. The PT boat glided along on the glass smooth water and up to the beach. Even wet land is preferable to being lost in the ocean. Ted and Chuck caught a ride back to G.R.S. headquarters, and "Home."

Needless to say, the Lieutenant was none too happy to see them back, but no more Corpsmen were sent to Iboki Plantation.

There was no more lovely beach and clear ocean water to bask in; it was back to the dreary, morbid, cemetery and camp area. Back to the leaches in the stream, to the mud and mold that permeated everything and everyone.

Now there was about as many bodies coming in to be "processed" from accidental death as there was from being killed by the Japanese.

Huge trees or limbs fell on, and crushed men working or bivouacked in the jungles. Trucks or gun carriages trapped men trying to help clear them from the mud holes. Cables broke on bulldozers or tow vehicles and entwined anyone within distance. Against all possible odds the accidents, as accidents always do, took their toll. A few men just couldn't take the environment any longer and ended their own lives.

New Britain would be a very poor place to get killed - Because of the incessant rains the grave mounds had to be rebuilt daily

Those pesky crabs that Ted had picked up in the "out house" on New Caledonia just kept coming back and multiplying. There was no Camphophoenique to combat them within any of the "sick bays" that Ted was able to visit. Daily, he plucked them and their "eggs" from his pubic hair, and from under his arms. One day he found one inhabiting his eyebrows and that was just too much. Lacking any medication to kill them, he hit upon the idea of using gasoline. Taking a piece of rag and wetting it in gasoline, he proceeded to swab down all of his hairy areas. Pubic, rectal, under arms, eyebrows, everywhere he could reach. In the tropic heat and moisture the gasoline blistered the skin. Much of it peeled off leaving some nasty spots, but the crabs never bothered Ted again.

Things on Southern New Britain settled into routine business. There were a few skirmishes with scattered bands of Japs. A few patrols went inland, and of course, the constant patrolling of the First Marine Division's perimeter to see that there were no unexpected surprises from the nips that might be hiding there.

The work at the cemetery went on, clearing the area and mounding over the graves. It was a constant job for the rains pounded down and washed away the mounds about as fast as they could be formed. Ted accompanied the Marines into the deep jungles for several days as they procured truckloads of long poles. These were hauled back to the cemetery and stacked up in a pile, and everyone wondered what they could be for. Having no duties except to render first aid to any Marine that might hurt himself, Ted was free to explore. It didn't take much exploring to find out that he didn't think much of the place, and was not about to wander off too far.

One day the whole detail decided to go to the beach for a swim instead of gathering poles. It was a rather pleasant day until they arrived back in camp without a load of poles to show for the day's labors. Ted wasn't allowed to accompany the detail any more. Seems that somehow he had gotten the blame for the day's escapade.

A week or so after the poles were gathered the reason for gathering them became apparent. One morning several truckloads of Natives were brought to the cemetery. They started constructing a huge log (pole) chapel. They erected a huge framework of poles, tying them in place with vines and rope. They were really agile, climbing all over the framework, and it hardly able to stand upright. When they finished, it was as sturdy, or possibly more sturdy, than if the Americans had of constructed it. They gathered great bundles of the Kuni grass and fastened them to the roof, making it really waterproof. Quite a construction job, even though it looked like it would be crude in the beginning.

One day a truck driver came back from the supply dump with a case of pork chops. This was the first and only fresh meat the G.R.S. section had seen in about three months or more. There was an "old" Corpsman, in his thirties, who was Jewish. He walked over five miles each way to see a

Rabbi, to get permission to eat a pork chop for dinner that night. He got permission, and probably ate the first, and only pork chop of his life. It was quite a treat and ended in a very festive occasion.

Somewhere, someone had procured several gallons of pure vanilla extract. They had it in a five-gallon Billy can, that night they came to the Corpsmen's tent and "shared" it all around, pouring it out into their canteen cups. The high, one was supposed to experience, lasted only a few minutes before everyone got deathly sick. The smell of vanilla lingered for weeks in the canteen cups, and served as a constant reminder to steer clear of the stuff. Chief Van Horn refused to believe that "his" Corpsmen would partake of such a thing.

It was on New Britain that Ted learned to play Pinochle. This was a card game that was to occupy many, many hours of a long, monotonous, tour of duty in the South Pacific. Without Pinochle, cribbage, and poker the days and weeks would have been unbearable, especially back in the "rest camps."

Rain, mud, more rain, and more mud. It was a welcome relief when orders came to pack up and leave New Britain. The nightmares of memories would remain forever, but were they real experiences, or only that, nightmares, that would haunt one for the rest of their days.

PAVUVU I

April 25, 1944 Boarded USS Wayne

It was with great expectations, and no remorse, that Ted's division started its withdrawal from New Britain.

For some weeks the scuttlebutt had been rampant. The division was going back to Australia, to Melbourne, where it had reformed and staged, after the Guadalcanal campaign. They were going to Hawaii; they were only going to New Guinea. They were going all the way back to the States (no one believed this one, only hoped.) To northern Australia, every hour brought a new rumor, straight from some clerk at headquarters, who had access to certain secret documents.

The great hope and expectation was to go back to Melbourne. That dream city, where Marines were welcome by all, except Australian service men. Back to where there were bright lights and young ladies, especially, young ladies.

Fresh milk, fresh fruit and vegetables, back to Paradise, six months of war wouldn't be so bad if there was a rainbow at the end of the journey.

It was a rather forlorn, grubby-looking bunch of young Marines who gathered their few remaining possessions and loaded into trucks for the final journey to Borgan Bay. Here they waded aboard Higgins boats for the trip out to the large troop transports, anchored in the smooth and shining harbor. Ted would always remember and marvel at the smoothness of the ocean in those waters. No swells, no surf, no whitecaps, just smooth like glass, but of course it could rage, like any ocean in a storm. Climb up the cargo nets, and down into the stifling holds of the waiting liberty ships. Dump his gear on a bunk, and back on deck to stake out a little homestead. The names of the ships were always different, but the routine was always the same.

The third day out everyone was greatly disappointed; the convoy of ships was heading east, and not south. Melbourne was not to be, this time. Hawaii was still a slight possibility but the rumor mill had now focused on "Guadalcanal." Was it possible that Guadal was to be their "rest camp?" For what ever reason the 1st. Marine Division was ever to remain a loner. Seldom did anything good come their way, except by accident.

A few more days sailing and one morning the ships steamed through a narrow opening, into a beautiful bay. The bay was quite large and could accommodate many ships. But except for when the Division was coming or going, there was seldom more than one ship anchored there, and often none at all.

Coconut palms waved behind a white sandy beach. There was a lovely blue-sky overhead and absolutely nothing else what so ever in sight. Gather the gear and over the side, down cargo nets and into the landing craft for the trip to shore.

April 28, 1944

No Australia, no Hawaii, no anywhere, only little Pavuvu, (PA-VU-VU) Russell Islands (a few short nautical miles from Guadalcanal and part of the Solomans chain) for a "Rest Camp." First Service Battalion, of which G.R.S. was a part fell in and marched about half a mile up the beach, and back into the coconut plantation. There was absolutely nothing there. The plantation had been abandoned for several years because of the Japs. Weeds, grass, brush and undergrowth had taken over.

Shortly a truck ground up the hill; loaded with tents. The Marines were soon busy off loading and starting to clear an area for the tents to be set up in. The ground was all mud and slosh, and it was covered with rotting coconuts that had fallen from the trees. Every time a Marine would pick a coconut up to toss it out of the way, it would fall all to pieces, spilling rotten coconut, and fermented milk all over him.

What a place for a "rest camp." Better to have stayed on New Britain. Some joker must have flown over the island, seeing the plantation and the lovely white beaches he thought it would make a good camp. Certainly, no one had bothered to explore the island.

As was the custom, the Corpsmen were allowed to do nothing in the way of physical labor. The Marines had to do all the clearing and setting up of the tents.

As soon as the tents began to be set up a truckload of cots and thin G.I. mattresses arrived. Ted and the other Corpsmen were soon sacked out, in the first tent up. Such was protocol that the Corpsmen got everything first, often an embarrassing situation. Next were the non-commissioned officers, Master Sergeants, Gunnery Sergeants, and just plain Sergeants. What, if any was left went to the Corporals, Privates First Class and just plain Privates.

Even before the first tents were up the rains came, and drenched everything, and everyone, but this was nothing new to men accustomed to New Guinea and New Britain.

By nightfall everyone was under somewhat soggy canvas. The weeds and brush were being trampled down into the soggy earth, and the Marines were slipping and sliding around on a muddy surface that was slipperier than ice. The foot or so of dirt covering the coral atoll would soon become a giant skating rink.

Along the beach, and back from zero to possibly fifty yards the land was flat, and only slightly above the high water mark. From this point it sloped up to a second plateau, which was some twenty or thirty feet above the beach level. This whole area was one huge coconut plantation, and the various battalions, company's etc. were set up in their own respective areas.

Ted's company was set up on the outer edge of the second plateau. This offered a lovely "view" of the beautiful blue bay, and of any ships in the harbor. It was also on the slope, and this would soon become a giant otter slide. The rains would start suddenly. A deluge would come down for possibly a minute, or fifteen minutes, then the sun would come out bright and clear. Ten minutes later it might start all over again, day and night. Just like someone was turning a big faucet on and off.

The cooks had set up a couple of tents in the flats along the beach and had "attempted" to prepare some hot food for all hands. The cooks tents, and later, the mess hall, was a long block from the nearest bivouac tents. It was necessary to traverse the lip of the ridge to reach them. It was virtually impossible to go up or down this slight incline without slipping, or falling, from once to several times.

Never (or so it seemed) at this time, was "food" served when it wasn't raining. Since there was no place except one's own tent to be under cover, it was necessary to traverse the slope going and coming. One would put a poncho on, go down and stand in line for twenty or thirty minutes (due to their rank the Corpsmen were permitted to go to the head of the lines but virtually never did) to get a mess kit full of hot "C" rations. Dehydrated potatoes and carrots and coffee or "battery acid." (Lemonade from powder)

The only way young stomachs could be filled was by getting both halves of the mess kit full. This left it wide open, and the rains would pour into it, and overflow the trays before, if one was lucky enough, they could get back to their tents. What was more likely to happen was that one would fall and spill their "food" all over themselves. Then they would have to go stand in line again, and start all over. It was virtually impossible to make one's way up that slope, trying to hold their mess trays under their ponchos.

This routine would go on for many weeks before screened in kitchens, and mess halls, could be constructed. Then, for the first time in many months one could sit down to a table, and finish a meal that wasn't mostly water.

With the coming of darkness came screams, curses, slamming and banging, from all up and down the rows of tents. In the daytime there was no slightest sign of living creatures, but as soon as it got dark, literally millions of rats, and billions of land crabs, came out of their hiding places. They (especially the rats) swarmed over everything, and everybody.

The screams usually came when a rat would run up the inside of a man's pants leg. It would bite him when he grabbed it with both hands and tried to squeeze it to death. A very harrowing experience, but one most everyone had before they learned to take measures to stop it.

During the night there would be screams when someone would be woke up by a rat chewing on his ear, nibbling at his nose, or perhaps taking a chunk out of a toe.

The sound of the land crabs crawling all over, banging their bodies and their claws together, or fighting over some morsel of food was terrific. It sounded like dry bones being rattled together. All night long the screams, the yelling, and the cussing, kept up as person, after person was "attacked by the rats." Better the fighting on New Britain, at least one could fight back there.

With the coming of dawn the creatures disappeared, but every time someone stuck his foot in a shoe or boot he would scream like a banshee. Every shoe was filled with land crabs, or rats, or both. From that day forward the first thing one did in the morning was pound the heel of their shoes down to dislodge any crabs or rats, for any dark or sheltered spot was full of them. Every conceivable hiding place was packed with land crabs, and the tops of the coconut palms must have been alive with rats. Move a pack and there would be a dozen or so land crab's hiding there.

War was declared on the filthy things. They were squashed all over every thing. Every step one took they were on parts of the crabs. The flies (where the swarms came from Ted never knew) swarmed over the squashed carcasses, and the smell became horrible.

The next day mosquito netting was brought into camp, and there was a great scramble to procure poles to stretch it over one's cot. The mosquito netting helped as much to keep the rats off, as to keep the mosquitoes out, and there was swarms of both. Having to bring food back to the tents to eat didn't help anything either.

Things got so bad from a sanitation standpoint that a clean up was necessary. Fifty-gallon gas drums had one end cut out and filled part way up with sand. This was saturated with oil and gasoline, and then set afire. The Marines scooped up all the dead crabs and rats and burned them. For more than a week there was a contest to see which group could find and burn the most crabs. Finally, by hacking away all the cover, and turning over everything in the tents each morning to get the one's hiding there, they began to thin out somewhat. Hundreds of thousands of land crabs, and tens of thousands of rats, were burned in this manner. The fires went night and day. The smell was horrendous. The crabs were finally brought somewhat under control, but the rats would remain a hazard as long as the Marines remained on Pavuvu. Even though they were thinned out with killing, and poison, and every conceivable method of trapping them.

The troops coming out of the recent combat were real lethargic at first and would only do what was really necessary. The Corpsmen would spend twenty-four hours a day in the sack, and would hardly crawl out, even to go to chow. For the first week or two, one would usually try to negotiate the slope leading down to the mess kitchens and bring back as much food as he could to share with the others.

A road was bulldozed out along the beach area. The coconut trees were shoved out of the way, and it was reasonably leveled. The whole thing became one big lobloily after a few days. Trucks had to be dragged along by bulldozers; their wheels so buried and clogged up that they didn't even turn. They just slid along like a big sled, digging into the ground as they went. Persons trying to walk this road would sink up to their knees. One had to pick his spot carefully to cross it, as the battalion had to do to get to chow.

Some weeks later a coral pit was opened not far from the mess tents. A bull dozer scraped off the top soil, and would push up mounds of the coral to be loaded on trucks, and hauled away for paving. Throughout the Pacific coral was mined and used as blacktop. It was like small gravel and would pack down just like black top or cement. All roads, airport runways etc. were made from it. Without the coral paving the mechanized units of the Americans would have been in big trouble. The C-B-s could do in hours with coral what it would have taken months to do with blacktop or cement, and it was almost as efficient.

Bucket brigades of Marines were formed to carry cans, or buckets, or helmets full, of the coral across the road to First Service Battalion's area. The Corpsmen for once even volunteered to help in this task. The very first thing to get coated was the "hill," so afterwards one could go to chow with a reasonable chance of not falling. The company "street" received a sprinkling as well as the hill. So precious was this material, at this time, that guards were posted on the "pit" and wouldn't let anyone take any, except to pave the main roads. It would be a long, long time before the rest of the company streets and the tent floors, etc. would be paved, so one wasn't slopping around in mud ankle deep.

Eventually, all the roads and streets, and even a "parade ground" did get paved. One could get from one area to another pretty well and trucks and jeeps whizzed along the road. Still it was necessary to make the long walk to the mess tent to get some chow, which would only be wet slop by the time it was carried back to his tent. Then one returned to wash the mess kits in half drums of very hot soapy water with fires kept burning under them when possible. An unwashed and unrinsed mess kit was a sure enough invitation to a severe case of dysentery. After one such bout, no one had to be forced to thoroughly clean his mess kit.

Open pit toilets were dug outside the tent areas. Lime was sprinkled on them to keep down the smell, and the flies. Later they would build a wooden box, with holes, and lids, but they would not be covered and screened in on this trip to Pavuvu. Wait for a rainsquall to blow over, then make a dash for it, and hope it didn't start again until you were finished. Soaking wet boards don't make the most comfortable of toilet seats, however, they do beat no seat at all.

There was no water piped in, and no showers anywhere. There was no fresh sparkling stream to bathe in either. The only way to bathe was to be ready when the rains started. Hop out and lather up, then hope it kept raining long enough to rinse off, which it seldom did. How in the world could rainsqualls know when one was fully lathered up? After a few sessions of being caught thus, Ted and his friends loosened one corner of their tent flap, this formed a reservoir that would hold five gallons or so of fresh water. This could be dipped up in a helmet cover and used for bathing, rinsing, washing clothes, or shaving. Soon all the tents were used in this way. Drinking water still had to come from a trailer at the mess tents. It would be a few months before water was piped in, and an open shower was built, but no hot water was ever available on Pavuvu.

It was astonishing to see the creativity of the young troops. Each tent soon had a crude table and some stools, blocks of wood, or even chairs. Racks to keep packs and rifles up off the ground, and best of all, lights soon appeared. The most efficient light was a ketchup or coke bottle filled with gasoline. A wad of rag was stuffed in the top, with a piece hanging down in the gas for a "wick." It was necessary to pack the top really tight, to stop the gas from exploding. This gave off a good light, could be moved from place to place, and would last a long time. There were not many bottles available however.

The next most popular light was simply a can filled with sand and saturated with gasoline. This flared up quite wild when first lit and gave off lots of heat, which was never welcome in the South Pacific. It was also difficult to move from place to place. Placing the can on a board and just moving the board finally solved this. Also the can smoked more, but both were welcome additions to the tents. Now one could stay up after dark and play cribbage, blackjack, pinochle, and write letters. The days were extended, and the long dreary nights, nights without female companionship, were shortened.

Crude tables or stands were soon attached to a coconut tree in back of each tent. These, like the tables inside, were made from sticks, poles, scrap boards from crates, or anything else one could wire, nail, or tie together. Each person took their turn going out to wash up, shave, brush teeth, do laundry, or what ever else might please them. The helmet cover, that most versatile of all the troops equipment, was used as a wash basin, a tub for washing clothes, a bucket to carry water, a pot to cook food in, a coffee pot, and any one of a million other uses. One could even crawl completely under it, if he got scared enough, and most did.

Mostly the troops did all their shaving, laundry, or just lounging around in the nude. It was too hot and sticky to wear clothes, and they would be wet within minutes anyway. Occasionally, a modest soul would wrap a towel around his waist. A pair of shorts (cut off dungarees or khaki pants) was the uniform of the day. Nude or dressed, one always wore his shoes, for the coral was sharp and stobs were many and cuts just didn't heal in that wet sticky climate.

It was almost like Russian roulette standing under a coconut tree, shaving, doing laundry, or whatever. There was absolutely no warning. "Thud" and a coconut hit the ground, maybe inches, maybe twenty feet away. A great number of people were hit and badly injured. They either got it on the head, or in the middle of the back, as they bent over shaving, or doing laundry.

It was a completely different sound when the coconut hit someone, instead of the ground. Everyone laying or standing around would make a wild dash out to help revive, or carry the poor devil that had been hit back inside. Some were hurt quite seriously but Ted never knew of anyone being killed.

Several who had come through Guadalcanal, New Guinea and New Britain stuck their rifles in their mouths and blew the tops of their heads off. Paviivu was just the one straw too many.

PAVUVU II

In spite of the disappointment of not going to Australia, of the rats and the crabs, and of the rotten coconuts, life still goes on.

The troops soon began making the best of what few assets they had. The most important asset of all was their youth. Youth will nearly always pick it's self up from whatever depths of despair or adversity that has befallen them, laugh at themselves, and start all over again. This is why the very young are fed into the wars!

Camp and sick bay were set up under the exotic coconut palms

A Marine "Division" is in many respects like unto a large city or county, or state. It has some unit that will take the place of any business one can find in any thriving community.

First and foremost were the infantry regiments. In the First Marine Division these were known as the First, Fifth, and Seventh Marines. Each unit was made up of three battalions. Each battalion was made up of three companies. First = A-Able, B-Baker, C-Charley, Companies. Second = D-Dog, E-Easy, F-Fox, Companies. Third = G-George, K-King and L-

Love. Each of these units was broken down into three platoons, the platoons into squads. Each unit is under a successively lower rank of officer. When one knew their divisions, it was as simple as knowing their A. B. Cs to identify the different units. These infantry regiments (line companies) could be compared to the factory workers, or farmers, or whoever produced the "cash" crop, that all the rest of the city survived on. They did the actual fighting in nearly all instances.

Next came the support units, heavy weapons, machine-guns, bazookas, flame thrower units, tanks, war-dogs. Then came the supply units.

The supplies ranged all the way from ammunition to shoe laces to toilet paper, with a rare bit of luxury thrown in. There were cooks, bakers, butchers, and shoe repair shops, canvas shops, service stations, garages, machine shops, demolitions, hospitals, and yes, cemeteries. Water supply units, ice house, library, ships stores, you name it, and somewhere within a division it could be found. Generally each battalion and each company had a small section of each, drawing upon the main unit at division level. Each company was almost a complete unit within itself. A Marine Division was known as a triangle division; (compared to the army square division-four each of every unit) because they were divided into threes, three battalions, three companies three platoons. There was a total compliment of some thirty thousand troops. Of this only about twenty thousand would make the actual invasions of the various islands.

A city of thirty thousand covers quite a large area and so does a division of Marines. They were scattered over several square miles, with each unit like a city within a city. Each having its own toilets, showers, (if any) mess kitchens, sick bays, offices, officers quarters, bivouac areas and any other "business" one could think of.

Each unit had that salvation of all the "Pacific Paradises," a movie theater; consisting of a screen, a crude shack for the projectionist, and coconut logs placed in a semi-circle for seating.

On Pavuvu there were a number of theatres, with a large division theatre by the parade ground along the beach. These theatres were the salvation of, and probably preserved the sanity of all the troops in the South Pacific, as well as the crews of the war ships that ferried and supplied them.

The evening "movie" was the social event of the day, week, month, or year. It was a brief period when one could lose him-self in another world that real world, or that make believe world. It was a connection with home, the one that brought back memories. Memories of when one had met "their girl" at the movies, had sat close, and possibly held her hand, or stole a kiss. Most of all, it was "something" to do.

Going to the movie was the social event that told one who their friends really was. As the evening came on, the "invitations" started going around. Want to go to the movie? (Everyone was going to the movie; there was nothing else to do.) Let's go over to Seventh Marines theatre tonight, they have so and so picture. Want to go down to Division? "Big Deal" it was probably half a block to one's own company theatre. The main thing was "SOMEONE" cared enough to include "you" in the invitation.

A "friend" would no more go off to a movie without asking their best buddies than they would have abandoned them on the battlefield. "Friends shared everything." They were closer than family, for they were "there."

Friends cued up to go to the movies. Usually a group of three or four, or maybe seven or eight, formed out in the company street. They waited for the "always late" ones to get ready, then sauntered over to the movie together. They shared a coconut log under the stars, and came back "together." Banter and laughter was rampant on those journeys, these were the few times one put all things out of their mind except their friends. Cares of the days and nights were left back in the tents, to be retrieved on returning.

A poncho was a "must." Nobody, but nobody went without one, even though the sun might be shining bright, and the sky absolutely free of clouds. Everyone knew it wasn't for "if" it was for "when" it rained, for it always rained through part, or all of a movie. Rain was just a part of life in the islands.

When the rains came, the ponchos went over one's head. Arms and legs were spraddled out to hold the poncho away from their body to allow a little air space underneath. The rains were never cold. The humidity, plus one's own perspiration soon rendered them about as wet as if they had not of used the poncho.

One lesson that was learned quickly at Pavuvu was to tuck the pants legs into one's socks, as "soon" as he sat down. Demoniac, banshee screams came from all around, as the rats "invaded" the place. They would run up the inside of men's pants legs. The person would jump up screaming and holding the rat inside his clothes with both hands, trying to squeeze the life out of it, while it bit and clawed his leg. Some were always careless, too lazy, or too stupid; to tuck his pants legs in. Though it tapered off, there were always two or three screams a night, but that was better than the fifty, or a hundred or so at the beginning.

Most of the films were old, sometimes one had seen them ten or fifteen times, but it was still something to do. It was better than laying in a deserted tent while everyone else was out laughing, joking, and having fun. The nights were long enough without adding anything to them.

The best part of going to the movies was the horseplay with one's friends, and the kibitzing from the audience. With no ladies around the language became kind of wild, but the "timely" remarks were amusing.

When there would be a love scene, some one would invariably yell out instructions to the guy making love to the girl. Not that way stupid! Put your arm around her waist! Hold her closer you fool! Those dumb civilians, why don't they let a Marine play that part.

If the heroin got killed, or died, it was a sure enough invitation for some wild remark about "making love to her while she was still warm" or some such. This was one of the few times the troops found much to laugh about on Pavuvu.

A trip to the Division Theatre was a more formal thing than just going to the company theatre to see a movie. The division theatre was only a couple of blocks away through the coconut grove, it had coconut logs to seat a great many people, possibly several thousand. It had a large screen and a stage where "local" talent sometimes performed. It was the only spot where the very rare "stage shows" such as the Bob Hope Show would ever perform. The division band would sometimes have some people there to play before the movie started.

Dungarees might be worn to the company theatres, but one's best khaki was a "must" for the division theatre. A clean pair of khaki, slept on for pressing. It wasn't mandatory but one got dressed up to go out, it was a change. People started gathering in at division an hour or two before show time. One could usually meet some of their former "buddies" that had gone to other battalions, or companies. There was a chance to "visit" and get the latest scuttlebutt. One found out what was going on on the rest of Pavuvu.

Besides all the visiting, Division usually got any "new," old pictures first, but most of all, it was getting dressed up and going somewhere, with someone.

After the movies everyone drifted back to his respective area, and the card games soon started. Nearly every tent had some kind of a game going; poker, cribbage, pinochle, hearts or what have you. Many times the poker games would have several thousand dollars in the pot or on the black jack tables.

On Pavuvu the division went back on U.S. currency. No more French Francs or Australian Pounds. Also, many went back to playing cards for nickels and dimes, instead of for pounds, about three dollars at that time. Foreign money just meant nothing, and was used much as play money would be.

There were a few "serious" games that went on every night. It wasn't unusual for they're to be thousands of dollars on the table for each hand. These players never went to the movies. Their games started at dusk and went to the wee hours of the morning.

Preparations for another campaign were getting under way. It was time to get into both physical and mental condition for the "ordeal" ahead.

Somebody was going to get "hurt."

THE HUNGER

PELELIU

Aug. 24, 1944 - Embarked on USS Fayette, arrived Guadalcanal Aug. 26, arrived Tulagi Aug 28, arrived Florida Island,Sept 1, arrived Guadalcanal,Sept. 2, practice landings and resupply. Left Sept 8, arrived Peleliu, Palau Sept. 15

The tiny fleeting moment of reverie was over. Ted had recalled how he had come to be in this dreadful situation. It was now time for him to return from his vision of the past and once again face that deadly gunfire. From behind the burning amtrac on Peleliu's bloody shore Ted could see the Jap mortar rounds walking back and forth, up and down the beach, with only seconds between each explosion. Machine gun bullets from the rocky point were churning up the sand. There was no way anyone could

last many minutes here. He had to get off that beach, up and make a run for it, with rifle at the ready.

. To know that someone was shooting only at you stirred different emotions. Occasionally it was exhilaration; sometimes one got just plain old mad, most often it was fear. This day it was great fear.

The Japs were literally coming out of the woodwork. They had coconut log bunkers, they were coming out of caves in the rocks, and they were being brought forward from the hills and the valleys. It seemed the massive naval shelling and bombing had done little, if any, damage to they're prepared fortifications. They had simply buried deep and waited for the raids to pass by, possibly dazed, and in shock, but they're fighting abilities still intact.

If they had of been able to react even a few minutes quicker they could have overwhelmed the thin line of Marine's and rolled them right back into the water. Twenty or thirty yards off the beach was a long ways that first morning.

All at once Ted realized there was another enemy besides the Japs. The sun was bearing down something fierce. The snow-white coral sand reflected it back up, and the sand became so hot it would nearly blister.

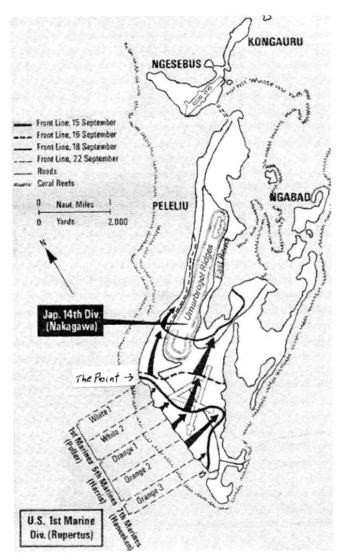

Map showing the order of attack and daily advance

During the destroyers shelling and diversion, another wave of amtracs, and Higgins boats, had ran the gauntlet. More had reached the beach this time. The amtracs crash right up onto or past the beach, and Marines spill out over both sides. A welcome sight! The Higgins boats ran aground in shallow water, dropped their front ramp, and Marines came swarming out in a mass. A lovely sight when you needed help, and on Peleliu it seemed like one always needed help.

Mortars, machine-guns, or grenades, seemed like one or the other, or all three, were coming in all the time. No water, no shade, no nothing, but

The Japs had the beach and lagoon zeroed in with their boat guns and mortars - There was amtracs burning all around and dead Marines littered the water and the beach

plenty of Japs. Their rifle and machine-gun fire came in from every conceivable direction, taking its toll of young men's lives, or wounding them horribly. Every last person on the beach that morning must have had some sort of wound, but only the really severe ones were attended to. There simply wasn't enough Corpsmen, time, or opportunity to look after, the lightly wounded. Many, many, of the severely wounded kept up their firing also, for it was sorely needed if the Japs were to be kept off the beach.

At the time Ted didn't realize it, but looking back he was sure the Japs were as hot, as miserable, as scared, as unwilling to die, as the Marines were. He was sure they needed they're Banzai, Banzai screams to bolster up their fogged brains. However, to this day he wouldn't really give them credit for having one. He is still not less convinced, now, more than then, that the only good Jap was a dead one!

What had once been lush growth and large trees had been virtually demolished by the exploding shells and bombs.

Absolutely nothing but shreds of trees and a tangled mass of debris could be seen in all directions.

There were little trails of toilet paper marking "safe" passage through the mined area, just above the high water mark. The Japs had literally sown the strip with one hundred, and five hundred-pound bombs, and land mines. Ted could see little black points sticking up all around where the dirt had been blown away by the mortar and shell explosions. Most were set to explode under the weight of tanks, amtracs, and trucks, but some triggered on people. Ted didn't know which step might place a weary foot on one of them. Just because a Marine with a mine detector had negotiated the path didn't mean they had spotted everything, for they were running for their lives, also. It also didn't mean the toilet paper was still in the same place where it had been strung. There were equally as many spots where it was torn, curled up, or just plain missing as there were marked trails. Not many of the Marines with mine detectors survived the trip in, and the withering fire, coming from just back of the beach area.

No one was immune to a bullet, and a mortar shell launched from afar was not particular what it reaped. Dead bodies littered the whole area, and were floating around in the water, rolling back and forth with the tide. It would be most of three days before many of the dead Marines could be gathered off the beach, and be given a "proper" burial.

All day the mortar shells kept walking up and down, up and down the beach area. No place on the sand was immune. Inland, small arms and machine gun fire never seemed to cease. Sometimes the heavies won, and sometimes the light nambuls won. As soon as one Jap emplacement was overrun another sprung up. It was foot by weary foot, yard by weary yard, as the day drug on, and on, and on. For too many though, it had come to a very sudden end, there on the blistering white-hot sand.

Finally, after hours of torment and hell, Ted came face to face with the enemy. The first dead Japanese he had seen out in the open all day. That little monkey face didn't look so frightening in death. They really were human and could be killed. They were not just ghosts, drifting in and out of holes, sending those deadly projectiles to rip and tear the young Marines flesh. And to drain their blood in the white-hot sand, where it quickly turned black, and the swarms of huge green and black flies, began to gather.

More and more Ted saw evidence of the Japanese soldiers, a pack, a rifle, pieces of equipment, more dead, and parts of dead Japs. They had penetrated the Japs first line of defense.

The Marines had advanced "almost" to the runways of the airstrip, which was the main purpose of securing this damnable piece of real estate. In retrospect, one wonders if another "unoccupied" island wouldn't have served the same purpose. Could not the C.B.'s have bulldozed an airstrip in far less time than it took to secure Peleliu?

Could not the Jap garrison have been starved out, much like at Rabaul, New Britain. Was it really necessary for so many young men to bleed and die; at the time it seemed a necessity and not one person questioned the reason for being there?

A screech, a groan, a clanging, something very strange was going on just in front of the lines, but out of sight. The sounds grew louder, and louder. The firing along the line was picking up. Straining forward, Ted could see a cloud of dust rising along the edge of the runway, then he could make out three trucks rumbling his way, but wait, that wasn't trucks, those were tanks. The clanking and groaning was coming from their tracks, as they hauled full bore for his position.

This was the first Japanese tanks Ted had seen in action, and they looked more formidable all the time. What could stop a tank? Certainly not a little peashooter! Was there anything ashore to combat these tanks with? Ted had heard the firing of several light artillery pieces that have been brought ashore during the afternoon. Could they be brought to bear on those rapidly approaching machines? If the tanks penetrated the Marine's lines, all the days labor, and shed blood was for nothing. The end was very near.

The clanking and groaning grew louder, and louder, but the Jap tanks were still some distance out, barreling along at full speed, straight down the line.

All at once, in the midst of all the confusion and noise, a great cheer arose. It was almost like the great exhilaration of the bugle call of charge, to the cavalry, for out of nowhere had materialized two of the Marines tanks, (Shermans, Ted thought). The increased clanging was coming from them.

Just in the nick of time it seemed, they lumbered up to the edge of the runway, stop just short of exposing themselves to the full view of the incoming Jap tanks, and to the artillery pieces in the hills.

Their turrets swiveled right, a little to the left, a little right, up a little, down a little, and then they belched fire and smoke. They jumped and shuddered, but the firing went on. What was happening? Ted could see nothing for the smoke and dust was swirling up all around. Where were the Jap tanks?

A great cheer went up, the dust settled slightly. Ted could see three hulks, stopped dead, not far out on the runway. Smoke was billowing up from two of them, and Jap bodies dotted the landscape. The tanks were covered with Jap infantry, riding in to do combat with the Marines who are holding the line.

Twilight was beginning to fall, a slight letting up of the fierce heat from the burning white sands. The Marines clothes were caked with white salt streaks. Ted's mouth was dry, he was covered with dust, and dirt, but he was still alive.

A little beachhead had been occupied; maybe seventyfive, or a hundred yards wide. Reinforcements had managed to land during the afternoon. They were taking their places to help fill a few of the spaces left empty by the Marines who had been killed that day. The Marines were there to stay, but the Japs still hadn't been told.

The word was passed; dig in for what would be a very long night. Not one person on the beach doubted that fact, and events were to prove them more than right. All knew their ranks would be thinned greatly before the night ended.

Dig, and dig, the sand fell back in almost as fast as Ted could throw it out. It was not the easiest thing to do, to dig a hole while laying flat on the ground, peering intently around for Japs, or for the next rounds of fire that will be coming in.

Ted gathered every piece of coral, every rock, every scrap of wood within reach, to help reinforce a barricade in front of him. When one was fighting for his life, he never seemed to feel that he had done enough to protect it. One more shovel of sand, one more scrap of wood, that last shovel of sand just might be the one that would save the day, or night. Even a blade of grass seemed an effective shield when there was nothing else in front of him.

There was a lull in the firing from both sides of the line. All at once Ted was tired and famished. There hadn't been time to think of such things before. Fish in his combat pack for a can of cheese, and some hard K ration "crackers," the only food in the K ration packs that was fit to eat, and about the only thing kept by most of the Marines.

When the food packs were issued aboard ship, they ripped them open, took out the cheese and crackers, saved a few bars of the dry, hard, tropical chocolate, and threw the rest away. A practice they would sorely regret before they left Peleliu.

As darkness sat in Ted could hear, or sense more activity out in front, and on all sides. He knew the Japs were up to something, and whatever it was, it was not designed to be pleasant for him.

The Japanese soldiers must have been equally as exhausted as the Marines. Where as in the daytime they had been on the defensive, with the coming of darkness they would go on the offensive. They would try to retake their lost ground, and throw the Americans back into the sea, or kill all of them.

Night brought but little relief from the stifling heat of the day. The white coral sand had stored up the sun's rays, and was still burning hot to the touch. There was no cool water to slake a burning thirst, or to wash some of the dirt and sand from the dry mouth.

Two destroyers had moved in close to the reef again, from their vicinity Ted could see a small streak of light sail overhead. There was a pop, and out burst a parachute flare. These burn with a fierce light and illuminate the whole area. Sometimes things were real bright and clear. Other times everything was real weird and full of creepy shadows. What was real, and what was only imagined by young minds in mortal danger?

The flares drifted down slowly and as one began to fade another took its place, but never in the exact same location. The shadows were always changing position, and moving around. As soon as one thought they had spotted something alive, and creeping towards their position, the shadows changed. They had to readjust their eyes, and try to pick out that little, imperceptible movement they thought they saw. A good portion of the time the movements were only imagination, or some dancing debris. But all too frequently they ended with a splash of grenades, and a hail of bullets.

Ted waited, and waited, and waited and listened. At times he could hear loud screaming voices. At other times only low jabbering, then complete, total, silence. Not a gun, not a voice, not a scrape, nothing.

How long did it last? A second, a minute, an hour, who can say, or did it even happen at all? Ted knew they were coming at him, he just didn't know at what second it would start.

Pass the word along, everyone alert. Hold your fire; don't reveal your position. Wait until they are in close. My God! Ted could hear them jabbering and walking. How much closer could they get without moving into his foxhole with him? Somebody was going to get hurt.

Ted heard a soft thud, thud, thud, and buried himself in the sand. Almost simultaneous with the thuds, the grenades began to explode all around. The ground shook and dirt flies, the Japs screamed, and made a wild charge.

The smell of powder, and of death, was all around. Pull the pin; hurl a grenade with all your strength. Those shadows that were creeping are no longer creeping; they were running, darting, and falling.

Start squeezing that trigger, or this is it. It seems all sound stops when you start squeezing the trigger. Grab another clip, shove it home, and squeeze some more. Over and over, then all at once there is nothing before him.

They had vanished as suddenly as they appeared. Some are lying around on the ground, some have retreated, and a few have made it through the lines, for Ted could hear the scattered firing picking up behind him.

A corporal, or a sergeant, came strolling along. Checking on who needed help, and who was beyond help. It was amazing how those squad leaders had the nerve, and the knack, for checking on "their people." Forever, and always, you are, "their people," and they will never forsake, or abandon you. In combat there was a greater percentage of Corporals, Sergeants, and Lieutenants killed than any other rank.

They were sending for more boxes of grenades, and for more cases of ammo clips. This night had only begun and was far from over yet. The — — (stuff) will hit the fan, many, many, more times before this night ends.

All up and down the lines Ted could hear similar firefights, and knew all too well what was happening. First from one direction, and shortly from another, the charges were wild and vicious, but sporadic. If they had of made a coordinated push on all sectors at once it was certain they could have rolled up the Marines lines.

All night long the battles raged, sometimes at Ted, sometimes to one side or the other. Occasionally, only in some other companies' perimeter, but always, there was the sound of death, moving up and down the lines, on both sides.

Just before dawn, it seemed the Japs had finally mounted that coordinated attack against the ever-thinner Marine lines. From all directions came the boom, boom, of artillery and the swish, swish, swish, of mortars and the splash of grenades, and the never ceasing cracking of machine gun and small arms fire.

They seemed to literally come up out of the ground. One second there was nothing, the next they were almost in Ted's hole. Grenades, grenades, grenades, would they never stop?

There was absolutely no time to be scared, to run, (for where would you go) to do anything, except the thing you were trained to do. Grab a clip, slam it home, jerk a shell into the chamber, and start squeezing the trigger. Hurl a grenade, and squeeze some more. Pray without ceasing.

Daylight finally crept in, and as mysteriously as they appeared the Japs had again disappeared into the ground. It was very, very, close, but the Marines lines had held. There was no more than a third of them left in the front lines that had started the night.

Every available man was pressed into the lines to fill the gaps. The night had finally ended, but the day was just beginning. The Marines desperately needed some of the high ground, from which the devastating mortar fire was still coming, and everyone knows; hillside real estate never comes cheap.

The heat began almost before the sun crept over the horizon. By the time it was full up, the sand was beginning to open its hungry jaws to swallow the full force of the burning rays.

The canteens were collected and a party sent back to the water cart that had been brought ashore. The water would be hot, and taste of metal and paint. But it would help quench the nagging thirst, and wash a little of the sand and grit from the mouth that had collected during the night. The remaining water was hoarded as no precious gem has ever been hoarded, for who knew where the next drop would come from. And this day promised to be even fiercer than the last.

Ted finished the last can of cheese with a few crackers, and prepared to move out. The tangle of the demolished jungle, and the bodies of the dead Japs in front, didn't look the least bit inviting.

Just yards ahead, Ted passed mangled and twisted Jap bodies from the night's clashes. There was probably some Jap flags, and great souvenirs to be had, but one dared not move them. Ted knew many had been booby trapped by pulling the pin on a grenade, and wedging it under the body so it would release the arm, and detonate, when the body was moved.

Another twenty or thirty yards and swish, swish, swish, and the whumpf, whumpf, whumpf, of exploding mortar shells. The mortars were zeroing in. Scattered small arms fire began picking up the tempo. The calls of Corpsman, Corpsman, at fifty yards the lines ground to a halt. It would be a long, long day.

Things were settling in, it didn't seem as though the Marines got careless as much as it just became routine, crawl a little, fire a lot, and crawl a few feet more.

Swoosh; swoosh, the searing flames leaped out from the flame-throwers and into the caves and bunkers of the Japs. Most had died instantly, but a few had let out mortal screams as the flames devoured them. A very few came charging from the caves all-aflame, to be cut down by the Marines rifles.

It seemed funny, but in the daytime on Peleliu, there was seldom a clear shot at a Jap. The grenades bounced down and the mortars whumped all around, the rifle and machine gun fire came in. But the only time Ted saw a Jap was when he darted from one cover to the other. Or possibly he came out of a cave or bunker screaming, and full ablaze, after being doused by a flame-thrower. Few survived the original blast when it could be directed into their holes or caves. But several that did came out screaming until it would turn ones blood to water.

It was no big deal to see a Jap shot, or to shoot one for that matter, but it was something else to see someone engulfed in total flame, to hear their screams end in a dying gasp.

The canteens were getting much lighter, and the water was so hot it almost burned Ted's mouth, but it was still the most precious thing on earth.

Possibly a hundred yards of ground had been gained on that sector, while next door the Marines had crossed the runway, and had came up against the fortifications, and pill boxes, guarding the airstrip terminal.

Great concrete fortifications, so strong, the shells from the huge navy sixteen-inch guns just bounce off them, and go screaming into nowhere.

They had gained the lower slopes but know the ground will become untenable when the counter attacks start after dark. It was either move forward or back off and let the Japs reoccupy the positions that had been so dearly won. The Marine Corps has never been known for backing off.

About 1600 hours (4:00 o'clock) the word was passed to get ready to move out, and don't stop until you reach the high ground. By 1900 hours the Marines were seen on the ridgeline and preparations for digging in for the night were begun. The forty-eight hours had past, and they were hardly a stones throw off the beach.

Again water became the most pressing need as every one was starting to dehydrate, and many had passed out from heat stroke, or heat prostration.

Many lines would be breached that night, but there was enough men and material on the beach to ensure it staying in Marine hands. Many of the reserve companies had been brought ashore, and had been used to fill the gaps in the lines left by their fallen comrades.

Now, also, many minds started thinking about all those K rations that had been discarded aboard ship. The three-day supply had been reduced to one, and now it, was long gone.

They were thirsty, exhausted, hot and miserable, and not a bite to eat. It would be another long night. Another night, another day, one packet of K rations to eat that was found in a dead Marines pack, and this shared with two other buddies.

What would one give for a big tall glass of ice water? Most would have sold their very souls for one tiny sip, much less a whole glass full.

Faces and hands blistered, the lips cracked open and bled. Eyelids were sunburned and swelling shut. Was this the glamour of war? Now it was a battle just to stay alive long enough to get off that filthy, stinking island. Indeed, it had already started stinking from all the dead bodies lying around, both Marine and Jap.

Ted was relieved late the third afternoon and sent back to G.R.S. headquarters that was still on the beach. By this time dehydration, lack of food and water, and a fearful fever from a head cold, was extracting a great toll from what had once been a very healthy, strong body.

These were the men who had the responsibility of gathering, identifying and burying the dead - They were overworked

On the way back from the front, he passed a little gully that had evidently concealed many Japanese at one time. There was a great deal of equipment, packs, clothing, papers and so fourth lying around. On top of one of those piles was of all things, a slab of bacon. It didn't look too much the worse for wear and tear, so he picked it up and took it along.

When Ted finally found the H.Q. bivouac (only a bunch of fox holes dug in the sand just off the beach, it was nearing dark. Mortars were still walking random patterns up and down the whole terrain. They were not as thick as before but just as deadly. He only had time to scrape out a hole and fall into it before another miserable night.

The next morning Ted found there was plenty of tepid, warm water for drinking, but no rations were available. He was told there was a field kitchen set up about a quarter of a mile up the beach, but they only served food in the evening.

Washing off the slab of bacon, he sliced a few pieces and put them in one half of a mess kit and fried it over a little fire that some of the fellows were using to heat water for a cup of instant coffee. The bacon smelled delicious and brought several curious Marines over to cop a meal. When they heard where it came from not one person would touch it, for fear of it being poisoned.

At some point in time, it is necessary to abandon caution and to opt for survival, or to what will be, will be. Ted had never in all his life tasted anything so good. He gobbled every last crumb of it down. If it was poisoned, so be it.

That batch of greasy bacon had not been down for five minutes when it all came back up with a gush. That was the beginning of four or five days of vomiting and diarrhea that almost never ceased. This took a further heavy toll on an already weakened body.

Finally, one evening, Ted was able to make his way to the field kitchen. The only food was what they called "Lima Bean Soup." A virtually clear liquid that no one ever found a bean in, but it was hot and gave just a little nourishment to a starving body. Every evening it was lima bean soup, lima bean soup, but as it turned out this was the only thing that would stay down.

Time after time Ted tried heating some C rations. These consisted of two things. One was a greasy cross between pork and beans and baked beans. The other was called meat and vegetable stew; a greasy concoction made of mutton and vegetables, for it was processed in Australia. In both cases they would no more than go down, before they would come back up, and the diarrhea would start all over again.

He found an occasional can of K ration cheese and some crackers in dead Marines pockets and field packs. Between these and the evening meal of Lima Bean Soup, he started holding his own and gaining a little strength back. In spite of being so weak and sick he was working a full ten to twelve hour day in the broiling hot sun; fingerprinting, dental charting and identifying the dead, that were pouring in faster than they could be processed.

Although it was a grisly, stinking, backbreaking job Ted's company of Graves Registration People could be proud of their record. They had very few "unidentified" bodies to their credit, (Ted later received a meritorious promotion based on the efficiency of his identification efforts in three campaigns.) even though many, many, were horribly mutilated, and often there was only a few "parts of a body" to work with.

GRS Corpsmen labored twelve to fourteen hour days in the boiling hot sun - Notice the devistation, hardly a tree was left standing from the bombs and shells

Only a day or two was needed in the broiling hot sun, for a body to swell to huge proportions. The skin would crack open, and could be removed like a garment. Often, the only way to get a good fingerprint was to slip the whole skin off a hand, put it on like a glove, then print it from his own fingers.

One day Ted was sitting on a log processing just such a case. A few feet away there was a bulldozer working to clear the debris, and level an area for the extension of the cemetery. The dozer hit one of the multitudes of bombs, or mines, that were "planted" all over the place, one that the mine detectors had failed to find. The explosion wrecked the tracks, and the underside of the bulldozer. It blew the operator several yards high, and away, almost like an ejection seat. It blew Ted over backwards with an unbelievable force. When he came to, it took several of his people to clean the dirt from his eyes, nose, mouth and ears.

Most of the fighting by now was confined to the ridges and valleys in the interior of the island. It was hand-to-hand, rifles, grenades, and flame-throwers, vicious and fierce, cave-by-cave. The Japs were extracting a heavy toll for every cave taken. Just enough rounds of mortar or artillery fire fell in or near the cemetery area to keep every one jittery, and on their toes. The nights still brought patrols and skirmishes, and little sleep was to be had.

Day in, day out, week in, week out. Where had that seventy-two hour schedule gone? The Japs were still resisting as stubbornly as ever. They had holed up in the mountains, in the center of the island. This was a jumble of jagged peaks, sharp cliffs, criss cross valleys and a very inaccessible area at the very best. At the very worst it was a death trap for the Marines attacking it. An area the Japs had worked on for years, and in fact, at one time had a Korean work battalion slaving on it.

It was literally honeycombed with caves and tunnels, most interlocking, and all inner supporting. Many of these caves were several stories high, or deep, and connected by tunnels in all directions.

The Japs could surface; fire a few rounds, then duck back in and surface on a totally different level, and at a different position. This labyrinth was well stocked with food and water; so all they had to do was sit back and wait for the Marines to come at them.

It seemed the only way to defeat them was to burn out, and seal up, every one of the thousands of openings they had dug in the mountains. Invariably, when the Marines started for one area the crossfire would come in from another direction and take its toll. Whatever else one might care to call the Japanese soldiers in the islands, they could not call them cowards. They nearly always fought to the very last man.

There was one particular Jap sniper who was holed up in the ridges overlooking the airstrip. He was a deadly shot and invariably hit his target "right between the eyeballs." He killed at least thirty-five Marines, including a full Colonel, before the Marines finally got him, right between the eyeballs. At least, it was a fitting end.

Nearly all vegetation on the island was destroyed - From the high vantage points the Japs could zero in on the marines

One day an ambulance driver asked Ted to go into the "valley" with him to pick up a load of dead Marines. Thinking this would be a good chance for a little ride to rest up from his duties, he jumped at the chance. As it turned out Ted found that the driver wasn't doing him any favors. In the first place, a field ambulance ride, at break neck speed, over broken terrain, is about like trying to ride a bucking horse. You come out so battered you think someone has been beating on you. In the second place Ted found out his duty was to ride shotgun, through a stretch of no man's land. (Later known as "death-valley,") It was kind of like running an Indian gauntlet. If the Navy planes dropping Napalm (fire) bombs didn't get you, the Jap snipers or mortars would. Once they started into the valley, there was no way to back out. If stagecoaches bounced as high, and hard, as that field ambulance, there is no possible way those cowboys ever hit an Indian riding on one, or on a bouncing horse.

Instead of a quick pick up, turn around, and back out again, Ted was "shanghaied." Casualties were so high in the line companies that virtually anyone stupid enough, whether on business, or whether curiosity, or especially souvenir hunting, that went into the "valley," was immediately put on the front lines. Corpsmen were in very short supply at that time, and the number of casualties dictated they have every one they could get.

No lima bean soup there, only K and C rations, the diarrhea and vomiting started up again. The big problem was, one didn't stop to heave or drop their pants when a nip was shooting at him.

One morning Ted's squad followed a tank into a deep ravine. They were told that there was a squad of Marines on a little plateau of Mount Umurbrogol, (later known as Bloody Nose Ridge) that had several casualties, and needed help bad. Following a Nippon trail, up an almost sheer cliff they came to a little open glade. Scattered all around the edges, behind every bush, every rock, in every depression, was a wounded or dead Marine.

No way to go up, and no way to go down. Evidently the Japs had written off the Marines who were on this ledge, as they had virtually stopped firing into they're midst. When the Japs saw the five people, two Corpsmen and three Marines, crawling amongst the wounded, they literally opened up with everything they had. The little glade was covered from every conceivable direction. The bullets came in like rain, and there were no umbrellas on that cliff-side.

Before Ted could bat an eye, one Corpsman, and two of the Marines had been hit. There was absolutely no way one could get back down the trail alone, much less dragging a wounded Marine. There was no way up, and the fire from all directions was hitting some men over, and over again. The only possible way off was to jump over the straight up and down cliff. It was a good one hundred, to one hundred fifty feet, straight down. Maybe they were not going to survive the jump, but there was no way they were going to survive on that ledge very long.

Have you ever seen a Marine that the Japs have tortured and mutilated; Ted had seen them cut off their penises and stick them in their mouths. They stick them in the eyes with bayonets, to give them slant eyes. They are stuck all over like pigs.

There was no way those people were going to be left to such torture, and besides, in the Marines, one just didn't leave a fellow Marine in need. It just wasn't done. No one will ever know how many gave their lives trying to help a fellow Marine, whether one knew them or not, who needed help. If necessary, they would kill them their selves, if they lasted long enough.

The only way out was over the ledge; they would help as many as possible. They were able to convey their intentions to most of the wounded. Those who were able crawled to the edge of the cliff. Methodically, Ted began to push and roll them over.

Ted did not remember one single person protesting, screaming, or crying out, (no doubt the noise of the great explosions, the flow of adrenaline and a "closed mind" wiped them out) even though many were horribly wounded, and the pain must have been excruciating. The Corpsmen were out of morphine the first five minutes on that ledge, so about all they had been able to do for those MEN, was to try and stop the bleeding, put on sulfa powder and bandages.

By some totally inhuman effort, they were able to drag and carry the more seriously wounded, the unconscious, and the dead, to the cliff's edge, then throw, drop, or roll them over. Ted had no faintest idea if any one of them survived, or if most or all survived.

By this period of the battle Ted was no doubt below one hundred pounds, and even though all the Marines had deteriorated somewhat, many, or most, out weighed him by fifty to seventy-five pounds. It was a task that once started became automatic, and he didn't even realize he was doing such a thing until it was all over.

The valley floor, below the ledge, had been covered with heavy timber, and tropical growth. But during the prolonged naval shelling and bombing, and the attacking Marines fire, nearly every tree and shrub was reduced to scraggly, broken, twisted, splintered hunks of debris.

One of the most vivid memories Ted has was etched indelibly in his brain, as he stood up to hurl a man over the side. There, standing out in bold relief, was one of the Marines, impaled on one of the splintered shards of a tree. It had gone completely through him, from back to front, and his entrails were all pushed out and hanging down. If Ted were an artist, he could draw you that picture in minute detail to this day.

Finally, there was no One left on the ledge to suffer more, or to beg with their eyes for Ted to end their untold suffering with a bullet.

Another quick survey of that damnable ledge just to be sure no one was left stranded there. Ted turned and ran full tilt, hoping to jump far enough out over the ledge to miss the rocks, and crags, and land on the floor of the ravine.

He heard the swish, swish, swish, of the mortar shell. He even recalled a sharp click, then felt the searing blast, as he sailed out into a merciful oblivion. Ted remembered nothing more except awakening in darkness, and of being entangled in a mass of broken limbs and vines. He recalled the weird patterns of the shadows cast by the flares from the ships, and of wondering if he were dead, or alive.

The pain that wracked Ted's body, as he tried to sit up and crawl away, soon let him know that he was not dead. Knowing that which ever, Jap, or Americans, that controlled this gully, if they saw movement, would probably shoot first and ask questions later, he was very cautious in his movements.

After crawling and stumbling some yards out, towards where he imagined the Marines lines to be, he became aware of a tantalizing odor. All at once he was ravenously hungry. Searching around by the light of the overhead flares, Ted discovered the source of the smell. There was a Jap soldier, he could tell by the split toe'd shoes, about the only thing left on him, who had been cooked by a flame thrower, probably from a tank.

Involuntarily, or voluntarily, Ted knew not which, his fingers reached out and touched the burned flesh on the Japs thigh. It smelled so good, and as he pinched it, a chunk came loose in his hand.

As Ted slowly raised it towards his mouth, the odor became even more tantalizing, but when he opened his mouth, he heaved all over the place. His stomach had rebelled, not at the thought of eating human flesh, for it looked, and smelled, better than any beef he had ever smelled before, but at the prospect of receiving such rich food.

The Marines found him (or he found them) the next afternoon. By that time he had recovered enough to walk proudly, if humbly, and wracked, from that gully, and back to the forward lines. He found that instead of being gone two days and one night he had been gone three days and two nights. Most of that time was a total blank, but the few hours Ted remembered make up for the ones lost.

He managed to talk his way aboard the next ambulance load of dead Marines to leave the valley, and arrived back at his company, just in time to go for the evening meal of lima bean soup. A few mouthfuls of this was all that would go down, but after a few days he began to regain a small measure of strength. However, laboring about ten hours a day, in the broiling hot sun, in the filth and stench, continued to take its toll. Ted's weight kept dropping until his body was wasted away to skin and bones.

One afternoon a Japanese patrol was caught passing near his area. Several, if not all were killed by small arms fire and the use of a flame-thrower on two that had gained the "protection" of a small gully.

Again that tantalizing aroma of cooking flesh drifted down and gnawed at the empty vitals. Unashamed deeds could have been done that night.

A few days later an army division relieved them. There was only a small pocket of Japanese left alive on Peleliu to be mopped up, but the army was welcome to them.

After forty five-days, starved, emaciated, they were leaving that most dreadful of hellholes but more was to come.

Peleliu Cemetery - The Japanese defenders reaped a fearful toll of young Marines lives - Many comrads and buddies buried here

They boarded a Dukw (amphibious truck) just at dark, to take them out to the transport ship, for a return to Pavuvu. The Coxswain missed the hole in the reef, and the Dukw flipped over, dumping them all in the ocean. By sheer strength of will they managed to hold onto it throughout the night, and were picked up the next morning.

The following day after boarding the transport, a large work party spent the whole day carrying crates of fresh turkeys, that had spoiled, up topside, and dumped them overboard. How they would have been cherished on Peleliu. The irony of some things was almost too much to bear.

Peleliu had almost devoured the division of some thirty thousand young Marines. The toll in dead and wounded was great and hard to accept, but it also took a heavy toll on the physical, and mental, condition of those who still remained.

Some two months after leaving Peleliuls shores, after he had been on "normal rations," and in their rest camp recuperating, Ted was in the back of the mess hall one day and found a large pair of scales. He had gone from one hundred thirty-five, to one hundred-forty pounds, and was now exactly eighty-six pounds.

There was a saying:

A Marine who had served on Peleliu died and went to heaven. When St. Peter opened the gate the Marine saluted and said, "Another Marine reporting sir, I have already served my time in Hell."

Of such a place was Peleliu.

ONE NIGHT

PELELIU

All day Ted had labored at a task few could stand and no one would relish. He was finger printing, dental charting, and identifying the dead Marines who were pouring in on Peleliu's deadly shores.

The terrible heat the snow-white sand reflected up had become almost unbearable. Many of the Marines and Corpsmen were passing out from the extreme heat. Heat stroke and heat prostration were becoming a real enemy to battle. On Peleliu one needed not another enemy the Japs were enemy enough. Some of the ships standing by with equipment and material had sent in some of their precious supply of apples, and fruit juices to help relieve the symptoms of this awful heat. These luxuries, or delicacies, would never have been shared with the Marines except in extreme circumstances and often not then. As precious as an apple was to one that had not seen fresh fruit for months, and as hot as it was, there were many Marines who came to the cemetery with an apple in their pocket. Someone had passed them around, but they didn't have a chance to eat it before being killed. Peleliu was that kind of a place.

After the third day on Peleliu's shores the question was no longer in doubt of whether the First Marine Division could hold onto the island, but the toll of wounded and dead young bodies was beyond belief. Absolutely no one was immune. Every able body, and many "walking wounded" were pressed into the front lines, which, on an island only about two miles wide, and five miles long were seldom out of rifle shot, or mortar fire range.

Take absolutely nothing away from the MEN of the line companies. Though they make up only about twenty five percent of a divisions manpower, they do ninety-nine, and nine-tenths (99.9%) percent of the actual fighting in times of combat. "Seldom" does a GI of the support units ever get to fire a shot at the enemy, unless for some reason or other, they get attached to a line company for a brief period. Probably less than one man in ten in the Marines, or army, has ever fired a rifle at the enemy. It took a tremendous number of support units to keep a man on the front lines.

There was no "safe" place on Peleliu, either by night, or by day. Even the support units were well within the Japs field of fire. Everyone was extremely nervous, probably the "rear echelon men" more than the ones in the front lines, if possible. At least the line companies were much more "disciplined," and one was "reasonably" safe from their own people when in their ranks. How many thousands of troops were killed in combat by "friendly fire?" No one would ever know! Many Marines in the support units were killed by so called "friends," when they would crawl out of their holes to urinate or go to the bathroom. In other words, too many were trigger-happy. Many lives could have been saved by not issuing weapons to any but the front line troops, letting everyone else take their chances. The only problem was that everywhere was front lines in Peleliu's first days.

Young Ted Alexander had come to that dreadful shore with a big handicap. He had a fearful head cold. It seemed a cold always picked the worst possible time to happen. No one needed one when they were trying their best to stay alive.

After performing Herculean tasks by day, and occupying a hole in the wet sand at night, Ted's cold had become progressively worse, and was on the verge of, or had already became pneumonia.

Ted's lips were cracked open and bleeding. His face and eyelids was sunburned, from exposure to the heat of the burning white-hot sand. Sweaty, dirty, thirsty, (oh for one swallow of good, fresh, cold water!) The stench of the dead and the smell of cordite mingled to dull senses. The day finally ended, with nothing but a canteen cup of weak lima bean soup, (no one ever found a lima bean) as a reward for the interminable days labors.

Jap mortars were still splashing here and there at random, up and down the beach, and around the perimeter. Taking their toll of anyone unfortunate enough to be in their path. Big guns, little guns, rifles and grenades, some Marines, and some Japs all added their special sounds. It was incredible how one could distinguish between the sounds of the different army's weapons. Each has it's own distinctive sound, one that a person never forgets.

Tired, exhausted, miserable, Ted found "his" hole in the ground. It was much deeper and larger than a normal foxhole. Also, it had a hole dug much deeper in the bottom at each end, for body waste, and as a possible receptacle for grenades which might come his way. Reasoning that it just might be possible to kick it into the hole at one end or the other, to help absorb the concussion, and to help keep "some" of the shrapnel from his body.

As darkness sat in, the destroyers moved in closer to shore, and started their long night of keeping parachute flares over the battlefront. All night long, one after the other, the parachute flares streaked overhead, opened, and drifted to earth. Casting their bright light over the entire area. As one went down, another went up, keeping everything in a weird pattern of light and shadows. Everything seemed to be alive and moving, yet never got closer, or farther away. Young minds, in mortal danger, could see strange shapes and movements in the night. Some of them were real, some only imagined. Japs liked to infiltrate under cover of darkness.

To most Americans, darkness itself was something to fear, to Ted, who before entering the service, had roamed the back roads and tasted the swamps at night, darkness itself held no fear. What he needed that night was rest, and relief from the terrible pain in his head and chest.

Crawling into his hole in the sand, Ted attempted to curl up and get some rest. Content to let some one else watch for the night, or beyond caring. After some time the sands began to cool slightly and the dampness penetrated Ted's body. Deciding it was just as well to die in comfort as to lay in that wet hole and die of pneumonia, Ted called out to his friends in surrounding holes. Informing them that he was going to be moving about, and for them not to shoot him. He crawled out of his hole and strung his "jungle hammock" (A beautiful piece of equipment for the tropics. It had mosquito netting all around, zipped up one side, and had a top of waterproof material. One could sleep in them in real comfort) between two scraggs of shelled down trees. He crawled into same, zipped it up, and was fast asleep from exhaustion.

Oblivious to time and place, Ted slept, for how long he knew not. The next thing he knew something had bumped into him. Instantly, alert and awake, by the glimmering light of the overhead flares, and only inches from his face, he saw another face. Flat, dark, it had to be a Japanese soldier. Springing erect within his zipped up mosquito netting, he grabbed for the forty-five pistol he had tucked inside his hammock.

Fear, amazement, everything happened so suddenly, like it might be happening to someone else and he was only a spectator. At the instant the forty-five whipped up, and within a hairs breadth of the trigger squeeze, a faint, undeniably, Mexican voice, called out "Help Me". Just as the face collapsed in a heap on the ground.

Ted never remembered if his greatest fear was from seeing the face, or from the fear that some of his friends would fill him full of holes. Completely forgetting the "password," his first thought was to call some of his buddies to help. With Smith's, Jones, Brown's, Chuck, Joe, all around, the only name he could frame was "Hercowitz," a Marine of very limited acquaintance. Nevertheless, Hercowitz, then a couple of others, Chuck amongst them, came to his assistance. Try as they would, they could get no help from their Company Commander and the rest of the Company Elite. Holed up in their own private little bunker that the Japs had abandoned, and were scared to death to come out, even to help a buddy. It was one of the few acts of cowardice that Ted was ever to observe.

The young Mexican Marine had been shot through the upper chest. From what Ted could tell in the darkness, it was a "relatively" clean wound, having gone in the front and out the back. Ted found his medical bag and gave him a shot of morphine. He then dressed the wound as best he could under the conditions, to help staunch the flow of blood.

After regaining consciousness the Marine explained that he was part of a communications team. They were stringing wire to a command post when they were jumped by a Japanese patrol, only about fifty yards in front of Ted's position. Rolling a corpse from a stretcher, Ted and his friends carried the wounded Marine through the minefield, and out to the beach. They were able to get him on a Higgins boat that was evacuating wounded Marines to a "Hospital Ship" standing by just outside the reef that surrounded Peleliu. They never knew if he made it, or if that was his final ride.

Making his wary way back to their area, Ted crawled into his hammock. Being totally exhausted he fell into a "deep sleep" not to awake until the dawn.

When Ted emerged from his hammock the next morning his friends were astounded and could hardly believe their eyes. They, supposing him to be dead, for as they explained, there was the biggest "fire fight" most of them had ever seen when a few minutes after Ted crawled back into his hammock, that Jap unit came through this area. His friends had called to him several times when it started, trying to rouse him from a sleep of the dead.

Ted had heard not one sound during the interval, and yet when they examined his hammock, they found seven bullet holes that had gone completely through the mosquito netting. Some, it seemed, would have passed through his body, and yet he had not a scratch.

Ted would always assume that this was "one of the nights" his mother had prayed from dark to dawn, and her prayers had been heard, and answered.

(An assumption later confirmed.)

Ted with a hard earned Jap flag. Notice the nose of a bomb sticking out at his feet.

HOT LIPS BROWN

There was one in every outfit. He never stopped talking long enough to hardly breathe, much less eat. They were a friend to everyone, yet had no "close" friends of their own. Maybe that is why they talked constantly, yet never really said anything.

His last name was Brown, so it was only natural to call him Brownie. In Australia he had picked up the name "Blue," for this was they're nickname for anyone with red hair. The nickname used most often needed no explanation, "Hot Lips."

There was usually a crowd around "Hot Lips." He was always the center of attention for everyone loved to hear his "stories" and he always had the latest scoop on any scuttlebutt going around.

The only time old Hot Lips was ever silent was after mail call, when he would get a letter, or letters, from his mother, whom he dearly loved. At least then, he would stop talking long enough to read and digest them, but only just.

He was a tall, strong young man of possibly twenty-one or twenty-two. He would always do his share of work without shirking or complaining. He was one Ted could really count on in a "fire fight," when the going got tough. Old Brownie always showed up with some "extra" ammo clips, or a few "spare" grenades. He was almost like "home," he was always going to be there.

Old Hot Lips always had an answer for anything that was said. Sometimes it was a little wild but from his lips it never sounded lewd, or vulgar, only funny.

Brownie had been fighting the Japs from the days of Guadalcanal, New Guinea, New Britain and now Peleliu. He was overdue for rotation, and was counting the days until this campaign was over. He was due to go home as soon as the very first replacements arrived.

As the days on Peleliu drew to a close, Hot Lips began to talk (and Ted was sure, dream) more and more of going home to see his mother.

The fighting had been reduced to little pockets of Japs; back in the honeycomb of caves, and tunnels, in the rugged hills. No more did the mortar shells walk up and down the beaches. One could stand upright, walk around, and do their daily deeds without fear of a sniper bullet ripping him apart. It was true, the dead were still pouring out of the hills, but for those not in the line companies, it was virtually all over but the loading up, and getting away from this dreadful place.

An army Division had come ashore to relieve all that were left of the First Marine Division. Their respective units were setting up as speedily as possible. They were certainly welcome to any and all of Peleliu.

Before they had hardly got into the lines, their dead began to trickle back down out of the hills, mingled with the dead Marines. It was said they set up loud speakers to tell the Japanese they were Army, and not Marines, they could surrender and not be killed. For the Marines throughout the Pacific it was virtually "no quarter given." Seldom was a live person ever taken prisoner by either side, Marine or Japanese.

G.R.S.s relief came ashore and set up right beside them with all new tents and equipment. Normally they would have been stripped clean of equipment, guns, food and anything else that was movable. On Peleliu the Marines were too happy to see them, and too anxious to get away, to "procure" any extra gear. In the Marines it was never considered stealing when one took anything from the army. It was just "drawing small stores."

The army G.R.S. personnel were about as nervous and scared as they could be. The sight of row upon row of white crosses driven in the sand; and the mounds of dead bodies waiting to be processed gave them little to be confident about.

Oct. 28, 1944 just before sundown of Ted's final night on Peleliu, him and several of the Marines, including "Hot Lips Brown" started up the way to the field kitchen for their daily ration of Lima Bean soup. They must needs go through the Army camp of five or six new tents. As they passed the last of these there was a pistol shot.

"Hot Lips" sank to the ground, a bullet through his heart. A green recruit, playing with his pistol, had ended another life and no more words would pass those lips.

The next morning, Oct. 29, 1944, tears flowed down hardened cheeks as they laid him in the ground. For now those lips had grown cold and silent.

How close he had come to seeing his mother again, and planting a kiss on her warm cheek.

A few hours later they left Peleliu's shores, but never more would "Hot Lips" laughter and banter sound throughout camp to warm their hearts.

RETURN TO PAVUVU

1420 Oct. 29, 1944 Aboard U.S. Army Transport Willard A Holbrook

The First Marine Division's withdrawal from Peleliu was not the glorious, swaggering event of a victorious army. It was a solemn affair, more the withdrawal of survivors, rather than of victors.

True it was, they had triumphed in one of the great battles of the Pacific War. One that would equal, or exceed, most any battle of the war, or possibly of all time.

More than thirteen thousand lives were expended on Peleliu, the majority of them Japanese, but the Division had also paid its dues in blood. That was an average of three hundred lives a day for the forty-five days the Marines spent on Peleliu.

Great numbers of Marine casualties had already been evacuated to the Hospital Ships standing by just outside the reef or to hospitals on the remote islands which the Americans controlled in the Pacific. Some of the worst wounded had even been returned to the states, but many were planted there, under the burning hot sand. Their flesh already consumed by the maggots that seemed to appear almost spontaneously with death.

As an effective fighting unit the First Marine Division was washed out. There had been too many casualties in the "Line" companies. Too many leaders of all ranks were gone but especially, Sergeants, Lieutenants, and Captains, the backbone of any fighting unit. They were devoid of their veteran Privates, and Privates First Class, the ones who do the actual fighting, and most of the dying. The ones who knew how to take a pill box, or storm a ridge.

Ted was never able to understand how or why, Generals, or Admirals, should get the credit for winning battles. They never fire a weapon, they sat back in the lap of luxury, in Australia, or Hawaii, or else they were sitting out on a large ship. Safely out of range of any harm, and yet it was proclaimed that, McArthur won a battle, or that Admiral Halsey won a battle. No slightest mention of the ones who bled and died is ever made, no credit is ever given, but then, I suppose, such menial lives meant nothing anyway.

The physical and mental condition of the troops was nearly gone after forty-five days and nights of almost continual combat. Had they been called on, they would still have been a formidable force, but much of their real effectiveness was gone.

The strength and stamina to get back aboard the troop transports, standing by outside the reefs, was about all the troops had left. To Ted and his companions, who had spent the night in the water, it was almost more than they had.

There was a story that made the rounds, it proclaimed. "As the Marines boarded the transports, a Sailors asked if they had any souvenirs for sale," one of the Marines patted his fanny and said. "The only thing I am bringing off of Peleliu is my Ass, and that is the only souvenir I ever want of this place." That pretty well summed up the feelings of most, if not all of the "Survivors of Peleliu."

Just the thought of Peleliu can stir some very deep emotions. A nightmare that will never vanish as long as one survivor exists, and possibly not after they all have perished. This, from a Graves Registration Corpsman, not even a combatant, what must the feelings be of the front line troops.

About the only thing Ted could recall of the trip from Peleliu to Pavuvu, was the dumping of tons of spoiled turkeys overboard. How this rarest of rare delicacies would have been cherished to the near starving troops on Peleliu, rotten or not. And the scuttlebutt, that something "Great," was waiting for the Division when they returned to Pavuvu.

The usual rumors started making the rounds. The Division was going "Home." They were going to Hawaii. They were going here, they were going there. No longer were the seventeen to twenty-year olds so gullible as to believe these rumors. However, even the Chaplain aboard confirmed that "Something Grand" would be waiting when the troops got back to Pavuvu. The rumor finally settled on, and most "men" wanted to believe, was that the whole Division was going to take turns going to Melbourne, Australia for a thirty day leave. This sounded reasonable, and was something surely deserved. How the spirits did soar. What great plans were laid for, "When we get to Melbourne," what a cruel hoax was played on the young Marines, by the trusted Chaplains for letting them believe these rumors.

0820 Nov. 7, 1944

One early morning, the ships steamed back into Pavuvu harbor, and there lay the camp, "Home" just as they had left it. The neat rows of tents, the parade ground, and the movie screen, even the row, upon row, of coconut palms looked inviting, to young Marines who were going to Melbourne.

Down the cargo nets into the higgins boats and amtracs for the trip to shore. The first troops ashore were forming up into squads, and companies, and marching off to their respective camps. The parade grounds were a beehive of activity.

Part of the Division band which had returned earlier, or possibly, had been left behind, to police the camps, while the Division was away, was playing some lively tunes that seemed out of place, almost lewd. The Death March, or Taps, would have been more appropriate, for everyone remembered, and were greatly humbled, by the thoughts of their friends who were not coming back. A part of everyone lay buried in Peleliu's bloody red waters, or in its burning hot sand.

When most of the G.R.S. people were ashore, they were formed up and started to march off to their camp. Part way across the parade ground they were halted and the Chaplain proclaimed. "O.K. Guys. Here is your Big Surprise." He seemed all proud.

Lined up at some make shift tables, passing out little cups of tepid, powdered grapefruit juice and battery acid, (powdered lemonade) were seven Red Cross women. All of them were old, (probably twenty-five to thirty-five) and dressed head to toe in Marine khaki and boondockers.

Ted was sure the Chaplains and the women meant well, but their presence was about as out of place as a belly dancer at a funeral. It was almost revolting. Ted didn't recall any member of G.R.S. accepting a drink, which was no doubt very rude, but this was not the time, or the place. No "outsider" would be allowed to share in this mourning period. It was a time when only the ones who had paid their "dues," would be allowed to enter. Another bitter disappointment swept the Division.

How different was Pavuvu from the first time Ted came ashore there. The great Parade Ground, Division Theater Area, the Highway, all paved, with the shining white coral. The G.R.S. Company "street" was paved, along with the hill. The tents and the cots were the same, and this was where the exhausted, emaciated, troops headed.

For days, and days, the weary troops hardly stirred from their cots, even long enough to go to the now enclosed mess hall to eat. Only when it was absolutely necessary did they stir from the comfort of their cots, their own "Private Little Worlds."

The coming of the Red Cross women had wrought many changes. The outdoor toilets (heads) were now screened from view. No one was allowed out side their tents without at least a pair of shorts on. The "Big Surprise" was a "Big Pain."

Grim faces and gaunt ribs mark the Corpsmens faces after the return from Peleliu

Gradually the "Walking dead" came back to life. Some one of the Corpsmen suggested they go over to Division Hospital, to visit some wounded friends. This led to trips to First Marines, Fifth Marines, Seventh Marines, until all of their acquaintances were accounted for.

Groups of the Corpsmen made the rounds, talking to the survivors, the wounded, and the friends of the dead. Hearing, and telling, how so and so caught a mortar round. So and so got it with a grenade. So and so lost his arm or legs to a machine gun.

The stories went on and on. So and so was in the hospital on Guadalcanal, or Binika. So and so was recommended for the Silver Star for bravery. Some got promotions, some this and some that, but most of the real heroes never got anything. The one's who could recommend, and verify their deeds had been killed, also. There was no one to tell. Uncommon Valor was so prevalent on Peleliu, that it became common. But many, many, never left Peleliu's shores, of this the G.R.S. Corpsmen could attest.

Gradually, the movie areas, abandoned the first few weeks began to fill up again in the evenings. The mess hall, now lighted, began to fill with men playing cribbage, or poker, or hearts. The young men were gradually coming back to life, they wanted, and needed, to be together again.

The only place that remained almost deserted was the new Red Cross Library and Recreation Hall that had been built while the Marines were dying on Peleliu. The Marines avoided it like a place that had the plague. The few times Ted had ever seen one of the women, was when they would be whizzing by in a jeep, with an officer, or armed guard, accompanying them. Their compound was enclosed inside a high wooden fence, with armed guards patrolling. It was between G.R.S. and the Division Theater. By mutual, unspoken consent, the men made a wide circuit of this place when going to the movies, so as not to have to look upon it, or them. It was as though bringing those women there was a violation of one's self and certainly it was a violation of one's privacy. The armed guards were an extra-added insult to one's honor. No Marine of the First Division would ever be accused of being "A Red Cross Commando." God forbid.

A couple of weeks after the return from Peleliu, the tales started making the rounds. Someone in such, and such, outfit woke up screaming. Some one was standing over him with a bloody knife. Day and night these stories ran rampant throughout the Division. Some one with a Knife slit the mosquito netting off, and tried to kill some one. On and on, and on, every morning there was a new wave of stories about the exploits of what "He" had did last night. "He" became known as "Jack the Ripper." More and more people kept waking up screaming, and the whole Division was in turmoil. No one went out at night alone. Armed guards were posted to patrol "all" the company streets at night. A fear permeated every camp and company.

It was only after several weeks, with no one being wounded or killed that it was realized these were only "nightmares" of the young troops coming out of a bloody, prolonged combat. The legend of "Jack the Ripper" finally died down, and the camps came back to normal.

The arrival of replacement troops probably helped pull the veterans out of their stupor as much as anything could have done. There was a temporary camp set up for the replacements that were arriving regularly. It was on the right of the G.R.S. camp, just off the beach. Here the new, mostly raw, troops spent from one to three days while their fate was being decided.

Most of these seventeen year old "Kids" (to the nineteen year old Veterans of three campaigns) were right from the states and boot camp. This was their first taste of field life, but at least they would have the benefit of two or three months to train, practice, and get acquainted with their respective units. They would not have to go directly into combat right off the ship as Ted and his companions had done.

Almost invariably, virtually every one of the new replacements came down with dysentery, stomach cramps and vomiting. Their drinking coconut milk and eating their greasy field (hot C) rations from a mess kit that wasn't properly cleaned caused this. One of the first lessons learned in the tropics was "clean that mess kit, but good."

The G.R.S. Corpsmen, being closest to the replacement camp, had the responsibility of treating there sick and seeing that they kept a "sanitary camp." It (the dysentery) usually started about nine or ten o'clock at night, and it ran for two days and nights. The Corpsmen set up day and night watches and were kept busy administering Bismuth and Paregoric. Bismuth was for the diarrhea and Paregoric for the stomach cramps that accompanied it.

This, along with bandaging and sewing up the cut and bruised hands of the recruits, trying to open coconuts for the first time, kept the Corpsmen occupied for a few days and possibly made them feel "needed."

The new recruits were assigned to the various units to replace the injured and dead from Peleliu. The "Old Salts" took them under their wings and started their initiation right, with "tall tales, and stories of bloody combat." The poor recruits sat wide-eyed, listening to these "mostly true," if somewhat exaggerated stories for several days and nights. The replacements brought the latest "dope" (news, not drugs) right from the states, for which the veterans were starved.

With the coming of the replacements, quite a number of the veterans from Guadalcanal days were relieved to go home. Some would return as combat replacements during Okinawals last days, and make the supreme sacrifice, after surviving the bitter and lean days of being the first to lead the way, on the road to Tokyo.

A troop transport would steam into the harbor, and the next morning, the Division Band would set up on the parade ground. They would play lively tunes all the time the veterans were going aboard ship. They continued to play until the ship started to move out, then they would strike out loud and clear, "San Fran-cis-co Here We Come."

Ted and his companions, lying in their bunks, could see most, and hear all of this activity. They were happy for the ones "going home," for it showed that "some" did make it. But it left a very sad heart, as the ship steamed out of the harbor, around the point, and suddenly, out of sight, and one was left to Pavuvu's lonely days and nights. Although some good and true friends sailed aboard those ships, the moment they were out of sight was almost like they never existed. One seldom if ever saw, or heard from them again. Only "Memories" were left, and "Memories" will more often than not, lie to one's soul.

Although Ted, and the group he came over with, longed for a big "send off," or a "Welcome Home Band," the only greeting they ever received was when "The Man" once said, "Welcome to New Britain" as the bombs fell, and the bullets zinged through the trees.

Packages of Christmas "Goodies" were beginning to arrive, along with the huge bags of mail that had backlogged when the troops returned from Peleliu. Every day brought more and more packages, as the home folks responded to the "mail early" urging from the post offices.

Weeks, sometimes months old cookies, cakes and candies were eagerly devoured by the troops, accustomed to only the G.T. K and C rations. The mothers, sisters, wives and sweethearts, using of their precious sugar rations was greatly enjoyed, and appreciated by all.

Ted's sister Vera, sent him a box of divinity, the best he had ever before, or after tasted, one of the few items Ted never shared willingly with everyone, especially Chuck, for two of his big hands full, would have cleaned it all out. One effect the mail early had was that most all the goodies were long gone before Christmas arrived.

Some one, or group, in First Service Battalion, fashioned a Christmas tree from coconut fronds, and Christmas Eve brought a big "sing along" and a few skits to go with the evening movie.

Holidays it seems, should be renamed "Family Days," Any Holiday without the family present, is just another day, and means absolutely nothing. Holidays are for "going home" or for having the family "come home."

Christmas Dinner that year was a great feast. The company cooks outdid themselves with the meager supplies and equipment they had to work with. There was fresh baked Turkey, dressing, and gravy. Real (not dehydrated) mashed potatoes, corn, cranberry sauce, and other goodies. To top it off there was fresh baked pies, the first ever offered in the Division while overseas.

Church services had been held in the mess hall prior to lunch. Separate services for Protestant, Catholic, and Jews. The "Lords Supper," a small wafer, dipped in wine, was offered all around. The Chaplain drank all the remaining wine in the cup; everyone thought he filled it extra full to start.

The G.R.S. Corpsmen, having so little to do, still spent too many hours sacked out each day. They had too much time to think, and dream, of the one Christmas present no one could receive, the touch, the feel, the sound, the smell, of a lovely, soft girl. Oh how the long hot afternoons, and the weary, moonlight nights drug on, and on, and on. Men, especially service men, were notorious for talking about "girls," but the "Need," on Pavuvu, went far beyond talk, and there was not one thing anyone could do about it. Except do like a few did, take a rifle and blow the top of their heads off. The "Need" was that strong.

The dreary months, slopping around in rain, and mud, and filth, and stench, without seeing even one female in a dress or skirt. Her hair trailing down, and the clean, sweet smell of perfume, had left a loneliness a "Need," out of all proportion to "Normal."

The evening meal, the movie, a late card game, helped to relieve the pain for a few precious hours, but then, one was alone (amongst thirty thousand men) again, to watch the moonlight playing on the waves in the bay, or dancing on the swaying palm fronds. Or, feel the spray of the rain splattering down, and see the lightning sparks leap up and down the tent ropes.

The afternoons, and the nights, without a female companion to share it with were interminable. Sleep usually came in the wee hours of the morning, but quite often, it was interrupted by one waking up in a cold sweat, from hearing a grenade thump, a mortar swish, or a banshee scream in the dark. Dream sounds, which still bring the same results.

What would Ted give for one night, one hour, one minute, one second, on Melbourne's shore? The States, Home, seemed something unreal. A place one would never see again. But Melbourne was a "Fairy Land" one dreamed of, and might possibly be attainable, sometime.

Things were picking up in the Pacific. No longer were a few lonely divisions holding the line against the Japs. Great American Aircraft Carrier fleets were dominating the seals and the skies. Men and material were pouring in, new trucks, new jeeps, new tanks, and new guns.

No longer was the food totally slop, about twice a month, a refrigerator ship steamed into the harbor, and for two or three days, there would be fresh meat. A beef roast, a rare steak, and rarer yet a pork chop. To the starved, emaciated troops, it was Eden. The usual "goat," (mutton) greasy meat and vegetable stew, dehydrated potatoes, and carrots were not half as bad when there was an occasional meal of fresh food.

Right after Christmas the whole Division seemed to come alive. A new Division Commander, new replacement troops, new equipment, and then the whole tempo picked up, slowly, imperceptibly, until it was a swelling tide.

It was time to make both mental and physical preparations, for another bitter campaign.

Who would be the living? Who would be the dead? Who would be the hero? Who would be the coward? Only time would tell, for certainly, no one knew, except God, and He wouldn't ever tell.

MALARIA

Like a hurricane it roared in and consumed even the strongest bodies. This virus carried by the tiny female anopheles mosquito could lay waste to a whole division of troops. In most of the divisions of Marines fighting in the South Pacific there were more casualties from malaria than from the Japs whom they were fighting.

So prevalent was this disease that the divisions had special Malarial control officers and units to combat it. A Marine was just as (or more) effectively put out of combat by malaria as by a non-fatal wounds from a bullet or a fragment from a grenade.

Mosquitoes require water to lay their eggs in and to reproduce in. In the South Pacific there was no shortage of water except to drink. The very nature of the jungles made them ideal breeding grounds for mosquitoes and they took full advantage of the opportunity. The immense swamps and mangrove areas were ideal habitat for the mosquito. When one invaded their habitat they usually paid the price.

The Poncho, a sort of rain cape was one's best friend. It went everywhere with him for out of a clear blue sky could materialize a cloud and drench the earth it seemed.

In a matter of minutes a foxhole would become an unwelcome bathtub. It filled to overflowing and one wallowed in the mud and water until he "almost" welcomed the chance to rise up and face the other enemy, the lesser enemy, the Japs. The only consolation, if it could be a consolation, was that the Japs were having to endure the same weather. The same diseases and the same conditions as oneself, but at this time there was certainly no sympathy lost on the Japs. Only curses.

On the island of New Caledonia there was no malaria because of some certain tree that grew there. Ted never knew the name of the tree. He did not remember if it killed the mosquitoes or just the malaria virus.

On many of the most affected islands there was a joke going around. "The mosquitoes are so big here that they will turn a Marines dog tag over and check his blood type to see if they like it before they bite." Certainly some of them seemed large enough to do it, too.

Outside the combat areas the troops usually had mosquito nets. These would hang some four feet above the cot. The sides and ends would be rolled down at night and tucked in to keep the mosquitoes out. No doubt they helped but there was no way of keeping all of them out. They could, and would find the smallest of openings and then pour in.

On one island Ted had a mosquito net that had developed a tiny hole, less than one quarter of an inch across, right over his head. Every morning, just at daylight the mosquitoes would discover this hole. They would circle above it for all the world like a swarm of little dive-bombers. One at a time they would peel off and dive straight down through the hole. Ted would lie below and smack them between his hands as they dived through.

Any kind of an illness or wound in an all-male society is bad. It seems that "man" needs the sympathy of a woman when he is sick. Men and especially young men just don't have the empathy that a woman has. A field hospital was an abominable place to be. Even though the Corpsmen tried their best, about all they were able to do was to give medication and change bandages. They simply did not have what ever it was that women or girls have to nurse a sick or wounded person back to health.

Quinine, a substance obtained from the bark of the cinchona tree was the prime treatment for a person with malaria. It didn't stop the malaria as much as it would finally allay the fever.

A substance known as Atabrine had been developed to combat the malaria bug. All troops were required to take one each day. These were little yellow, bitter pills. Though not as bitter as quinine, they were never the less, unpleasant tasting. There was a rumor that they would render the taker impotent going the rounds, so many of the Marines simply took their pills and threw them away. This practice became so wide spread that Corpsmen were finally stationed at the head of the chow line. Everyone that went through from Private to General was required to open their mouths and the Corpsman would toss a pill down their gullet as they passed by.

Malaria struck like a freight train. The fever skyrocketed and the chills started. In the tropical heat one could not possibly get enough blankets over them to keep warm. Massive doses of Quinine were given four to six times a day and night but it was of little effect for several days.

Complete exhaustion, fever and chills raged through one's body. It seemed the very joints would separate from the shaking and the aching that invaded his bones. There was simply no relief from the chills and the fever.

Only the most severe cases were admitted to the division hospital for no one wanted to go there if they were not forced to. It was the custom in Ted's outfit for the Corpsmen to take care of the individuals in their own tents. This also included the Corpsmen them selves, for they were not immune to the ravages of the malarial fevers that prostrated so many of the Marines.

Several times Ted was struck with the fever. His friends, especially Chuck Lasalle would force the quinine down him and start piling on blankets. Each person had a blanket, to sleep on, not under. These would be gathered up and stacked upon the one with the fever. The sweats would start and one would be wringing wet and still the chills would possess him.

If (or when) one was having a malaria attack "all" of his friends stayed with or near him. To stack blankets on, in the sweltering tropics, or to wipe a fever-ridden brow with a cool cloth.

One of the Corpsmen might get a damp cloth and wipe his brow, another hold his hand and talk to him, but for the most part he was left to himself. There was just nothing more they could do to alleviate the fevers, the shaking and the aching. It would take several days for the malaria to run its course and for the quinine to take effect. Often the affected person would be out of their heads from the high fever. They would toss and kick and talk in their feverish state.

When the fever abated one was left in such a weakened state that it might take several days for him to be able to get up and walk about or go to the mess hall for meals. One of their friends would bring them back a mess kit filled with what ever might have been served that day.

One of the big problems with malaria was that it stayed in a person's system for years and might pop out at any time. For many years after the troops returned home the fever and the shaking would occasionally over take them, though they were never as severe as when in the South Pacific.

Occasionally one would have a severe attack right when it was time to go aboard ship for another combat operation. The doctors would sign a slip for them to be left behind. For most Marines and Corpsmen this was about the worst thing that could happen. Though no one welcomed combat, only a very few would condescend to be left behind when their buddies were going, and everyone was needed. Of course there was always that few who would do most anything, including committing suicide to keep from going.

Ted was to see several Marines with everything from malaria to broken legs sit and beg the Doctors to let them go. If it was at all feasible the Doctors would usually relent and grant permission. Some of them never returned.

MAIL CALL

Of all the events taking place in the service "mail call" was definitely the most important in most if not all lives. It was the greatest event of the day, or the sorriest. Depending on whether one got mail, or whether they were standing empty-handed when all the morsels were passed around.

In the pacific theater mail call was the most eagerly awaited event (outside of going home) that ever took place. When one was shipping over it took weeks for their mail to catch up. Often they received much later mail than the first posted. After one was permanently assigned to a Division or Post it arrived fairly regularly once their correspondents got the correct address.

Ted was one of the more fortunate of the young men stationed overseas. His mother wrote to him daily. His brothers and sisters were faithful to keep letters on the road. He had many friends with whom he corresponded so when there was a mail call he usually got his share and a bit more most of the time.

On Pavuvu's lonely shores mail from home was about all that kept the young men from going stir crazy. Pavuvu was such a tiny island and was occupied only by the First Marine Division, so there were very few things that came directly there. Most things arrived at Guadalcanal or Banika and were transshipped on to Pavuvu; mail was no exception. There was no airport so the only planes that could land were piper cubs that landed on the road by the beach after it was finally paved with coral.

Each day the mail boat left for Banika and each afternoon it returned. If successful it was piled high with many bags of mail. The mail boat was about the only regular link with the outside world. As well as the mail, it carried personnel and small items of equipment, or other freight back and forth between the islands. Ted was a fairly regular passenger, accompanying dead Marines over to be buried, for there was no cemetery on Pavuvu either. He would spend the remainder of the day visiting with acquaintances stationed there. It was amusing to spin tales of combat terror to those poor "rear echelon" troops. They would fairly cower in the corners of their tents at the stories, mostly true, but possibly exaggerated a little, if that were possible. Hearing possibly made their hum drum lives bearable, for nothing was worse than the boredom of the rear echelon life. Certainly Ted could never have survived it.

The mail boat was usually sighted coming into the bay and the word was passed along. If there were mail it would be off loaded to the Division Post Office. The individual Battalions, Companies, etc., would secure it from there and it would finally filter on down.

At long last the cry of "MAIL CALL" would ring out throughout the company perimeter and everyone would gather around. The mail orderly would start calling off names loud and clear, even if mispronounced. Occasionally, one's name would come up quickly, but usually it could not come up quickly enough. If one person should get two or three pieces of mail fairly close together there would be a great chorus of boos. Occasionally one's name would not come up at all. Then a sad, brokenhearted young man would slink back to his tent and try to pretend that it didn't matter, while all the others were reveling in their "messages from home."

These letters brought the only real contact with the outside world, they were a constant reminder that "Home" was still there and might some day be attained again. They brought joy, sorrows and heartaches and tears. They brought the news from the "real" world. Pavuvu was only a nightmare, a bad dream to be endured.

Service men and the girl's back home wrote some of the most outlandish letters. Great tales of love poured forth to one's they had never even seen before, and the young ladies, bless them, answered in kind. It was a relief, a diversion, something one could hold on to. The big lie seemed very real in the monotony of Pavuvu. One wanted to believe every thing and what wasn't said was imagined, and stored away. Most of the young men wrote to several of the young ladies, whom they had never seen, and never really expected to see, but at the time you could never have convinced them of this fact. It is virtually certain that most of the young ladies also wrote to several of the fellows, though neither one would ever mention it in one of their letters to the other. It was part of the unwritten code, and everyone played the game by the rules.

One could become very disturbed when there was no letter from some certain person, or from a person whom they thought a letter should be due. Occasionally, a young lady would write that she had found her true love and would write no more. This was a great blow to one's ego, even though they had never even met, and one might curse both him and her mightily.

If one got several letters, as Ted usually did, the procedure was to take them in order of importance. Mom's letters came first, then sisters and brothers, and finally, the letters from young ladies. The letters were opened and quickly scanned to pick up any "real news." They were then tucked away and when one got time they would methodically go through them to digest the real, or imagined meaning of the contents. Letters of import might be read and reread over a period of days. It was as though one was trying to digest every last word, trying to see if there could be any hidden meaning, in any line of the letter.

The letters from the young ladies would be memorized, and stored away for a moment in the dark, when one might imagine the hugs and kisses promised were being delivered. One wanted so very much to reach out and touch, no, to hold someone soft and warm. The slight whiff of perfume on a letter was worth ten thousand times its weight in precious gems or gold. The physical desires of young men were always there, but the spiritual desire to be with someone of the opposite sex was even greater, if that were possible.

The Marines spirits waned or soared according to the news contained in letters from home. For those who were married the mail was even more eagerly awaited. It brought news of births of their first-born and occasionally it brought news of first-borns, some two years after they had been shipped out. This would sow devastation beyond many of their capacities to endure. That was the main reason for Ted's trips to Banika on the "mail" boat.

The letters might bring requests for divorces from the young ladies to whom they were married, after only knowing them for a day or two, marriages that had no possible chance of lasting. Marriages that were made because of the "old fashioned" idea that one only went to bed with some one to whom they were married.

It was hard for the troops to accept the fact that life went on back home, even though they were not there. It seemed that time should have been suspended while they were away. Though one was happy for their families it was hard to digest that they might be enjoying some event without them present to enjoy it, also. Events that could have been happy occasions if they had been there became nightmares when they were away. Was it jealousy or maybe possessiveness or possibly that one just longed to be there with them, most of the guys wanted to know that they were missed or needed, not that the family was enjoying life without them.

Censor-ship was fairly strict and all outgoing mail had to go to the censor before it could be posted. Tokyo Rose might be proclaiming that you were headed for such and such a place, and she was seldom wrong. But you were not permitted to even hint that any activity was about to take place. A few times Ted attempted to tell about some of his "experiences," but the letters were returned. One had a note attached that stated. "You will have your mother in tears," destroy this and write her another more pleasant one. Ted could make up great lies to tell, but he could not tell the truth about combat, or Pavuvu, or what was in his heart.

Pictures of the girls one was writing to was the only means he had of really telling what they might look like. Pictures in bathing suits were really treasures to behold. Everyone sent descriptions of them selves, but pictures told the real story. They didn't lie too much, but then, who has ever sent a picture of themselves that wasn't at least a little flattering to their egos. Pictures of ones families were the means of telling how much their little brothers and sisters had grown and matured. A couple of years in an adolescent's life can make great changes. The pictures of mom and dad were always there for one to commune with, to assure them that everything was still all right.

When the time to go into combat came all the rules changed. The training, the sense of urgency, the activity, pushed the need for "mail" to the back burner. It was still important but not the necessity it had been. Before going aboard ship however the final letters were thoroughly digested. Everyone knew it would be a long time before there was more, and for many these would be the final ones.

During the final days before boarding ship everyone tried to find time to dash off a few last lines to everyone with whom they corresponded. Usually, it was rather short, terse notes. So many, many things one wanted to say, but was restrained either by conscience, timidity, or the censor.

Last Wills had long ago been filed and stored away in the Division records, and there was no use to remind anyone back home of the possible need of these. Only a few vague hints could one pass on, but surely the loved ones at home could "feel" the change in tempo and know that something was about to happen, also. When the letters ceased to arrive they knew then that something was in the works. Only those who have waited can even imagine the anxiety with which the mailman was awaited, or the thrill of a "Fleet Post Office San Francisco" postmark on an arriving letter.

Even aboard ship one could write home but the letters would not be "mailed" until the ship arrived at some distant port, sometime in the future. Most everyone had one final morsel to get off on the last night before "D" day arrived. It was a somber bunch that sat on the bunks and dashed off these last notes. Possibly the last time one would get to commune with mom and dad, sweetheart or wife and children.

When the divisions were locked in combat for a prolonged period of time, and the First Marine Division's lot always fell this way; mail would eventually arrive. It would be weeks old, but it was mail from home, and eagerly awaited. There was probably no greater morale builder than the sacks of mail that arrived during combat operations.

One of the things that touched Ted deeply was to find unopened mail in dead Marines pockets or packs. Often the line companies would get a mail call just as they went into the lines, and would have no time to even open a letter before they would be killed.

When the division returned from combat there would be huge stacks of mailbags waiting. One might get thirty or forty letters, mostly several weeks old, but a letter is a letter, no matter how old. Just as news is news, the first time one hears it. One would separate the letters by postmark, date and person. Retire to their own private little world in a tent filled with other Marines doing the same. They're to have a "Mail Orgy" quickly opening and scanning the contents. One would go over everything later to really digest it.

Packages from home were eagerly awaited. They came separate from the "mail." It seemed they were put on the slowest boats possible, and would take several weeks to arrive. The contents might be stale and crumbly but they were welcome. Cookies, candy and other delicacies were devoured; it was the "taste of home."

Mostly one shared "everything" with their buddies. The contents of packages were no exception most of the time. For the most part even letters, except for the ones with the most intimate messages were shared around. One would read them aloud after they had read and reread them several times themselves. Service buddies, and especially combat buddies, were "family" and shared virtually everything, even their inner most thoughts at times.

Ted's sister in-law gave him a packet of stationery the night he left for the service. In it were two poems, one of which he can still recite word for word "almost."

> You will say you had no news to write me
> And this possibly may be true
> But without news one has always
> Something to say to those with whom
> One desires to have anything to do
>
> Lord Chesterfield

Even without news to write, a letter said, "I Care," and what more could one possibly say to someone they love.

PREPARATIONS

Indeed the tempo was picking up on Pavuvu. Every morning Ted would awake to the sound of close order drill that was being performed by the various units on the parade grounds.

The Line Companies, First, Fifth, and Seventh Marines were starting to whip their men into shape, and what better way than close order drill, and calisthenics. Day after day, hour after hour, atwo, areep, afore. As the sound of rifles changed positions on the shoulders and to the rear march echoed across the tiny island. Quick time, double time, hit the dirt, then up, and start it all over again.

Inspections for the Marines became a weekly event. One day the G.R.S. Marines were having an inspection. Many of their number were off on some other duty so they had very few to stand in ranks. The Corpsmen were never (or almost never) required to stand these inspections but a Sergeant had jokingly said, "why don't you guys come help us out," so Ted, Chuck, Lee and Frances picked up their rifles and joined the ranks. When the Lieutenant took Ted's rifle and looked down the barrel he at first turned all red, then green, then repressed a smile and said. "I think you should take this rifle back to your tent and clean it." Back in the tent and Ted sighted down the bore, there was a big old spider with a nest. No one ever asked him to "help" stand inspection again, and he never volunteered again either.

About that time a real epidemic started through the camp. Great masses of big, yellow, puss pockets started appearing in everyone's armpits. With the hot humid weather, and the lack of bathing facilities, these proved extremely difficult to heal. The Corpsmen were kept busy cleaning, doctoring, painting, and giving pain pills.

In an effort to keep the armpits dry, the Corpsmen rolled gauze around big wads of cotton and taped them under their patient's armpits. Soon everyone looked like they had a Kotex under each arm.

Ted finally came up with these puss pockets under his arms and found out first hand how painful the "Chinese Crud," as it had become known, could be. The pain was excruciating. He finally painted his armpits with a strong solution of salicylic acid. The pain was great and all of the hide peeled off. Ted took massive doses of Codeine, Phenobarbital, and everything else on the sick bay shelf. It did kill the "crud" however, and

Ted used this extreme medication to heal several of the Marines whose infections would not heal with only merthiolate and such. The "Chinese Crud" lasted for weeks and virtually every officer and enlisted man alike contracted it.

One afternoon there was quite a flurry of "activity" on the parade ground around Division Theater. Word soon passed around that Bob Hope, Jerry Colonna, and a troop of "girls" were going to put on a show that evening. Needless to say, everyone not on duty was into they're best khaki and at the Division Theater early.

The First Division Air Force, four or five Piper Cubs, came in for a landing and out popped Hope, Colonna, and several girls. They put on a great show; it was a real morale builder throughout the Division. So isolated was the First Marine Division's "Rest Camp" that almost none of the U.S.O. or camp shows ever showed up at their island.

How Hopes writers could always get the latest jokes, nicknames of officers, pet peeves of the troops, never failed to amaze Ted. Bob always knew the appropriate thing to say to get a big chorus of groans, such as. "They told me there were so many girls on this island that I really didn't need to bring these along." One of the greatest things about the Bob Hope shows was that he would never let an officer be seated until "all" the enlisted men were seated. The enlisted men got the front rows and if there was any room left, the officers could have it.

Fresh supplies were pouring ashore from the ships that appeared in the harbor almost daily. One item that came ashore under heavy guard and much ado was the "New Secret Weapon." It was the then new infrared scope for night vision. One was supposed to be able to see in the dark with it. Although they did help they were not that effective for there were not enough of them for wide distribution. Ted never understood why all the secrecy from the troops who were supposed to get, and use this item.

There was a huge cache of Coca-Cola and beer stacked and fenced off, with guards patrolling the fence. Everyone was given two cokes, and two beers a week. Ted "usually" traded his beer for cokes. Just before leaving Pavuvu, to clear out the supply, everyone was issued five cans of beer. There was a lot of drunk "kids" that night, and a lot of sick ones the next morning.

There was a new "Ice House" in service and supply. On coke and beer days the G.R.S. Corpsmen "always" found two or three people with "sprained" wrists or ankles. They would requisition several blocks of ice, so that "all hands" might have ice-cold cokes and beer after the evening movie, or while playing cribbage, poker, or hearts.

The pace seemed to quicken with every passing day. All hands had to have several rounds of shots, and with each new round of shots came new scuttlebutt (rumors) as to where the Division was going. Everywhere from Perth Australia, India, the Philippines, (to help McArthur) to Formosa, to China. Everyone had the "straight dope" and the latest information, right from some one in headquarters. Except no one but Tokyo Rose knew the real destination. She always announced weeks and months in advance where every division was going. Each evening she would come on the air with the latest "Hit Songs," right from the states. And comments like. "Marines, do you know where your wife is tonight? Do you know what civilian's arms she is lying in right now? Do you really want to go to such and such an island to die for Old Man Roosevelt?" She had a great program, the best in the Pacific. Possibly this was because she had the only one beamed at the Pacific.

The mornings continued to resound to the cadence of close order drill, but the afternoons were given over to softball games. The G.R.S. crew would dump twenty or thirty barrels of high-octane aviation gasoline on the field and burn it to help dry it out. This, when gas was so strictly rationed in the states.

Pavuvu's monotony remained, but things were seldom dull now. Everyone was busy repairing packs, getting new shoes, plenty of new socks and clothing for the coming campaign. Every day brought something new.

The G.R.S. Corpsmen, in addition to their regular Identification satchels, carried a supply of bandages, sulfa powder, merthiolate, and morphine. In addition to their regular packs, they crammed their "Gas Mask" pack with more large compresses, slings, codeine, and above all a huge supply of Morphine Hypodermics, for now they had wised up. The dead could wait, but the wounded needed attention at once.

Mornings often found the Corpsmen on the rifle range, sharpening up their skills. All hands took their turns on the firing range. Rifles, automatic weapons, machine-guns, everyone took turns firing, loading, and cleaning up afterwards. Everyone, even the Corpsmen, had to master the art of disassemble and reassemble blindfolded, for a rifle (never ever say gun) was much more apt to jam on a wet muddy dark night.

A dip in the bay was a real respite after a morning at the firing range. Then, it was back and hit the sack for an afternoon nap. How easy it was just to "do nothing" in the tropical heat.

As the weeks on Pavuvu came to a close, more and more troops stuck a rifle barrel in their mouths and took the quick way out. Several times a week some G.R.S. people had to make the boat trip to Binika, a nearby island, because there was no cemetery on Paviivu.

Ted could never understand why anyone would rather die than take they're chances in combat, but then Pavuvu could provoke some pretty weird thinking. A "Dear John" letter from home might just tip the scales.

The evening movies became a little more crowded. The Sunday Church Services better attended, as everyone started making their own individual preparations for the ordeal ahead. Meals became more sumptuous as larders and warehouses were cleaned out, for this would be the last trip to Pavuvu. "Last Wills and Testaments" were checked to be sure they were up to date. This was a rather depressing chore for everyone knew that for many it would be truly a "Last Will." Pairing up of "Best Buddies" became more intense. Everyone needed someone to be close to.

One morning a large number of Big Troop Transports, Cargo Ships, L.S.T.'s (landing ships tank) and L.C.I.'s (landing craft infantry) appeared in the harbor. Suddenly the harbor seemed too small to hold all the ships anchored there. Never before had there been more than three or four at the most. The bay was a beehive of activity. Higgins boats, Amtracs, Dukws, anything that would float was ferrying men and material to those ships. There was jostling, bumping, and pushing all around.

This was the day, stow your sea bag, roll your mattress pad, knock down your cot, don your combat pack, grab your rifle, and fall in. Just like that, Pavuvu was to be abandoned just as it had been occupied. Only the tents were left standing for the "Rear Echelon" people to take down. Then they would follow the combat troops.

Into the Higgins Boats, out to the ship you were assigned to, up the cargo nets, stow your pack and rifle and find a little piece of "real estate" above deck to stake out. Next morning Ted stood at the rail watching as the beautiful harbor disappeared. Then Pavuvu itself became a tiny speck, and finally disappeared, to remain, "only a memory of life's little journeys."

Although this "preparation" was for Okinawa, it was typical of the preparations for all of the First Marine Division's campaigns.

TO OKINAWA

Feb. 25, 1945 Aboard U.S.S. Magoffin

As the ship steamed away from Pavuvu's lovely harbor for the last time, young Ted Alexander, now an "old man" of nineteen, stood at the rail contemplating on the past, and considering the future, if there was to be one.

What havoc had life reaped that a lad of such gentle stock had now become a "hardened veteran" of three bloody campaigns? Could take the life of another human without batting an eye, that could sit on a dead comrade's chest and eat the meager rations from his pockets? Or, on occasion curse a person mightily because he was so mutilated or decomposed that identification was near impossible. Yet, could have love and compassion for the wounded and maimed. What did the future hold?

Somewhere Ted had heard that a statistician had figured out that each time a person went into combat, his chances of survival were exactly equal to everyone else, be he veteran of several campaigns, or a raw recruit. Probably not one veteran of several campaigns would agree with this "logic," right or wrong. Virtually everyone considered that if they had survived three or four battles, in which twenty to fifty percent of the participants had been killed or wounded, they had already beat the odds. The percentages in their favor had already ran out. Common sense, if not logic, told them their numbers should come up on this invasion, and facing another campaign was not easy.

Pavuvu faded into the distance, along with such thoughts. More important things were at hand, a cribbage game, a few rounds of poker, stand in line for two or three hours, on a broiling hot deck, to get some slop in the mess hall.

Each person was assigned an abandon ship station, a boat station, and a landing group section. Preparations were made for a practice landing (staging) and as previously, it was to be held on Guadalcanal.

March 1, 1945. The ships steamed up to a now familiar sight, the outline of Guadalcanal and Tulagi. The pounding white surf on the snow-white beaches became visible. Here the ships could stand in close to shore so the passage wouldn't be as long. On a hostile island, the ships had to stay several miles off shore to be out of range of any shore-based artillery the enemy might still have in operation.

As the ships approached their assigned positions, their decks became a massive swarm of activity. The P.A. systems blared out, "Now hear this." "Boat crews, man your boats." Boat crews manned their boats and were hoisted over the sides. Cargo nets were lowered all along the sides of the ships for the "invading" troops to disembark on. By the time engines were stopped, and anchors dropped, troops were swarming over the sides and filling the landing craft, thirty-five or forty to a boat.

A practice landing has very little resemblance to an actual invasion. Probably the most valuable experience is to the boat crews, many of whom have never been in combat before. It also gives the "Beach Masters" (who have absolute authority in their sectors) and their crews, experience in untangling foul ups, and working together. The main benefit to the combat troops is that the new men get a little better acquainted with the veteran's ways.

They say practice makes perfect, but every invasion Ted was on looked like a mass of organized confusion. The combat troops have not the slightest idea of the planning necessary to support an invasion. Although there was the inevitable foul ups and many mistakes, the people in planning had a monumental task. Every last item of food and equipment, every last person, every ship, and fuel for same had to be planned into the operation. Just think of packing up and moving a city of several hundred thousand people, several thousand miles. They must be transported, fed, and maintained. Everything from ammunition to toilet paper must be accounted for. Every ship, every boat, every person, every piece of equipment, was assigned a priority number for the landing, and a certain spot on the beach to be landed. It was mass confusion, with a purpose.

To the veteran troops the landing was just a big nuisance. A lot of effort expended for nothing. The only resemblance to a real invasion was the very real possibility of a broken limb, or serious injury going down the cargo nets and into the bouncing Higgins boats. As the ships buck and bounce, one has to climb over the side with all their equipment, rifle, pack, etc. Hang on to the rough rope "ladder like" nets as he descended thirty, forty, fifty, feet down to the water. The landing craft were bouncing around like crazy in the swells and in the churning water. Try to time his release from the net to coincide with the boats momentary pause on the top of a swell. If one misses this momentary pause, the boat dropped out faster than he could fall. It may be ten or fifteen feet below when he hits the steel deck, or worse, gets crushed between it and the ship. An experienced Coxswain handling the boats can do wonders, but they can't control the swells and the waves being churned up by the milling boats, waiting their turn to be loaded.

The tension, the uncertainty, the smells of gunpowder, the belching of flames from the big guns is missing. There was no sounds or the concussions of the huge shells being launched on their way. The sight of the planes strafing and bombing the beaches, the explosions, the smoke and haze, everything is different. It was about like watching a battle scene or invasion in a movie.

Movies always look so fake no matter how much sound, how much smoke; explosions, mud, dirt, mutilations, or drama are included. Actors are still that, just actors, the electricity the tensions are just not there. The first thing Ted sees in an actor's performance is his eyes. Try as they may, actors and make up personnel just can't duplicate the look in the eyes of one facing death. The determination of near exhausted troops, the will to continue on in spite of fear, or thirst, or hunger. Eyes do not lie. If the opportunity ever arises to view combat troops, look at their eyes to tell if the movie is real or fake.

Everyone knew what was waiting on Guadalcanal, two cans of warm beer, not Japs. Two cans of beer held no fear over the "invaders."

Guadalcanal had changed in about the same fashion as Pavuvu. Wide coral paved highways; not muddy ribbons for roads, neat rows of tents and warehouses, headquarters buildings, signs announcing the identity of each group, or company, or building.

Throughout the Pacific, the massive buildup of men and material was snowballing. After this one final assault the Japanese home islands would be next.

Ted spent most of the day touring around with a group of Marines who had been in the original invasion of Guadalcanal. They stopped by Lunga Point and the Matanikou River crossing, where so many thousands of Japanese had died, trying to overwhelm the Marines lines. They found old foxholes and dugouts. The veterans discussed how swarms of Japs had crossed the river, night after night. How machine guns had jammed from burning so hot. How mortars had come in blanketing their positions.

Now the Japs had came so close to overwhelming their positions at every point.

Certain officers or men were killed here, or wounded there. Their reliving of the events and emotions went on, hour after hour. The airport, now big, and broad, and busy, was the next stop, all remembered when it was only a trace, the mud, the rains, fevers, deprivations were discussed.

Every person could point out places and areas they had been in close calls and hilarious events. Virtually every person could take you to the "exact spot," find a slight depression from an old foxhole, or point to a spot and say. "I was right here." Not close to here, but "right here," that they had spent one particular night.

The night a fleet of Japanese Battleships, Cruisers, and Destroyers, boldly steamed into the channel between Tulagi and Guadalcanal. For hours and hours they steamed slowly up and down, up and down. For hours and hours these steel monsters released broadside, after broadside, of naval gun shells from the equivalent of five, eight, and sixteen-inch guns.

The ponderous sixteen-inch shells were particularly devastating. They tore up huge tracts of real estate, belched death and destruction, and threw fear into every heart. I was "right here" they would say. A spot they would never forget.

The final stop was the cemetery. Somewhat unkempt, by First Marine Division standards, for now it was under Army control, and not the Marines.

Up and down the rows and rows of crosses. "Here's Old Tom, or Bill, or John, or Orville," rang out from person after person. So and so should be over in that corner, or a little more this way, or that way. They were planted there among the coconut trees, but as long as this generation lived, they would never be forgotten, possibly they're names and the dates but not the person.

In the absence of flowers or other momentos, some of the Marines placed a coconut by the little wooden "Crosses," or "Stars of David," Some placed rows of palm fronds over the graves, in a noble, but futile effort to shield their fallen comrades, "buddies," from the incessant rains.

Ted has often wondered what it would be like to revisit one of the islands he helped invade. There were several spots he could walk to and say; "I was right here."

Back aboard ship and the next morning the ships weighed anchor and headed in a somewhat northerly direction.

The usual rumors had persisted, but until now none of the troops knew their destination, they only knew they were going to meet the Japs again. The most "logical" destination from the few maps available, and from Tokyo Rose, seemed to be Formosa. Every scrap of information available on Formosa (now Taiwan) had been ferreted out and digested by the troops. Every few minutes some new bit of information came filtering through the grapevine.

All the Corpsmen were notified via the Ships P.A. system. "Now Hear This." "All Pharmacists mates will assemble in the mess hall at 0930." The Corpsmen were all issued "Anti-Venom" snakebite kits. The only problem was the instructions for use were all in Spanish, and no one spoke or read Spanish. These kits came from some South American country and no doubt cost untold millions of dollars. The deadly "Coral Snake" was supposed to abound where ever they were going, but neither Ted, or any one he heard of ever saw one, or for that matter, any other kind.

March 8, 1945, Banika Island. After a week of the landing maneuvers the ships larders were restocked and their fuel tanks were topped off, the what seemed a large convoy again headed north.

March 15, 1945 Left Banika. Briefings were held, and each person was assigned a "wave" number (what position they would have in the landing) and told what beach they were to land on. But no destination was given. The only thing Ted knew was that before he could step off on solid ground, there was a long boat ride. At the end of the boat ride was a high "sea wall" to be scaled by tall ladders. Some one was going to "Get Hurt" going over that sea wall, "The Man Said," it would no doubt be covered by machine gun, mortar, and artillery fire.

A few days later, steaming in drizzling weather and choppy seas, the convoy steamed into some kind of an anchorage. There was many ships anchored there, for the outlines could be seen through the clouds and rainsqualls.

1600 March 21, 1945 arrived Ulithi Atol.

The next morning it was bright and clear. From a vantage point on deck there was a sight never before seen, and one that will probably never again be seen. It was viewed with awe, and amazement, by "all hands."

Stretched out in every direction, as far as the eye could see, in the great Ulithi harbor, for such was their anchorage, was hundreds, and hundreds, and thousands of ships of every conceivable size, shape, and description. Great Aircraft Carriers, Jeep (small aircraft) Carriers, Battleships, Cruisers, Destroyers and D.E.s without end it seemed. Masses of Troop Transports, Supply Ships, Tankers, laden with fuel oil, Landing Craft Tank's, Landing Craft Infantry. More ships it seemed than ten worlds could contain.

The greatest fleet gathered together in "in one place, at one time," in the history of the world. It was totally impossible to grasp the size of this fleet. Where had they come from? Where were they going? Surely such a vast armada could only be sailing for Tokyo Bay itself.

The harbor was a mad house of activity. Fleets of fuel tankers were topping off each ships fuel supply. They came along side and their smelly hoses were linked up. The ships P.A. blared. "Now Hear This, The Smoking Lamp Is Out Through Out the Whole Ship during Refueling Operations." Ammunition Ships, Supply Ships, all taking they're turns visiting ship, after ship, to replenish their stock of supplies. There was Mail ships and messenger boys carrying Captains and Commanders for briefings and orders. Who could possibly be directing this, what seemed mass confusion?

Billows of smoke would announce getting under way preparations for a dozen or fifty, or a hundred ships. They would sail off in orderly fashion, to destinations only they knew. Each group had its own flotilla of heavy escorts, and small carriers and cruisers. Swarms of sleek new destroyers were buzzing around on the fringes, searching for enemy submarines or aircraft. They were "Big Brothers" protectors, and in turn "Big Brothers" aircraft was their protector, each group was mutually supporting.

No sooner would a fleet sail off than twice as many came in. Ships were arriving and leaving every minute of the day and night.

Great vociferous, if somewhat good-natured arguments would break out among the troops lining the rails, as to what type of ship certain ones were. The names of the huge Aircraft Carriers, or the Battleships that cruised by; with their great turrets of sixteen inch guns bristling in the bright sunlight.

A great swelling tide of pride as one viewed this majestic armada spread out before them. Certainly, there seemed nothing on the seas could be feared, but every Marine and Corpsman always knew, a mortar round, a grenade, or a tiny twenty-five caliber bullet might just be the one with "His Name" on it.

Ted and his friends never tired of watching the comings and goings of this marvelous fleet. There was always some thing new going on. Signal lights would flash out their messages of dots and dashes, too fast for the untrained eye to read. Semaphore flags would blossom forth, and signalmen would dash off a message. Signal flags would be hoisted from the masts of the great ships, and always, the activity grew more urgent by the hour.

How different this great fleet from the three lone LSTs that carried Ted to his first taste of combat, without even an escort of any kind. How different it was from the occasions when he saw four, five, or eight ships in a "large" convoy. How far the war had advanced since the resounding, "Welcome to New Britain."

After about a week of sitting in Ulithi harbor, one night the ships P.A. system blared out. "Now Hear This." "Early mess will be served at 0430 hours for the Getting Under Way Section."

Every one of the troops realized what this message meant. Whatever they're destination and what ever their fate, come daylight they would be on their way; the hands of time were counting down.

So gradually during the past several days had the great Line Carriers and their attending heavy, fast escorts slipped away, that they were hardly missed. Great Armadas of ships and planes had gone to pound the coasts of Japan itself. Gone to destroy as many planes and airports which would repel the invasion as possible. Gone to bomb, to shell and strafe the landing beaches, and support areas. Gone to places and duties totally unknown to the troops aboard the transports.

Early the next morning the P.A. blared out, "Revile for the Getting Underway Section." A few minutes later it was, "Now Hear This," "Chow is now being served for the Getting Underway Section," in the crews mess hall.

A short time later and it was, "Now the Getting Underway Section report to your duty stations." Time for Ted to get a position at the rail to watch, as ship after ship silently glided by, churning up a white froth from their great propellers, and finally, the tell-tale shudder of Ted's ship. One feels a slight vibration and hears the groaning of the winches hauling up the huge anchor. A shudder, a lurch, a bump, and the ship joins the mass exodus from Ulithi harbor and takes up position a uniform distance from the column in front, and glides out to sea. As they hit the slight ground swells and the ship is lifted into the air, Ted can see no end to the neat row upon row of great ships, all bobbing along like rows of ducks or geese on a pond. Everything looks so symmetrical, so uniform so unreal.

Mar. 26, 1944 Left Ulithi

Hardly had the transports cleared the harbor before the troops were called to muster, then sent below to the mess hall for briefings on their destination.

A giant map covered one wall of the mess hall. Big bold letters proclaimed. "Okinawa Shima, Ryukyu Islands." Where in the world was Okinawa, or the Ryukyu Islands? Shortly, the officers in charge unveiled another large map. This showed the whole Pacific and Okinawa's nearness to Japan itself. Not much wonder the radio station, later activated on Okinawa opened its broadcasts with, "This is Radio Okinawa, A Stone's Throw from Tokyo."

Okinawa was hundreds of miles closer to Japan than Formosa, and had been a Japanese possession for ages. It was practically one of the home islands.

Everyone had their own opinion as to what this would mean to the invading troops. If the Japs had dug in and fortified Peleliu in such a short time, what had they done to Okinawa, one of their very own?

A big relief map of Okinawa was wheeled in. The various units landing positions were pointed out. The scope of the operation began to take shape. The First Marine Division was no longer alone. Two more Marine Divisions and three Army Divisions were going in together. These would be known as "Tenth Army." An "Army" is a lot of Divisions under the same overall command.

First Marine Division's lot had fallen smack in the middle, right at and between Yontan and Kadena airports. A High Seawall covered the whole beachfront and ladders would be necessary to scale it. (The purpose of the ships carrying these masses of extremely long ladders was solved.) If the seawall were not enough, the ground behind the seawall rose gradually upwards to the heights of Yontan airport. The Japs would have the high ground. "Someone was gonna get hurt (never, ever, say killed, it is a bad omen) going over that seawall." Of this there was not the slightest doubt.

When the briefing officers finished their presentations and asked for questions, virtually every question was about that seawall. To those that had waded the blood red waters of Peleliu, the seawall looked to be an impossible barrier to scale. Even if anyone survived the inbound journey long enough to get that far. Someone was going to get hurt for sure. That seawall just had to be covered from every conceivable direction with machine-guns, rifles, mortars and artillery. Many other bits and pieces of information were given that day, but the topic of conversation that night by the ships rail, was on "The Seawall."

For the next few days it was briefings mornings and afternoons. Everyone knew they're intended routes by heart. Where day one objective, day two objective, day three objective was. What they were expected to do, and when, but always, when they walked from the room, the seawall loomed bigger and higher. It seemed surviving that seawall became the prime objective, but many had already surrendered to it.

The Chaplains never failed to mention the "Seawall" in their prayers. The impromptu church services, and "Prayer Meetings," in the holds at night, always ended up with, "Protect Us, or Help Us, or Guide Us, on the seawall." Quite possibly that is why events turned out as they did, when the seawall was "Conquered."

When the ship sailed from Ulithi the ships company Chief Petty Officers, invited all troops of the same rate to share their quarters and mess hall. They needed some "extra" help to accommodate these people. Chief Van Horn asked Ted if he would like to take care of the coffee maker and cold drinks for them. In exchange for this minor duty he would be permitted equal access to all of their facilities. They had special food, cold drinks, a lounge, and a spacious place to sleep. Sure would beat sleeping on a blistering steel deck, and standing in a chow line for hours each day. From the very first this proved to be a great arrangement for Ted.

The food aboard ship was greatly improved in both quality and quantity to what it was in "the old days." No longer was it just greasy mutton stew, or roast goat and dehydrated potatoes and carrots.

The Chief's drew their rations from the regular mess and also from the officer's mess. They usually had baked ham, roast beef, fried chicken, or other delicacies available. Delicacies never experienced by the Marine Divisions in the Pacific. Cake or pie was usually served for dinner. Ted having access to all this food before the C.P.O.s usually managed to get a portion set aside. Ted's job was to take care of the coffee and cold drinks, but after meals he had free reign in the galley. His buddies up on deck generally fared nearly as well as the C.P.0's did. He always managed to carry up a stack of ham sandwiches, a pie, or cake, to share with his less fortunate buddies.

For the first time ever, Ted spent most of his time below decks, in the soft chairs of the lounge, sipping ice cold coke or lemonade, in the little galley, or just loafing around. Every time he went on deck he was amazed at the numbers of ships to be seen in all directions. They stretched from horizon to horizon all around.

One morning Ted went on deck to find cold wind, rainsqualls and cloud cover. The ocean was a mass of white caps and froth. The ships were beginning to roll a little in the troughs that were forming. The next time Ted went topside, around noon, it was even worse. Soon the ship was screeching and groaning, as it rode over, and through the great swells that were picking up. One second the ship was picked high up on a rolling swell, and one could see hundreds of ships. The next second it would plunge into a trough, and he could see only the ships next to it or none at all.

Each time Ted went on deck or talked to someone coming below, the seas were running higher, the winds blowing harder. Word was passed to "Secure all gear, batten down all hatches, and close all watertight doors." All of the troops were restricted to below decks. Crews were summoned to string lifelines all around the ship's decks. Truly they were in a great typhoon.

Night came on and the heavy-laden transports were bobbing and dancing like corks in a windstorm. One moment they would stand on their sterns, the next they would plunge down at the bow, or roll from side to side, twisting and dancing like a bucking horse. The screeching and groaning of the ships steel plates became louder, and louder. No one slept that night. Everyone was battered and bruised from being thrown against the bunks, bulkheads, and passageways. One dared not move without having a firm grip on something solid. All night long the ship rolled and pitched and tumbled. It moaned and groaned and Ted could hear water sloshing around inside the vitals of the ships holds. How much longer could it stay afloat? How much longer could it keep from breaking up? The groans and screeches of metal plates, on metal plates, had become horrendous.

In one of the holds a church service was being held. They were singing, "Oh Prepare to Meet Thy God." Everyone was making preparations, either for this night, or for the time when they would wade the surf, and scale the seawall.

Ted managed to keep the coffee makers brewing, and served hot coffee to all the C.P.O.s and Master Sergeants gathered in the mess hall, for no one wanted to be alone that night. Also, hot coffee was offered to anyone coming off duty, or to any troops who passed that way. It was a time to share.

Somehow the ship managed to ride out the angry storm throughout the night. Come daylight, and Ted managed to make his way topside, again. Reports from people coming off duty were that the seals were "viscous," they were not exaggerated.

Below decks things had seemed bad, but topside was much worse. Great frothy swells were engulfing the ships. One moment the ship was riding the crest of the swells, and Ted could see down hundreds of feet to the bottoms of the troughs below. The next moment it was in the bottom of the troughs and all he could see was the great swells, towering hundreds of feet above the ship, and about to crash down upon it. When he could see the other ships of the now scattered convoy, they were pitching around in an unreal fashion. One moment they were standing on their sterns, the next they were down at the bow, their sterns totally out of the water, the great propellers churning nothing but thin air. A more frightening scene Ted was never to see. Life jackets, those horrible nuisances, were one's prime asset.

All day, and most of another night, the ships were battered and tossed around, by the viscous typhoon. Many ships with their crews, and loads of troops overturned or broke up in the battering. Post war records show that the little (by comparison) Destroyers, and Destroyer Escorts, (smaller) took the worst beating of all.

Next morning the skies were clear, but great swells and troughs still lingered. The ships would ride up a swell and almost stall out, then race down into the valleys, as the swells fell off.

The ships were battered and scattered, but the great invasion fleet was mostly still intact. Ships were scattered and out of position in their ranks. It would take several days to gather the flock together again. Somewhere, there is an old hymn that goes something like:

Pray for the ships upon the sea
When mighty billows roll
Pray for the souls within the holds
When mighty ships overturn

The storm abated, but the mighty seawall grew taller, and more formidable, every hour of the day and night, as the ships approached. "Someone was gonna get hurt."

L—LOVE DAY

OKINAWA

April 1, 1945 - Arrived at Okinawa

They had changed the designation from D-Day to L Day to denote the day the troops would be storming the beaches at Okinawa. L or Love Day sure sounded much better than D or Dying Day? (Ted never really knew what the D stood for.) It sounded better rolling off the tongue, but it didn't feel any better in one's gut. Everyone knew that some little officer back in the states could change a designation. But when it came time to face the Japs it was still going to be "Dying Day" of this there was not the slightest doubt.

Again, whether by fate, or luck, or malice, the First Marine Division had drawn what seemed to be the worst possible assignment. (Ted was sure every Army or Marine Division, and every Ship considered the same.) They had to scale the high sea wall, there was high ground in back, leading down to the ocean. The most important Airport was sitting on top of the hill in back of all. Would not the Japs defend this position with all their might?

Okinawa was the same as Japanese home territory. That high sea wall, which had to be scaled by Ted's Division before they could get to solid ground, loomed taller and taller. Someone was going to get hurt going over it.

Our "government" did its utmost to keep the facts and figures of the dead and dying from the nation. There was still enough information that seeped through the cracks for the lowly G.I. to munch on, and figure what his fate might be. G.I.s in the Pacific knew little of what had transpired in the European Theater. Yet, they had still heard of the slaughter on the Normandy Beaches, when the Soldiers had to scale the cliffs. The sea wall was a monstrous cliff to be scaled, at least in one's mind.

It was pitch black when the transports glided to a halt, and the anchor chains ground out their ominous sounds. Ted had the coffee makers brewing early that April 1, 1944, April Fools Day, Easter Sunday. While the coffee was brewing he went topside to see if there was any visible sign of their destination. After one has been at sea for several weeks they are always anxiously awaiting that first glimpse of land, just to know there is still something besides water in the whole world.

Up on deck and it was dark as the Pits of Hell. From no vantage point could Ted see anything except the outlines of various "ghost" ships anchored all around. Everyone wanted to crowd up to the bow, assuming the ship was pointing towards their destination, Okinawa Shima, Ryukyu Retto Islands, "Japan."

Suddenly, the night sky was rent asunder by flames. A huge Battleship anchored nearby had opened up with its giant sixteen-inch guns. By the time the first big sound waves, kaboom, kaboom, kaboom, drifted in on the crisp cool morning air, there was monstrous flashes from all around, clear to the horizon which was now becoming slightly visible.

It seemed there were hundreds of Battleships, Cruisers, and Destroyers cannonading the beaches. Or what one assumed would be the beaches, for there was nothing visible to go by. A tiny part, and yet literally hundreds of ships of the great convoys which had sailed from Ulithi Harbor had gathered there. No longer was it one old Battleship with a couple of Destroyers and six or eight transports carrying the troops into battle. It seemed this huge Armada of ships was without number.

The early dawn sky was lit up by the great guns belching flames and smoke. The kabooms, kabooms became one massive roar. The concussion waves swept over the whole of the fleet. Any Japs on that beach were surely taking a beating. Evidently the Big Brass had finally realized, what the Marines knew all along. Little damage was done to the Japs dug in on the various islands by the shelling before the invasions. The First Marine Division could well remember Peleliu, and the fiasco at Iwo Jima was fresh in mind.

It would have been "nice" just to remain there on deck, a spectator, and watch the proceedings, but that old nemesis, the ships P.A. system blared out. "Now Hear This. Chow is now being served in the enlisted men's mess."

Ted dashed below, but he had stayed topside much longer than anticipated. The coffee carafes were empty. Indeed, two of the glass pots had melted to the electric burners and broken, but who cared about that. This was still D, for Dying Day, regardless of designations.

A sumptuous breakfast by comparison to what the troops were accustomed was offered up, but regardless of the offerings, they would not go quite all the way down. A long boat ride, the sea wall, and death, were waiting only a couple of hours away.

The brief interlude in the Chief's mess was quickly forgotten. It was time to find one's buddies, to stay close, to hang together. At times like that one needed someone too lean on, to hold on to. Someone they can trust with their very life.

"Now Hear This." The P.A. blared. Boat crews stand by to launch all boats. Time was swiftly running out. "Now Hear This." "All troops in the first wave, Lay To Your Debark Stations." Not yet! Ted's turn was coming next, in the second wave.

Check for the hundredth time, both canteens completely full. Plenty of clips of ammunition for the Carbine, the Carbine, and a 45 pistol strapped to the side. The Graves Registration identification pouch, crammed full of bandages, sulfa powder and morphine syrettes. A field pack with clean "dry" socks, and a few packets of K rations. The helmet and helmet liner, which one will unstrap before hitting the beach, for the concussion of a bomb or big gun could rip one's head off. Ted looks and feels like a pack mule sweating in the stifling holds, waiting, waiting, waiting.

All too soon, yet it was a relief to be doing something. "Now Hear This" All troops in the second wave, Lay To Your Debarkation Stations. Up topside there was crisp cool air to breathe. The smell of gunpowder, cordite, fills the air. It was an all too familiar smell. Ted had smelled it before, it smelled of death, and destruction, and dying.

It was a bright clear day, but the pall of smoke from the huge guns was hanging over everything. Ted could still see the flames belching from the muzzles of the guns, and the kabooms, kabooms, were still floating all around. The kabooms, kabooms, were impersonal sounds, they were meant for someone else. At this stage one is waiting to hear the personal sounds. The roar of the Higgins boats motors, the whish, whish, whish, of mortars, the chatter of machine-guns, the crack of rifles. These were the "personal" sounds, sounds that kill.

The square-nosed Higgins Boats were milling around in the water like a swarm of dragonflies. The "first wave" was forming up and starting to pull away. From every transport, and there must be hundreds of them, the boats were swarming around, leaving little white trails of wakes. Close at hand the exhaust smoke was starting to become stifling and the kabooms were beginning to sound more ominous. It was no longer an impersonal thing. Ted was no longer just a spectator. The small boat Coxswains maneuvered they're craft along side the Transports. They were bobbing, jumping and drifting in every direction. The ship was rising and falling on the swells, everything was a jumble of turmoil. The ocean was a churned up froth from all the boats milling around.

From the direction of the island Ted could see huge pillars of smoke billowing up, see the swarms of fighter and bomber planes working over the beach area. Okinawa looked like a mountainous country. It was huge compared to the tiny islands invaded before. It loomed up out of the smoke and haze, but it didn't look as forbidding as the deep dark jungle clad islands of the south. But then Ted was still many miles off shore, too far away to really tell just what it would really look like.

Somehow or other, the Coxswains managed to get the awkward Higgins Boats along side the Transports, and under the cargo nets, which the Marines would descend on. They were pitching and bucking like wild horses as they tried to hold station. "Now Hear This. Second wave, commence debarking." Up, over the rail and onto the cargo nets that dangle over the side of the ship. The ship is pitching and swaying, the Higgins Boats were really bouncing. Hang on for dear life, (literally) for to drop down on the steel decks or sides of the boats would be fatal. If Ted fell between the ship and boat he would be crushed. Many mishaps and near mishaps occurred. Broken and twisted limbs were a real possibility, if not a probability. Watch out or the guy above would step on your fingers, or you might step on the fingers of the Marine below. Down, down, down, one rung at a time. Hang precariously over the Higgins Boat, waiting for just the exact moment to "launch" yourself aboard. One must be cautious and catch the timing just right. Just at the top of a swell there was a moments hesitation, before the boats plunged down again. If one could time it just right, they would (with the help of those already aboard) drop on board without landing on someone, or breaking a leg.

The engines were roaring; the Coxswain was bellowing orders, confusion reigned. Yet, within minutes the three dozen or so Marines who fill a boat were aboard. With a great roar and a crash or two into the side of the ship, the boats were free at last. Still bouncing and bucking, for now they were out in the deep water riding the swells, pitching and yawing. It was a mass of organized confusion. Each boat was assigned a group or "station." As they filled up and departed the mother ship they formed up into groups, usually circling around and around, the only way they could keep station was to keep moving. Waiting for the last of their group to form up.

The first wave was already moving toward shore, all strung out in a straight (nearly) line so as to hit the beach as near the same time as possible. Each string of boats was called a wave, for they came crashing upon the beach kind of like the waves of the ocean, and about as consistently if they were not blown out of the water first.

Whether by design or by accident Ted never knew, but the boat in which he was riding maneuvered right beside a giant Battleship. They cruised right under the big guns that were belching fire and smoke, launching a thousand pounds or so of steel towards the shore. The noise and concussion was tremendous.

What with all the smoke, fumes, and noise, it seemed the little boats were hardly moving, but soon they were out in front of all the large ships. In a no-man's land, between ship and shore. Far ahead Ted could glimpse the "First Wave" forming up and circling, then they fanned out and headed for the beach. As they move out the "Second Wave" takes their place. There was a sort of emptiness in the pit of Ted's stomach. It was not really fear, probably more like anxiety. What was waiting on that beach?

Bouncing around and smelling the fumes made some of the Marines seasick. The waiting seemed like hours, but in reality it was only minutes. Ted's wave formed up and headed for the beach. What was happening up ahead? He could only guess, for they were still too far out to see clearly, and the smoke coming from the island had obliterated most of the landing area.

The big kabooms, kabooms, had been going for hours, but now Ted was miles out in front of them. They seemed more like an echo than the real thing. They had lifted their trajectory to cannonade the rear of the Japs positions, or have ceased altogether. This was an ominous sign to the Veterans. The first waves were about ready to hit the beach, or to get hit before they reach the beach. Dying day was now.

The little landing craft sat so low in the water that it was difficult, if not impossible to see what was going on up ahead. Everyone was huddled deep in its bowels, just waiting for the Japs big guns and mortars to start coming in. A pall of smoke hangs all over everything. The smell of burned gunpowder permeated the air along with the fumes from all the landing crafts motors.

Although everyone was admonished, yea, ordered, to stay down, it was only human nature to want to peek a little to see what one was heading into. Now there was a trickle, soon to become a wave of Higgins Boats returning from the first wave. They were barreling along at full speed. Now empty, their flat bottoms rose up and smacked down each time they crossed a wake or wave. They were going like the devil himself was on their tail. Their wakes made the incoming boats bounce and sway even more. Was this a good sign, or an ominous sign? Was the First Wave ashore, or had something happened to them? How many was washing around in the tide. How many were lying at the foot of the ladders propped against the sea wall, or would there be any ladders against the sea wall?

Ted sneaked another peak over the gunwale of the landing craft. There ahead was the white froth of the breakers crashing upon the beach. He could see the ladders against the sea wall, and tiny people ascending them, reluctantly. In Ted's boat an Officer or Non Com. bellowed out, "Hit the ladders, and don't stop until you are over the top."

Ted was in the front row, if it could be called a row of troops aboard the boat. He was scrunched, banged and bruised between the press of Marines, rifles, packs, canteens, and the steel bulkheads of the boat. There was a mighty roar of engines and clashing of gears as the Coxswain forced the boat motors into reverse, so he wouldn't go too far up on the sand or rocks and be stranded. There was a sudden slowing as the boat touched ground, but the forward momentum carried it a few more feet through the sand and surf.

There was a great forward surge of humanity as the boat came to a sudden stop. Simultaneously with the stop, the front ramp crashed down, and Ted was propelled out upon the beach by the press from behind.

There was no dead Marines lying all around, none in the water, none at the foot of the ladders. Something was dreadfully (delightfully) wrong. No time to deliberate, Ted plunged forward to the ladders ascending the sea wall and climbed up. Only a few scattered sounds from machine-guns chattering as he went over the top, and out upon a dark green hill. The First Wave of Marines were formed up and strung out in a skirmish line as far as Ted could see. It looked like another "practice" landing.

No big guns boom, no mortars swish, no hand grenades, no screaming, no dying. "April Fools Day, Easter Sunday!" What a beautiful clear, delightfully cool morning it was, for Ted was still alive. The sun was still shining. Was it at all possible the planners were right, and this was "L-Love Day"?

FIRST DAYS

OKINAWA

What a blessed relief! The First Marine Division, of which Ted was a part, had made the landing on Okinawa with only a few minor skirmishes. The great slaughter that was expected, and accepted, of a landing and going over the sea wall, had not materialized. Many were still alive who had already surrendered to death.

After one had surrendered to death, it took a certain measure to return to life. Excessive giggles, loud boastful talking, wild tales, much swearing, (the same words, but not filthy cussing when it was relief) and other measures of letting off the unrealized pressures.

The Battalion Ted had landed with made a forced march all the way across the island. There had been only a few "minor" skirmishes on the whole march. Mile upon mile they traveled on foot, seeking out the enemy who was supposed to be there.

There were civilian farmhouses and a few tiny villages captured. This was something new, no where in the islands had the First Marine Division encountered civilians except for a few Gooks. For the first time there was a few souvenirs to be "liberated" besides the Japanese soldiers personal effects and flags.   There was scarves, handkerchiefs, lacquer bowls, porcelain bowls, and dishes. There was any number of things that had been hastily abandoned when the civilians fled for the hills, or were taken to the labor battalions by the Japs.

One afternoon the squad Ted was marching with got several miles out in front of the Battalion. It was turn around and double time all the way back. Everyone was exhausted from the day's forced march. The double time return was almost too much for troops who had been confined to the ships for such a long period. At every pause there was a hasty searching of the combat packs for items that could be discarded. So desperate was he to lighten his load that Ted even threw away two or three tiny silk handkerchiefs. It was a moral victory even if not a physical one. It seemed that every last person was at their total physical limits when the Battalion was finally reached.

As Ted recalled, it was water that was so desperately needed on the march across the island and the return trip. The canteens were constantly empty. On the rare occasions when a water trailer would be brought up there was a mad scramble to fill the canteens. The line would be a block long waiting each ones turn. Heaven help the person who spilled a few drops. Water was just too precious to waste; it was the very essence of life itself. It was a hot, dry, physically exhausting trip.

Ted was happy to rejoin the G.R.S. Company that had set up headquarters in a farm complex near Yontan Airfield; which was already doing a thriving business.

The First Marine Division still had not really encountered any of the one hundred and ten or twenty thousand Japanese soldiers who were supposed to be occupying Okinawa. Was it possible they had abandoned the island altogether?

There was nothing for the GRS Corpsmen to do. Ted dug deep, along with everyone else, and built a bomb shelter. Though the Japanese soldiers had not been found, the same could not be said for the Japanese airplanes with suicide, or Kamikaze pilots.

There was almost constant air activity. Except for the Kamikaze planes diving on and sinking ships, they did little physical damage on the island itself. There was a regular pattern of bomb dropping and planes strafing, but the damage was mostly to one's nerves. Many nights there was no respite at all. Later in the campaign it would be necessary to give the G.R.S. Marines a day off because of the constant air raids.

The Marines had prepared slit trenches for toilets but for all the months spent on Okinawa there was only water that was brought in trailers. There was no baths taken in all the four or five months except sponge baths. The times when it was raining Ted would strip off, lather up and rinse off by the rain. The only real baths Ted ever had on Okinawa were in "The River of Life" and even then there was no soap, only sand to scrub with.

There were herds of goats roaming all around the G.R.S. camp. These were the farmer's goats that had been turned loose. There were also roving bands of the little Okinawa farm ponies running wild. They had grouped up and ran in herds of two or three to a dozen or so. They were almost wild mad from the wounds they had received from the falling shrapnel of the big antiaircraft guns, and from the bomb fragments. When the guns would start sounding off the ponies would become frantic. It is doubtful there was a Marine on the island that did not try to ride at least one of those ponies in the first days.

Ted and Chuck and several of the other Corpsmen caught some of them and decided to have a race. With rope bridles or rather halters, they had little control over the ponies. They were racing up a little dirt farm road and it made a turn at the end of a cabbage field. Ted's horse made the turn but he didn't. He went headfirst into a drainage ditch that paralleled the road. Didn't feel good at all for several days.

No bodies, no graves to dig, so little to occupy the Marine's time. They built a baseball diamond, (where they got the material for a backstop Ted never guessed) had baseball, or rather softball games, and everyone gathered around and cheered. It was much better than dying on a lonely beach. Ted pitched a no-hit game, but his team got beat by like eight or ten to nothing in about five or six innings. An air raid thankfully broke the game up. Needless to say they didn't have the very best fielders or basemen.

Chuck and Ted had found a little plaque with Japanese writing on it and hung it on their doorpost but no one had the faintest idea what it proclaimed. They told everyone it said, "We Have A Son in the Service" just like people "back home" had in their windows. Ted and Chuck built a table to wash clothes on, racks to hold helmet covers full of water to wash in and many other little conveniences.

The first couple of weeks on Okinawa were known as "Honeymoon Weeks," but like real Honeymoons, all too soon they drew to a sudden halt. The First Marine Division, along with the other Army and Marine Divisions had found the Japs. They were holed up, and deeply dug in, on the southern part of the island. They were just laying and waiting for the U.S. troops to come at them.

All at once great truckloads of dead bodies began to arrive at the cemetery. The place was permeated by the smell of death. There were hundreds of graves to be dug in the iron hard clay. From early morning to late night Ted and the other Corpsmen were kept busy finger printing and dental charting the corpses. Ted was sent to the front lines to help in the identification of the dead Marines there, before they were returned to the cemetery.

The "Honeymoon" was truly over. Death, and dying, had arrived on Okinawa. No longer was there laughter, and banter, and joking. The cussing began in earnest.

THE KAMIKAZE

OKINAWA

One day as the great fleet carrying Ted to Okinawa steamed north; they passed close by a small flotilla of ships that were steaming south. In the heart of this flotilla of Destroyers and Cruisers was a huge Aircraft Carrier they were shepherding along. The convoy was barely making headway, as they drew near, the reason became readily apparent.

The Carrier was just a burned out hulk, sitting low in the water, and down at the bow. She had been hit by several Japanese kamikaze, (suicide planes.) Her decks were a mass of twisted, steel girders. She had great gaping holes in several places, and she was charred black from stem to stern. How her crew had managed to bring the fires and explosions under control was truly a miracle.

They had lost hundreds of crewmembers and it was readily apparent that her gallant crew had been through an inferno of Hell. All hands aboard Ted's ship stood at attention and gave the U.S.S. Franklin, for such was her name, and to her gallant crew, a salute for their heroism.

Normally, Marines envied the sailors, as they had a dry bunk, relatively good food, hot showers, and they died clean. An infantryman wallowed in the mud and dirt, ate poorly, died filthy, ragged, and with a stubble of beard. Okinawa was not one of the places to envy the sailors in the "Line Ships."

The great Japanese fleet that had scourged the Pacific was now gone. Crushed by the might of the U.S. fleet and its host of fast Aircraft Carriers in a horde of viscous sea battles. The "Fly Boys" had paid a great price, but they had literally bombed the Jap fleet out of existence. The U.S. Submarines had also taken their toll. They had deprived the Japs of all merchant goods from the Philippines, Borneo, Sumatra, Malaya and Indo China. Their source of rubber was cut off, and that most precious of war commodities of all, "oil" was gone.

The Japanese armies were relatively in tact, but daily, huge fleets of B-52 bombers were dropping thousands of tons of firebombs and explosives on Tokyo, and the other large manufacturing cities of Japan. Of the great sea battles, the submarine warfare, and the air war the Marines knew so very little.

The Japanese high command had been trying to buy time, to sue for an "honorable" peace, but they were down to their last defense, the airplane. Shoot down a U-S-plane, and dozens more rose from the decks of the mighty carriers. Sink a carrier, and hundreds of planes, and pilots, were out of existence. Bombs were effective when they could hit a dodging, twisting, bobbing ship, but a more effective method was to crash dive a planeload of bombs onto a ship.

The young Japanese pilots were poorly trained but they could get a plane in the air, and they could get it down. It was said they were given a party, and a bottle of saki before their missions. Their planes were loaded with bombs and just enough fuel for a one-way journey. No one was to return alive. To die for the emperor was supposed to be a divine death. To surrender was unpardonable.

The kamikaze pilots got all the glory, but was there really any difference between crashing a plane on the deck of a ship than making a Banzai charge, or fighting to the death of all the defenders of the myriad of islands?

As soon as the troops had secured enough of the Okinawan territory, hundreds, and possibly thousands of 155 M.M. Anti Aircraft guns were installed on the island. Some air raid sirens were also installed, but the first Ted usually knew of the air raids was when the boom, boom, boom of the big guns started, and the black puffs started filling the sky. Usually, they began way off, then came nearer and nearer. The planes seemed to move slowly and the big black puffs exploded all around. So many thousands of shells expended, and the planes still inched closer and closer.

Occasionally, a plane would explode and disintegrate, or spiral to the ground, trailing a great plume of smoke, but mostly they just circled on around. When they were out over the bay they would appear to be hit and plummeting towards the ocean. All too often a great billow of black smoke followed. Another ship was scratched from the list back in Honolulu, or Washington D.C. where they knew nothing of the burns, the screams, or the dying, of the personnel aboard, and cared less.

Dogfights between the American and the Jap planes became a commonplace thing. Most of the ones Ted saw, it was the American planes hot on the Jap zeroes tail. Tracer bullets were licking out; soon the Jap planes would crash and burn. Several passed so close by that Ted could see the Grumman's shells tearing up the ground as they went by.

Of the hourly battles between the Jap planes and the little D.D.s or D.E.s on the picket lines surrounding Okinawa the Marines knew very little.

G.R.S. was set up in a field of cabbages, carrots, and other vegetables that the Okinawans had planted, for life must go on, war or no war.

Most of the Okinawan civilian's who were not behind the Japanese lines were put into camps in the northern part of the island. Being a farming area, the houses were well scattered along little dirt roads, with canals or drainage ditches bordering all. The houses were the center of the farms, with goat, chicken and pigpens almost touching the house and all connected within a courtyard. Each pen occupied a minimum of space. Only room for a pig to stand in but not enough for it to turn around, or walk in. A high bamboo hedge that had only one opening going into or out of it surrounded each of the houses.

Ted and Chuck Lassalle had explored most of the complexes. In one, about a quarter of a mile across the cabbage patch from camp, was a big fat pig. It probably weighed five or six hundred pounds, and an old rooster that was running loose. Goats, and the little farm horses ran wild everywhere, especially the goats.

One day Ted decided, (against orders to not molest the civilians animals) to catch that old rooster and make a "chicken stew" with some of the cabbage and carrots. He meandered down to the house, and sure enough, the old rooster was still there. Ted tried to coax him close but he was wary. Around and around the house they went, just as Ted grabbed for him, he zipped out the opening in the bamboo hedge. Ted had ducked under a telephone wire that the Marine communications people had strung when they first passed through the area, when he entered the compound. In the heat of the chase he forgot about it. It caught him right under the chin and nearly took his head off. While he was nursing his wound, and catching his breath, the old rooster sauntered back in. That was too much, so Ted set in pursuit and finally caught him. He wrung his neck and after he stopped kicking headed back "home."

About half way back across the cabbage patch Ted heard a Jap plane, (Japanese planes sounded totally different from American planes) coming in fast. He turned and looked backwards. There was the Jap plane, big, bright red, rising sun balls on its wings, heading his way. Possibly the Jap pilot decided this was too good a target to pass up. The planes nose tilted, and flame started spewing from the wing guns. Ted hit the ground and

166

absolutely, literally, crawled totally under his helmet, (Don't say it can't be done) as if his helmet would have been any great protection. The plane roared past, its shells kicking up dirt on both sides of Ted, as he lay there, scared. The plane pulled up and circled out towards the bay. Not one gun on shore had fired, but as the plane approached the bay, every gun, on every ship in the harbor opened up. The Jap plane turned nose down and dove, a big plume of black smoke rose for hours. Scratch one more ship. This was the only time in Ted's career that a Jap plane had singled him out. Always before it was an impersonal thing. The planes strafed and bombed, at random. One might possibly be a victim but this time there had been only one target, Ted.

Ted arrived back at camp with his rooster. He cleaned and boiled it in a helmet cover for hours and hours, but that old rooster was still so tough he couldn't have ground him with a meat grinder. The vegetables were tender and tasty though, even if they were fertilized with "night shade." (Human waste)

Someone in G.R.S. managed to rig up a short wave receiving set. Nightly, crowds would gather around to listen to the crackle of the voices from the night fighters, and from the ships on the "picket line." The reports came in calm and business like. A voice would proclaim, "six boogies, (Jap planes) bearing so and so, nine miles out." Sometimes it was one, or three, or just many boogies. The receiver would answer "Roger" then many minutes later the same calm voice. Scratch three boogies scratch seven boogies, one time it was scratch seventeen boogies. The Japs were paying a terrible price, but so were the Americans.

The air raids went on, day and night. There was seldom an hour passed that one or several Jap planes, Zeros, Zekes, or Bettys, weren't over the island or over the ships in the harbor.

For the first weeks the great fleets of planes from the Carriers had the responsibility of patrolling the air space at sea. They brought down hundreds and hundreds of Jap planes. Once the Japs planes were over land they became the responsibility of the land-based guns.

Huge batteries of 155-MM guns were set up all over the island. Great banks of searchlights to pin point the enemy planes at night were installed. Both guns and lights was radar controlled, so they could latch onto a plane and follow it all over the island.

Mostly the daytime raids were just a nuisance to the infantrymen; the greatest danger being from the falling shrapnel of the A.A. guns. The real casualties were the ships at sea.

Nighttime was a different matter. The Japs always sent hoards of planes in to bomb and strafe the airports and the fuel storage tanks. Ted's unit was set up right between the two main airports with fuel tanks scattered all around.

Within days of the landing, both Yontan and Kadena airports were cleared and enlarged, and became operational for literally thousands of American planes. Kadena was said to be the busiest airport in the world at the time.

From just before daylight until after dark, there was a constant flow of squadrons of aircraft, coming and going. Their drone overwhelmed most other sounds. There were "Graumman Hell Cats," the Navy's fighter planes, squadrons of P38's. The Armies fighters, Fighter-bombers, Torpedo planes, Light two engined bombers. It seemed there was no end to them.

Soon, several squadrons of "Night Fighters" equipped with radar, were brought in. At dusk, they would take off to patrol and intercept the Jap planes coming in. All night long the groups of four to sixteen would come back to refuel or rearm, then off again. Quite often there would be gaps in the formations. One or two planes missing, for though they were extracting a heavy toll, they still had to pay the price.

Nighttime was show time, if one was not on the front lines, but it was also a deadly time. As soon as a Jap plane was over the island, the big anti aircraft guns would open up, boom, boom, boom, and the searchlights started pinpointing it. Often ten, twenty, thirty and more lights would have the same plane "locked" in from every direction. Their beams created a great pyramid with the plane shining silver bright at the very top. The planes seemed to be frozen in position by the lights, just sitting still, way up high in the night sky.

The boom, boom, booms continued, and after what seemed hours, but in reality were only three, four, or five seconds, the big black puffs started appearing. Sometimes, if the plane was some distance away the big black puffs appeared first; then the sound would kind of come in, in slow motion.

At first there was just a few puffs here and there. Then there was dozens, and hundreds, and thousands. The boom, boom, booms of the distant batteries drifted in on the night breeze. Soon the sky was filled with little black and gray puffs, like a mini storm cloud drifting over.

Sometimes the planes were totally engulfed in black puffs. Sometimes a shell exploded hundreds or thousands of feet below and it looked like the plane had just disappeared. Occasionally, a flash of fire could be seen when the plane was hit, and it would go tumbling off, trailing a stream of smoke.

Mostly the planes just creeped along through the black puffs, drawing slowly nearer until Ted's neck was curved back, and his eyes were looking straight up. Show time was over it was time to pay the price of admission, for getting to see this great outdoor spectacle.

One of the first orders of business after setting up a "Permanent" (for a month or two) camp on Okinawa, had been to dig and construct a bomb shelter.

When not in the front lines it was almost like home

These differed from fox holes in that they were dug four or five feet deep, roofed over, and a couple of feet of dirt piled on top. The entrance was just big enough to dive through. It was placed at right angles to the main hole, for the obvious reason that bullets or shrapnel don't go around corners, most of the time.

The shelter was just wide enough and long enough for Ted to lie down in. The wider and longer they were, the more vulnerable to caving in and one being buried alive.

Try as Ted would, he could never keep the shelter dry. The floor was always wet at best, and after heavy rains might be covered with several inches of muddy water. The roof seemed to always be leaking, and there was drip, drip, drips that he tried to keep his body out from under, but seldom succeeded.

When the planes crawled to an overhead position, and the black puffs filled the sky, there would be a pitter-patter as of raindrops. Then a plink on the helmet as the first pieces of shrapnel came falling back to earth.

Ted would stand, or sit in the entrance to his shelter, until the very last second before he would dive deep into that muddy, wet hole. Possibly part of it was playing "Chicken" with himself, and part of it was just the inborn instinct of rebellion everyone seems to possess. Just daring fate to do something about it. Most of it was the knowledge he had gained of when to sit tight, and when to go to cover. For Ted learned that when danger was a few dozen yards away, it didn't affect him. Let someone else do the worrying.

When Ted had stood outside longer than was prudent, or sensible, a head first dive was made into his hole, but if he went in early, he would back in, crawfish style.

The rain of shrapnel would fill the air, and the whump, whump, whump, of bombs exploding would be heard, but all too often they would also be felt. The ground would jump and heave, and there would be a concussion blast as the explosion wave spread out. The close ones made Ted know why he buried deep in that wet, muddy, hole. Ted never knew of one bomb hitting any of the fuel storage tanks, but their near misses seemed to always be in the cemetery area where his hole was.

Sometimes it was only necessary to stay down for minutes, and sometimes it was necessary to stay down for long periods, even hours, if the raids were exceptionally heavy. Occasionally, Ted would be in and out of his shelter and up for nights and nights in a row, until he would be exhausted. He would crawl deep into the shelter and go to sleep. A sleep so deep, he would only awake if he were bounced around by a real close whump.

Early on in the campaign for Okinawa, Ted and Chuck, having nothing better to do had "procured" several big room dividing panels from an Okinawan home and had built themselves a little "house." This house was very snug and dry and warm. They had built stretchers up off the ground for beds. Their blankets and gear were dry for the first time in months upon months. On wet rainy nights it was sure a task to force one's self out of a soft warm "bunk" and dive out into a wet muddy hole.

One afternoon, a group of four Grumman fighters came in for a landing. One of the planes was making a "funny noise." Just as they were near overhead, the pilot of that plane climbed out of his cockpit and jumped. The planes were not more than two or three hundred feet above Ted's head, and everything seemed to be happening in slow motion. Every move of the pilot was clearly visible. The plane seemed to fly straight on for a few seconds, as the pilot plummeted straight down. So low was he when he bailed out, his parachute didn't have time to open. When he hit the ground only a couple of hundred feet from Ted, his parachute fluttered out behind him. The plane continued on a few hundred yards, then nosed over, crashed and burned.

So broken up was the pilot, that he was just like a blob, with no bones. The other pilots from his squadron, who came to G.R.S. to see him, even though there was almost no external wounds couldn't even identify him from his appearance.

Things were different on the three nights that the Anti Aircraft batteries had the duty. On those nights, Jap planes more or less came and went at will.

It was also on those nights, that one would add a few more scoops of dirt to the top of their shelters. They would bail out as much water and mud as possible, for long hours would be spent there during the next several nights. Many nights there would be a continuous flow of planes so one spent many more hours in their shelters than in their beds.

The planes just seemed to flow through the lights and clouds of shrapnel. When overhead they would release their bombs. So close did many of these bombs fall that it was necessary to dig a second opening into the shelters to let the concussion blasts flow out. Concussion blasts from shells, mortars, or bombs, just seemed to overwhelm the whole body. A great air blast, that affected the head, and ears, sort of like going into, and out of high attitude. It was amazing how those concussion waves could even travel underground, or else they flowed into the openings of the shelters, Ted never knew just which.

One rainy, wet, night after returning from a few days and nights on the front lines Ted was getting a much-needed rest in his bunk. Even while asleep he heard, or was conscious of the sounds around him. Four of the U.S. planes came circling in for a landing, but there was something different, peculiar, about their sound. A wave of cold fear swept over Ted and a cold sweat popped out as he realized what the sound was. A Jap plane was flying along with the formation. Ted's sensitive, alert hearing had picked it out of the drone of the other four planes.

Evidently, the U.S. planes spotted the Jap zero. For though they were sort of drifting in, under low throttle for a landing, all at once they powered up to full speed, and the zero did the same. Ted seemed momentarily paralyzed, but as the planes bore closer, and closer, he sprang up and headed for his shelter. As he went out the door, he slipped and fell headlong in the mud. Before he could scramble up the planes came roaring over, so low they almost touched the ground.

The Americans planes guns were spitting fire as they bore down on the zero. A second or two later, and a couple of miles off, the zero crashed in a ball of fire. The U.S. planes circled on in for a landing, as though nothing unusual had happened.

So shaken was Ted from this, another Kamikaze planes near miss, that he spent the rest of the night in his bomb shelter. Next morning he found the blanket on his stretcher bed all wet. One of the planes cannon shells had gone right through the roof, and through Ted's bed, not five feet from where he lay in the mud. Could anyone deny that God was watching over him that night?

A few days later, while a Jap plane was threading its way through the clouds of flack, which were reaching up for it, there was a "tremendous explosion." The whole island shook and trembled and great clouds of black smoke rose up from some ten or fifteen miles back in the hills from Ted's camp.

A huge ammunition dump had exploded, whether from the Jap bomb, or from U.S. shells, probably no one alive will ever know. The explosions, smaller in scope, but still strong enough to be heard and felt for many miles away, continued for at least a week. There was always a column of smoke, as another bunker, or rack, or stack, of great shells or bombs would explode.

Possibly hundreds or thousands of Marines or Soldiers were killed in that explosion. But like always, in wartime, no slightest hint of the casualties or losses were made known.

The Kamikaze raids continued right through Ted's last night on Okinawa, and that was one of the things he wasn't sorry to leave behind.

THE WOMAN

A few days after landing on Okinawa, G.R.S. Headquarters was set up in what would become their permanent location.

Things were exceptionally quiet from a fighting standpoint in that area. Occasionally, an Okinawan civilian man, or woman, and sometimes one of each would pass by. They carried huge loads of clothing or household belongings suspended on poles set across their shoulders. Their knees looked as though they were going to collapse as they chop-chopped down the road. Their burdens were so great it seemed they had to trot to keep moving. They were bringing some of their possessions out of the caves in the hills where they had secreted them before the American invasion.

Moving day - Civilians bringing their posessions out of the hills

Some nights there had been occasional spats between roving Japanese patrols and the Marines. Sometimes with Ted's own people involved, and sometimes in surrounding companies perimeters. These usually lasted only a few minutes. The machine guns or small arms fire of both sides would flare up, then quickly die down. The Japs were no doubt only looking for information as to where the Marines units were, and not for a fight. Possibly they were Japanese soldiers who had become separated from their units by the invasion and were trying to make contact with some of their own people.

One night there was a few rounds of firing right in the G.R.S. camp, from a Marines M -1 rifle, but there was no answering fire.

Next morning there was an old woman, or so she seemed, dead beside the road, right in camp. She had been shot in the stomach, and was sprawled on her back. Between her legs was an almost full-grown baby that had gushed out of her. The umbilical cord was still attached.

They lay there for three days with flies swarming over them and were stinking up the whole camp. Finally, a Marine detail was sent to roll them over in the ditch beside the road and to cover them with dirt to keep down some of the stink.

Ted was reminded of a passage from Matthew 24:19 in the Bible. "And woe unto them that are with child, and to them that give suck in those days."

THE OLD MAN

OKINAWA

One day while on detached duty, it fell Ted's lot to accompany a detail escorting civilians to the rear lines. Back to where they would be turned over to the civilian authorities.

Okinawans, being Japanese, it was impossible to tell who was civilian, and who was Jap army. The older ones were usually considered to be civilians, but the Japs were not above donning civilian clothes and infiltrating the Marines lines, along with hoards of civilians. Once inside the Marine lines they would whip out grenades or rifles, then start shooting and running.

There were about fifty "civilians" of all ages in the bunch, old men, women, young girls, and kids. All were loosely herded up the road and away from the front lines. There were six or seven Marines, besides Ted, to look after this group of people. As they strung out down the road, it was impossible for one person to see all of them at one time. The Marines would yell hubba, hubba. Meaning, hurry up, or faster, or good looking, or anything else one wished it to mean. A word about like Gizmo, meaning, "anything" with, or without, wheels. Move it, move it, keep going, keep going, they called, not having the slightest knowledge of the Okinawan language.

The civilians were frightened, not knowing if they were being taken away to be shot or tortured. The Japanese had told them the Marines would kill all the men, women, and kids, and rape all the women and girls. They were more than a little reluctant to be herded away.

After a couple of hours, and perhaps two or three miles, a group of the women and girls kept lagging behind and pointing to the trees, or hills, or something. They just kept pointing and jabbering, but it was all-Greek to the Marines.

After some time, the Corporal in charge of the Marine detail told Ted, a Corpsman, to take a couple of them up the hill to see what they wanted for they were getting pretty persistent.

Ted selected two, but several wanted to follow and had to be restrained with threats from a pointed rifle. Wailing and jabbering erupted.

Up the bank and behind a stand of pine trees, and it was quickly learned what they wanted. Ted started laughing and yelled back to let the rest of the women come up, for they only needed to use the bathroom. It seemed even an Okinawan woman needed some privacy, even in the midst of a war.

An hour or so later and it became apparent they were not going to reach their destination before long after dark. It was decided to find a place where the small detail could keep an eye on the bunch of civilians for the night.

An isolated farmhouse soon hove into sight and it was decided to spend the night there. The buildings were pretty well shot up, but had somehow managed to stay erect with all the shelling and bombing. The house and adjoining buildings, pigpen and chicken coops weren't too spacious but it was decided to put all the civilians inside, and the Marines would loosely circle the place. The civilians were given some K rations for food and left to their own devices to make the best of what they had.

Some of the Marines were set to digging pits for the guard detail to spend the night in. These circled the farmhouse compound, and were in the edge of brush or trees.

Just at deep twilight there was the splash of two or three grenades, and small arms fire was coming from one of the buildings. Two or three people broke and ran for the trees, speeded on their way by the crack of M-1's, and Ted's carbine, for that is what he was carrying that day.

Shortly, from out of nowhere a squad of Marines with War Dogs came charging up. They had been bivouacked nearby and heard all the commotion and had come to help. After being told where the Japs had gone, they dashed headlong into the trees and brush, never hesitating the slightest. They were off in full pursuit, being dragged along by the anxious Dobermans, and Shepherds, which they had trained for just such circumstances.

Ted and the Marines never knew if these Japs had accompanied the civilians, or if they were hid out in one of the buildings and only chanced to be there when the bunch of civilians arrived.

The guards found their respective holes and settled back for what would be a long night. Ted was paired with a young Marine and they were to take turns standing watch, and sleeping.

Just before total darkness set in, an old man came out of the house, looked around, and started towards Ted and his companion's foxhole.

178

They yelled at him to get back in the house, but of course he probably understood nothing they said.

The old man had one hand inside his kimono, and he just kept walking towards Ted and the young Marines fox hole. The young Marine yelled, "Look Out, He's got a Grenade!" so Ted shot the old man, right in the chest.

He fell to the ground groaning, and he lay there all night, groaning. No one in they're right mind was going to crawl up to him to see if he had a grenade that he would pull the pin on or not. There was several good Marines buried on Okinawa who trusted what they thought was an innocent civilian, or small child.

Sometime later there were shots heard from the direction the Marines with the War Dogs had gone, so they had probably caught up with the Japs that had escaped the building.

The next morning Ted made the old man stand up, and take off his kimono, before he approached him too closely. He put some sulfa powder on the wound and a bandage around the old man's chest; he was loaded on a jeep and hauled away. No grenade was found.

Sometimes his groans still sound in the night, when one wakes from a fitful sleep.

THE LITTLE KIDS

OKINAWA

Have you ever seen fear? Real fear? Words cannot describe the "fear" in the eyes of the little Okinawan kids. It seemed that every little kid from four or five on up would have a little brother, or little sister tied on their backs. They were the protectors, the keepers, and they would die rather than put one of them down or give one of them up.

The Japs would round up a whole herd of hundreds of civilians. There were old men, and old women, with bundles of clothing and probably all their worldly possessions tied on their backs, mothers with babies in their arms, and the little kids. Then they would mingle amongst them and try to infiltrate the Marines lines. They would always come through at night so detection would be harder.

Ted Thought families or what was left of them were doing their best to stay together. When the Japanese soldiers started "pushing" them through the Marines lines, and began firing at the Marines, the flares would go up to light the area. The Marines did their best to protect the civilians and the little kids, but when the grenades started coming, the mortars splashing and machine-guns chattering it was everyone for them selves. For a short time all Hell would break loose. There was screaming and yelling, firing and explosions. Dying! It would be a wild madhouse of a melee. The screams, the cries, the confusion with people running here and there, and everywhere. It was impossible to tell who was a civilian, and who was a Japanese soldier wearing civilian clothes. The barbarianism of the Japs was impossible for "Civilized" people to comprehend. The playing of "catch" with babies, on the ends of bayonets in China, the torture and mutilation of prisoners. Death marches in the Philippines. The tying of wounded prisoners to hospital beds, then setting the beds on fire. The gouging out of little children's eyeballs, then smearing them on walls. What were a few thousand civilians and little kids to such people?

Ted watched the little kids with their precious burdens as they came on and on, some of them were horribly wounded by the shrapnel or bullets; but they just clung the tighter to the one on their back. Often the tiny one on their backs was already dead, but they would never be abandoned.

When all the Japanese soldiers were either dead, or had retreated, the job of gathering up the civilians would begin. To minimize the senseless slaughter it was necessary to get them herded into the rear echelons before the Japs would start another drive. The Japs seemed to have absolutely no regard for their own people, even women kids, and babies.

Daylight invariably found the Marines with a group of those kids, who had become separated, lost, or were possibly the sole survivors of their families.

The hardest job (but the most rewarding) Ted ever had during the whole war was seeing and treating a few of those kids. The fear in their eyes as Ted or another Marine approached them was horrible. There was uncontrollable trembling, as bandages or medication was applied to their wounds. The younger ones strapped to their backs were trembling as bad, if not worse than the ones carrying them; but there was never a cry, or a scream. It was as if fear had totally overwhelmed them. Tears there were, streaming down little brown cheeks, but outcries were seldom heard.

Soft, soothing words for these victims of war was the best medication Ted ever found, food, candy, even chocolate, would just be clutched in their little brown hands, and remain there, unnoticed.

The little ones, as well as the old had been told the Marines would torture and kill them. It seemed most had resigned them selves to this fate. It would take much unraveling to straighten out these little minds.

The sight of a hypodermic needle to give them a shot, (Tetanus for the wound, morphine for the pain) was almost beyond their capacity to bear. How the little lips quivered, the little hands trembled, and the unseeing eyes did stare. The little kids stood around in groups, more or less back to back, shielding each other. They never, ever put their burdens down. How they bore them hour after hour never ceased to amaze Ted.

Many of the little kids had that far away stare in their eyes, and could seemingly look right through Ted. It seemed the smaller (but not much) ones on their backs must have been attached to the same umbilical cord. Every emotion was "instantly" conveyed to the other. If one little mouth puckered, the other puckered. If one grimaced from pain, the other grimaced at exactly the same time; it was uncanny how their emotions were so shared.

Even though these kids probably had no food for days, their little trembling hands would not hold still long enough for them to feed themselves. They could not control their trembling lips and jaws enough to take a bite of the sweets offered.

It was a sorrowful relief, when the Army Civilian Control units bundled the little kids up into the back of a truck or ambulance. Then conveyed them off to a place and fate that Ted never knew.

RAMAH

"Jeremiah 31:15"
"Matthew 2:18"

The barbarism of the Japanese has been known from time immortal. The imperial Japanese regime was a cruel, ruthless band that had no soul or spirit to guide them. They had absolutely no regard for human life, be it man, woman, or child.

In the Pacific War, it was sometimes necessary to become almost as ruthless as the Japs in order to stay ahead of them in combat, but the American G.I.s were raised with different set of values than the Japs. It was necessary to become ruthless and hard, but the Marines could never apply the degree of cruelty and torture the Japs practiced daily.

One day while out cruising the back roads and trails of Okinawa, in a Jeep, looking for a Company of Marines who were in heavy combat, Ted and four stretcher-bearers came upon a scene that was almost beyond belief.

Rounding a curve and coming out upon a precipitous cliff, they came upon a squad of Marines who were trying to force a large group of civilians back from the cliff's edge. It was a scene of utter chaos and calamity.

At first glance it looked as though the Marines were trying to assault the civilians. As they drew closer, it was plain to see the Marines were trying to console them, and to move them back from the edge of cliff.

Some of the civilians broke away from the group as Ted and his companions watched in horror. Three women, mothers, hurled themselves over the cliff's edge to join their babies whom they had already thrown over.

What weeping, wailing, and lamentations, the mothers, fathers, and families who were left did do. "Rachel crying for her children, but her children were not."

"Their tears were stained with blood" as they slowly grasped the meaning of the great hoax perpetrated upon them by their own soldiers. What horrendous deed had they done?

The Japanese soldiers had convinced the civilians that the Marines would torture and kill all their babies, would torture and rape their young

183

girls and old women. This being exactly what the Japanese soldiers would have done.

They were in the process of hurling their babies and young people over the cliff when the Marines burst upon the scene of carnage, and did their utmost to stop it.

Ted walked to the cliff's edge and looked over at a scene that would haunt him, and all who had seen it for the rest of their days.

There upon the masses of rocks, exposed by the low tide, sloshing around in the tide pools lay dozens upon dozens of dozens, of small babies, little children, young girls, and old people. Some with their insides gushed out, and some with their heads broken open. Their legs and arms were twisted in grotesque shapes. The children lay broken on the rocks below; their small bodies rent asunder, and scattered around like rag dolls. But these were not rag dolls.

NAHA

SHURI'S RUBBLE

The battle for Okinawa had been raging at a furious pace. The Marines and Army troops were trying to crack the Japanese army's main line of defense. This defense line had become known as the Naha, Shuri, Yonabaru line, for it stretched across the island roughly paralleling those towns.

The hills rose up sharply behind Naha and made an excellent defensive position. The town itself was battered until there was not a whole, and only a very few parts of buildings left standing.

Unbeknown to Ted and the other Marines, the air and sea war had been raging over and around, Okinawa for weeks. An old Okinawan man who spoke fluent English, as many of them did told Ted late in the war. One day five hundred American planes, he raised his hands and spread his fingers, came over. He lowered his hands, then lifted them palm upward. "Naha (The capitol of Okinawa) no more," he said. Ted was to spend many days and nights in the rubble of Naha, where only a few hulks of bombed out buildings remained.

Naha - No more

Battle ships Cruisers and field artillery had battered the town until it was only a heap of burned buildings, shell craters and mounds of rubble when Ted first entered it. Mostly the fighting in Naha itself had ceased, but the Japs were still shelling the town with their big guns from back in the hills.

The shells would come screaming over and Ted would dive for cover, even though it was usually too late for that. Most of the time if he could hear it, it was already past, or he was already dead. After some days one would become somewhat complacent, and just go on about their everyday business unless the shells started dropping too close. Then they would hit the nearest hole available. There one would curl their bodies up in as tight a little knot as possible. Thinking Ted presumed, that the smaller the target the less chance of being hit, but mainly it was just the natural reaction, for everyone did it.

Ted was to make many trips to and through Naha. It was here one day he and a couple of marines came upon a Buddhist or Shinto Temple that had been virtually destroyed. About the only thing not demolished of the building was the entrance posts. Two huge beams placed crosswise on two upright beams that looked somewhat like a Japanese writing symbol.

In the rubble they found numerous grotesque statues of varying sorts and descriptions. They were carved of wood, and stood about three feet tall. Most had pot-bellies, hideous faces and were painted in ancient

Japanese style. Ted assumed they were the gods the Japanese worshipped, but they had not kept harm from this temple.

Idols from Shinto or Buddist temple destroyed in Naha

Ted, Chuck and another Marine went on a trading expedition out to the ships in the harbor. They were "heroes" to the Navy personnel; they had met the Japs eyeball to eyeball.

In the Marine Corps, "anything" what so ever belonging to the Army or the Navy was fair game. If one could beg, borrow or preferably steal it, that was O.K. It was just "drawing small stores" from the warehouse. There was always "open season" on any item of Army or Navy gear that was left unprotected.

Trucks and Jeeps were both prime items one could "liberate" from the Army. G.R.S. camp began looking like a motor pool because so many vehicles had been brought in. Theft of vehicles got so bad that the M.P.s started putting up roadblocks and checking I.D. numbers. This affected G.R.S. very little except for the nuisance of delay. They merely took their vehicles to the service and supply garage and had the I.D. numbers changed to correspond to the ones of their issued vehicles.

Getting to Naha from the cemetery was quite an experience after the rains started. The roads were quagmires in many places, great bottomless pits or stretches of mud and ooze. Even though all vehicles had four-wheel drive and low ranges there were many spots they would sink in so deep it would take a bulldozer to pull them through. There were numerous spots along the road that every vehicle had to be towed through. There was huge D-Eight bulldozers stationed at each one. A chain would be hooked on if one could find the hook for the mass of mud rolled up under the vehicles. Then they would be towed up to the next "dry" spot. Many times Ted was to see the dozers themselves become bogged down so badly that another would have to be summoned to free them from the quagmire. There would be long lines of trucks and jeeps waiting their turn to get towed through these places and it took several hours just to go a few miles distance.

When returning from Naha the same routine was experienced in reverse. The only difference was that many Army trucks were also returning, filled to capacity with boxes and crates of supplies for the supply depots. It was standard practice to pull up behind these trucks until they were almost touching. One person would crawl out on the hood and relieve the truck of a few of its boxes. One never knew what they might come up with.

The rains came down and the typhoons roared across the island. Virtually everything became a sea of mud. Nearly all motorized transport came to a halt. About the only thing that could move was the infantryman and even that was with great difficulty. One's shoes soon became great balls of mud. It was near impossible to pick one foot up and place it in front of the other.

Death still stalked the front lines. The huge trucks stacked high with bodies like cordwood were towed through the near impassable mud holes, and would finally reach the cemetery. Here the Corpsmen sought to fingerprint and identify them. The G.R.S. Marines dug holes and they were laid to "rest" in a soggy, muddy hole.

Trying to fingerprint and do the paper work in the pouring rain was extremely difficult. The old reliable Poncho did double duty by providing a somewhat less wet environment in which to complete the forms.

The only good thing, if it could be called good, was that the bodies didn't decay quite so fast, and the maggots didn't infest them as soon. The rains helped keep the stink of the decaying bodies from permeating everything for blocks around as it did in the hot, dry weather.

The rains continued and Naha could get no wetter. The dirt roads leading into the hills became like otter slides. Going up, the trucks sat and spun their wheels, and coming down they slid as if they were on skis.

Service and supply had set up a few tents in the rubble of Naha for the use of its personnel. G.R.S. personnel who were a branch of the Service and Supply Company had the use of them, also. These were hastily thrown up and soon flapped in the winds and sagged at the corners where great pools of water collected. Often the stakes loosened and the tents would blow over. Everyone would have to dash out and try to hold it up while the stakes were moved to a "firmer" spot, and the ropes restretched.

These tents had about eight folding cot's set up in each one that the persons lucky enough to get one could sleep on. There were no blankets supplied so it was necessary to furnish one's own. One soon learned to take a combat pack, or at the very least, a poncho and blanket when going to or through Naha for the chances of getting back before night were slim.

It was also in the rubble of Naha that Ted got drunk. So many rear echelon troops and fly boys were then on Okinawa that Jap souvenirs were at a premium. Everyone wanted them, but no one wanted to go to the front lines and pay their dues to procure them. Any souvenir was worth twenty to fifty dollars. A Jap flag was gobbled up at a hundred dollars. This when the lowly GI made fifty dollars a month.

Ted and his friends decided to make some "more" Jap flags and sell them. Somewhere in the rubble they found some red and black paint, and white material. A big red spot was painted in the middle with what seemed appropriate lettering in black around the edges. They were roughed up, dirtied, and some holes poked in same, to make them look "genuine."

Several of these quite obviously fake flags sold for a hundred dollars each, but one fly boy wanted to trade a quart of "Philippine-Seagram's Black Label" for one. This was a very potent "White Lightning" bringing a hundred dollars a bottle, very rare, and hard to come by at that. The trade was made, the bottle taken back to the floppy tent and hid under the combat packs. A "party" was planned for that night.

That afternoon the four Marine stretcher-bearers in Ted's group took the truck to the front lines and picked up a load of "bodies." Ted was left to look after the equipment, and to "guard the bottle." Who knows?

The pressures of war, the small prospect of seeing home again, sometimes made one live for the hour. When Ted's friends returned there was still plenty left for them to get drunk on, too!

One thing Ted could never figure out was why; the farther away from the front lines one was, the more elaborate their efforts at preservation became. On the very front lines, where the bullets flew, and mortars, and grenades thumped constantly, one had only a shell hole, a stump, or a rock. The next line dug shallow foxholes, the next covered over their holes, like Ted's. Back at headquarters, they had massive shelters; all sand bagged around, neat and orderly. Why did the lights blaze all night in the combat zones, when they were having blackouts thousands of miles away in the States?

There were no bomb shelters and few foxholes in Naha. When one flopped upon a cot with their wet, muddy clothes and boots on they fell asleep. If the Japs shelled the town, or bombs fell, so what. All the tents had numerous holes from the Anti Aircraft flack that had fell and pierced them. One felt lucky just to have a shelter over their heads. If they spent the night in the forward lines they "slept" in a wet, muddy foxhole, where the grenades thumped and the rifle and machine guns chattered most of the night. It was a real blessing to get back to a nice, dry bed in Ted's little "house" at the cemetery.

The roads continued to be bottlenecks all through the Okinawa campaign but the engineers were feverishly working to pave the main arteries with coral. Eventually the main north south highway that ran from Naha to the Yontan and Kadena airports and passed right by the cemetery was widened and "paved" with coral. One could drive fifteen or twenty miles per hour on it, a hair-raising speed after the weeks and months of mud.

THE RIDGES AND VALLEYS

The ridges, always there was the ridges. Ted dreaded the beachheads and the landings but the exhilaration, the excitement, the fear, the turmoil, seemed to take some of the edge off of the landings. One expected, and accepted the death and destruction on the beachheads. Someone was going to "get hurt" going in, and everyone knew this. There was nowhere one could go after leaving the Higgins boats or the amtracs except into the face of machine-guns, mortars and grenades.

After a firm beachhead was established it was a much different world. All of the support troops poured into the vacuum left by the advance of the "Line Companies." Except for occasional forays, these troops were out of harm's way. They were beyond the rifle and machine gun fire, on the fringes of mortar and light artillery fire. For the most part they were safer than he was in his own home. Although he might not have the option, now there was somewhere he could go to escape the death and destruction of the front lines. This was the daylight to dark, work-a-day world. They usually had part of the nights to rest.

For the line companies their jobs had only just begun. They were usually bloodied and decimated on the beachheads, but now they were faced with rooting out the deeply entrenched Japanese armies. Their work-a-day world became a twenty-four hour a day task, just trying to stay alive. The High Brass was always asking for more pressure, more pressure, but more pressure meant more dead and wounded. It was easy enough to call for, yea, demand more pressure when one was safely out of harm's way. It was something else when he was the one who had to apply the pressure.

Okinawa, as has been previously explained, was a totally different experience for the First Marine Division. The almost total lack of resistance on the beaches, and in the first weeks, had left a false sense of security. Now, no one was all pumped up; ready to accept death or maiming.

By mid April all the tranquility of the first couple of weeks came to an end. The two or three divisions of Army troops had found the Japanese. They were dug in and entrenched, in the southern portion of the island. The Army Divisions were stalled, and the Navy Brass was screaming for pressure. The Navy was taking a terrible beating from the Kamikaze suicide planes in its efforts to protect and supply the ground troops.

Army troops fought differently from the Marines. Most assuredly, take nothing away from the Army Infantryman, he was just as brave as anyone was; but the Army philosophy was different. The Marines stormed the ridges and the caves, believing that produced the fewest casualties. The Army took a more subtle approach; they waited for the heavy stuff to soften up the Japs first, then went in. Which was best, no one will ever know. To the Infantryman, both Army and Marine, it was still one on one, eye ball to eye ball with the Japs who were dug in.

The First Marine Division was ordered south to take over part of the line. All too soon the casualties mounted. The cemetery crews went from nothing to do, to a pressing twelve to fourteen-hour day trying to keep up with the identifying and burying of the corpses now pouring in. Ted was dispatched south to help in the initial gathering and identification.

On one of Ted's trips south, he arrived in the early morning hours at Machinato Airfield just as the Marines were mopping up a segment of Japs who had tried a nighttime amphibious landing to get behind their lines. For once the Marines were on the giving end of a landing instead of the receiving end. The Marines had burned out many machine gun and mortar tube barrels, but the landing was crushed. Only a relatively few of the Japs made it to shore alive, and these holed up in caves and places of concealment. Ted's Jeep was halted near a large cave where many Japs were firing out at the Marines who had them cornered. Ted added the puny fire from his little Carbine to the M-1 and machine gun fire being poured into the cave. A Marine demolition crew worked its way to a ledge above the cave and swung a demolition charge from the end of a rope into the mouth of the cave. It was detonated and no more fire came from the Japs within.

First it was a push towards Naha, but the inland ridges were just too well defended, and too tough to crack. The Sixth Marine Division was called in to take over the push for Naha, and Sugar Loaf Hill. The First was moved to the inaccessible mid section of the island. There, the Japs were truly dug in. Thousands of caves and bunkers, their positions such that they could defend all of the ridges and valleys. They had masses of heavy and light artillery, and it seemed there was mortar battalions without number. All these were set up so that when a Marine Platoon, a Company, or a Regiment attacked one ridge or valley, many of the Japanese defenders could bring their weapons to bear from the opposite ridges. As usual, the First had again gotten the short end of the stick, not that the Marines and Army troops on their flanks had a picnic.

Hill Nan, and Hill 60 had taken their toll and it was in Death Valley and Dakeshi Ridge that Ted first caught up with the Line Companies.

There was just no possible way Ted could describe the fierce battles that raged in the valleys and the ridges. Each individual had his own little battles of "Armageddon." His own taste of Gehenna. (Places of torment) So many young minds succumbed to the horrors of death, and fear, and destruction that a special hospital was set up to deal with their mental problems. This is one of the glories of war the Governments never mention, "The Wounds that Don't Show."

Day and night, night and day, it seemed the kabooms, kabooms never, ever stopped. Great thundering explosions from both the Jap and Marine artillery, incoming and outgoing mail. Battleships and Cruisers sitting off the coast of Naha were adding their mighty rending thunder to the din as they hurled huge projectiles into the Jap positions on the ridges. With the coming of daylight the bombers came in to make their contribution to the horrendous explosions. There were great sheets of flame from the Napalm bombs. Smoke, dirt and debris from the high explosions filled the air.

Fleets of rocket launching trucks come barreling up to discharge their hundreds of rockets into the enemy lines. So many explosions it seemed, the whole ridge would be completely destroyed; just wiped off the map. It was quite fascinating to sit back a couple of ridges and watch the world's greatest war machine at work. It was a totally different thing when Ted was to accompany the Infantryman into the valleys, and up the ridges that had been so pulverized.

So many ridges, so many draws, so many hills, so many valleys, each dealing out its own particular dose of death and destruction upon those attackers, and those defending.

The official histories of battles only give the overall picture of the attacks. So-and-so Company attacked such-and-such a ridge. But for the individual it all came down to a very small sector; one draw, one gully, one knoll, one cave. Conquer a machine-gun emplacement, a mortar crew, an anti tank gun, rifle pits, bunkers. Each had to be taken individually, and yet, in many cases simultaneously, for so many were able to bring they're withering fire upon the attackers of the other ones.

Attack one ridge or valley and the fire would come in from the opposite ridge, to reap devastation upon the attackers.

Ted was to spend a relatively few days and nights in the ridges, compared to the Men in the Line Companies.

The closer Ted was to the front lines the more confused everything got. Trying to find the various units in all the valleys and ridges was near impossible. It was a real miracle that there could be any kind of coordination among them.

First there was Division Headquarters where one was comparatively out of harm's way. Next came Regimental Headquarters (for the 1st Division these were the 1st, 5th. and 7th. Marines) Here one was only rarely in harms way. Each Regiment had three Battalions, each having a Headquarters. Here one was quite definitely beginning to feel the heat. Surrounding each Battalion was all the support units, Tanks, Mortars, Hospital facilities, Engineers, Water supply, Field Kitchens, Service units, Motor Transport and on and on and on, all in support of the Infantryman.

Each Battalion had three Companies, each having a Headquarters. Here one was definitely in harm's way. From this area the Men were sent forward into the ridges and valleys. Each Company had three Platoons, and each platoon had three squads. Now one was finally down to the very basics. It all came down to each individual, or small group of individuals, attacking some small segment of the line. This was where War became a very personal thing. Each individual must then summon the courage to walk, crawl, or run into the withering wall of fire coming from the ridges, or the valleys, or out of the next ravine.

There was two kinds of weather on Okinawa. Either it rained for days and days and everything became a quagmire, then jeeps, trucks, tanks and bulldozers bogged down in the bottomless mud. They slopped along in the mud, slept in the wet fox holes, cold and miserable. Or, it was so hot and dry that they blistered from the sun. Then there was dirt and dust and they were miserable from the heat. It would make Ted downright mad to think of the Japs living in a nice dry cave while he braved the elements in the ridges.

There was a few things Ted learned quickly when "working" near the front lines. Of course, the number one lesson was, "never, ever, volunteer for anything." The second was "Always have a valid excuse for being where he was, or make one up, fast, else he would be shanghaied into a Line Company." The most valuable lesson one learned when in the forward Company lines was, "Stay away from the Captains." The Captains were the one's who controlled one's fate. They ruled with an iron fist. In the front lines they held the power of God Himself. You go here, you go there, there was no talking back, no excuses accepted. To run a foul of a Captain meant almost certain front line duty, for they were always short of troops, and especially Corpsmen.

On Okinawa there were no big tank battles that Ted was aware of, but the Division tanks were an integral part of the Division's infantry. Tanks and Infantry operated as one unit when at all possible. They went into the "Ridges" together, they came out together. They trained as one unit: the tanks protected the Infantry, and the Infantry protected the tanks. Although they drew a large portion of the "incoming mail" it was sure comforting to have that big hunk of steel to crouch behind. Their machine-guns and especially their flame throwers could "neutralize" most of the many caves and bunkers. They could protect the Infantryman while he crept up and delivered a grenade, a satchel charge, or a burst from his backpack flame thrower.

When Ted had to abandon the safety and comfort of a jeep or truck and accompany the "Foot Soldiers" into the ravines, the valleys, or the ridges, the whole scope of the battles changed. It was no longer an interesting or amusing thing to watch. Ted was never to overcome the "taste of fear" which accompanied a trip into the valleys. Not the fear of death, but possibly the fear of life. What was going to happen there today, or tonight?

The fear of the unknown was often worse than the actual event. There was a certain taste, a smell, the adrenaline began pumping. Most of the time Ted was not really afraid, but was infinitely aware of the possibilities, and the probabilities, of a bullet, a grenade or a mortar having, "His" name on it. Ted had not the extra training, or the courage of the Infantryman. He was more a spectator than a participant in the day's activities.

On New Britain it was Hill 450, Hill 150, Suicide Creek, Hill 660, Aogiri. On Peleliu it had been, The Brothers, The Sisters, The Valley of Death, Bloody-Nose Ridge. On Okinawa it was Hill 57, Hill 55, Hill 69, Dakeshi Town, Dakeshi Ridge, Death Valley, Wanna Draw, Wanna Ridge, and above all the Town of Shuri, Shuri Ridge, and Shuri Castle. Much of the time Ted never knew the names of the "Ridges" or "Draws" at the time, or of their great significance or insignificance in the battles outcome, or on history. He only knew they were another place of "fear" he had to conquer.

So many Ridges, so many caves or bunkers, so many ravines. Ted could not remember in exactly which spot each episode transpired, but the episodes themselves would remain indelibly imprinted on his mind. He could not remember just which Company or squad of Brave Men he had been with at any particular time, but he would never, ever forget their business-like actions. Or, their heroic deeds in "neutralizing" some of the positions. He would never, ever, forget the terrible wounds, or the Supreme Sacrifices they sustained either. In his mind's eye, Ted could take you to the exact location of many caves or ravines. He can see the rocks, the bush, the blade of grass that he hunkered down beside of for "protection."

For Ted, a typical, (if anything could be called typical or average, for no two times were ever the same) trip into the Valleys or Ridges usually began with his joining up with some particular platoon of Marines. A few bites of K rations, or an occasional meal of hot C rations preceded the filling of canteens. He never went anywhere without two FULL canteens of water. It would become a valuable asset when the inevitable heat overwhelmed his body. Sit around, or lay around waiting for a Lieutenant or a Sergeant to come along with orders. Sit and wait as the Artillery and Mortar Battalions "softened" up the target. The Sixth Army, of which The First Marine Division was a part, had some twenty-seven Battalions of artillery on Okinawa that could be called upon for support of the ground troops. The First's own battalion of artillery, the Eleventh, was in direct support most of the time. Ted had a friend, buddy, in the Eleventh who told him they had already fired well over one hundred thousand rounds of heavy artillery shells into the Japs on the ridges, and this from only one of the battalions.

The "word" would be passed. OK let's saddle up, and move-em out. Thankfully, Ted and the litter bearers could more or less bring up the rear. The Line Company marines and Corpsmen led off. All too soon there would be the sound of rifle fire, the chatter of machine guns, especially the sound of the Japs light machine-guns, and the battle was engaged. Sometimes the whole area would erupt in firing, tanks, machine guns, and rifles; sometimes there was only one gun involved.

The swish, swish, swish of Jap mortar rounds, coming in, filled the air, take cover, if there was any. A call for covering fire and soon the Marines

60 and 81-Millimeter Mortars were blanketing the ridges, but still the machine guns and rifles chattered.

The "Big Stuff" both Jap and American joined in the fray. Ted could hear the screaming and whistle of the artillery, incoming and outgoing. There was smoke, dust, dirt and noise, the calls of Corpsman, Corpsman, Corpsman.

The clamor of the tanks, the great swooshes of the flame throwers, the whump, whump, whump of bombs and the huge 155-Millimeter artillery shells add to the chaos of the battlefield.

The Marines went about the "business" of attacking caves or bunkers in a very deliberate way. To see them in action one would think these farm or small-city lads were performing a task they had performed all their life. But for all too many, it would be their last performance. Lying sprawled around in a radius of some hundred feet might be ten or twelve Marines. Their grotesque shapes told the story. Their days of torment were over.

There was a whole new smell that enveloped the front. The acrid smell of the bombs and artillery shells exploding. The smell of dust and dirt and smoke, the smell of burned flesh from the flame thrower attacks. Then there was the all too familiar smell of death. Blood and Guts and fresh torn flesh added their own peculiar smell and one would never forget it.

All too often, when a person was hit "just so," and Ted never knew what that "just so" was, their whole bowels just "flushed." Every last thing within them just gushed out. It was the most degrading thing that could happen to a person. The smell was horrendous, and one never had to examine them to be sure they were dead. The smell told the whole story.

There was a saying that went throughout the Division when they were in combat. The dialogue between Ted and his friend Willis T. the last time Ted was to see him alive was typical. They had spent a pleasant few minutes of visiting and reminiscing and had said their good bys. Ted had turned and walked eight or ten steps away, when, in a gruff voice, Willis yelled. "Hey, Ted!" Ted answered, "Yeah!" Willis said, "Keep your Ass Hole Tight—Buddy!!!" Meaning, don't go getting yourself killed, for I care for you. Ted answered in just as gruff a voice. "Yeah, well, the same to you too, Willis T.!" The corners of Willis' eyes glistened as he too turned away. It was a saying of love, not one of vulgarity. Ted truly hoped that Willis T. had been able to keep his "Ass Hole Tight," when he caught a bullet later that day.

One often tried to distance them selves from someone who was killed or dying. It was as though they had an infectious disease that might be caught, or that they might bring bad luck. Sometimes it hurt so deep when one lost a "Buddy" they would curse him mightily for "letting" himself get killed, as if he could have prevented it. The hurt was so deep they had to blame someone, and there was no one else to blame.

Two canteens of water seemed real heavy when Ted was carrying them. Two canteens of water didn't go very far towards slaking his thirst in the valleys and ridges. Ted was always thirsty, but he had to hoard his water for it might be twenty-four or thirty-six hours before he could procure more. How he longed to rise up and pour a whole canteen of water over his head and down his throat. How dry and parched his body was, and yet he dared not even lift a finger. The bodies all around spoke of the danger! Was a Jap sniper zeroing in on him at that very instant, just waiting for one more inch of his body to be revealed? As the Marines moved on up the ridge, Ted must rise up and move too, or be left there all alone with the dead.

The days seemed to pile one on top of the other, but the nights were interminable. All day long the Marines struggled to take a ridge, or gully. Their comrades were strewn all over the landscape. Sometimes the wounded could be evacuated, sometimes they couldn't. It was often more hazardous to get out of a valley than it had been to get in. With the coming of evening the Commanders must make a choice, neither of which would be very pleasant for the troops. Could the Marines hold the ground they had taken, or should they retreat, allowing the Japs to reoccupy the caves they had lost. If they stayed on the ridges or in the valleys they would be counterattacked all night long. If they pulled back they would just have to start the whole process over the next morning.

Usually the Marines spent two to four days and nights in the front lines, if there was enough of them left to hold that long, before being relieved by another of their units. Being in the front lines at any time was bad, but to spend nights there was an experience none would ever forget. Most would like to wipe the experiences from their minds but they just would not be erased.

A typical night on the lines would see the Japs coming out of their holes or caves, or being brought forward to counterattack. At any given moment one could expect the attacks, often preceded by a knee mortar barrage. Then came the grenades, the satchel charges, bayonets, knives or rifle butts. Over, and over, these attacks came, then they melted away, only to be repeated at some other position, or more likely, back at the same position a little later in the night. Often the dead Japs were stacked several deep in front of a Marine's position.

Jap dead were just tossed into a hole and bulldozed under

People who came out of the night attacks had a look in their eyes that one could not mistake. Their bodies were scarred and bruised from without and from within.

Faces and lips were cracked and burned from the blistering sun, or else the hands were wrinkled from the constant rain and mud. The hands, elbows, and knees were scraped and bruised from sprawling headlong into the ground, the gravel and dirt, or from crawling, crawling, crawling. Exhaustion, Ted could not start to describe as the hours and days dragged on, and on, and on.

So many Beachheads, so many Valleys, so many Ridges. Who can say how many a young mind could take before it would seek release?

TOO YOUNG TO DIE

To Ted one of the real tragedies of war were the battlefield replacements. Okinawa, being a very long and viscous campaign seemed to draw more than its share of these.

Due to the great number of casualties, especially in the Line Companies, it was necessary to supplement their numbers with fresh troops.

There were generally two classes of these replacements. The veterans of several battles, who had been rotated to the states, had their period of leave and recuperation, and then were reassigned to the battlefields again. These twenty-two or twenty-three year old, "Old Salts" knew the ropes, and took care of themselves as much as possible. It didn't seem quite right though, that those who had "survived" the early battles should have to come back and die in the final round, even though many had volunteered to return. They, not being able to accept the "security" of stateside duty and life. There was a comradeship, a togetherness, a kinship, amongst combat troops that could not be equaled anywhere else in the universe. Many sought this unison elsewhere, but in vain. Much like the wedding vow. Forsaking all others, mothers, fathers, brothers, sisters, they clung together, they were one.

Probably they were looking for that "something" which was no longer there. During combat, friendships and kindred spirits joined everyone together; a certain bond was formed. This bond lasts forever, though these people may never see each other again. One could not take this spirit or bond to the next outfit for it was an invisible thing, like the love of a man for his wife, or of a mother for her child, or of a soul and God. When the principles of these bonds were scattered, the memories remained, but like yesterdays, they could not be called back, try as one would.

The other class of replacements was the "Kids," the raw recruits, barely seventeen years old, and some probably not that.

For the most part those Kids had no possible chance of survival. Too brave and too cocky for they're own good. They never had the chance to learn what fear was. Their curiosity carried them right to deaths door, and the old enemy death, was waiting to swallow them up.

Many of those Kids had only six to eight weeks of "training" and knew only the very rudiments of attack, and of defending themselves.

Probably most of them believed their drill instructors admonishments, "You Are Tough, You Are a Marine."

There was a total difference between bravery and ignorance. Any person on the front lines was seldom-permitted even one mistake, for they would not live to make another.

Most of the green troops were given the short end of the stick. Few officers or non-coms were going to send their "Soul Brothers" into the inferno's of Hell, when there was unknowns to send out as "cannon fodder." Even so, many of the veterans sacrificed their own safety and lives to protect and initiate the Kids into the ranks.

The regular replacement troops were integrated into the various units at the rest camps. These had the extra training from the seasoned troops. They learned quickly to follow instructions, and the examples of the veterans. They at least had an equal chance at survival.

It was easy to distinguish between the corpse of a battlefield replacement and the regular troops, no matter how badly mangled they might be.

Everything aged quickly in the Pacific. The "Men," their uniforms, their equipment. The Men quickly turned a deep dark tan, and their complexions aged quickly from the rigors of the land, and from combat. For many, like Ted, their skin not only tanned, it turned yellow from the Atabrine they took daily to help protect from the malarial fever. Ted's skin turned so yellow that many called him the "Atabrine Kid."

The uniforms quickly faded and had that certain look which bespoke the rains, and the scorching sun. They faded and aged out almost as quickly as did the troops who wore them.

A rifle, even though kept perfectly clean "aged" they had the inevitable nicks and scratches on the stocks. The wear spots from being handled constantly; these all told their stories to one who bothered to observe them.

The "Kids" right out of boot camp, their faces all smooth shiny, and white, their uniforms bright colored and "clean" showed no aging at all. Their weapons, many had never even been fired in combat lay beside them. All glistening with the unmistaken glow of newness showing through the "new" dust and dirt, that spread over them.

Those "Kids," whether heaped high on a truckload of rotting corpses, picked up fresh on the battlefield, or naked from the field hospitals, stood out like sore thumbs. In death they were still fresh, many not even old enough to grow a beard.

It seemed such a total waste of life for these Kids to be slaughtered. Many, if not most, never even saw the enemy or fired a weapon at him, before they were mowed down. They didn't know the rules of the "Grim Reaper." He took anyone who was not prepared, and many who were.

Ted always hoped, against all reason, that the world would know what those "Kids," and their families, mourning at home, had given for its freedom.

PREMONITIONS

From where do premonitions come? Are they revelations from some higher form? Are they silly beliefs? Was one really able to tell what was going to happen, hours, days, or months in the future?

During the months of war, Ted had heard many predictions from fellow Marines: they were going to be wounded, or killed, on the next beachhead, during the next battle, or even the next night. Such thoughts were never very far from anyone's mind. Ted never knew what to make of those premonitions, for "most" never came true. Had the knowledge of what was to happen been used by the Marines to help protect themselves, or had they only thought something could possibly happen to them?

One such premonition happened on Okinawa. Ted had been given a New Testament by his parents and his oldest brother and sister-in-law when he first entered the military. He usually kept it open on his bunk and would read from it, as he had been admonished. The inscription on the inside cover read, "Ted, read from this book, and know what God has for you." One day Ralph, a Marine of limited acquaintance, came into Ted's little shack and said, "I have seen you reading the Bible, and I want to talk to you."

Ralph proclaimed, "I'm going to get killed tomorrow and I want to know what happens after death." Ted jokingly said, "We will gather you up and bury you out there in the cemetery."

Ralph said, "Oh, I know that, but what will happen after that? Is that the end of things, or will something else happen?" Ted was somewhat uncomfortable with this line of questioning and was wondering if Ralph had gone psycho.

Ted asked, "What makes you think you are going to get killed tomorrow?" Ralph answered, "It is just something I feel inside. I know it is going to happen tomorrow." He went on to proclaim, "I will be shot off the back of a truck and my body will be tortured, and mutilated. Don't ask me how I know, I just know, and I need to know what happens after that. What does the Bible say will happen to a person after they die, or get killed?"

Ted tried to explain that the Bible says a soul will live forever, and it will either go to Heaven, or to Hell, according to what preparations one has made before they die. Ralph said, "How does one make preparations?"

Ted told Ralph of his "Experience of Salvation" when he was Saved before entering the service. He read him the few passages of scripture he could think of, and told him to pray to God, and God would hear him.

Ralph said someone had told him that anyone who had killed a person couldn't go to Heaven; and he was sure he had killed some Japs in a firefight earlier in this campaign. Ted told him that Japs didn't count as people, and besides, soldiers killing the enemy wasn't the same as murder, even though Ted sometimes had doubts on this subject himself.

Ralph talked awhile then said as he turned and left "Just don't let that little S.O.B. of a Corpsman cut my fingers off."

The next day Ted watched as Ralph left on the "mail run" instead of on the truck to the front lines, and he thought, see, he was just having hallucinations about dying.

That night when the mail truck returned, Ralph wasn't on it. The driver explained that they had run into a Jap ambush along the road, and there was a lot of firing going on. The other fellows on the truck reported that Ralph was either shot, or fell off the back of the truck, and the truck driver wouldn't stop so they could rescue him. Either way, he was gone. When the mail truck returned later that day Ralph's body was nowhere to be found.

The next day, when a squad of Marines went through the area to clear out any Japs, they found Ralph's body some distance from the road. He had been shot; he was bayoneted through both eyes, in the forehead, and several times in the chest and stomach.

Ted made sure he was the one to fingerprint Ralph, so the little S.O.B. couldn't cut his fingers off, because he was too lazy to work the rigormortis out of the stiff limbs.

Ted wondered how Ralph knew just what was going to happen to him. He also wondered if Ralph found God before he died, or was the other person right: one who has taken another person's life cannot go to Heaven. But then, with all Ted had seen, he still didn't believe that Japs counted as real people.

THE VALLEY OF DEATH

Did you ever hear of the "George Medal?" Chances are you never have and few people except the original recipients even remember hearing about one, or of seeing one.

The medal was struck in Australia when the First Marine Division went there after the battle for Guadalcanal. It was meant to depict the fate, or commemorate a fact, that George Company and the First Marine Division as a whole, always drew the short straw when assignments were passed out. Nothing good, or easy, ever seemed to come their way. Whether by accident, or by design, Ted never knew but probably by both since George Company and the Division had the reputation of getting the job done; what ever it might be, and at what ever the cost in lives spent.

The famous, or infamous, "George Medal" depicted a whirling fan with a cow defecating into it. One side said, "When the —— (Stuff) hits the fan." (A common saying denoting a viscous fire fight.) "LET GEORGE DO IT."

The bronze colored medal was about the size of a silver dollar. The bearers of this medal, although not an "Official" government issue, can be proud for it certainly depicted the fate that seemed to invariably befall George Company, for George Co. could, and did do it.

No Japs had been found on the beaches as the Marine and Army troops stormed ashore. Now they were beginning to see why they were allowed to land so easily.

The Japanese high command had opted to fortify the southern end of Okinawa and defend it to the death of every one of their soldiers. They had literally honeycombed the area with caves, bunkers, and trenches; all with tunnels connecting and inner connecting the defense system.

It was in one of the long open valleys near Shuri Castle that George Company, which Ted was with, drew the unenviable task of attacking the Japs that were dug in on a hill on the opposite side of the valley.

The rains had been coming down for days and everywhere was a quagmire of mud. It was difficult for the infantry to slog along in it and almost impossible for the mechanized units to move at all. This was probably why the company of Marines was sent across the valley to attack the heights beyond without tanks or other armored vehicles to spearhead the way.

There was a massive artillery attack on the ridges where the Japs were dug in but it did little damage to the well-entrenched troops.

Everything about the battles on Okinawa was different from the ones on New Britain, Peleliu and the other remote islands of the South Pacific.

Now it was the U.S. industrial might against the Japs feeble efforts. We now possessed thousands of ships and airplanes where as before we had only two or three, or none. Now there were whole batteries of artillery as against two or three small field pieces in the beginning of the war.

Now there were tanks, rocket launchers, flame-thrower tanks, and artillery without number it seemed. The whole scope of the war had changed in the Pacific in the last two years. Material and troops were now catching up with the lonely divisions struggling through the jungles attacking the outpost islands the Japanese armies were so fiercely defending.

Massive air raids would bomb and strafe the Jap positions before the Marines would attack. But for the Marines, in the end, it still came down to the same old story, eyeball to eyeball with the Jap infantry, and someone was going to get hurt.

The valley floor was pockmarked with bomb and shell craters. The brush and trees had been blown to shreds by the violent explosions.

Crossing the valley was no easy task, but as events were to prove, it was much easier to get across, than it was to get back across. The Japs small arms and machine gun fire raked the valley from every conceivable direction.

It was run a few feet and dive into a shell hole. Run a few feet and dive behind a bush, or a blade of grass, or any possible thing the imagination might depict as being of some protection. Fire a few rounds, at nothing, to keep the courage up, and dash on again.

By the time Ted arrived at the foot of the rising ground, the platoons of George Company were already there and fully engaged in fighting the Japs. From every side came the sounds of battle, in fact, there was no spot on that side of the valley which wasn't directly engaged in the fight for life. It seemed every inch of the terrain was being splattered by bullets and by mortar fire.

The calls of "Corpsman," "Corpsman," rang out from every side as more and more Marines fell, wounded or dead. The Line Companies Corpsmen never faltered in their duties, and at extreme risk to themselves, rendered every possible aid to their fallen comrades. A large percentage of them paid the "Supreme Price" for their devotion to their "buddies," and to their duty.

Ted, as always, had carried a limited supply of bandages, tourniquets, morphine syringes, and sulfa powder along with his identification and fingerprinting equipment. These meager supplies were quickly decimated and it was just use whatever was at hand. All the troops carried a couple of bandage packs and a package of sulfanilamide powder on their ammunition belts to fill the gaps in such emergencies. These were quickly exhausted also and it was just use anything that was at hand. A couple of times Ted was forced to stuff handfuls of dry grass under bandages to try and staunch the flow of blood from badly wounded Marines.

Many people were trying their best to give aid to, and to evacuate the worst of the wounded. But there was simply no where to shelter them from the murderous fire coming from the heights, that swept the terrain from every direction. Every time the stretcher-bearers tried to remove a wounded Marine some would be hit, then there would be two or three wounded instead of one.

It seemed there were more beyond help than there was still alive. The less wounded continued to help keep up the firefight as best they could. Every gun was vital if the Japs were to be kept from overwhelming the Marine positions.

By that time the Jap mortars had the valley completely engulfed in coverage and it was just as impossible to get reinforcements in, as it was to get the wounded Marines out.

So well entrenched in the caves and bunkers were the Japs that the Marine's fire was having almost zero effect on them. The best defense against caves and bunkers was flame throwers, but one had to get close to them before they became effective, and no one was getting close to anything except the ground that morning.

The Marines were huddled in their hastily dug foxholes and shell or bomb craters, doing their best to ward off the horde of Japs; but they were downhill with practically no cover and the withering fire was pouring in from every conceivable direction.

Many of the Marines were being hit over and over again, and there was absolutely nothing anyone could do about it. Jap machine gun, rifle, and grenade fire was splashing all around; and it seemed that nothing could be worse. But then things can always be worse, and certainly they were to get worse, and soon.

A couple of tanks managed to get across the valley but were unable to maneuver in the bottomless mud. They were drawing volumes of mortar and anti-tank fire. In desperation the drivers opened their emergency escape hatches and the Corpsmen loaded as many of the critically injured as possible through them. They lumbered away, back across the valley, taking a rain of mortar fire with them.

Possibly by coincidence, but probably because of the tanks, the Japs threw more infantrymen, more mortar platoons, and more field artillery pieces into the fray, as if they didn't already have more than sufficient to annihilate George Company.

Along with the small arms fire and grenades, the Japs began to saturate the front lines with mortar fire. Swish, swish, swish, whump, whump, whump, the mortar rounds came in, so thick the swish, swish, swish, was almost drowned out by the explosions. Not one inch of territory was immune, not one person expected to walk away from this saturation shelling. Not many actually did.

Ted hunkered in a little hole expecting every second to be his last. There was no possible way to help himself, much less to think of someone else. The whole area seemed to be just one big explosion as the Japs threw untold rounds of mortar fire into the area.

They would do with mortars and field artillery what they had been unable to do with their infantry. No doubt their infantry would swarm in as soon as the mortars lifted, for few Marines could survive this shelling with such meager protection.

The ground shook; the dirt, mud, and dust flew. The air was thick with the smell of gunpowder exploding. Ted hunkered deeper and deeper into the dirt and rubble of the battlefield. Great waves of heat and concussion flowed forth from the explosions, battering both mind and body.

Whenever one has done everything he can possibly do and it isn't sufficient, then he must resign himself to fate, or to whatever destiny God has for him.

When Elijah had done all he could do, God sent a still small voice to console him. When Ted had done all he could do, God sent a wee small spider to preserve his sanity, and to take his mind from the fear that was permeating the air.

There, amidst the background of the battle was Ted crouching in his little depression, with all the noises and confusion reigning terror down on everyone present, when the tiny spider appeared.

It was trying to carry a huge bug back to its lair, wherever that might be. It would lift, tug, and pull from every conceivable direction, to move what for it, was a massive object.

Ted's mind became riveted on the struggle of the tiny spider and was completely removed from the terror of the battlefield. It was such a fascinating thing to watch that he completely forgot to be afraid, or to even be aware of where he was.

How long he lay watching the struggles of the spider he had no idea, possibly an hour, but probably only a moment. What is time anyway?

The next recollection Ted had was of one of those indomitable Marine Sergeants coming down the line, telling everyone who was still alive to be ready to withdraw, (never say retreat) and to take some wounded person with him.

Most everyone had some kind of a wound, but only the most serious would be carried out. Ted and another Marine found a young man with a leg and a hand missing. They placed him on a poncho and started to drag him along like it was a sled. The pain must have been horrible but except for grunts and groans he made no complaints, or else Ted remembered none.

They passed a youngster who was all shot up, full of shrapnel, and he had been blinded. He had the most piteous wail. Mama, Mama, Mama, Mama, he was calling, over and over, but from the looks of him he would never hear his Mama's voice answer, much less see her again.

The battalion commander, not being able to get reinforcements across the valley, and seeing George Company being decimated, had ordered the withdrawal. They had blanketed the valley floor with smoke grenades for cover. It was through this smoke screen that the remnants were able to withdraw to the other side of the valley.

Mortars still rained down and explosions were all around. Ted could feel the heat and the concussions of the detonations but the smoke was so thick he couldn't see from whence they came, and was able to muster the blind courage to dash through the withering fire. He was feeling "almost safe" for he could not see out, and it seemed reasonable to think the Japs couldn't see to hit him either.

The floor of the valley was littered with the dead, and parts of the dead, from beginning to end. At almost every step Ted had to walk on or around some prostrate form.

Somehow, miraculously, Ted and the Marine managed to drag and carry their burden all the way across the valley and turn him over to a collection team for emergency treatment, and for removal to a field hospital. As usual, Ted never knew if he survived or not.

Just when it seemed the nightmare was over, the very same Sergeant who had called for the withdrawal came through the smoke. He was "asking" for volunteers to re-cross the valley, to help more of the severely wounded men across.

How easy it would have been to disappear into the smoke, and to leave that valley behind. No one would ever have known, and certainly no one would have blamed anyone for taking that route out. No one would ever have known but Ted himself, that he had just walked away, but that voice kept ringing in his ears, "Mama, Mama, Mama."

Choking, coughing, his eyes burning from smoke and tears and it was back into the jaws of hell.

The valley floor was full of shell and mortar holes. There were pieces of equipment, bodies, and debris everywhere. The mortar shells were still raining down, and bullets zinged by, but the little spider had done his job well, and Ted was no longer afraid of death.

So thick was the smoke and dust (the great explosions would dry the earth) that Ted could not tell where on the battlefield he was, or where he had last seen the blind youth. Try as he would, he could not be sure where he had last seen him, and had to abandon the search.

The Jap infantry had over run most of the Marines former positions, and there were a very few wounded to be found at all. Ted could only hope someone had found the blinded lad and had been able to cross the valley with him before the Japs found him, or that he was already dead first.

Beating a hasty retreat, Ted stumbled onto another Marine who was shell-shocked and completely disoriented, he was just staggering around, not even aware of where he was. Ted led him back across the valley to a waiting field ambulance to be evacuated to another place.

A few days later, the Marines stormed the ridges from another direction and drove the Japs out. The G.R.S. stretcher-bearers brought in bodies for over a week, which they gathered from the valley floor, and from the foot of the ridges. Truck load, after truckload of bodies, all bloated and swollen from lying in the sun.

Certainly George Company re-earned the right to wear the George Medal that day. They had stood in the face of such extreme odds, and in the infilading fire.

They made an orderly withdrawal, and above all, the ones who were able brought out their weapons and the wounded. Many of the dead were evacuated from the battlefield before it was rendered impossible to remove them.

In that brief four to six hour ordeal, George Company sustained over forty percent casualties, and this included the personnel who didn't even get in the "fire fight."

The squads engaged in the fierce fighting had probably suffered sixty or seventy percent casualties. It would take a major rebuilding job before George Company would again become an effective fighting unit, to take its place beside the other companies.

In spite of these overwhelming casualties there was one thing you could be sure of however. "When the —— (stuff) hit the fan," George Company would be right in the thick of it, to do their share and somewhat more.

NO GREATER LOVE

"Kim Li, Li Kim, Each night my soul with you it dies again."

Come sit here beside me and I will tell you a story. This is a story of a love so great that words cannot begin to disclose the depth of it. It is a story that cries out in the night to be revealed; and yet it is so secret, so personal; so sacred, that it can only be told to those who can understand the depth of it. Those who feel the pangs of torment, and the joy of two hearts suffering and singing together.

This is a story that must be told before my Soul can go to its Maker and find peace. My Soul would suffer torment in Hell if I fail to tell of the love of Kim Li.

It must be related before it is gone forever, or perhaps it should remain the secret of the two hearts that shared this love. You be the judge!

This story starts some fifty years ago during the Great War, known as "World War II." It is a story that will live through eternity in the hearts of the two youths that experienced it, Li Kim and Ted Alexander.

Perhaps you just might grasp the spirit of love they shared and it will dwell in your heart forever more also.

This story came to me through a very direct source so I will humbly try to relate to you the facts.

Oh that I was a master of language so I could take you to the depths of despair and to the heights of glory these two hearts shared. That you might share the moments of ecstasy and the deep dark void of torture their souls endured.

Try if you will, to let your heart feel what their hearts felt. Bury deep inside these two souls and let their souls become your soul for a brief period. It just might be that on some dark and lonely night the tears will flow upon your pillow, as they do on mine, when remembrance comes, as they are flowing upon the pages of this epistle now as I try to relate it to you.

Young Ted Alexander, at nineteen, had already become an old man, having spent two bitter years fighting the Japanese in the jungles of the South Pacific.

He had tended the wounded and helped bury the dead and he had spent some few days and long nights with the Line Companies in fierce combat.

213

His days had been full with the companionship of other young Marines, and they had been lonely, lying in the rain, mud, filth and stench of the battlefields.

He had experienced the exhilaration and the fears of close combat, and the backbreaking labor of the support units. He had tasted the hum drum monotony of the rest camps, and he had survived the deep dark sweltering jungles. The rain, and the rain, and the rain!

Ted's two years in the tropical heat, the rains, the scorching sun on the snow-white coral; of storming the beaches in the face of Japanese machine guns, mortars and grenades; of malaria and malnutrition had no doubt taken its toll, both physically, and mentally.

Ted, along with his companions, was just looking to survive this one more campaign, and then they would be relieved to "go home" if there was such a place.

It was Ted's fate, one night in the waning days of this Great War to draw duty with a forward guard post in the rubble of Shuri Castle, on the island of Okinawa. The last Japanese bastion in front of their home islands.

Of Kim Li I know so little; in fact, I do not even know if her name was Kim Li, or Li Kim, for Ted was never really sure.

One time her lovely sing song voice would proclaim Kim Li, and the next time it would be Li Kim, but then perhaps in the Okinawan language it could be either way.

Which was her surname, and which was her given name, Ted never knew, but it really didn't matter. Two young people of such diverse nationalities, of different languages and customs, and yet their hearts became entwined as one. Maybe it was Gods way of giving relief to two minds that had gone astray.

How old was this lovely urchin of the wilds? Ted could not tell, and certainly in her demented state she was not capable of telling. Perhaps thirteen or perhaps twenty-three, but Ted would always figure in the lower range, near fifteen or sixteen.

Her well-formed and firm body proclaimed a young age. A body that was never covered by clothes. Yet in her total innocence and trust, she could never be called naked.

Naked is a frame of mind. If one had no concept of being clothed, or unclothed, they could not qualify as being naked.

If cowardice had not overtaken Ted they would never have met.

214

SHURI'S SHADOW

The rains and typhoons had ceased, and the battle for Okinawa had settled in. The Jap main defense line had been established along a ridge roughly paralleling the towns of Naha, Shuri, and Yonabaru. These towns were situated in the foothills of a range of mountains that crossed the southern tip of the island.

The Japanese defenses were extensive, taking in every possible place of advantage. The high ground, and every foot Soldier, or Marine, knows that high ground is expensive real estate. It will be paid for in blood. They had the rubble of the towns, burial vaults of the dead, and networks of inner connecting tunnels to fight out of.

Okinawan burial vaults offered concealment for Japanese troops

This was the line in which they had prepared to stop the invasion, and to buy time for their leaders, weeks and months of fighting and delay. Every Sailor, Soldier, and Marine knew this battle wouldn't end until every last Japanese soldier was dead, and the Japs knew it, too.

During these weeks and months more than one hundred thousand Japanese soldiers died, only a small handful would surrender. One Hundred fifty thousand civilian men, women, and children were killed or injured. Hundreds of thousands of Japanese in the home islands were killed by the massive air raids and fire bombings, as city after city was demolished, and the Japs ability to wage war came to a stand still.

The leaders of both nations sat safely back in Tokyo, Washington D.C., Honolulu, Brisbane, etc., in massive palaces built of concrete, underground, stocked with gourmet food, servants, and their women. They plotted strategy and took credit for the battles won.

The Sailors sailed the seas and fought hourly battles with the kamikaze suicide planes. The Soldiers and Marines slogged through mud and dirt, lay in wet foxholes, and met the Japs face to face. They died with their boots on, filthy dirty and dog tired, with no soft hand to comfort and no one to know of their sacrifice.

The infantryman knows little of the overall strategy of a campaign, and only a slight bit of his own division's role in that campaign. His knowledge comes down to his battalion, company, and squad level. He is most concerned with his own platoon's involvement. For wars are won or lost by a multitude of little, personal battles; one ship, or one division, one company, and finally, one individuals own personal efforts, or lack of them. It is eyeball, to eyeball, and somebody is going to get "hurt."

Though armies, divisions, and individuals receive medals and commendations from time to time, many of the real "heroes" never get recognition. They do their job, pay the price, and, except for a mother, father, wife, brother, sister, and a very few close friends, are soon forgotten. Like the prodigal son, they could vain fill their stomach's with husks, and no man would care.

The town of Shuri, with the huge battered castle towering over it, stood smack in the middle of the Japanese defense line. A more defensible position would be hard to find. The rubble, the bunkers, the caves, and tunnels, all made excellent places of concealment for the defending forces.

It was the First Marine Division's lot to draw this area to attack and capture. It was a slow, agonizing task, for the Japs were extracting a heavy toll for every foot of ground surrendered. They held all the aces. It was up to the Marines to dig them out. Machine gun nest, by machine gun nest, bunker by bunker, cave by cave, they had to be killed, burned out with flame-throwers, or met hand to hand. Attacks, and counter attacks were furious, a life and death struggle for both sides.

For weeks and weeks the fighting had been fierce, and every foot of ground had been paid for in precious blood. The Marines kept hacking away at the almost impregnable defenses of Shuri Castle, the Japs holding on to their dying breath.

Late in the conflict Jap prisoners were used to help dig graves

So many badly mutilated Marine bodies had come in from this area that Ted was posted there to help identify them. There was also a shortage of Corpsmen, so Ted's duty became twofold.

One night, Ted, along with four Marines, was assigned to a forward guard post, guard post number seven. This seemed an innocent enough assignment as the Japs had been on defense, instead of offense. The Japanese soldiers were buying time with their lives and the longer they could hold off the Marines the better it would be for their country.

As fate would have it, this was the night the Japs decided to counter attack. Shortly after dark, jabbering, shrill voices could be heard, and the rattling of equipment told everyone that something besides defense was about to take place.

Every rifle was checked, and the flaps on the pockets of the cartridge belts were unsnapped to make the spare clips of ammunition more accessible. A fraction of a second can mean life or death when one has to reload.

Ted's group had set up in a shell or bomb crater, a hole three or four feet deep, and possibly eight or ten feet across. They were in the rubble and debris of Shuri Castles outer walls. At this moment they should have pulled back to the main Marine lines. But then, they had no inkling of what was to come, and not often in the front lines does one get a second chance to rectify a mistake.

Ted was sitting in the bottom of the hole smoking a cigarette, with a poncho over his head to shield the glow, when the first shells from the Japs big guns began to come in. They had let loose with everything they had to offer.

Big shells were screaming like banshees, passing low overhead, then they started landing all around. Ted had heard it said, "The shell or bullet you hear will never kill you, for it has already passed over, or passed by."

The ground shook, and the concussion of exploding shells lifted Ted off the ground. Deeper and deeper into the hole he and the Marines crouched. The dust was so intense they could hardly breathe. The great explosions walked back and forth, back and forth, their thunder rending the air. Every second was an hour of torment as the flashes and heat of the explosions swept over them.

Rocks, dirt, and shrapnel was falling like rain, and the little hole seemed to be a cistern; catching more than its share of all that came down. It was too late to return to the main lines now.

Almost instantaneously the Marines big guns took up the challenge and started answering with everything they could bring to bear on the Jap targets. The rumble, din, and concussions were horrible. The guard post was being straddled with shells from both the Japanese and Marine bombardment.

While the big guns were belching their destruction, the swish, swish, swish (Ted will never forget the sound) of the Jap mortars started joining in. The swish, swish, swish of the mortars can kill you, for they are still coming in, and close. All Ted can do is hunker deeper in his hole, squirm farther under his helmet, whisper a prayer, and hope there is not a direct hit.

After an eternity of time, and yet possibly only a matter of ten or fifteen minutes, the Japanese big guns lifted their trajectory to shell the rear lines, trying to knock out some of the Marine's big guns. Their mortar fire traveled a few yards farther to the rear, and picked up its sweeping intensity.

The Jap soldiers work very close under their own mortar and shell fire, so Ted and the others knew it was going to be time to pay their dues, again. It seemed that it would be only a matter of moments before they faced eternity.

Parachute flares had been doubled up, and as the dust and smoke began to clear the whole battlefield became "almost" as light as day, except for the weird, dancing shadows, as the flares drew closer to earth.

Bayonets were fixed to the rifle barrels and all hands were crouched and ready. Ted knew things were going to get sticky, and someone was going to get hurt, (Never say killed.) All at once the Japs are rising up out of the rubble, almost on top of the guard post.

All five rifles start firing at once, the Japs start hurling grenades, and firing their rifles and machine guns. Banzai cries and screams of "Amellicans you die, Amellicans you die," pierce the night; and go to the very marrow of ones bones.

Now the Marine's mortars blanket the area and no doubt it is a lifesaver, but they are just as deadly to friend as to foe. Jap bodies are falling everywhere, as they go swarming by like a plague of locusts. They are after the main lines, let the mop up crews take care of the guard posts later.

> Guns did bark Grenades did splash
> Upon the ground they lay like logs
> Their blood spilled in the dust
>
> Banzai's they screamed the mortars came
> Grenades splashed all around
> And when our guns burned hot and stopped
> The tide had been turned round

> They will come again those little fiends
> They only wait for orders

Machine guns, rifles, mortars, and grenades, are exploding like crazy in the rear, but there are still too many Japs around to worry about what is happening in the rear.

The main attack flows on by, but there is one dead Marine in that hole; whether he was killed by the shrapnel from a Jap grenade, or from a "friendly" mortar, Ted would never know, and indeed, it didn't really matter. He was no more.

> But in that hole lay one dear friend
> His life had now gone from him

All night long the attack kept up, the Marines lines were pushed back somewhat, but they still held firm. All night long the assault on the guard post kept on. Jap bodies are strewn all over the place, some inside the hole, and some on the very edges. In the shadowy light from the flares, the bodies looked like clumps of rocks, or logs, scattered around on the ground.

> Your eyes will lie your ears will too
> For they see and hear things
> That just aren't true

> The shadows move, weird shapes they take
> The mouse makes a noise, like an elephant

> Wait and wait and wait and wait
> Will morning never come?

A night without end it seemed, yet, after an eternity of time, the dawn finally began to break over the island. By the early morning light it was determined the ammo was almost gone, there were only a few clips left.

Ted and his comrades gathered in all of the dead Japs rifles and ammo that was within their reach, for it appeared that it would be a long time before their supply would be replenished.

What was nearly as bad, or possibly worse, the canteens were almost empty. How had anyone found time to drink during the interminable attack, but one becomes excruciatingly thirsty during close combat, and he often does things automatically, without even realizing he has done them.

All day the battle in the rear raged, the Marines trying to retake what they had lost, and the Japs trying to hold on to what they had gained. All day the Marine's artillery and mortar shells rained down around the guard post. All day the Japs attacked it with machine gun and rifle fire. How the four occupants had survived this long was truly a miracle.

The day burned fiercely hot and the water was soon gone, shared to the last drop with each other. Ted and his friends were down to firing only when absolutely necessary to keep the Japs out of "their hole." So low was their ammunition they would wait until the last possible second before expending another round. More than once a Jap soldier came hurtling into the hole, there to be dispatched by one of the Marines bayonets.

> The ammo low the water gone
> There is nothing to do
> But try to hold on
>
> I'll go for help the youth did say
> It seemed to be the only way
> The dangers great the chances small
> And still he stood both brave and tall

The second night the youngest of the marines volunteered to try to go for help. He and the others knew his chances of slipping through the Jap cordon and into the Marines lines were very small, if indeed, there was any chance at all. He knew the chances he was taking, and the probable fate that awaited him out there in the Jap lines, but he never faltered. He stood both brave and tall. A Marine's Marine, a "Man" if they're ever was one.

He didn't make it a hundred yards before his screams could be heard. They still reverberate throughout the dark lonely nights, chilling one's blood. The sounds of the young Marines unbearable pain were one Ted would never forget as long as he lived on this earth.

We heard his screams we heard his call
But not one gun could answer at all
To give him the release he so deserved

Into our nest the enemy pressed
More determined than ever
To get the rest

No water today
No relief has been sent
Oh where in the world
Could our comrades have went?

Morning's light revealed the Japs had staked him up to a shattered stump of a tree. They had pierced his body, they had pierced his neck, and they had pierced his eyes with bayonets. The sons of bitches!

To move is to draw more deadly fire
But oh for one drop of water
For a parched burning tongue

The charges come the charges go
And still no relief

All day the sun was fiercer still
The lips were cracked
The mind drew dim

The noise the screams
The big guns roar
Until the hoard is at the door

The ground does shake
The dirt does fly
Until it is hard
To see the sky

All sound stops when you start
Squeezing the trigger

The nights they came
The nights they went
No relief did come
None had been sent

Early on the third night a Jap sneaked up close to the hole and threw an explosive charge into it. One of the Marines, seeing the danger to Ted and the other Marine hurled himself up on it. He lay there covering the charge with his own body. He was shaking and quivering like a bowl of Jell-O. It was only the twinkling of an eye, but Ted remembered every last detail. The explosion came and his broken flesh sailed out on high. He freely gave his life that they might live.

From Shuri's shadow they did crawl
The creeping yellow bastards
They crawled up to that little hole
And threw there in a bundle

He lay upon it in the sand
His body it did quiver
His broken flesh sailed out on high
He died that we might live

A Jap bullet through the head stilled the other Marine. He never even knew it hit him. What a beautiful way to die.

The final rounds of ammunition were gone that night also. There was nothing for Ted to do now but play dead, and hope the Marines soon retook this position.

Four lives they had give that he might live, to die a coward.

THE COWARD

Alone, alone, two days and nights Ted lay there. One small flask of water, which he had found on one of the dead Japanese soldiers, was the only sustenance he had. His body was dehydrated to the point of collapse. His mind was beginning to hallucinate. If relief didn't come within hours it would be too late.

From where do the great swarms of enormous green, and black flies come? It almost seemed they were like buzzards circling overhead, just waiting for someone to get killed. From out of nowhere they appear and start their grisly task of feeding, and laying their billions of eggs, to propagate their species.

The dead bodies in the hole, and all around, both Marine and Japanese, were swollen to huge proportions. They were two or three times their normal size. Only an hour or two in the broiling hot sun was needed for the decaying process to set in. The stink permeates everything within a great radius. The smell is one that a person will never forget.

> The filth the stench
> Lay all around
> His body it was listless
>
> They start in the nose
> And then to the mouth
> The eyes begin to crawl
> Soon there is nothing left
> But a squirming mass
> Of what was once great and tall
>
> There are many things worse than death

Some months before Ted had written home for a knife. There being no good knives left on the market, his brother made him an excellent knife from an old file. Ted kept it as a backup, in his pack, back at camp.

His daddy, being a blacksmith, made him a double-edged knife of the finest steel that could be had. Its edges were honed to razor sharpness. Ted treasured this knife, and wore it on his belt constantly.

Sometime, during this second night, a Japanese soldier slid into Ted's hole. His bayonet was only inches away from Ted's chest, when Ted ducked under it. The bayonet nicked Ted's rib cage at the same instant the razor sharp edge of his daddy's knife, the only weapon he had left, cleaved the Jap from his crotch, till it lodged in his breastbone.

It is probably still there, dozed under with the Jap, and possibly with a high-rise condominium, or a shopping center built over them.

Ted's daddy never knew what became of his beautiful knife. Possibly Ted should have told him it had served him well.

The hot entrails spilled out upon Ted's body and entwined his feet, and his hands were wet and sticky with his, and the Jap's blood. The bayonet gash in his chest burned like fire.

> That night his honor it did fall
> He trembled, shook, and cowered
> Until at last he broke and ran
> To ever be a coward
>
> He ran and ran, his sides would break
> Like fire it burned within him
> He stumbled, fell, and ran some more
> Till blood gushed out upon him
> His body wracked with pain and woe
> His life would not go from him
>
> At last fatigue had took its toll
> His legs would go no farther
>
> He lay down to die

It was there, in a far off wilderness, that Ted fell beside a babbling stream, and surrendered to death. Too weak, and too demented, to even partake of its life sustaining water.

A coward that must face his Maker.

SCREAMING

Ted returned to this life slowly, and in fact didn't even recognize that he was returning. Sick of heart, sick of mind, and sick of body, he still only wanted to die and have this horrible nightmare ended. Had he not paid his dues? Why? Oh why could not the gates of Heaven, or of Hell, be opened just long enough for him to slip inside?

His eyes surveyed the surrounding area but his body was unable to make the slightest move. He lay like a wild animal trapped, as indeed he was. His Very Being was trapped within a broken body, and his mind had slipped off the pendulum and escaped into that deep dark void where only true love can enter.

The bright light of the morning sun filtered through the treetops and its warmth began to penetrate his body.

The instinct of survival held his body in submission and not a muscle twitched as his eyes slowly, methodically, roved around the area where he had fallen and surrendered to death.

It seemed to be a world devoid of sound, and yet the sounds invaded Ted's body. He could hear the big guns roar, the swish, swish swishing of mortar shells, coming in; the explosions of grenades and the popping of small arms fire.

He closed his eyes to drown out these noises but the tighter he closed his eyes the louder the sounds became. Now he could hear the shouts of triumph, the mortal screams of death, and above all came the penetrating, screaming, Japanese voices that could not pronounce the "R's." "Amellicans you die, Amellicans you die, Amellicans you die." "Malines you die, Malines you die." As if from an echo chamber the voices just kept screaming and screaming, louder and louder and louder. "Banzai, Banzai, Banzai," they penetrated his whole body.

Ted screamed and screamed (whether audible or inaudible he knew not) and closed his eyes tighter and tighter to block out these sounds of horror. All at once the sounds stopped, but a far worse scene replaced it.

Again that horrendous bayonet was entering his chest. His knife flashed and the red-hot entrails fell down his body and entwined his feet. Ted raised his hands and they were dripping blood.

Again that uncontrollable shaking seized his body and was shaking it as a dog might shake a snake. He screamed, and screamed, and screamed to force these sights and sounds from his battle weary mind. Why, why, why could he not die?

Sensing, or feeling some presence, Ted opened his eyes and let them rove again. They took in the trees, the rocks, the hills, and came to rest on the little stream near at hand. He lifted his vision a few inches and there "She" was, sitting on a small rock, as naked as the day she came into this cruel world, but at this juncture Ted could no more comprehend her nakedness than did she.

Sitting there totally void of the slightest expression on her lovely face was a young Okinawan girl. How long had she been sitting thus, listening to his silent or audible screams? How long had she been watching over him? He knew not. Was she, in her demented state, reliving some torment of Hell also?

Their eyes met. She arose and waded across the stream, then sat down by Ted and lifted his head onto her small lap. With her hand she trickled a few drops of water on his parched lips as she began to rock and croon a strange lilting lullaby.

He closed his eyes and the sights and sounds vanished. His body stopped its quivering and shaking. He slept; her compassion had soothed the pain and the torment that had wracked his body.

He awoke and she was not. In and out of the horrible nightmares his ravaged mind raced. Each time his Very Being went out of control she would appear at his side and guide him back.

Somewhere in the terrible episodes was a little red light. Each time the deep, dark, horrible void would open wide to entice his mind, there was a tiny red light. It would whirl off into the universe taunting, "You can't catch me, you can't catch me, you can't catch me."

The faster he raced to catch it, the faster it would whirl away, taunting, "You can't catch me, you can't catch me, you can't catch me." It was whirling, spinning, whirling, faster and faster and faster. A thousand times a second, a million times a second, a billion times a second, it would whirl completely around the universe, taunting and taunting and taunting.

Each time he would reach to grasp it, it would draw him deeper into the deep dark pits of purgatory, but before the dark doors could close about him She would be there to pluck him back. Each time his mind raced off, a few drops of water on the lips, and her soft soothing hands would calm his soul. How many hours or days this was repeated he knew not.

Again Ted awoke, and his still wide-with-terror eyes searched every inch of the glade he was in. No enemy was in sight; no sign of the young girl was to be seen. Had he, in his time of need only imagined, or dreamed that she existed? Had his tortured mind and afflicted body invented her as a means of escape and respite? In vain his eyes searched every inch of territory within his sight.

With great difficulty he rolled over and got on his hands and knees. He crawled to the river's edge and drank deeply of its refreshing waters. He drank time-after-time and lay in the water, too weak to move away and not really caring.

Ted rose to his knees and leaned over to drink, at that moment he felt the presence of some one near. No fear overwhelmed him, but his eyes lifted to cautiously search, as only a wild creature would do.

There on the opposite bank, not more than twenty-five feet away, and directly in front of him squatted the girl. Where had she come from? How had she managed to draw so near without Ted, accustomed as he was to danger, not sensing her presence? Was it possible she could have walked to this position directly in front of him, without him seeing, or had she simply materialized out of nowhere?

So absolutely still did she sit that except for an occasional twitch of her eyelids, Ted would have thought she was a statue, something un-alive?

For a long time they sat this way, unmoving, as if transfixed. Ted again feeling her gentle hand stroking his brow, and hearing her voice croon the lullaby. He could again feel the deep compassion she had for him when he was unable to care for himself. She was still sitting, unmoving and staring without the slightest expression on her lovely flat face. It was as if she were looking right through Ted, and not seeing him at all.

As the evening shadows crept across the stream and engulfed the young girl in their darkening shade, Ted managed to negotiate to a kneeling position, then to a somewhat upright stance. He talked to her but she merely stared at him, unmoving, yet unafraid.

He took a cautious step into the river and started to cross to her side. It was only a few short steps across the small stream, but as Ted looked up again, she had vanished. He didn't even see her rise, he only glimpsed her lithe movement as she entered the dense pine forest, in the twinkling of an eye, she had just disappeared completely.

Why had he frightened her so? Had she not sat and cradled his head in his time of need? Had she not trickled water onto his parched lips, when he was unable to care for himself? Why had she deserted him?

Ted did not know that something in the night winds wrenched and tore at her soul, and bore her away to places and deeds beyond his comprehension

ANGEL OF MERCY

Ted staggered through the rocks and brush in the direction he thought he had seen her disappear. He called and he called, come back, come back. Don't leave me, don't leave me, don't be afraid, all to no avail.

Neither could she understand English, nor could she have comprehended what he was saying even if she could have, for the Night Winds had called her.

Ted, having been nursed back to life was left to surrender to death all over again. Anyone who says a person can only die once has possibly only lived once. It just doesn't seem fair that after a person has surrendered their "Very Being" up to death they should be required to turn right around and do it all over again.

Perhaps surrendering to death is like surrendering to God. One must die before he can find everlasting life. Ted did not realize that his surrender to death would be the birth of his everlasting love for Kim Li.

No doubt, if his mind had not of strayed into those horrendous pits of Hell, She would never have found him, and surrendered Her compassion, Her love, and Herself to him. As with God, death brought a love that would live throughout eternity.

Still weak from the days without food or water, Ted was unable to pursue Li Kim into the hills whence he thought he had seen her disappear. He turned and somehow managed to make his way back to the little glade by the stream.

Here, utterly exhausted, and too weak and tired to take another step; he collapsed in a little spot of sand at the streams edge. Too weak to even partake of the cool water he was partially lying in.

God had guided him back to "The River of Life" but his "Angel of Mercy" had disappeared.

DEEP DARK PITS

Ted lay for some time, partially in and partially out of the small stream. He was too weak to move in either direction, and did not really care, or realize where he was, or what was happening to him.

His battered and emaciated body needed rest, but each time he closed his eyes, the horrendous noises would start again. The death throes would seize upon his body. It would seem his joints would be rent asunder, from the shaking, and the trembling, and there was no Kim Li to soothe his troubled mind.

From deep within the Pits of Hell the Torments raged and tore at Ted's mind and body. The maws of the deep dark void opened to swallow his soul; and the little Red Ball beckoned him come. A fear beyond all fears enveloped him, as his mind raced to bury itself in the deep dark pits that have no end.

The fearsome, black, abominable, "Thing" stretched forth its arms to gather him in, to devour his whole Being. It would possess him forever, and forever. Why could he not die?

A horrible thought flashed through his fevered brain. He was already dead, and his "Soul" had gone to Hell.

God had turned his back, for He could not look upon the unspeakable things that were happening in this place.

So deep, and black, and devastating, were these agonizing attacks, that they can completely overwhelm Ted's very Being, when they flash back from time to time; for no apparent reason other than to torment and haunt his soul.

Hell had not gained a complete soul, but neither would it ever relinquish its hold upon that part which it had possessed.

Of a truth, "Hell is a place where their Worm dieth not, and the Fires of Torment are not quenched." They burn for ever and for ever.

"For Eternity" is a very long time, of this Ted's soul will attest.

THE CAVE

As the evening shadows lengthened, the night chill began to settle over the little glade where Ted lay by the babbling stream. The coolness penetrated his wet clothes and his quivering body. It seemed to revive, or at least bring his troubled mind back to the necessities of this life.

The survival instinct of all forms of life is so strong it can override the desires of the mind. Ted's desire to "just lay down and die" was slowly being replaced by the need for warmth and shelter.

Slowly and painfully Ted got to his feet and began to search the fringes of the glade for some form of shelter; downed trees, dense shrubbery, underneath trees with low hanging branches, large rock formations. He was looking for anything which would offer some measure of protection from the cold breeze that had now sprung up to add to his misery, as if his misery needed any additional help.

Seeing nothing within the glade that looked even remotely like shelter Ted started out on a faint trail that led up stream.

The stream came from out of the mountains or foothills, as we would call them. At this point above the little glade the hills ran up steeply from both sides. There was only a relatively narrow flat floor. In all the millennium's of ages the water had washed and eroded away the high mountains as it meandered around with the floods and the droughts.

The old streambed was covered with downed trees and undergrowth. It was with great difficulty that Ted was able to follow the faint outline of the trail.

So exhausted and listless was Ted that he sat down on the end of a fallen log to rest. A wave of heat, then of cold, flooded his body. A cold sweat popped out on his brow and overwhelmed him. The smell of something sweet, as of cherries or strawberries or some such fragrance possessed him. The little red ball sped away into outer space and a wave of nausea flooded his Very Being, as he retched and passed into unconsciousness. Later, that exact same smell sometimes overwhelmed Ted's soul and he had to fight with all his Being to keep from crossing over into that deep, dark, impenetrable void. Sometimes he lost the battle.

Again Ted, when he revived had no realization of how long he had lay there, probably only a moment as we count time.

He raised his weary head and supported it with his hands propped up on his elbows. He was still retching water and mucus for there was nothing solid to retch up after so long a time without food.

The evening shadows had become deeper as Ted had been searching and lying here on the ground. The nausea and retching subsided somewhat and he lay with his head still propped up on his hands.

His eyes lifted from the ground in front of his face and through a break in the foliage he saw what he had been searching for. There was a darker spot, an overhang or a hole in the side of the mountain. Ted lowered his head and it was not visible. He moved his head from side to side and it was not visible. Only in the prone position with his head propped up on his hands could he see the opening and he began to think it was a figment of his imagination, a part of the horrible nightmare that was gripping him and would not turn him loose.

Slowly, cautiously, Ted began to part the undergrowth and creep towards this possible place of shelter. His strength was ebbing fast and he was about to turn back for he had now became convinced that he hadn't seen anything but a dark spot in the foliage. He parted another clump of bushes and there it was; a tunnel someone had dug in the bank at the foot of the mountain. Was someone living here?

During the past months Ted had seen literally thousands of these tunnels, which the Japs or the Okinawans had dug as shelters. The Japs used them all along the fighting fronts to fight from. The civilians used them as shelters from the dreadful bombing and strafing that had been going on by the airplanes from the American Aircraft Carriers that now steamed at will throughout the Pacific.

Ted had ventured inside several such tunnels. They all seemed to be of the same pattern. A small opening ran straight back for several feet then made a sharp right or left turn, opening up into varying size chambers. Most shelters were of this similar design for everyone knew bullets, bomb fragments or antiaircraft shrapnel traveled in a somewhat straight line and could not turn corners unless it ricocheted off a rock, or tree, or some other such obstacle.

Ted stood unmoving for several minutes straining his eyes and his ears for any slightest sound or movement. He sniffed the air for the smells of danger and of cooking foods but found nothing suspicious to alarm him.

Like a wild animal he was poised for flight at the slightest sound or smell, but he had no strength left with which to flee.

Methodically, he let his eyes study the bare ground in front of the tunnel. There was only the tracks of birds and small animals in the dust and no sign of human footprints.

Convincing him self the tunnel was not occupied, and too weak and sick to really care, he staggered inside, into the dark void. He felt his way along the tunnel to where it made a right turn into a large chamber. Here he leaned against the dirt wall and waited as his eyes gradually accustomed themselves to the gloomy light that was coming through the tunnel.

The only thing Ted could ever remember seeing that night was a stack of Okinawan sleeping mats placed against the wall nearest to the light. On top of the mats, folded neatly, was two sleeping "quilts." Ted picked up the quilts, they smelled musty and of dust. Truly, they had not been used in a long time.

He collapsed on the mats and laboriously got the quilts over his trembling body. The sweet smell of cherries came again and overwhelmed his body. This time there was no fighting it. He was beginning to feel the warmth of the quilts and he surrendered to the dark oblivion that swallowed him up.

Ted awoke suddenly as had always been his custom. Instantly he was fully awake and aware. He opened his eyes slowly and let them search the surroundings before another muscle of his body so much as even twitched. Next his instincts surveyed the situation for any feel or smell of danger and only then did he sit up.

Full daylight was streaming down the tunnel shaft and Ted's eyes searched the interior of the chamber he was in. Except for the sleeping mats the chamber was void of all furnishings; but, hanging from the ceiling on strings attached to two wooden poles was some sort of bags and some clusters which looked like onions or garlic and other dry vegetables.

The chamber itself was quite large by the average that Ted had been in. It was approximately eleven or twelve feet across and more or less rectangular in shape. The ceiling or overhead was only slightly higher than Ted's head and in a few spots he would have to be careful not to bump his head on it.

Ted just sat there on the sleeping mats staring into space, trying to let the events of the past days come into focus. Where was he? How had he got here? He closed his eyes trying to remember and the horrendous sounds drifted back in. Swish, swish, swish, Whump, whump, whump, Banzai, Banzai, Amellicans you die, Amellicans you die.

Certainly there were no sounds here. Had he just awoke from a bad dream? Had all the sounds and thoughts that flooded his soul not been real at all? This had to be the answer; it was just a bad dream. But why could he not wake up and where was he?

He opened his eyes and let the scenes unfold. It was as though he was watching a movie and the characters were only actors. The main character looked familiar so he let the scenes roll on; the guns, the roar, the dust and dirt, the smells, the screams, the bayonet piercing his side, the bloody hands. Then came his surrender to fear, the running and running and running, the falling and falling and falling, and the surrender to death.

His body was heaving great convulsions and moaning and sobbing and wave after wave of torment rolled over him as scene after scene unfolded.

He flopped onto the sleeping mats and covered his head with the "quilts" to force away the picture. Exhausted, he again fell asleep.

An hour or two later he awoke once more and staggered to his feet. He assayed to check the bags and the bundles hanging from the poles.

In the first bag he found some kind of bread, probably rice cakes or millet cakes or some such. Almost involuntarily he bit off a small corner of this dry hard substance.

He chewed and chewed and chewed until it became soft enough to swallow, then he did it again. After about the third bite his mouth became so dry and sticky he could not swallow and found it even hard to breathe.

Some instinct, or a thread of memory, told him there was water outside and he stumbled along the tunnel until he came out into the bright sunlight. Cautiously he made his way through the undergrowth until he found the little stream. Here he fell prostrate and drank of its cooling water.

Somewhat strengthened he sat upon a stone and again tried to sort out the past few days events to no avail. He found the faint trail near the stream, but, try as he would, he could not see the opening to "his" cave, nor could he find a path leading up to it.

After several unsuccessful attempts at finding an opening in the undergrowth he finally came out at the tunnel by pure accident.

Exhausted from these efforts he crawled back through the tunnel and again flopped down on the sleeping mats and was soon fast asleep.

Days later, Ted, having regained his strength somewhat, set out to explore this little spot where "His" cave was. From no point on either side of the mountain and from no place along the stream could he see the tunnel or find a path leading up to it. Never again was he able to lay on the ground and look through the underbrush to see the opening.

To find a place some Okinawan had so laboriously prepared and stocked with subsistence food was truly a miracle.

Who was he, or they? Ted would never know. Had they already been killed? More likely they had been put to forced labor by the Japanese army and died building the defenses they had so skillfully prepared.

Only later did Ted comprehend that the Mysteries of God are so great, and His methods of revealing Himself are so diverse, that the carnal mind can not even begin to discern them.

Had not the sweet smell made Ted so sick that he had to prostrate himself on the ground, at that exact spot, he would never have found the "Haven in the Wilderness." Quite probably he would have perished from exposure in his already weakened condition.

God, in His infinite mercy had prepared a "Rest" for a weary troubled soul.

THE LIGHT

Ted lay very still on the sleeping mats trying to let his mind come into focus. To sort out what was real and what was only a "bad dream" or imagination.

Where was he? What was he doing here in this dim dark cave? Who was he? The questions just kept flowing on and on.

Slowly the events of the past few days began to return to his troubled mind. The roar the explosions of the big guns massive assault made as they walked back and fourth, back and fourth. They were straddling the guard post and ripping up the turf, rending asunder anything and anyone in their path; raining down rocks and dirt and huge chunks of jagged shrapnel. The waves of heat and the concussions that lifted him off the ground, then slammed his body back down into the dust and dirt; bruising both mind and body.

He recalled the swishing of the mortar rounds coming in and the shock of the grenades exploding all around. The tat, tat, tatting of machine guns and the pop, pop, pooping of the small arms fire, each having it's own little peculiar sound that will never die. The screams, the moans and groans of the wounded and dying and the piercing screams of "Amellicans you die, Amellicans you die, Amellicans you die."

So he was still alive, and he was still in that shell hole on the battleground, only he wasn't really hearing anything. Was everyone already dead, Japanese and American? Was he the only person left alive on the whole earth?

He trembled and shook as more memories came into focus, the smell of the dead and decaying bodies. The maggots squirming in and out of mouths and eyes and noses, the huge swollen bodies undulating as their masses fed upon the flesh beneath the skin. The screams of a comrade tortured far beyond endurance. The bayonet in his chest, the blood, it must be his blood. Then he was not really alive; he was dead. Whoever had buried him had not done a very good job, for there was still a tiny bit of light filtering into this, his tomb.

His whole Being went out of control and from somewhere within himself he heard the sobbing voice proclaiming. "No, no, no, don't bury me, don't bury me, I am not dead."

An immense surge of fear overwhelmed him and he was running, running, running, screaming, screaming, screaming, he fell again, and again, and again. In a little glade by a babbling stream he fell, and he died.

It was in the glade that "She" had found him. She had gathered him into her tender arms and restored him to life.

Nausea and the feeling of suffocation almost overcame Ted. He threw back the musty sleeping quilts and sat up. He had had a bad dream; that was what it was, just a bad dream. He had to get out of this dark hole and into the light or he would suffocate.

If only he could get to the light everything would be all right. His mind would clear, his fears would go away, all of this dreadful nightmare would disappear. He would awake and it would all be gone, gone, gone, forever gone.

Staggering forth Ted fell in the gravel and dirt at the entrance to the cave, It was past mid-day and the hot rays of the sun penetrated his cold body. It warmed and restored him; he was awaking. The bad dream was over at last. It had all been just his imagination after all, but why was he so tired? Why was he so weak? Where was he?

The stillness of the place startled Ted as he began thinking again. His reasoning was beginning to return.

If this was not a dream then there was a small stream not far away. He was unbearably thirsty, and his thirsting bade him rise and go to the stream, which some inner feeling or recollection told him was only a few short yards away.

Not many steps down the slope and Ted stopped short, listening, ever wary. There was the unmistakable gurgle of water flowing over stones and splashing away down stream, making it's way to the mighty ocean.

Almost heedless, he plunged the last few yards to the stream's edge. There he knelt and drank deeply of the refreshing water. The water burned his lips, and feeling, he found they were sunburned, cracked, and bleeding.

Somewhat revived Ted stood and surveyed the area. It looked familiar and yet so strange. Where was he? Where were his friends?

By a dim path Ted began working his way down stream. Suddenly, he halted in a thicket on the fringe of a small glade.

A bolt of fear ran through him as he suddenly realized this was the exact same glade he had seen in "his dream." The same one he had lay down beside of and died. The very same one where "She" had cradled his head and sang lullabies as she placed drops of water on his parched burning lips and on his feverish brow.

He poised to flee but something held him fast. If the stream was real, and this glade was real, was it not possible that "She" was real, also. He knelt and searched with his eyes but no sign of her or any other human occupant could he find.

Slowly he ventured out into the glade and sat down in the warm sunshine to rest his weary troubled body. There was no strength to get up and walk away from this place which was so mysterious, frightening, and yet at the same time it was soothing and compelling him to stay.

The balance between sanity and insanity was still teetering back and forth, back and forth, and Ted seemed to have no power to control it. He was oh-so-close to crossing the bridge to the other side, to enter the deep dark pits. Yet, some power within held fast, quite probably the prayers of his precious mother that never ceased. He could not let go to cross over and lose control forever and forever. Each time he ventured forth the tiny silk thread would hold fast and pull him back.

He closed his eyes trying to force out the evil that was possessing his very Being, the darkness that had engulfed his soul, compelling him to cross over.

A tiny speck of light began to glow somewhere in the outer universe. He arose to chase it. He had to reach the little light, to grasp and hold it fast or else it was all over, and time, and sanity, would be no more.

How easy and painless it would be to surrender to this evil horror that was devouring him bit by bit. Just turn loose, quit struggling and it would all end. He seemed to have lost all will to escape, to fight back. Each time as he was going down into the dark void the little light would twinkle in the distance and some power as of gravity would propel him towards it.

The pinpoint of light grew brighter as he chased it across the void, but the faster he traveled the faster the light moved away. They were spinning, spinning, spinning around the earth, faster, faster, faster they whirled away.

The little light started taunting him, "You can't catch me, you can't catch me, you can't catch me, you can't catch me."

Faster, faster, faster, a million times a second, a billion times a second, they whirled completely around the universe. Faster, faster, faster, spinning, spinning, spinning, whirling, whirling, spinning, whirling, spinning, they sped away into nothingness.

The light grew brighter and brighter. It turned into a whirling red ball or rising sun and Ted reached to possess it.

In that instant a wave of nausea overcame him, and when he awoke, or returned to this life, or form, he lay by the little stream retching and vomiting. The sickest he could ever before or after remember having been.

The evil form within must be disgorged, gotten rid of. He must needs cleanse his body and his soul of this horror-of-horrors. He screamed, and he screamed, and he screamed, and he screamed.

Two gentle arms enfolded him, drew his head onto her soft breast. The crooning of a lullaby, the gentle rocking back and forth, the feel of a soft hand on his fevered brow and the bitter thrashing and turmoil from within subsided.

He opened his eyes and looked up into two dark eyes that showed no emotion, but they gave peace to his troubled mind. He slept, and then he awoke, and "She" was no more.

Was she real; was she alive? Why did She only appear when he was crossing over into that never-never-land, never to return?

Each time he was so near to surrendering his mind to the evil one, she had appeared and guided him back.

Why did she leave him when he needed her so? Ted had not the strength to fathom that at some time past she had already crossed over the dark void; into a place that only those who have crossed over, or have came so near to crossing, as Ted had come, can even imagine the horrors of.

Somehow she had given him the strength to overcome the dark evil thing. He had caught the bright red ball and held it fast, but on a bad night, or in the midst of a gala affair; it will sometimes whirl away and start screaming. "You can't catch me, you can't catch me," and the deep dark void will swallow it up ere Ted can catch and hold it.

The nausea abated, Ted rolled over and again drank of the water of life that the little stream offered.

He searched and searched for "her" but the only trace he could find of any human habitant was one small bare footprint in the soft earth beside the stream.

Ted returned to the cave and ate a few mouthfuls from the bag hanging on the overhead.

He sat and considered, dreams leave no footprints. Tomorrow he would find her, and know for certain that "She" was real.

He wrapped in the sleeping quilts and slept the sleep of death, for indeed, he had died in many ways these past few days.

AWAKE

Awaking from the deep sleep, Ted comprehended that a great weight had been lifted from his soul. The burden of despair was lifting, and the turmoil from within him had tempered its hold.

Though not fully recovered, if indeed he would ever be fully recovered from such an ordeal. His mind was free, and clean within. His power of reasoning, that tiny speck which separates man from beast, was returning. He sat contemplating the events that had led up to his fleeing to this habitation in the wilderness.

He relived the terrible few days and nights of the battle in the shadow of Shuri Castle and the feelings of aloneness, after all of his fellow Marines were dead, the stacks of dead Japs; in and around that little hole in the rubble. The taunts of the Japanese, "Amellicans you die, Amellicans you die," "Malines you die, Malines you die."

He remembered the craving thirst, and the torment of blistering, burning days and nights without water, the total futility of it all.

He again felt the uncontrollable shivering and trembling as his mind and body surrendered to the cowardice that overwhelmed his Very Being.

He recalled the wild flight from the battlefield, and the total devastation of his bruised and battered body as he lay down by the little stream and surrendered to death.

He remembered "Her" and her gentle touch, as she guided him back from the brink of destruction.

Then he remembered a prayer he had prayed before his first taste of combat. "Who will be the hero, and who will be the coward. Please Lord, let it not be the coward."

God had surely deserted him when his "need" was the greatest.

He wept.

THE SEARCH

It would be a sultry, hot day, for as Ted sat in the mid morning sun, the heat and humidity was already building. Though his body was dehydrated, the perspiration began to trickle down his armpits and to dampen his forehead.

The combination of the dry food that he had eaten and the heat made Ted long for a drink of water. He arose and made his way to the now familiar stream and he drank freely. He was nourished by the good night's sleep, the food, though strange in taste and texture and the refreshing water from the stream. He sat on a rock and began considering for the first time how he was going to get back to the Americans lines and to his "own people."

He must proceed carefully for it was almost certain he was in territory controlled by the Japanese armies. He must work his way out of the mountains and to the northwest, but how far, he had not the faintest idea. It seemed he could recall running and running for hours, but in his weakened condition he may have covered little distance, or he may have been running in circles. He had no comprehension of how long, or of how far he had ran when the terrible fear was upon him.

He would take his pockets full of the food hanging from the ceiling of the cave. He would set off in the direction he hoped would bring him out into the Marines lines, but first there was something pulling, drawing him.

He had to know if "She" was a real live person. He had to find Her, regardless of what risks might be involved.

Inching his way along, Ted would move a few feet down the faint trail then stop and watch and listen, move a few feet more, then do the same. Over and over he repeated this procedure until he was at the glade.

He squatted for some time, drinking in the shape and form of every rock, every bush, log, tree, and any other protrusions within sight.

There was nothing. "She" was not here, no one was here, and indeed it seemed, no one had been here. With careful steps Ted emerged and searched the soft earth and sand along the streams edge.

Only his tracks were visible, and nothing more. Had he only imagined he had seen the small print of a bare foot in the sand? Had he wanted to find it so bad it had appeared, or had his imagination conjured it up?

Ted set off down stream, searching every inch of the way. Not one footprint, not one broken twig, not one flattened clump of grass could he find. He made a wide circle and came back to the glade and still there was not the slightest sign of anyone passing this way.

It dawned on Ted that somewhere in his "dreams" he had seen "Her" come from across the river. That was it; she had crossed over here, and had come to him when he needed her most.

Anxiously, Ted waded the stream and began to search the opposite bank. He inspected every sandy bare spot but no sign could he behold. Once again he circled the glade searching as he went.

The only sign he could find was the imprint of his own Marine boondockers coming and going into the forest beyond. How had his footprints gotten here? Possibly in his wild flight he had passed this place more than once before he had returned and collapsed by the stream.

Perhaps many things had transpired while he was in such a demented state that he could not remember. Perhaps, perhaps, perhaps, his imagination could run on and on, and on.

Crisscrossing the glade, up and down, back and forth, he looked and he looked and he looked. He went up on the hillside in the pines and searched, but still there was nothing to indicate hers, or anyone's passing. Only the tracks of birds and small animals revealed that there was any living thing besides Ted in this territory. For several hours he searched and searched but it was all-fruitless.

Returning to the glade he re-crossed the stream and sat down by the water's edge. Doing his utmost, he recalled everything he could of the dark evil period which had invaded his Being.

In his mind he could hear her strange, soothing, crooning voice. He could feel her soft breasts as she clasped him to her bosom. He could feel the cool hand stroking his fevered brow. And he could see those strange dark eyes, so full of compassion, as she looked upon his troubled countenance.

How had she been able to materialize, then disappear so suddenly? He contemplated and contemplated, then the revelation came to him. "She" was a Ministering Angel, sent from God. So God had not abandoned him after all.

His cry had gone up to Heaven and God had sent a Ministering Angel to watch over him, in his time of need.

The bitterness towards God abated, and a bit of peace came into his heart.

FIRST GLIMPSE

As he sat by the stream in the hot sun, meditating, Ted suddenly realized he was covered with perspiration. His forehead was wet, his tattered clothing showed dark stains and something smelled awful.

Looking at himself for the first time, in he didn't know how many days, Ted realized that the "something" was him. From head to foot his clothes were caked with dirt, blood, and offal from the dead Jap. His clothes had become the receptacle for the waste his own body had discharged without his even knowing it.

He stripped off every last thread of clothing, waded into the stream and washed the filth from them as best he could. He scrubbed them inside and out with rocks and sand, and rinsed, and rinsed, and rinsed.

Spreading his clothes on the hot rocks to dry he waded back into the stream to wash his own body which was every bit as foul as his clothes had been.

The little eddy in which he sat turned brown and red from the filth he scrubbed off himself. It floated off down stream and disappeared in the greater volume of water.

Ted leaned forward and scrubbed his face and neck then immersed his head to wash the caked earth from his hair and scalp.

He came up wiping water from his face with his hands. He opened his eyes and there "She" was, as real as life it's self.

His heart leaped within him as he realized she was here, she was alive. She was real after all.

Where had she come from? How had she gotten there? For there she sat on a large rock, not more than ten or fifteen feet in front of him, her feet dangling in the water. She was as silent and unmoving as the stone she sat upon.

Ted would have dashed to her side and held her fast, but something within bade him remain motionless, also.

The two of them sat for some time, eyeing each other. Both as bare as the day they came into this world, and yet neither having any shame, or awareness of being naked. Their relationship had transcended the carnal things of this world.

Her small body was almost as dirty as Ted's had been. Her hair was matted and tangled and bore pieces of leaves and twigs. Heaven only knows when she had had a bath, or had had on clothes. Her olive brown skin was covered with blood from the many scrapes and scratches to its delicate surface.

Ted spoke soothing, quiet words to her, for somehow or other, if it was his last act here on earth, he had to know for certain if she was real. He must touch her; he must repay the tremendous debt he owed this lovely creature of the wilds.

Ted moved ever so slightly and she bolted erect, ready to flee. No fear showed on her countenance, but every muscle of her lithe body was poised for flight.

Ever so slowly Ted stretched forth his hand and beckoned her to come. The battle that raged within her soul must surely have been fierce; for Ted could discern the struggle she was going through. Instinct bade her flee, but his and her compassion, bade her stay.

Softly Ted spoke and stretched forth his hand to the limit. Finally, ever so slowly, she took a small step into the river. Cautiously she waded near, small step, by small step. She was ready to flee at the slightest alarm.

She sat in the water, as Ted was sitting, and their compassion for each other allayed the fears of each.

How long they sat thus Ted never knew, but it seemed a lifetime. Silently they sat, just letting their spirits or souls commune. Two broken minds at peace with each other.

Where had this beautiful, filthy little creature come from? What were the forces that had warped her mind? Was she born this way, or had the pits of Hell destroyed her mind temporarily, as it had Ted's?

It is quite certain she had no family or friends in this area, but in her demented state of mind, had she roamed and wandered and just "accidentally" been in this place. Or had God, in his Infinite Wisdom, created and placed her here for the sole purpose to console Ted, in this, his dire time of need.

Where did one so delicate and fragile find the sustenance to maintain life in this battle torn land? Did she eat the herbs of the fields, or did she receive nourishment and food from above? From whence came the strength of body and limbs she was able to maintain?

Ted's mind drifted back. When he layed down by the babbling stream to die he had not the faintest concept of where he was, nor did he care.

How long he lay there unconscious he knew not. It may have been minutes or hours, or it might have been days. He dimly remembered her standing over him, her hand dripping water onto his parched lips, and her cool wet hand stroking his fevered brow. He seemed to sleep, then awake again, and always she was near by.

Ted's first real memory was of awaking with her cradling his head in her arms. She was rocking back and forth crooning what seemed to be a lullaby. The words were foreign, but the melody was soothing, and he had no fear. He opened his eyes and looked into hers, and in that fleeting moment, a bond was formed. A bond that even death could not destroy. How many times he slept, and how many times he awoke, he never knew, but each time he returned to consciousness she was always there, a part of his dreams, and a part of his waking. Had he ended up in Heaven, or had he ended up in Hell. Certainly he was in no condition at this time to tell, or even consider.

The tiny silk thread that holds the pendulum of sanity, or insanity, is fragile. It maintains such a delicate balance that Ted never knows in which direction it may swing. What will be the event that will start it swinging from side to side and going completely out of control, what might be the incident that will tear it from its moorings and let the mind run at will.

Slowly Ted arose and walked the few steps out of the river to the hot stones where his clothes reposed. Picking up his skivvie shirt, he turned to offer it to her, but she was not. In that moment of his back being turned she had completely vanished. No slightest sign could Ted find of her going; or of her ever having been.

Was his troubled mind only imagining things? Was the Evil One playing tricks, just waiting for one more chance to consume him?

He had found Her and he had lost Her. Bitter dark spirits descended upon his soul.

Cursing mightily, he dressed and searched and searched, then he gave up and returned to the cave.

Throwing himself down upon the sleeping mats he tossed and turned, and threshed about. All night long he wrestled with the evil within, the bright red ball, the deep dark pits, the empty void. Such turmoil one who has not experienced it can not fathom. Why, oh why, could he not die?

He cursed the Devil, he cursed the gods, and he cursed Her, for had she not kept him here. Except for her, he would already be dead, and in the torments of Hell, which must be mild compared to what he was going through.

It was daylight when he awoke. His face was wet with tears, and his body was weak, but his mind was still his own. One more time he had triumphed over that abominable evil thing. How close it had come to consuming him.

Memories of those dark moments would torment Ted for the rest of his days. Even at the gayest of times, the dark shadow of memory would sweep down from nowhere, and that rush of fear would overwhelm him completely.

GUARDIAN ANGEL

Ted roused himself from the mats and ate heartily from the bag of dried cooked rice and vegetables that were hanging from the ceiling of the cave.

No longer did the taste and smell of the strange herbs and spices affect his eating. He was becoming used to the old, hot, garlicky taste, and the spices they used to cook or to preserve the food.

He had not become used to the "old" taste of the few slivers of meat that adorned the concoction. It appeared to be ham or pork of some sort, but in its present state he could not tell which, and certainly he was making no complaints. If anything he was blessing the hands that had prepared this repast, and placed it here where he had found it. The taste of the fiery hot peppers and the dry food, as usual, made him aware of how thirsty he was and he sauntered off down to the river to drink. He longed for a container to bring water back to the cave so he could sip it as he ate the food. His still slow functioning mind had not yet perceived of taking the food to the water. That thought would have to wait for a later, clearer time, for it to take effect. For the present only instinct was guiding his thoughts and steps, and only the inborn instincts of survival had kept him going.

Still weary from the long night of wrestling with the Evil Dark Thing that kept trying to possess his body, he made his way down to the little glade.

There he reposed against the rocks, letting the rays of the early morning sun penetrate and warm his cold, cold heart and soul.

The abominable dark shadow was still hovering over his head, just waiting for one more moment of weakness so it could pounce upon him, and possess him forever. He simply did not have the strength, or the will, to fight it.

Where was his Guardian Angel, the only one who had the power to repel the Dark Pits when they would open wide and bid him come?

Some how he had to figure out a way to take her with him, when, and if he was ever able to leave this place. How deep, dark and selfish were his thoughts. He had not yet come to the realization that her predicament was even worse than his, if that could be at all possible. Her mind had already crossed over into that never-never land, and might never again be able to return.

Ted bade her to return to him now. He willed her to come, he begged her to come, he even demanded that she should come.

Having no name to call out, for as yet he only knew her as "Her" he walked about the glade calling softly so as not to frighten her if she should be near. But how she could be near and him not know it, he was not able to figure out.

Thinking she had gone away and would never return again (if indeed she had ever been there in the first place) he went back to the rocks and sat down.

Up and down the riverbanks his eyes roamed, taking in the full detail of every bush, tree and stone. Presently his eyes fell upon a large rock by the river where he had seen her sit; dangling her feet in the water, and it startled him to no end.

Some things his mind could arrange so perfectly clear and plain, but most things were still in a fog, or dream, or just floating around all jumbled up. They simply would not settle down in one spot and take shape. Over and over he turned what details of memory he could recall, trying to bring them into focus. He was trying to sort out what was real, and what was only hallucination.

Ted removed his clothes, and folding them neatly he placed them upon the rocks. Having done this he waded across the stream and inspected the large stone upon which he could remember her sitting.

What he expected to find there he knew not. Possibly he thought she was still sitting in the exact same place, invisible, and she would materialize when he approached.

There was no sign upon the stone to show that she had ever been there, and search about as he would, he could find no footprint or other sign of her ever having been.

Why, oh why would his warped mind recall her so clearly? How could he recall so vividly her gentle touch and her soft crooning voice? What a beautiful, horrible, nightmare it was, and now he was convinced that this was all it could ever have been. He struggled and struggled to awake. If he could only awake he would be back safe in camp with his buddies, and all this turmoil would be past and forgotten. Probably he wouldn't even remember dreaming this dream.

Ted stood by the rock where she had sat, and he willed her to come forth. Could it be possible she was one of these stones, and could come and go at her pleasure? How could she simply appear, and disappear, like a wisp of the wind in the tree tops?

In his heart he knew this little creature of warmth could not be a cold hard stone. Where did Angels come from anyway? Where did they live or stay when they were not in Heaven? There were so many things he did not know, or understand.

Ted had always thought Angels came from out of the sky, but he could not recall seeing her either ascending or descending, she had always just been there, in, by, or near the water.

Could she possibly be a Mermaid that she would live in the water? Ted had always thought Mermaids only existed in the ocean. Possibly she was like the mighty salmon and could come and go as she willed.

Possibly she had never been at all!

No Li Kim, though as yet he had no name for her, appeared to assuage the anxiety welling up within him.

Recalling that yesterday; was it only yesterday, it seemed so much longer, as he sat in the gurgling stream; she had appeared. She was sitting on this very same rock. Could it possibly happen again?

Ted returned to the center of the river and positioned himself so he could watch the rock without appearing to stare at it. If by any chance and the chances seemed nil, she should appear again he would be watching. He would know from whence she came, or from what place of concealment she had materialized. Not once would he bat an eye or turn his head this time. She would not be able to elude him again. He would know her secret of appearing and of disappearing.

To the casual observer he might not appear to be watching; but his vision never wavered. He kept the rock and the area surrounding it, and in the rear of it constantly in sight. He would know if there was the slightest movement upon any of this landscape.

Ted sat and watched, and watched, not letting his eyes stray. So intently did he watch that his vision would become blurred, and it would be necessary to bat his eyes, but immediately they would refocus on the rock, and the nearby terrain.

He scooped up a handful of water and washed his face and eyes for he was becoming weary of watching and waiting for that which it seemed certain was not going to appear.

Quite possibly, at one time or another, every living thing has had the "feeling" that something was watching them, when there was no one in sight at all. Something in the air carries the message and imparts it to one's mind. Something beyond our knowledge is able to impart this feeling to one of the innermost senses which we know not of. We only know it happens. We do not yet perceive of how it can, or does happen.

This feeling now came to Ted, but there was no fear or apprehension in it, as there is at most times. Only peace did he comprehend; and his soul "knew" before his mind could fathom what the instinct meant.

Turning his head ever so slowly he looked upstream and there, not ten short steps away, she came, tiny step, by tiny step. She was wary but not afraid. Probably cautious would be the proper word for it.

She approached as a deer might approach a water hole. She was aware of everything in her surroundings, and her nostrils seemed to waft the air for any hint of danger.

Nearer and nearer she approached until she was at Ted's side. Here she sat down in the water as he was sitting. Something from within seemed to be compelling her to seek one of her own species. Something was irresistibly drawing her to Ted, but she was ever alert, and ready to flee at the slightest indication of danger or alarm.

No trace of expression showed on her countenance, but her body was as tense as a huge spring, coiled and compressed. Ted knew that should he make the slightest movement she would be off and away. His Guardian Angel would be no more.

THE TOUCH

Sitting there in the river, so close to her, Ted thought his heart would explode. He dared not move, or make the slightest sound for fear she would vanish, as at other times. Doing his utmost to keep from frightening her, he very slowly let his eyes explore her features. Peeking ever so cautiously from the corner of his eyes, he slowly, methodically, drank in the infinitesimal, minutest detail of her countenance.

Her head was adorned with a thick mass of long dark hair that hung down over her shoulders. The front was cut in a "bangs" fashion, and the overall picture was to make her face look more square than it actually was. It looked as though it would be jet black if it were shampooed and cleaned. For now it was so full of dirt, and leaves, and grass that it was difficult to tell exactly what color it was.

Her face, although it appeared square from the haircut, was actually slim and narrow. There was a little pug nose above a small but ample mouth, surrounded by the beautifully formed lips. There was no hint of lipstick or other coloring upon her face, but her radiance and youth would have rendered them to none effect, even if they should have been there.

Probably her most striking feature was her eyes. They were large, oval shaped and set on a slant in her slim face. Deep dark brown, they seemed to see nothing at all, and yet they missed not the slightest movement. Ted had seen this look on so many faces in the mental ward, at Mare Island Naval Hospital, where he had received much of his training preparatory to being sent overseas. Young eyes, that had seen and endured too much, and had followed the mind which had slipped off into a never-never land. They seemed a deep dark void, that saw and recognized, but that did not comprehend. Yet her eyes held much compassion and a twinkle that Ted had never seen in eyes before. They seemed to be great pools that he could dive into and swim around in, so deep and round did they appear.

Her dark eyebrows were rather narrow and delicate in appearance. When she closed her eyes, Ted could see she had long curving eyelashes, lashes that could blot out the un-seeing, far off look that dwelt in her eyes. The ears protruding out from under her hair were rather small by comparison, but the size of her eyes probably over shadowed everything else. A high forehead, and a tapered chin completed what if scrubbed, and cleaned, would have been a real beauty amongst her own people.

To Ted she represented peace and security, and his only hold on reality. She was beautiful, but in a way that had nothing to do with physical attraction. She was his Guardian Angel.

Sitting thus, Ted was as unaware of her nakedness, as she was of his. Two minds that had crossed over the barrier of carnal things and passed into another dimension, of which only those who have crossed over can fathom. Yet, even they cannot understand. A deep, dark void, that transcends time, and space, and being. A place to be avoided at all costs; if one has the strength to withstand the evil forces that close in upon the mind; that has been put under too much stress. The place Ted was struggling so terribly hard to avoid, and yet, in spite of his struggles, was so very near to overwhelming him.

They were sitting here side by side, Ted facing east, and Kim Li facing west; both so acutely aware of the others presence, so close, and yet so distant, in so many ways. Possibly it was symbolic of their heritage's, one from the Far East, the other from the far west, and now against all possible odds the twain had met.

How Ted longed for her to take his head into her arms. Croon to him the haunting melodies that had so soothed his soul, in its time of need. How he longed to feel the comfort and warmth of her breast as she rocked back and forth. But for now he needed just one touch, to tell him she was real, and not just a part of his imagination, his nightmare.

The day was warm, but the peace within was even warmer. Li Kim and Ted just sat side by side, letting the peace overflow their souls. Neither one was moving or saying a word for there is no need of words when souls commune.

How much time elapsed Ted never knew, but finally, he could stand it no longer, being so near, and yet so far away. Ever so slowly, he raised his right hand to chest height, and slowly, slowly, let it inch towards her. Slowly, ever so slowly, her right hand responded and began to rise also. Fear permeated her very Being and Ted just knew she was going to vanish before his eyes. Nearer and nearer, their hands progressed towards each other. The expression or lack of expression on her face never changed. Yet, so tense, was her body, that he just knew she was ready to flee from this encounter.

Nearer and nearer, now their hands were only inches apart. Her small body was struggling with all the power it possessed to keep from fleeing this place. Closer, and closer, their hands came, until at last the balls of their index fingers brushed together. She was trembling and shaking.

In the moment of this touching, something magical happened. A bond was formed a union made that could never be broken. It was as though their umbilical cords had been joined. Their spirits were now one, joined permanently, they flowed freely, coursing through each others veins; making each mind, though horribly entangled, free.

Her love and compassion were flowing through him, and his hates and fears, were flowing into her. How could this fragile Angel absorb so much, and yet be able to give of her spirit freely. Surely it was a measure of her stature, of her bringing up, of her love, that a body so young, so tormented by the demons, could summon the strength and the will to go through the encounter with which she had just gone.

It is impossible to imagine the courage, and the strength it took from her body and her mind to accomplish this task. From where did this strength come? From where could she find the courage? Surely this child, from a pagan land was possessed of a God that was infinitely more powerful than any mortal. It is absolutely certain she was not the coward that Ted had proven himself to be.

The transfer of genes complete, their hands drew closer and closer together, until the palms touched. Little Kim Li's trembling was subsiding with each passing moment. Ted let his hand enfold her tiny one, and the bonding was complete. Now they would ever remain as one, her spirit was his, and his spirit was hers, and even death could never separate them from the love they had exchanged.

For a long time they sat thus, each reveling in the newfound friend they had. Each of them was just letting their love force out the dark evil fears that had so overwhelmed their bodies and souls. The two warped minds had formed a union. While they were together they possessed the strength to withstand the forces from that deep dark void which possessed them when they were apart. As long as their hands touched there would be a shield placed before their souls that would keep out all other forces. Two tormented minds; they were at peace with each other, and at peace with a world that had gone crazy.

For a prolonged time they sat thus, until finally Ted noticed that she had become weary. Her eyes closed and her head would droop to one side or the other. Ted did not realize it at this time, but the drain on her strength from the morning's efforts must have been terrific; and he knew not what rigors she had endured the previous night.

Clasping her hand firmly, Ted slowly inched his way up out of the water, and Li Kim, though apprehensive, gave no resistance but arose with him. Gently, Ted guided her footsteps up, out of the river and onto the path that led up stream. They stood for a few moments, letting the midday sun dry and warm their bodies; then, hand in hand they followed the faint trail the short distance to the cave.

Ted spread wide the sleeping mats and placing a quilt on each, he beckoned her to lie down and rest. She readily accepted the offer, and stretching out on top of the quilt, her eyes fell closed, as if there was no strength left to keep them open. She had given her trust to him, and there was no more fear to haunt her, while she was in his presence.

Ted layed down on his mat and let his eyes feast on his Angel of Mercy, whom he had found. This savior of his soul had rescued him from the Pits of Hell when he had not the strength to resist longer on his own. What would his fate have been if she had not of been there. Or, if she had not of used her strength to nurture him with all of her compassion when the dark evil thing opened wide its maws to receive him? For the rest of his days this question would haunt him in nearly every waking and sleeping moment.

He vowed not to sleep for fear that now he "found" her, she would once again disappear, and never again return. A few moments after closing her eyes, her small body began to twist and turn. Her arms thrashed around, flailing the air, as if seeking something they knew not what. What torments wracked her body and soul? What power possessed her very Being that there was no peace, even in sleep?

Fearful of frightening her more, Ted reached out his hand, and in her flailing, their hands touched. Instantly that spirit of oneness flowed through them. Her soft hand sought his and enfolded it. She ceased her thrashing around, and was immediately asleep.

Her troubled hands had found that for which they were seeking. A calmness flowed through Ted's veins and he too fell asleep; for peace had come to his soul at last.

THE NIGHT WINDS

To a person who has toiled all day in the high heat and humidity the evening breezes are a blessing direct from God. To a weary soldier who has fought all day in the blistering sun the night breezes are anxiously awaited. They are the one brief period when he takes a small respite.

The canteens may be refilled with the life sustaining water. Possibly there will be some K rations passed around and he might find time for a cigarette before digging in for the night. Ammunition clips will be replenished and the supply of grenades will be checked.

Daytime brings death and destruction that he can see. Night brings the unseen dangers; the counter attacks of the Japs who have been hiding or fighting furiously from the caves and bunkers all day.

From any point on earth it seems that twilight brings an evening breeze, a refreshing, a cleansing from the days activities. They also bring a foreboding of the events to come in the night. Ted learned to hate the night winds.

He awoke with a start; something had disturbed the sleep that he had not intended to take. How could he have fallen asleep at such a time as this? All the day long he had fought going into a sound sleep. Every few minutes he would rouse up and reassure himself that she was still there. Even though their hands had been clasped he had to reassure himself. Having found "her" he was taking no chances on losing her again.

No longer were their extended hands touching, indeed, hers were flailing and thrashing the air. Ted sprang to her side and grasped her hand but she awoke with a fearful fright in her eyes. She wrenched her hand from his and cowered on the edge of the mat, ready, as a wild animal might be to defend herself.

He tried talking softly to her, but to no avail. At the first twinkling of his eye she bolted for the entrance to the cave. Before Ted could recover and get to her, she was already out and away. He didn't even see in which direction she had gone, so swiftly had she disappeared.

He sped down the faint trail hoping to catch up with her; to somehow calm her shattered serenity. He didn't understand that he could no more calm her, than she could calm herself. It was late, and the "night winds" had called.

The Dark Evil Thing had possessed her soul and she must needs answer its calling. It was not Ted's touch that had frightened her; it was the fear of being restrained. When the Evil Thing called there was absolutely nothing mortal that could hold her. But then, at this time, Ted knew nothing of this and thought it was him she was afraid of.

What was this Dark Evil Thing that possessed her body and her mind? What was it that rode on the "night winds" and bade her come? What devilish horrors did the "night winds" inflict upon her of such delicate, fragile body, when they overwhelmed her? What joy did the dark evil spirits get from this torture?

During the daylight hours she seemed to be a totally different person. One full of love and compassion, one possessed of peace and tranquillity. But when the evening breezes stirred, something wild, dark, and evil possessed her soul. She no longer had the strength to overcome it.

A day or two later and Ted would realize that the Dark Evil Thing was the very same one that would have possessed him, if it had not of been for her and her tender hand that ministered to him in his time of need.

Was it the little red ball she chased, or was it some other abominable thing that called her?

Night winds can bring some terrible experiences. One never knows when they may be compelled to follow them off into that vast unknown, from which there is no returning. Once a person's mind has succumbed to the "night winds" they must needs be forever on guard; so that the dark evil thing will not slip in and claim its prize again. Sometimes it takes every ounce of strength one can muster up to keep them at bay and to withstand the forces that call, and call, and call. Sometimes one is not able to withstand the drawing and must follow them off into that great void. When they return there is only a vague remembrance of the horrors that prevailed; but the experience leaves deep scars and a greater fear of following again. Quite possibly, next time, they might not return. Never, ever, chase the little red ball or light that whirls through the universe at such a tremendous speed. There is no beginning and no ending to the universe, just as there is no beginning and no ending to a soul.

Ted found his clothes and dressed swiftly. He had to find her quickly for night was almost upon them. He raced around, up and down stream, calling and calling. He crossed the stream and entered the pines, still calling, but there was no answer to his calls. Indeed, there was no slightest sound of any kind. There was no sign of her having been at all, except in the feel of her touch, in the memory of his brain, which he would hold forever.

In vain he searched, and searched. Was it possible the Dark Evil Thing was still playing tricks on his mind? Had he only dreamed she had appeared and when he awoke he had willed her to be there? Far into the night he searched and called, and searched and called.

THE RIVER OF LIFE

A thing of majesty it was not. In fact it probably wouldn't even rate as a river, only as one of the myriad of small streams that flow throughout the world. On a scale of one to ten, it would no doubt rate less than a one. To Ted, it became the most important river in the whole wide world. It was the savior of his soul, the one common denominator between himself and "Her."

What was it about this stream that had the power to draw two hearts together? What mysterious power did it hold over the minds of two young souls that had gone astray?

What power did it contain that it could reach into the very Pits of Hell and snatch souls from the depths of torment? There are so many unexplained mysteries in the whole universe. There are powers that we don't even fathom, or have the capacity to understand, powers that govern many aspects of our lives and actions. Man in his infancy upon an earth many billions of years old cannot even begin to discern the powers that be. God, who created the heavens and the earth still rules His domain, and let no one forget it.

The tiny speck of knowledge that man has attained about God, and the powers He wields, should it be removed from off the face of the earth, would be less than taking one grain of sand from the beaches of the world. God in His infinite mercy sees all, knows all, and controls all.

The river of life for Ted will always be his "Garden of Eden," his place of beginning and ending. a place of beauty, and a place of devastation. It was here that he surrendered his life, and it was here that he found Her.

This tiny stream probably only bears a name given it by the local residents. It would not even show up on a map of any proportions; so insignificant was it by comparison to the other great and famous streams that flow and meander their way to the oceans of the world.

It seemed that Ted's life had been compressed into a space not much larger than a fair sized city lot. The stream was the sustainer, the giver of life. The little hidden glade that surrounded it was the perimeter of peace and tranquillity. Inside this small area there was serenity, and outside there was torment. It was as though the river carried the messages of the soul, from Her to Ted, and from Ted to Her. It gave each of them something to live for, something to hold on to, in their time of need. It was the one thing in the whole universe that they had in common.

Only about twenty feet across in its wider spots, and some eight to twelve inches deep, it wielded a power much beyond its size. It was a lovely, flowing, gurgling stream that meandered through the glade at this point. It contained pockets or depressions somewhat deeper, and it was sparkling clear. Its depth was deceptive for the clearness hid the small pools of deeper water.

The little glade extended possibly a hundred feet along the stream and thirty or forty feet back on either side. It contained rocks, sand pockets, small grassy spots and a few willowy bushes. Below and above, it was thickly covered with brush, logs, and trees. Rising up on either side, the hills were dotted by pine trees and scrub brush. It was just a tiny island in the vast universe, but something beyond his comprehension had drawn Ted to it. Some providence beyond understanding placed, or drew Her here, and bade her return to minister to him, when the dark evil thing would consume his soul.

After all of his searching and calling Ted finally realized that his only hope was to return to the spot where she had always found "him." There was something about this little glade that drew her back; that could alleviate her fears, and the torment that overwhelmed her. There was some unknown thing that drew her to Ted. The river of life was his salvation, for without her there was no life for him, no reason to fight on. Without her, he would just surrender to the evil thing and succumb to its powers forever more.

Surely God, or the Angels, or the Spirits, or mere providence had some purpose in drawing him here to this spot. Surely the drawing was for some purpose, but then, who knows what whims direct spirits? What invisible senses, or brain waves direct man along life's pathway and control his every move?

Fatigued, hot and dusty, Ted returned to the little glade beside the river. He removed his clothes and waded to the very same spot in the stream where he had sat the day before, when she came to him. He immersed himself in its cooling waters; then sat waiting for the "feeling" of her nearness to come. He had not long to wait. Where had she been secreting herself that he had not been able to find her? How was she able to materialize almost in front of his eyes? What power this stream must hold over the spirits that directed her life, and called to her when he was near, or in the water. What was it that frightened her away when he was not near it?

Ted was to learn that it was not him that she was afraid of when he was away from the river, but his clothes. Something about them repulsed her, shattered her serenity, and threw her into a state of fear. Possibly it was someone in uniform that had molested her, or killed her family, or some such, pushing her over the brink and warping her mind. Possibly it was the admonishing to fear the Americans, possibly, possibly, possibly. Whatever the reason, the effect was to forever ban her from wearing clothes. Or, to have anything to do with anyone who did, except when they were in distress, such as Ted had been when he first came to the little glade.

She came to his side and sat down in the river, also. There was no hint of recognition on her countenance but neither was they're fear. She sat straight and serene, the new scratches upon her skin had left spots of dried blood, and she was covered with dust and dirt. Her hair was tangled and matted upon her head. Overall it looked as if she had been through a very rough night.

Ted reached for her hand, and she responded eagerly. There was not the slightest hesitation as her fingers meshed with his. Again their love flowed freely from one to the other; they were at peace within. They were in the "River of Life" and it was producing its miracles.

Ever so gently he scooped up handfuls of water and began to wash the caked blood from her numerous scratches and she offered no resistance. The days, or weeks, and months of dirt and grime succumbed to his scrubbing as well. His hands progressed up her arms, then over her whole upper body. He found the splotches on her legs and feet and washed the filth from them also. As the dried blood and dirt gave way her skin took on a fresh glow. It had a light brown tint and was as soft and supple as a small child's skin. Though her countenance changed not, she seemed to revel in the cleansing. It was as though she had always had some one to bathe her and she knew not how to do it herself.

Next came her face and what a difference as layer after layer of dirt peeled away. Her cheeks were bright and rosy, and her lips a pale pink. She was radiant with the glow of youth.

Leaning her backwards across his lap he began soaking the dirt from her hair and scalp. All the time he was talking softly to her, as he had been doing while he worked over every inch of her body. The water turned a dirty color as the accumulation of filth drifted away. She had no fear as his fingers sought out the very roots of her hair and cleansed each tiny spot. He saw the skin beneath turn from black, to a soft golden brown. He plucked the twigs and leaves from her locks. With his fingers he combed the strands back and forth until there was no more dirt to be removed. His earlier summation had been correct, without the dirt and debris her hair was a deep, jet-black.

Raising her to a sitting position he surveyed his handiwork and what a transformation. If he had not of accomplished the task himself he would never have believed she was the same person. His lovely, filthy little urchin had become his Princess, she was truly radiant; she was beautiful.

In their total innocence they had performed one of the first rites of man. There was no hint of embarrassment, or of shame in either one; it was the natural thing to do. Ted had always heard that in the Orient they had communal baths, or possibly she had always had servants to perform the task for her. In a small way he was returning the love, the compassion she had shown for him, in his time of need, and most certainly she had been in need of a bath. Like salvation, the "River of Life" was there, but one had to partake of it them selves, before they could receive the benefits therein.

Her hands, beneath the layers of dirt were soft and gentle. They were not the hands of one who had performed manual labor or menial tasks. They were the hands of a lady.

Her feet, though she wore no shoes, were not the feet of one who spent days or weeks in the rice paddies, or toiled in the fields. If indeed she was not a real Princess, of royal blood, certainly she had come from a well to do lineage that had given her the protected life of a royal sibling. To Ted she would not remain his Princess, but she would become his Royal Queen, to have and to hold forever, and forever.

She put her arms around his shoulders and laid her head on his chest. His arms enfolded her, and they sat thus for a long time. Each was reveling in the closeness of the other. Each one renewing the spirit of their souls that had been stolen from them by the Dark Evil Thing. Their contentment, their ecstasy was complete, they were one. The hurts and the evil were gone from their minds and their lives. Oh the joys of the total bliss they shared thus, what blessed relief to two minds that had gone astray.

With elation in his heart he arose and grasping her hand, led her out of the river. Here they sat on the warm rocks until their bodies were dry, then he led her up to the cave. He pushed the sleeping mats together and they laid down side by side; each reveling in the warmth of the other.

What blessed peace it was, he had a friend.

TEACHING-LEARNING-TRUSTING

Lying there, enfolded in each other's arms, they dozed off to sleep until after midday. When they awoke, the warmth, the joy, the love had performed miracles to both of these young bodies. They were of one mind, and one soul, and their eyes communed with each other. Each had a friend, some one to trust, some one to hold, and someone to love. They needed nothing more. Theirs was a love from within, not one of a physical or carnal need.

Each brushed some stray hairs from in front of the others eyes and spoke softly as they did so. They were the first words Ted had heard from her lips, except for the vaguely remembered lullabies she had crooned as she cradled his head in her lap, while the torments of Hell were trying to possess his soul.

It was as if a dam had broke, each was trying to tell the other what was in their hearts. Each was overflowing with a love that would not be contained. Neither understood a single phrase the other uttered; and yet they had a perfect understanding. Love needs not an interpreter. The world was beautiful again, and they were a part of it.

No smile could cross her face it seemed, but her smile was in her voice and Ted understood. What was it that could have robbed her of facial expressions? What power still held a part of her in bondage? Some way, some how, he had to find the answer and then find a cure for it. To this task he would ever be committed.

They rambled on and on, each trying to out chatter the other. Each letting the hurts, the joys, flow from their lips to the other ones soul. Each doing they're utmost to tell the other the things that were in their hearts. Finally each one lay silent as the other poured out their souls, and each one grasped the essence of the others meaning, even though they knew not the words. Peace, joy and love need not a special language to be communicated between two lovers.

The afternoon fled away as they layed there side by side. Reluctantly, Ted arose and went to the food bags hanging from the ceiling poles. He got two handfuls of the rice and meat and brought it to her side. He offered her a portion, but she disdained it. He could only make a wild guess as to when she might have eaten last, yet she seemed not to be hungry. Possibly some water to wash it down might tempt her.

266

He grasped her hand and led her out of the cave, and down to the stream. Here he scooped up a hand full of water and drank. He bade her do the same, but again she seemed not to need it. He ate of the mixture, and drank of the stream, then offered her another helping to no avail. She simply needed not food or water.

Hand in hand they sauntered down to the little glade and reposed in a spot of warm sand. Her chattering had stopped, and the smile had left her voice. Ted could hardly coax a word from her lips. What could he have done that had changed her so? Was it the food that had reviled her, or was it something he had done, or had left undone? He was beside himself and at a total loss, for now they were unable to communicate. His words seemed to fall on deaf ears, for she paid on heed to his utterances.

He tried to persuade her to return to the cave with him. Maybe she needed to rest some more, for surely the few minutes of time they had both slept would not sustain her for long.

The sun crept over the hills, the evening shadows lengthened. Each minute she seemed to become more remote; agitated, almost fearful of him. Only one who has had a lovers quarrel can know how he felt. Yet they had had no quarrel, or at least none that he had understood. Was it possible he had missed some valuable clue as she poured forth her heart to him in the cave?

It was growing cool and her fragile body must need some warming. He would gather some wood and as soon as it was dark enough to hide the smoke he would build a small fire in front of the cave to keep them warm. For now, he would get his clothes and wrap her in his jumper; though he would hesitate to place such rough material over her delicate skin.

He walked the few steps to his clothes and quickly dressed in his skivvies and pants. He picked up the jumper and turned to offer it to her, but she was not. In the brief moment of his back being turned, she had vanished completely.

Unbeknown to him, her agitation and intense nervousness had been caused by the "night winds" calling. And he didn't yet understand the night winds power over her.

Hastily he searched and called to her, but this time he knew in advance that his efforts would be in vain. What ever it was that bade her come, he could hold no power over. But where could she have gone, or whom could she have gone to?

Her going bore mightily upon him, but unlike the previous times he now knew where and when, he would find her again. Early on the morrow he would be in the "river of life," waiting for her to come to his side. The love she had shown to him this day left a trust within and he knew for certain that the trust would not be denied. She would come to him tomorrow; or else he would find a way to go to her. Though he had not the faintest idea of where or how he would find her, he knew there would be a way provided. God had not willed him to this place without they're being a purpose for it, and God would provide a way. Though his faith in God had wavered, he still had enough trust to know that His will would be done.

Nights can be a very lonely time for one who is left alone, with nothing to do but wait for the morning to come. It was an especially long night that Ted spent waiting for the morrow. Many hours he sat watching the sky, the trees and the stream.

His mind and his reasoning were still mixed up. One moment he would decide upon a course of action, but in the next instant it would be something-different altogether. He devised plan after plan and yet everything depended on her returning and upon factors over which he had no control what so ever.

Sitting thus, he glanced up and noticed that the sky was darkening. Waves of great, angry clouds were gathering and swirling over the little glade in which he sat. Gusts of chilling winds engulfed him, and it seemed the sky opened up. A downpour so intense he was completely drenched before he could reach the cave descended upon his little world.

Where was his Guardian Angel, his little Princess? Had she found shelter from this downpour? Was she safely inside a nice dry refuge, or was she at the mercy of the storm? He went outside and called and called to her, perchance she might be somewhere within hearing. Some way he had to grasp and hold, no, destroy the Dark Evil Thing that possessed her soul; that took her away from him and devastated their serenity.

The downpour lasted only a short spell and the angry clouds vanished from the sky. Ted assayed forth and sought the desire of his heart. If she were out roaming the hills, the countryside, in this weather, she could very easily perish from the cold that descended after the rains departed.

As before, his efforts were to come to naught. The hills were muddy and slippery, he could find nothing to indicate that her, or anyone else was about. He returned to the cave and bundled up in the sleeping quilts for warmth. It was a long dreary night that he spent waiting for the morning to come.

Dawn finally came and with it the promise of an extra warm day. Ted snatched a few bites of food and headed for the stream that faith told him she would come back to. He positioned himself in the water as before, and waited, and waited, would she never come. Doubt began to cloud his mind and he was becoming anxious. Should he go search for her, or should he wait here, the only place where she had ever come to him. He would wait, for he well knew the futility of searching.

This time she came not up out of the stream, for Ted was watching and saw her enter the little glade from the opposite side. He gave a start, for he could hardly recognize her. She was not his beautiful little princess. She looked more like some bedraggled animal. From head to toe she was covered with mud. There were many scrapes and bruises over her body that bespoke of a night of roaming, of slipping and falling, of thrashing through the trees and brush. She had not found the safe, warm, dry refuge that Ted had willed for her, but she had come back to him.

Before she could reach the river Ted dashed to her. They fell into each other's arms and he knew the thrill of holding her again. How could he have ever doubted that she would come? By the time their embrace came to an end, Ted was almost as muddy as she, but what is a little mud between two people whose hearts were rejoicing at the presence of the other.

Jubilant at having her with him again, Ted led her into the river, to "their" very same spot. He washed the mud from his own body; then proceeded to bathe her from head to toe, as he had done the day before. This time the fresh mud dissolved away without so much scrubbing. Soon, except for some bruises and fresh scratches she was as beautiful as she had been yesterday.

They held each other close and whispered sweet nothings. The morning bath was to become their ritual and they would perform it every day they were together. Each morning she would come to him in the stream, if she had not returned in the wee hours of the morning and snuggled down by his side.

She looked so dainty and fragile that it broke Ted's heart to think of her roaming the hills and valleys at night and all alone. How he longed to go with her, to be her protector, to shield her from the scratches, the bruises and the falling. If only he could tame her soul!

They returned to the cave where Ted spread the quilts, they snuggled close and she was soon asleep. The night's exertions and cold had left her exhausted. Only the Angels in Heaven knew if she had any food or nourishment for her sustenance. His love had drawn her back, and her love had directed her feet.

They had learned a great lesson; they could trust each other.

KIM LI

Ted realized it would be necessary to have a form of communication other than their trust and instincts. It was imperative they each learn a few words of the others language if the bond between them was to grow and flourish. He had to be able to communicate with her before he could really help her to overcome the Dark Evil Thing that possessed her soul.

Youth has no fear of failure, or of trying to do the impossible thing. Some how there is always a way to overcome every obstacle put in one's path; if they will only put forth the effort to surmount it. Youth has not yet learned to mistrust life itself, or to question every step of the living and learning process.

He must needs have a name for her, other than "Her." If he knew her name and they became separated from each other he would at least have something to identify her by. It would also be nice just to know her name and be able to call her by it. They needed to be able to talk to each other instead of just letting their souls commune.

How could he start to learn or teach a language when there was no basic ground to start from? So far as Ted knew the Japanese, or Okinawan language did not use the vowels and consonants as did the English language. They didn't even use the same alphabet for that matter. The two languages had totally different sounds and utterances. There was no similar words to start from, such as yes, or no.

They were sitting in the river, having the morning's ritual bath when Ted hit upon the idea of word association, to try and communicate with her. So, it was only natural that the first word should be, water. "WAAA-terr, waaa-terrr, waa-terr." He would point to the water and repeat the word over and over. He scooped up hands full of it and repeated it time and again, letting it filter out through his fingers.

Her blank expression told him that she did not comprehend what he was doing or saying. He tried a different word. Hand, pointing at his hand. Over and over he repeated it. Haaannd, Haaanndd, Haanndd and still no association did she make. Word after word he tried to no avail. She was speechless and beyond approach.

Back to the beginning, Waaa-terr, Waa-terr, Waa-tterrr. She reached down and scooped up a hand full of water and some unintelligent grunts escaped her lips. Ted's heart skipped several beats. Though he didn't understand the word she had used, he knew that she had comprehended what he was trying to do. From now on it would all be down hill.

Over and over he repeated the word water, water, and finally from her lips emerged a sound that Ted took for water. It was not clear or distinct, but he knew she was trying to say it in English and he was ecstatic. They had made "contact" but there was such a long way to go.

Over and over he would point at different parts of their bodies and say the English word for it. She would counter with the Japanese word, which he could not in the least comprehend; or repeat. After several attempts she would come out with a sound that reasonably resembled the English version of the Pigeon English which he was using.

Deranged though her mind might be, she was still a much faster learner than Ted. At least she could repeat the English words much faster than he was ever able to repeat the Japanese words that she spoke. It seemed he could never get the accent on the words. He could not distinguish between one word and another, even when she repeated them over and over. It is just possible she had been exposed to some English in her schooling. Once she grasped the theory of learning the language she became quite adept at pronouncing the words and of associating them with their proper meaning.

Over and over he pointed to himself and repeated, "Teddd, Teddd, Teddd." Soon she was repeating the word but had not yet made the association; probably thinking it was Ted's chest that he was pointing to instead of himself.

The morning wore on and she began to be weary so they left the stream and headed for the cave. Here they lay upon the mats and covered with the quilts. She grasped his hand and snuggled close, more content than ever in their trust of each other and in their newfound knowledge.

She had been asleep for near two hours and Ted had dozed off a few times between his adoring watchfulness over her. Suddenly she sat erect; grasping both his hands she pulled him to a sitting position, also. She pointed at him, and in a very clear voice proclaimed, "Teddeee, Teddeee." Forever after, Teddeee he would remain.

She pointed to herself and proclaimed, "Kim Li, Kim Li," or so it sounded to Ted, so forever after she would remain, Kim Li, his Guardian Angel, the savior of his dark soul, his first love.

Some how, in her peaceful sleep she had comprehended, she had transcended the deep dark pits of Hell, and had overcome the Dark Evil

Thing for a brief period. She was in love also, and no doubt for the very first time, too.

The expression on her face changed not, but the gleam in her eye and the lilt in her voice, told Ted this was true. So overflowing was his heart that he thought he would explode.

THE FOOTPRINT

It was full light and she had not returned. How Ted's heart ached for her presence. The torments he suffered each evening when the night winds or spirits called her away were almost more than he could bear.

What if something should happen to her? What if she should never return? How would he ever find her if she became lost?

Not one moment of peace did his soul know when she was out of his sight! Somehow, somehow, he must tame that Dark Evil Spirit that had possessed her mind, which took her away each night, but first he had to find her and bring her back.

In near panic Ted dressed and set off through the forest to search. He was tempted to call out mightily for her, but dared not. Who else might be in this wilderness to hear he knew not, and caution prevailed?

Ted avoided the dim path that paralleled the stream. He had never so much as found one of her footprints on it. If someone else should come along and find strange footprints, would they not be curious and search out the owner?

Farther and farther from the glade Ted searched. Weaving in and out of the pines, he made no more noise than one of the forest creatures would make in passing.

It was nearing sun up and Ted knew he should be back in the cave, or at least back in the glade. He should be in a place where someone passing near would have less chance of seeing him, but at any risk he just had to find His Kim Li. He had to know she was all right. To touch her hand, and feel the love flow through their veins.

He skirted the brow of a hill and keeping well within the cover of the trees and shrubs, he continued to search. His eyes roved over the terrain seeking the desire of his heart.

Nearing despair he was about to terminate the search and return to the cave. Surveying the area one more time his eyes spotted what appeared to be a trail, or path, winding along near the foot of the ridge.

On the verge of abandoning his cover and going to inspect the trail, he suddenly froze in his tracks.

Something had alerted his senses to danger. A cold wave of fear swept over his being. He stood motionless, watching, waiting, testing the breeze, letting instinct take it's course. The tiny hairs were prickling the back of his neck, bidding caution.

Seeing nothing-amiss Ted never the less waited patiently. Through the years of danger in the South Pacific he had learned to trust and rely on this feeling. This sixth sense, or this warning from God. He knew not from whence it came, he only knew it had never been wrong. When it came there had always been some dire reason for it.

It seemed that when one's survival was at stake some inborn knowledge came to the surface and they reverted to animal instincts they knew not of.

Peering intently about, it was only a couple of minutes before the purpose of the warning became readably apparent.

Something sinister was on that path. At first it was only a blur, or shadow emerging from where the trail disappeared into a deep draw.

From where Ted stood, motionless, almost unbreathing, peering through the evergreen foliage, it appeared to be some kind of a large animal. His first thought was that it was a bear. Pre-invasion briefings had mentioned nothing of bears or other large animals, but then it wouldn't be the first time briefings had been wrong.

Slowly the mass emerged from out of the draw. Moving slowly, it was methodically inspecting the trail, then lifting its shaggy head and searching the terrain on both sides.

Step-by-step, it progressed on up the trail, looking, sniffing and searching. As it drew nearer Ted could tell it was some sort of man creature.

The biggest, hairiest, Japanese Ted had ever seen emerged into a small swath of sunshine. He was dressed in peasant clothes, was filthy and carried some sort of a large broad ax over his shoulder. He appeared to be heading into the hills to cut wood; so there must be a village or habitation of some sort near by.

Coming on, step by step, the hulk continued up the trail, checking for something which Ted knew not of. Behind a small bush the abominable looking creature stopped and squatted down, inspecting the ground or something on the ground.

What ever it was that he had found, it was no doubt the thing for which he had been searching. Rising up, he stood studying the hills and the valley below.

Finally, seemingly satisfied with what he had found, or what he had figured out, he strode on up the trail, a great evil grin spreading across his ugly face.

The hair prickled more on the back of Ted's neck. Some how he discerned that this filthy hulk bade no good to either himself or to Li Kim.

Silently Ted stalked the hulk on up the trail, over the hill, and into a little valley beyond.

He retraced his steps and sought out the spot where the hulk had stopped. Back and forth, up and down the trail Ted moved. Over and over he looked and looked and was about to creep away, when he spied the object that had so delighted the beast.

In a patch of soft earth beside the trail was a small bare footprint. Ted needed only a moment's inspection to know it belonged to Kim Li.

What had this hulking beast to do with her? A cold chill invaded the marrow of Ted's bones as it dawned on him; this huge hulking beast had been tracking her, and had evidently worked something out in his evil brain.

THE RESCUE

Darkness rolled in and she was gone. The deep dark fear flowed over Ted and his soul knew no rest. He must find and tame her wild spirit for he knew not of the forces that consumed her.

He couldn't wait for morning. He just had to find her now. It was exceedingly dark outside, almost as dark as inside the cave. Overhead the stars were bright but on the ground it was black.

Ted found and waded across the little stream. His night vision was beginning to adjust to the darkness and he was able to feel and find his way through the forest and over the hills.

He could only search by intuition for he had no idea where she fled too when the Night Winds called. The darkness deepened but the stars showed brighter. Soon he was able to move along at a fair pace and was getting farther away from the glade than he knew was prudent.

His heart longed to call out for her even though he knew there would be no answer. When the Dark Evil Thing possessed her body there was no communication between them. His words had not the power to penetrate the shield that engulfed her.

He must find and hold her, but how he was to accomplish this task he knew not. He had tried to hold her before and he knew the awesome fear that completely overwhelmed her. There had to be some other way but in his own demented state he was not able to discern it.

When, or if he was able to find her, surely the providence that had given her to him would provide a way.

Farther and farther away from the glade he roamed could he find his way back? He was beginning to be concerned for he knew how erratic was his directions, as he wandered over the hills and through the trees.

Coming out upon a bare ridge he saw the spectacle of the nights. Far to the north the sky was lit up by the crisscrossing of searchlights. They had a Jap plane locked in their beams. The white, gray and black puffs of smoke began to fill the heavens as the anti-aircraft shells exploded all around the plane.

It seemed as though the explosions would completely obliterate the plane. From this great distance it looked as though there was a solid wall of steel engulfing it.

The silver speck that was the plane was just creeping along, like it was just sitting still. It appeared to be just floating along on top of the beams of the searchlights.

A weird thought crossed Ted's mind. Was there fear in the heart of the Jap pilot, or was he rejoicing because he was going to meet his ancestors? Ted guessed great fear.

There was a flash of fire, the plane nosed over and started its plummet to the ground. One of the few planes Ted was to see knocked down by ground fire.

The moment of diversion was over and Ted was whisked back to his dilemma. His heart ached for the one he loved, but fear for her safety overrode his soul. How would he ever find her in this dark wilderness?

Ted wandered on, searching. How was it possible for her to just vanish off the face of the earth, for a period of time? Why had he never been able to find her when the dark shadows possessed her body?

A tiny moon appeared in the sky. It was not bright enough to light up the ground; it only helped sharpen the images along the way. Ted could discern the trees and brush a little clearer and hastened along to he knew not where.

From out of the darkness there came some strange sounds. At first they were so faint Ted was not sure he had even heard them. What could it be, or whom could it be that was moving around in this desolate place?

Was it possible Kim Li was out there? Was there a village or habitation near? The sounds grew louder and louder. All at once Ted realized what the sounds were. A body of men or people was moving through this wilderness.

Closer and closer they came. Now Ted could make out the unmistakable sounds of soldiers marching. They were extremely silent, but from a body of military there is always the sounds of moving troops. The sounds of rifle butts scraping against brush the squeak of leather; canteen rattles, always moving men make noises.

Were these Marines or Japs? Ted had to know which, though what he would or could do he hadn't considered. Frozen in the darkness he stood waiting.

The sounds grew nearer; he must seek cover. Even in this darkness his silhouette might be seen and he was not yet ready to reveal himself, even if they should be Marines.

That there could be Marines in this area Ted was doubtful, however, he needed to know for sure. If they were American troops it would affect his decision on what to do for Li Kim and himself.

If the Marines were in control of this territory it would be a simple matter to just walk into their lines. If the Japs were moving in he needed to clear out, find a safer place for him and Kim Li to hide. It occurred to Ted, how could he hide her out if he couldn't even find her.

Searching for a place of concealment he found himself on a dirt road or trail of some sort. The troops, Marine or Jap were coming closer, probably on this very same road. He must seek cover, now.

He backed into some trees and bushes beside the road and all at once the advancing people were upon him. It was too late to run now. Ted melted into the ground and peered through the undergrowth.

Now there was not the slightest doubt the troops were Japs. He could hear their muffled voices as they stumbled by. They appeared to be near complete exhaustion. Were they retreating, or were they merely trying to out-flank the Marines positions. Whichever, Ted knew he was in a precarious position. If he moved he might be spotted. If he stayed here he would be trapped if the Japs kept passing until daylight. What to do, the cowardly fear was gripping his soul, again.

He knew he should try to escape and find his own people to report this mass of troops moving. Indeed they had gone from a trickle to a swelling tide of movement. Great numbers of troops were on the move along this stretch of road or trail.

Ants or spiders or some sort of bugs were crawling up Ted's arms and were finding their way under his clothes. He wanted to jump up and slap them off but fear kept him glued to the earth.

The column in front of Ted halted. The weary troops were taking a break. Most of them flopped to the ground where they stopped. Some needed to relieve themselves. Ted could see and hear them moving into the bushes. He could hear the patter of men urinating. He was not ten feet from the road. Someone was advancing on his position.

The Jap stopped a few feet short of Ted and dropped his pants. The acrid smell of feces and urine almost overwhelmed Ted. He had a desire to jump up and run from this terrible position. Surely one of them would step right on top of him.

Was the whole Japanese army moving out of the lines? It was frightening to Ted to see so many Japs all at one time. Surely there must be a whole regiment, at least, on this road and who knew how many more to follow.

Shrill, commanding voices rang out. The troops stirred from their lethargic lounging. Ted could hear murmuring of what must be grumbling voices. The Japs were nearing exhaustion, either from the days and weeks in the front lines or from the long march. Ted knew not which and had no sympathy to waste on any of them.

How many hours had he been lying concealed here, or was it only minutes? His muscles ached and the cold from the ground was penetrating his body. How he longed to be back in the cave with her by his side.

The Japanese column more or less formed up and started moving off at a slow shuffle. What if it got daylight before the whole regiment passed. He would be trapped here with nowhere to hide. The cold dampness seemed to paralyze his mind and body. He needed to move now but fear held him in submission.

There was a sense of movement and Ted discerned the feel of body heat beside him. He was almost frantic for he had no weapon except his bare hands. Was this then to be his end, he did his best to melt into the ground, to literally become a part of the earth. Was it possible someone could be so near and not see him, or at least not feel his presence?

A gentle hand touched his shoulder. A wave of fear then of joy flooded his Very Being. There was only one person in the whole world that would be capable of this fete.

How, in this blackness was it possible for her to know where he lay? How could she come to his side without him or the Japs seeing her? How, how, how? This lovely little creature of the night was able to do so many super human deeds. Ted could not fathom from where she got her strength and guidance. Who, or what, was guiding her tiny footsteps?

What was it that could have guided her to him in this place of concealment? What was it that always told her when he needed help? Surely the devil would not trouble him self to reveal Ted's need.

Her small fingers found his and she gently turned him from the scene of the marching Japs. The fear melted away from his soul as they crawled into the darkness.

Every second Ted expected a bullet to shatter his shoulder blades. Every second was an hour as they inched their way along. As dark as it was it seemed to Ted they were spotlighted like the plane sitting on top of the powerful spotlights? Surely the explosion would come and they would be hurtling through space, just like the Jap pilot. For an instant Ted felt empathy for him. The first he had ever felt for a Jap.

A few yards traversed through the open terrain and she rolled into a slight dip in the ground. Here they were able to crawl on their hands and knees and were soon swallowed up by the brush and trees.

The sounds of the marching Japs faded away into the night. Still clasping his hand she rose up and they fled into the darkness, also.

How effortless she moved over the low hills and through the valleys. Ted was laboring to keep pace but she wasn't even breathing hard. It was as though something was carrying her on wings and her feet were not even touching the ground.

Her firm grip on his fingers guided him up, over and around. Had he wandered so far astray or was she taking him to some different place? What was compelling her onward?

Ted soon found out how she came in every morning so scratched and bruised. The limbs struck his face and slapped his body. She seemed not to notice them and ever sped onward.

Evidently, sensing his need to catch his breath she finally paused. Ted collapsed in the dirt and leaves of the hillside. He drew in great draughts of the fresh mountain air, reviving his strength.

Onward they sped through the undergrowth and the forest at a speed Ted could not have maintained. He was completely lost again and would have gone off in a different direction. He would never have found their little cave on his own. She reached for him and he got to his feet. Again she grasped his hand and led off in a direction Ted knew not. It felt like hours but was probably less than thirty minutes later when she led him into their little cave. He shielded his head and face with his arms but she walked unerringly to their sleeping mats.

Again that touch of fear came over him as he realized how utterly close he had come to the column of moving Japs. He doubted that he would have had the courage to crawl away had not she come to his side and directed him. He would still be lying trembling there beside the road or trail.

Utterly exhausted he collapsed onto the mats. She lay beside him and he snuggled into her warm body. Ted was soon into an exhausted sleep.

Instead of Ted finding her, she had again found and rescued him. Was it to ever be so? How could he protect and save her when she was always the protector.

THE HULK

Night after night Ted determined to follow Li Kim to see where she went and what she did that she would come in so cut, scratched and bruised.

She seemed to have the eyes of a cat or other night creature as she sped along through the forest. Over hills and through the trees she would fly at a tremendous speed.

Her lithe, agile form flitted in and out amongst the trees and her tiny feet hardly seemed to touch the ground. She sped up or down the mountain, on her way to only she knew where.

Time after time Ted had attempted to follow this lovely creature of the night. It seemed as though she turned into a different person when the night winds called and she would strike off down the trail in the darkness.

No longer did her mind rip and tear for she seemed to have a purpose. What could it be? Where did she go? What did she do?

Down the hill she sped, so fast Ted could not keep in sight of her, and he dared not call out, or thrash through the undergrowth. At the slightest sound she would bound off like a frightened deer, and instantly be swallowed up by the forest where she seemed as much at home as one of the forest dwellers.

There seemed no real purpose in her wanderings and no pattern in her going. One night she might go down stream and the next up. She would meander up and over the hills, searching, searching, searching. Ted would try to guess in which direction she might go and would shortcut to a place of concealment, but his waiting was always in vain. She would never appear, or possibly she would appear and he would never know of it.

So attuned to the night was she, that like the wild beasts of the forests she seemed to smell, or sense danger and would vanish. Not to be seen until daylight and she was ready.

It happened one night as the new moon rose earlier in the evening. Ted's loneliness and longing for Li Kim drew him farther from their little cave than he had ever been. He caught a fleeting glimpse of her amongst the trees.

More determined than ever he began to follow but was soon out distanced, even with the moon to light the way.

Fearful of wandering too far afield and of being discovered by some roving civilian, or possibly by a Japanese army patrol, Ted moved farther into the shadows of the pine forest.

A short time later he heard a noise as of voices far off. He turned to flee, but then he caught a familiar tone on the night breeze.

It was Kim Li; of this he was certain. Her lovely sing song voice was stamped indelibly on his memory. He would recognize it as surely as a mother can recognize the cry of her off spring in the midst of a horde of people or animals.

Using all the stealth that was in him, Ted inched closer and closer. Ever mindful of snapping a twig, stumbling over a rock or of creating any other noise that might cause her to flee.

There in the bright moonlight she sat, reposed upon a heap of stones in a little open glade. Her lovely shape radiated the moonbeams; and her raven black hair fell back off her white shoulders.

Her head was tilted back as if she were serenading the moon, or stars, or some ancient form of worship that Ted knew not of. From her radiant face and sweet lips flowed a strange, haunting melody. It seemed as though she was offering her soul, or her body, to the one that possessed her mind.

The words were all strange, but the rising and failing of the melody would live in Ted's memory. If he heard it again he could tell if one note was out of harmony.

Sitting on the hill overlooking the glade, Ted longed in his heart and in his very Being to go to her. to clasp her in his arms, and to hold her tight.

How his heart yearned to tame her broken mind that she might find the joy in her soul that she had put back in his. He started to her, but hesitated, knowing full well that she would flee from him.

In that moment of hesitation, Ted, his still warped mind almost as sensitive to the night winds, the dangers, as hers, felt, or saw, or sensed something was wrong. At the same instant there was a total change in Kim Li. Her form straightened. Her every sense and muscle became alert. The words of her haunting melody died in mid air. She was poised for flight.

The smell of fear was on the air, and, even Ted at his distant vantage point wafted it and it chilled his heart, his blood ran cold.

This must have been one of, if not the only spot that drew her back to wail her mournful pleas. Did she return here to search for the key that had twisted her mind? Was it here that it had happened? Was it here on this pile of stones, a cairn; that she had gone through the fires of Hell? Much as Ted had done at Shuri Castle that had left it's mark on him, though not as severely as it had on Li Kim?

Was she calling to father, mother, brother, or sister, or was it to the devil himself, who owned her mind, that she was calling?

These thoughts would torture Ted for the rest of his days, but he would never know.

From out of the deep dark shadows behind the mound of rocks it struck, as suddenly as a coiled snake. Those huge, hairy hands clasped round her, and held as tight as a vice.

He must have lain breathlessly in wait, night after night, knowing she would come to this spot, for there is no earthly way he could have approached without her knowing. Had he found her tiny footprints here in the dust, as he had found them on the trail? Had he, as Ted, just chanced upon this scene another time? That taking her was his sole purpose was without a doubt.

He began pulling her closer and this ugly hulking figure began stroking her lovely, naked, moon bathed body with those massive hairy hands. He would possess her here and now, after all those days of tracking and waiting. This truly had been his intent from the very beginning.

How many times had she been compelled to escape from him before? How many times had she been pursued throughout the night? Was fleeing from him the reason she had returned so scratched, bruised, and exhausted?

Possibly a scream, a moan, or some such escaped Ted's lips as he sprang up from the deep shadows to go to her aid. He remembered uttering no sound, but as he arose the giant hulk glanced up towards the hills, as if he had heard, seen, or sensed something.

In that instant of his glancing away, a ball of fury exploded. Scratching, biting, clawing and kicking. The tiny ball of fire took the great hulking beast by surprise. He loosed his grip on her and stumbled backwards a step. In that split second she was off and away a fleeting shadow that disappeared in the darkness.

Not once had she made a sound during the attack and she made none now as she sped away on feet as fleet as wings.

284

Ted crouched back in the shadows thinking he had possibly not been seen, but it is almost certain this monster had found his footprints in the mountains, as he had found Kim Li's. It is equally certain that he knew of whom he had seen, heard, or sensed on the hill. Who it was that had robbed him of his prize.

The hulk stood for a moment in the bright moonlight, looking for all the world like a mighty ape. Even at this great distance Ted could see the bitter anger and hate stamped on his ugly leering face. Entering the deep shadows he turned to the hill for a last glance as if to say, I shall have my revenge.

A cold chill ran up Ted's spine and the hair stood straight out on the back of his neck. The smell of fear vanished from the glade and Ted too turned into the shadows of the deep forest; to wind his way back to the tiny cave in the mountains.

Here he would spend a fitful night of waiting, longing and wondering if she would return.

How would he ever find her if she failed to return? What would he do without this lovely little creature of the night? The one that held the tiny thread that held the pendulum to his tortured mind.

The long torturous night convinced Ted of one thing. No matter how scared he was, no matter if he died in the doing. Tomorrow night, when the moon came up, he must find his way back to the battlefield he had fled. Surely the fighting had moved on by now and Ted knew there was always many guns and weapons left scattered around a combat zone.

He must have a weapon, for as sure as God was in the Heavens, that giant hulk would never cease his searching until Ted was dead, and he had possessed lovely Kim Li.

Ted sat for hours by the entrance to the cave, waiting, watching. He finally surrendered, and undressing he lay down on the sleeping mats, but determined not to fall asleep.

The moon was gone and it was as black as the pits of Hell outside. It was almost as black as Ted's heart when she was not near.

No sound did he hear; no slightest indication did he have that anyone was near until "She" touched his hand. Then, his heart knew that surge of sweet music that only two hearts in love can know.

How had she found her way back here in the pitch-blackness? How had she come to his side and touched him? Him who was so attuned to fear and watchfulness, to the smell and taste of death without his even suspecting she was near. Surely something higher than man guided her steps.

She layed down beside Ted and his arms encircled her cool body. She snuggled close and in the warmth of their love they fell asleep.

Two warped minds at perfect peace, and in harmony with each other.

THE WEAPON

It was early evening when the night winds called and her spirit answered. In a flash she was off and away, tearing through the undergrowth as though the night demons possessed her body.

One second she was by Ted's side and the next she was gone. Every day Ted would think he had stilled the turmoil that overwhelmed her soul each night.

He would think, tonight I shall hold her I will not let her go again. Each time he tried it was futile, her fear of being restrained was much worse than that of going.

Ted had neither the physical nor the mental capacity to hold her, and indeed, was often tempted to flee to the night winds as she did. To surrender to the power that was trying to engulf his soul, to let himself roam wild and free of the restraints of mankind.

Oh how it rended his heart each time she went. A large piece of his very Being would go with her.

Always there was the fear that she would never return and if she did not return, he did not wish to live longer either. He could never cope without her love to hold on to.

He must somehow retrieve a weapon to defend her with. For last night's terrible experience with the Hulk would not end until it was dead, or until he had vent his fury upon Li Kim and Ted, of this there was not the slightest doubt.

Cold shivers coursed up Ted's back as he recalled the evil, leering face, that from the cairn of rocks had stared up in his direction; that had made a silent, unspoken vow of hatred and revenge—a challenge of death.

From sounds and sightings Ted had reckoned his bearings. He must be in a little pocket of no man's land. He was well south of the American's lines and east of the Japanese defensive line.

From high on a hill he had seen the swarms of U.S. planes coming and going from Yontan and Kadena airports, way to the north. Fighters and light bombers were going out to help defend the fleet from the hordes of Kamikaze planes. They were going to bomb and strafe the Japanese defenses and a host of other duties assigned to each.

He could hear the report of the huge 155-millimeter guns and he could hear the return fire of the Japs.

Somewhere between these booming sounds lies the battlefields of the infantryman. If Ted were to retrieve a weapon it must needs be from one of these valleys that had been recently overran or abandoned.

Did he have the courage to return to one of these little valleys of Hell, where so many individuals had had to fight their own "Battles of Armageddon?"

From deep within he knew he had not the spirit or stamina to carry off such a task.

Possibly, just possibly, if he strolled off in that direction it would soothe the conscience of the coward within.

Ted could think of a thousand reasons for not going back to the battlefields. What if the Japs caught him and put him through the torture they had put the young marine?

Suppose he got lost and could not find his way back here? If they should ever become separated he would never find her again.

What if he should become the coward again and go off the deep end for good? What if, what if, what if?

That settled the issue. The what ifs had won easily, as he knew they would.

The vision of that ugly leering face and the thought of those huge, hairy hands, grasping her small body caused the battle to rage within.

The thought of that deep dark void, which had come so near to possessing him said, stay away, don't go, but something within said, it is all over if you don't at least try.

Looking around, Ted realized how little he knew of where he was. True he was on a little stream flowing out of the hills, but how many hundreds of such streams might there be in all of Okinawa.

He needed some real landmarks to pinpoint this place. With this in mind, and even though there was still too much daylight left, he set off to climb the highest hill which he had spotted in the area.

Keeping well into the trees and leaving as little sign of his passing as possible, Ted worked his way ever upward.

He crisscrossed back and forth, trying to confuse his trail. But within his heart he knew that if the great Hulk ever came across his tracks no amount of back tracking or crisscrossing would confuse him for long. Ted had to grudgingly admit that he was a woodsman of great skill. No doubt he had spent his whole lifetime in these hills; being by his very nature and bulk an outcast from the regular society.

At this time Ted had only fear and hatred for the beast. Later a thought would occur, what had made his life so lonely that he had sought after one so delicate and fragile as Her?

No doubt he was the laughing stock of all the local villagers. Conceivably no Okinawan girl would even have considered looking with favor upon one so huge, stooped and hairy.

Ted cautiously approached the summit being sure to keep as much cover as possible between him and the top. If any lookouts were on duty this seemed a good place to post them. It was the highest point for some few miles in any direction.

Being cautious to keep himself below the ridgeline so he would not be silhouetted against the evening skyline, Ted circled the high ground. He found signs of others having been using this high ground, as he surely knew he must.

All the sign seemed to be several days or possibly weeks old. Ted breathed a sigh of relief, but it lasted only a few moments.

Being pretty adept at tracking and hiding his own trail; he had been slowly working around the knoll. Checking out the lay of the land when he saw it. There, in a small spot of soft earth, was the barely discernible print of a huge split toed shoe. It was extremely fresh; else Ted would have missed it all together.

Ted froze in his tracks. Was the Hulk here on the mountain with him at this very moment? If so, he would surely know of Ted's presence. Though awkward and dim witted in some things, he missed absolutely nothing that traversed "His Land," and there was no question that this was "His Land."

With a supreme effort Ted resisted the urge to plunge headlong off this hill and be away, for the bitter taste of evil was on this knoll.

It was no longer a question of whether he would go back to one of the distant battlefields to find a weapon. It would be only a matter of possibly hours before the Hulk had found their little cave by the river. Then he must be ready at whatever the cost.

Ted did his best to pinpoint his location and its relation to what he thought was the Yonabru-Shuri battleline, as he had last known it. He searched right and left for prominent landmarks to come back to, more than to go from. The sounds of the big guns would guide him in the general direction. As he drew near the little intimate sounds of the battlefield, and the night flares blazing over head should zero him in.

He tried to imagine what the profile of this hill would be in the dark and of the distances he must travel to go and return if he was successful in this deed.

The distance itself didn't seem that far, but what obstacles, both human and topographical lay between; he had no way of knowing.

What would happen to Kim Li if he should not return? It devastated Ted's soul when he thought of her fate in the hands of that shaggy, plodding beast.

He would return or die trying, for it had become more and more apparent that his days would not be many unless he found a weapon, or returned to the Marines lines.

It would be simple to go and save him self, but to do so would sacrifice Her to a fate far worse than she was now going through.

Darkness settled over the valleys as Ted cautiously left the mountain, being careful to avoid any outcroppings of rocks, or deep foliage where the Hulk might be laying in wait.

Ted well knew his prowess in stealth. How well he remembered the snakelike quickness with which he had grasped Li Kim as she sat wailing her heart out there on the cairn of rocks.

It was slow going down in the valley for it was dark and Ted's eyes had not yet adjusted to the night. There were roots, limbs and any manner of brush to catch his pants legs and trip him up. Many many, times he fell; then would rise up and stumble on.

How labored his breathing, how exhausted his body; what did he think he was going to do anyway? He had to be crazy to be going back to those horrible places. What possible chance did he have of finding a weapon anyhow? The doubts and fears were almost overwhelming him.

It was about this time when he stumbled upon a trail of sorts. Going it seemed, in the same direction he desired to go. It was quite possible this was the trail on which Ted had first sighted the ugly hulk, trailing her up the mountainside.

Considering this possibility he soon left the path even though it was easier going. The prospect of stumbling into some habitation, or possibly a Japanese guard post was just too strong. Reluctantly he left the comparatively easy going and swung wide of what he thought should be his destination.

The timber grew more sparse as he descended out of the high country. Rounding a point of land, he was suddenly out of the trees all together.

Before him lay an open valley with ridges on one side and a high escarpment on the other.

From this point Ted could hear the sounds of the big guns talking to each other. He knew he had missed the area to which he had thought he was aiming.

The moon had risen and now was bathing the surrounding countryside in bright, almost daylight. The outlines of this valley looked somewhat familiar, but from his post at the end of the valley Ted could spot no landmarks that he could be really sure of.

For a long time he sat, contemplating what he should do, and where he should go. Inch-by-inch, he surveyed the scene before him. As far as he could tell there was no movement upon the whole landscape. He also knew how deceptive shadows could be. There was the possibility a whole army could be lying in wait in front of him.

Ted sat for maybe half an hour deliberating his predicament, trying to decide what to do. His body lacked the strength to reach the yet far-off battlefield, even if he should be able to drum up the courage to go there. He very much doubted his will to do this thing. The what ifs were still winning the battle of wills.

The moon ascended higher into the sky, the shapes and shadows of the surrounding area changed. It looked even more familiar to Ted.

Possibly he had not missed his intended destination by as much as he had feared. Possibly, in the few days he had been in the cave with Li Kim the battle lines had moved farther south. Conceivably, the Marines had mounted a huge counter attack and had driven the Japs deeper into the Shuri-Yonabru fortress.

Keeping in the shadows of the high escarpment Ted started working his way deeper into this valley. Everything was a tangled, twisted mass of roots and shrubs. The few trees standing were only skeletons. There was shell and bomb craters covering almost every foot of the valley. Certainly not more than a few days or weeks at most, had passed since this had been the front line.

Soon, Ted's nose told him what it did not need to be told. Many people had died in this valley, and on these ridges. Many of them were still rotting here. Probably they were dead Japs, for they were usually just tossed into a shell hole and bulldozed over when time would permit.

Somewhere on this hillside was what he was seeking. A rifle that was lost, discarded, or that the owner no longer had need of.

The smells of death almost overwhelmed Ted and the "fear" was upon his soul. It took a super human effort to stay in the shadows and proceed up the ridges rising beside him.

Presently Ted stumbled and fell headlong into a crater. He sat up clutching some cloth material his hand had grasped in the bottom of the hole.

Holding it to the light of the moon, Ted discovered it was a Marine dungaree jumper. In a side pocket he discovered an unopened packet of k-rations. In the top pockets he found two packs of cigarettes.

Further inspection of the hole revealed no more treasures. Ted pocketed the ones he had found and a little heartened he sat thinking.

He was oh so tempted to light up one of the cigarettes for it had been days since he had had one of these precious things. Time and again he pulled his trusty Zippo lighter from his pocket and came near to flipping the little wheel that would ignite the flame.

Reason prevailed, and as the moon was sinking farther behind the ridge he knew he must hurry and do what ever he was going to do.

Sighting a gully running between two ridges, Ted knew he had found the place to look. How many times had he seen the poor, overburdened stretcher-bearers hurl a rifle, a pack, or a bunch of grenades over a bank to lighten their impossible loads?

Searching along, more or less on hands-and-knees, Ted found the object of his search. Here was a Marines M-1 rifle. The stock was somewhat battered, but as far as he could tell the rifle (never, ever, say gun) itself was all right.

He removed the clip and found it near full. Elated, he pulled the mechanism open to check for a live round in the chamber. It held a live round and he released the breach. It slammed home with a click that could have been heard all over the entire ridge.

Ted heard a whispered jabbering voice. This one careless moment could cause him to lose his life. He had been alert for guard posts and patrols, but had never realized there might be Okinawan scavengers out searching, just as he was.

For several minutes Ted lay frozen to the earth. Faint sounds of two, three, or more persons moving silently away drifted down to his sensitive ears.

Hearing nothing more, and with the bitter taste of fear and panic welling up within, Ted held to the ravine and descended to the deep shadows of the valley below.

Glancing back up the ridges for one last look Ted again froze. The unmistakable call of MAMA, MAMA, MAMA floated down to him; and pierced his very soul.

This then was, indeed, "The Valley of Death" to which he had returned. Was it possible the dungaree jumper, and, or, the rifle could have belonged to the blind youth, whom Ted had been forced to leave on the ridge? Was it possible his spirit was still roaming this place of death and destruction? Calling for the one it loved most, MAMA, MAMA, MAMA?

Certainly Ted would never doubt the probability of any, or all of the above. Most certainly that voice would still be ringing in his ears for the rest of his days. Calling MAMA, MAMA, MAMA.

The fear of the coward overwhelmed Ted's soul. He fled back up the valley and into the hills, heedless of direction or distance. He ran and ran, and ran; then he collapsed on a hillside, too weak to run farther. Here he lay on the ground, sobbing and crying and there was no Kim Li to comfort his soul.

The moon had sunk behind the ridges and it was pitch black out. Ted was lost, totally, completely lost. Not only had his courage deserted him again, but all sense of direction had fled with the terrible fear that had engulfed his soul.

The desire to live was lost once more. Only the thought of her fleeting steps traversing those hills, with the great hulking beast in pursuit, stirred a desire to find her. He must take her the precious treasure he clutched so tightly in his hands. He had to find her again, had to hold her close and protect her from the Hulk and from the evil Thing that possessed their minds.

He forced back the great yawning, black abyss and the flashing red light that was trying to possess him.

Some how, some way, he must find her. He had finally realized it was not as much her that needed protection, as it was him. And she was the only one who could give that protection.

Without Her, he was less than nothing. Without Her, he would totally lose control and forever, his very Being would be condemned to chasing the little red light that was screaming. "You can't catch me, you can't catch me, you can't catch me, you can't catch me."

There are so many ways to be lost, and of a truth, Ted was lost in all of them.

SEARCHING

So close, so close he had come to surrendering but the tiny flickering flame had not gone completely out. Ted roused from his stupor. He thought of Kim Li, who even now might be back at their cave searching for him; this thought gave him the strength and the will to rise up and continue on with the task that he had set out to accomplish.

Ted listened to the big guns roar and did his best to take his direction away from them. Deeper and deeper into the dark hills he penetrated. He had no idea of where he was going, for the blackness had obliterated all landmarks. There was simply no way of telling where he was headed or of where he wanted to go.

He had no sense of direction and for all he knew, could be going away from the cave, or going in circles, or going in any other direction one might choose.

He at least had the presence of mind to keep working his way higher and higher into the mountains when possible.

Pausing to rest, he turned and looked back. There was an unmistakable lightening of the night sky. Daybreak was not too far off and something was irresistibly guiding his steps to the west. Possibly her spirit was calling to him, guiding his steps ever nearer, entreating his help. At this juncture he had no idea as to where he might be, or of where he would find her. He must trust the One guiding his footsteps.

Ted's body was so spent that he felt he could not take another step; the days without food or water, the nausea, and of mind-rending fear were taking their toll. Those were days he would like to erase from memory, yet within himself, he knew he had to find their little cove quickly or else take cover and hole up for the entire daylight period. It would soon be too light and too dangerous for him to be out traipsing the hills. Someone was bound to spot a lone figure moving around no matter how careful he was.

Forcing him self to get up and move on, he came out over the top of a ridge. In the valley below he spied a thin silver ribbon, possibly a half-mile away. A river flowed down there and Ted was excruciatingly thirsty.

As thirsty as he was, he realized the inherent danger of proceeding down into the valley. Rivers meant people; and there was only one person he wanted to see right now. Would he ever find her again?

How he longed to be back in her arms, and feel her warm body close to his. This was the thought, the desire that kept him going. The thing that gave him the strength to pick one foot up and place it in front of the other. The cement that held his mind together, that kept him from going completely off the deep end. His body was running on will alone. Nothing is impossible when someone needs you, and something told Ted that she needed him now, as never before.

Ted sat eyeing the valley, willing his eyes to see every inch of the terrain, to see if there was an enemy anywhere along the river course. Mostly though, he was just letting his inner self discern if there were people below.

Standing here, Ted remembered the K ration packet he had found on the battlefield. He reached into his pocket to retrieve it, but it was gone, somewhere in his wild flight from the "valley" it had bounced out without his having even realized it. How welcome even one small bite of the hard biscuit would be right now!

The two packs of cigarettes were still secure, buttoned down in his jumper pockets. He took a pack out and opened it. This time the temptation was just too strong.

Scrunching back under a low hanging evergreen tree he took out his Zippo lighter and cupping it in his hands to hide the flame, he lit the cigarette. Taking a long deep drag he slowly let the smoke out to filter up through the thick branches and disappear.

His head swirled up with the smoke; he was dizzy and almost overcome. The days without smoking had left his system devoid of nicotine. The deep drag he had desired so much almost made him sick.

Taking a few more short puffs he pinched the fire off and put the stub back in the package for future use. He well knew it might be a long, long time before he came into possession of more.

Leaning back against the trunk of the tree he rested a few moments. Then, stimulated by the smoke he crawled out and started for the stream below.

Something in Ted's Being warned that there was great danger in this valley, but something down there drew him irresistibly downward. Slowly, cautiously, he descended; using every bit of cover he could find to shield his approach.

Nearing the stream Ted's heart began to beat faster. Even though the terrain was different, the stream was of the right size to be "their" river. In his wanderings and going and coming he had crossed no other with anywhere near the amount of water that was flowing in this channel.

He had no idea if he was above or below their little cove, but he was almost certain this was the right stream. Now all he had to do was figure out whether to go up stream or down to find the cave.

Searching the horizon he could find no silhouette that seemed familiar. Possibly he was upstream, for the outline of the hills would be different when looking at them from the opposite direction, from the backside.

Being careful to leave no footprints, he made his way to the waters edge. There he knelt and drank deeply of the refreshing waters. He scooped up handfuls of the water and washed his face, letting some trickle down his sweat stained jacket.

Daylight had crept into the deep valley and Ted knew he should find a place to hide, but he just had to get back to their cave as soon as possible.

What if she had already returned this early, as she often had before? If she could not find him would she leave and never again return? Would he lose her forever?

The little inner voice kept warning of danger ahead, but her spirit kept calling out to him for help. She was in mortal danger, and he must needs go to her immediately. Something on the winds was telling him this, even though he knew not what. The communion of souls was taking place and she was entreating him to come to her side, to dispel the evil thing, or possibly, to protect her from the Hulk.

He wanted to stop and smoke the rest of that cigarette; how he needed it now, but there wasn't time. The thing that was calling him said he must hurry and find her, before something dreadful happened.

He felt a quickening of his spirit, a renewing of strength for the task ahead, whatever it might be. He would go to her.

Ted knew not from whence this renewing and warning came. He only knew that whereas, before, he had needed Her, she now needed him. He must go to her with all haste. Somewhere, her spirit was calling, entreating him to hurry.

He grasped the M-1 tighter, for there was no sling left on it. The strap had been severed near the top; an explosion, probably from a big shell, or a mortar round had blown part of the stock and the lower swivel away. Then he set off downstream to face whatever it might be that was waiting for him there in the wilderness.

Moving as fast as he dared Ted went down stream. No sign of human passage did he see, and what semblance of a trail he could find was even fainter than the one that led by "their" cove.

He must remember this spot, for it might possibly be a place of refuge in case they had to leave the cave they now occupied.

Not too far down stream and the canyon walls began to close in. They became narrower and narrower, until there were no banks left. Somewhere, a short distance below; he could hear the roar of a waterfall and instantly he was aware of where he was.

One night before, in his roaming, he had worked his way upstream from the cave. He was certain he had heard this same waterfall, even though he had not actually seen the falls either time.

The narrow gorge made it impossible to proceed farther down stream and Ted realized it was this same gorge that had isolated their little cove. This was the reason there was no main trail or road going up beside it.

Reversing his steps, Ted crossed the stream and started to work his way up and around the high ridge that lay in his path.

His spirit willed him to fly, but his weary body rebelled. It seemed he had to physically reach down and pick up each heavy-laden foot and move it forward, inch by precious inch. He was hurrying to her as fast as he possibly could.

Circling the steep grade Ted dropped off into another valley. Here he found a wide trail and knew for certain where he was.

This was the trail he had came across below their cove and no doubt it was the same one he had used briefly going to the Valley last night. The deep gorge was the reason it circled this longer way around instead of going on up the river's edge.

If he had only of known, he could have sped to the Valley and returned on this "almost" highway. He could have been safely back in the cave with Kim Li by his side at this very minute.

THE MURDER

The red flag of danger was still flying on the breeze, but her call was beckoning him on. He had to get back to their cave; he had to find her.

Some terrible thing was about to happen and he knew not what it was. If only he could find her he felt he could stop what ever it was from happening, for now he had this rifle which he was clutching so tightly in his hands.

Was not this the unforeseen thing that had willed him to return to the battlefields in spite of the incessant dread that had been upon him? What power from above or below had guided, indeed, forced his steps to the valley, and then returned him to this very spot?

Surely there was some magic there beside the river that had directed his compass, and each time drew him back without his knowledge of where he was going. Some power in her love and compassion was able to reach far out and lead his steps unerringly, back to that little cove beside the "River of Life."

Ted knew he should not be on this trail leaving footprints that the "Thing" would find. He also knew that no matter where he left a footprint the "Thing" would find them; and whatever it was that was drawing him onward had become more urgent. Hurry, hurry, hurry.

Almost he was able to run down this trail for something told him she was very near, and she needed him.

Possibly a quarter of a mile down the trail and Ted's breathing had become so heavy that he was compelled to stop and rest for a moment.

There was a huge pine tree standing in some rocks right beside the trail. Ted stopped and leaned his weary body against it to rest, and to catch his breath before he hurried on.

He stood looking up and down the trail trying to discover the danger that he felt so strongly. He turned and looked up the hill leading away from the cove and he had a momentary glimpse of something flashing between the trees and disappearing over the top of the ridge.

His soul leaped within and he started to yell out to her, for it could only be Kim Li. She was fleeing as he had never before seen her flee, as if her very life depended upon her speed.

Before the sound could escape his lips a chill ran up Ted's spine. The hair on the back of his neck bristled as it had never bristled before. He melted into the trunk of the tree, as if to become a part of it.

Ted looked up and down the trail, there was nothing. The next tick or two of the clock seemed like hours for he knew there was something out there, and he was certain he knew what that something was going to be.

He looked, and looked, and looked, to no avail. He came within a hair's breadth of stepping out to follow her up and over the hill. Then he took one last glance back towards where their little cove would lie.

His heart stopped beating, and his breath froze within him. There, not fifty yards away, and coming directly towards him was the Thing. His head was down and he was following what was probably Kim Li's tracks; where she had no doubt just fled from him.

Had he lain in wait for her in the cave, or had he just this morning found where her and Ted had hid out? It was inevitable he would find the place; and quite possibly he had ascertained it last night on the high hill overlooking the whole area.

Ted could almost see him standing on the hill with his slow-witted brain working out just where he would find the two of them. Not much doubt but the cove by the river was the only place he had not yet searched out. There was no question where the night or early dawn would find him. He would possess his quarry at long last.

Somehow she had managed to elude him Ted knew, for once those great hairy hands grasped her again they would never let go. There would be no second chance to escape.

What sixth sense had warned her away Ted had no idea. Probably it was the same one that had been calling to him this long morning. Urging him on, willing him to pick up one foot and place it in front of the other; guiding his steps back to this very spot. The Thing was so close behind her that he could only have missed by inches, or yards at the most.

Quite possibly he had hid in the cave and lain in wait. She had entered and at the last second had sensed, or smelled the danger, and had fled for her very life. The Guardian Angel was watching over and protecting her, too.

Ted could almost see the great Hulk bearing down upon her as she splashed across the river and disappeared into the forest. There was no doubt she could outdistance him in a brief burst of speed, but after her all-night's roaming and wandering over the hills, how much stamina could she possibly have left. The Hulk was big and awkward, but he could move at amazing speed when he willed. At times he seemed to almost glide up and over the mountains with no effort at all.

Ted chanced another peek, on and on he came. Surely he could hear Ted's heart pounding and his breathing at such short a distance. So much a part of the wilds was he that Ted was surprised he had not yet smelled him, this foreign thing in his territory. So obsessed was he with following her footprints that he never once looked up. This was the only thing that could have prevented him from discovering Ted's form, which was trying to melt right into the tree trunk.

Now Ted could hear his steps and hear his deep though unlabored breathing. The Hulk was going to pass within inches of him. There was no way he was going to be able to remain undiscovered.

Ted gripped the rifle tighter and tighter. His finger found the trigger guard and slid inside, then the thought came to him. He didn't even know if the rifle would fire or not. Had the explosion which severed the sling, and damaged the stock, ruined the firing mechanism, also. Why hadn't he tried firing it last night? He remembered the fear that had overwhelmed him in the valley and he knew why not.

There would be no second chance. Was the safety on or off? He let his finger check it out, and it was still on. He knew even the tiny click would betray his presence at this close range. His finger crawled upon the safety button and was ready in an instant to release it, and to squeeze the trigger.

Ted's Guardian Angel was working overtime this day; it guided the Hulks steps to the opposite side of the tree by which he was concealed. He stepped lightly out upon the trail, not two feet from where Ted stood holding his breath.

The Hulk looked up over the hill to see where her steps had led; then he glanced down at the trail, and there in the soft dust of the trail were Ted's fresh footprints.

He leaned over to take a closer look, and in that instant, the barrel of Ted's rifle came crashing down on the back of his head. Ted had swung with all his might.

The Hulk fell against the upper bank and rolled back into the trail face up. He let out a groan and stirred. As vicious as the blow had been, it had only stunned the great beast.

Before he could sit up Ted dropped the rifle and picked up a large rock. He grasped it with both hands and brought it crashing down on that great ugly head. In that instant, before the stone came crashing down, Ted saw the flash of fear, and of death, in his eyes.

Again, and again Ted brought the rock crashing down until there was nothing left of that ugly leering face but a mass of pulp, and blood, and hair. Never again would he be able to pursue little Kim Li, or anyone else for that matter.

So this was why her spirit had been calling him and warning of the danger that lay ahead. Even in her time of mortal danger she had been able to protect him also. If she had not of warned him, he would no doubt have blundered right into the hands of the mighty Hulk.

The deed was done; and Ted's knees turned to jelly. He was trembling and shaking beyond his control. Full panic almost took over, and virtually anything at all could have set him off into a flight of which he would never have finished.

If there had of been strength in his legs, he would have no doubt ran, and ran, and ran again, right into the maws of that deep dark void, never to return.

PEACE

Ted stood contemplating the cold-blooded murder that he had just done. It was one thing to kill someone who was shooting at him. It was an entirely different matter to hide behind a tree and bash him over the head, then beat him to death with a rock.

It wasn't necessary to beat his head to a pulp. The lust to kill had been upon him; and he just didn't want to stop. If it had of been possible, he would most utterly of destroyed the "Thing."

Even though he was sure the Hulk would have done the same, or worse, to him and Li Kim, this just wasn't the battlefield. He had become the coward and fled the battlefield. Now he had become the coward and done this dastardly deed. Was there no end to the torments he must suffer? Why could he not have died on the battlefield with the other Marines?

He sat down on a rock to think, and unconsciously, he reached for the pack of cigarettes. Withdrawing the stub he had put back earlier, he started to put it in his mouth when he noticed his hands were all covered with blood and matter. Indeed his jumper and pants were covered also. If he could have seen them, his face and hair was probably covered too.

Blood itself held no fear for Ted. He had smoked many packs of cigarettes, which he had removed from dead Marines pockets, with his hands bloody. He reached for his Zippo and lit the stub.

He wasn't as dizzy or nauseated this time. He smoked it down until it burned his fingers. He took long deep drags, exhaling slowly. He needed that, and it helped settle his nerves. As he replaced the Zippo into his pocket, he noticed it was also covered with blood.

With most evil deeds the perpetrators first thought is to hide them. This was Ted's first thought, also. He must hide this horrible thing that he had done. He must hide it from the world, even though; it would never be hid from his own mind.

With all the effort he could summon, he managed to roll the huge body over the bank and down into the small ravine. There he covered it with brush, leaves, and pine needles that he gathered from off the slopes.

This done he returned and did his best to clean the evidence from the trail, yet he knew that within a day his futile efforts would be to no avail. The putrefying body of the great Hulk would permeate this whole valley;

and lead anyone passing this way directly to it. It seems nothing smells as bad as a decaying human, but then Ted wasn't sure the Hulk was really human.

He picked up his splattered rifle and started off in the direction he had seen her go, then he realized how hopeless it was, for he would never find her. She was too fleet and agile; and she could go to places he knew not of, and dared not go.

He would return to the cave and wait, but he was sure in his heart that she would never again return. After the close call she had just had with the Hulk, it was almost certain she would give the place a wide berth.

His heart yearned for her, but at the speed she was traveling, she was probably miles from this place by now. Who knew what fate might await her in some other place? There was Japs in the direction she had fled and they could, and would be more cruel even than the Hulk.

Ted was heart sick and weary, there was no purpose left for his life. The only consolation he had was that he had saved her, this time. But why had he not returned sooner, and got to the cave before she did. Possibly he could have spared her the terrible experience she had been forced to go through.

The total futility of his situation came to Ted at last. Even if he should somehow, some way find her, what would happen to them. Sooner or later they were bound to be discovered; then what fate awaited them.

At the very best she would be locked away in a mental institution. And he would face a lifetime in a Federal Prison, or possibly, a firing squad, for running away from a combat zone.

With this thought gnawing at his vitals he sat and smoked another of his cigarettes. Then, heedless of leaving a trail he picked up the rifle and started off for the cove, in search of he knew not what.

If by any possible chance he should ever find her, he would see to it that they were never, ever, separated from each other again.

There was really only one solution. The rifle he held in his hands would take care of it, and it was the only way he could think of that it could be accomplished.

The deep dark abysses yawned wide, and the tiny red light was glowing in the far distance. He must hurry and catch it, before it whirled away and was gone, compelling him to follow.

Almost wild with fright and fury he dashed directly to the little cove. Here he searched, and searched, and called to the winds, for there was no Li Kim to hear him, or to heed his calling.

He went to the cave and searching, found evidence that the "Thing" had indeed been there. He found her tiny footprint at the entrance; and a wave of nausea and fear swept over him. Always upon leaving he had brushed away the tracks from in front of the cave, so he knew for certain she had returned this very morning. What providence had delivered her from the clutches of the terrible beast?

Returning to the cove, he drank from the river's waters. By this time he had convinced himself that there was no way he would ever see Her again. He had fulfilled his purpose in life when he destroyed the Hulk, who was trying to possess her.

In this demented, heartsick state, he determined he would wash the blood from off his face and hands. He would wash his clothes and dry them. Then being clean outside at least, he would put on his clean clothes. He would point the rifle into his mouth and end it all; as he had seen so many others do before him. There was nothing at all left to live for now. Without Her, he didn't want to live another hour.

He laid his rifle against a rock, then removed his clothes and waded into the shallow water and sat down to cleanse himself.

It was now past mid-day and the sun's rays beat upon his head and back. He lay back in the water to let it flow over him, for he had not the strength to dip it up.

He lay thus letting the water flow over his body, and his mind wandered. What would it be like over "There"? How long would it be before she could come to him There?

The loved ones at home would cry but a short time. Then he would meet them, also. Quite possibly he had already been reported as dead, or missing in action, so the sorrow at home would be no greater.

If only he could tell them why he was going to do this thing, he just knew they would understand and approve of what he was going to do. Oh, how the mind can justify the deeds one wants to perform.

He felt a gentle touch, but he dared not open his eyes or to even think. It was just his imagination, or perhaps a leaf, or a twig had floated by, or a small fish had bumped into his shoulder.

He opened his eyes at last, and looked into the shining eyes of his Darling Angel. How could he ever have believed she would not come to him, when he needed her so!

A feeling of deep guilt flowed over him, for not once in these many days had she ever failed him, when he "needed her." Her love and compassion had transcended that of a Mortal Being.

Ted wasted no time trying to figure out how she had come to him without his knowing of her coming. Too many times she had "materialized" out of nowhere, and was just there by his side.

Her gentle hands washed the blood from between his fingers, and from his face. As usual, her soothing soft touch washed away the hurts from within, as well as from without. The tempest assuaged, and the roaring in his head abated.

She placed his weary head in her lap, and crooning softly, she cleansed the caked matter from his hair.

They sat and lay long in the water this day. Just letting it wash the evil from off their bodies and souls.

Her voice was more vibrant, and her touch was more gentle; if possible, as she sat crooning and stroking his head. Something about her seemed different, as if a heavy load had been lifted from off her fragile shoulders. There was radiance about her that he had never seen before, sort of a freedom from within. A glimmer of hope sprang to Ted's mind. Could it possibly be she had recovered from the awful trauma that had been upon her?

Ted sat up and enfolded her in his arms. Long they sat just letting the water wash away the bitter taste of death, and the dreadful fear of the Evil Dark One that had been upon them.

The gentle breeze soughed in the pines, and they were at peace with each other, and with the world. As long as they were in each other's arms the Evil Dark One could not touch their souls. They belonged to each other, and to no one else. Nothing above or below would ever possess them again. They were at peace with themselves.

She arose and picked up his filthy clothes and washed them in the stream below him. She spread them on the warm rocks to dry. Then, hand in hand, they went to the cave, and curling up in each other's arms, they slept the sleep of a baby. They were "free" at last.

How his heart had yearned for this moment.

THE FINAL SURRENDER

The night winds called and she fought and fought against them, but night winds have a way of winning. No amount of pleading and coaxing or restraining could hold her.

The die was eternally cast, and Ted knew now what had to be done. He prayed long that God, who had not kept him from becoming the coward, would now give him the strength and the courage to do what he knew had to be done. There was really only one way they could be together forever. Only one solution remained; and on the morrow when she slept, he would end this eternal torment for both of them.

He needed to know if the rifle would fire, though he now had not the slightest doubt that it would. It was for a totally different purpose than he had thought that he had been willed to bring it here. It would be the means of their being together forever more, their salvation, free of the hurts of the mind that possessed both of them down here.

Heedless now of caution, for it would be only a few hours until it would all be over, and nothing on this whole earth could touch them ever again. No night winds, no deep dark pits, no whirling red ball, no memories of an ugly leering Hulk, no deep abysses. Nothing would ever disturb their tranquillity.

Ted pointed the rifle into the air and gently squeezed the trigger. A mighty rending roar echoed up and down the tiny cove, as he well knew it would. He took the rifle inside and laid it beside the sleeping mats, where it would be handy; when the time came.

A great sigh of relief flowed over Ted and he was at peace. He went outside and sat by the cave entrance. He smoked cigarette, after cigarette, taking long, unhurried, deep drags and ever so slowly letting the smoke out. He was savoring each and every puff.

He watched the crystal clear heavens, and tracked the stars as they slowly moved across the sky. The moon rose and bathed the little glade in a beauty he had never before seen. It set in the west and darkness was upon the land. Still he sat, just drinking in the beauty of God's Glory above. Not once did he sleep this night.

Daylight came, and finally the sun peeped over the ridge, flooding the little cove in its warmth. Ted arose and went to the stream. There he undressed and sat in the water for what would be his final bath.

Presently he looked up and saw her coming across the glade. She was moving so effortlessly; her feet hardly seemed to touch the ground. There was an aura about her that thrilled Ted's heart. On and on she came, bouncing over the stones as if they were not there at all.

As she drew near Ted saw a large red spot on the side of her head. He almost cried out, supposing that she had been somehow wounded.

She entered the water and sat by Ted's side, then turned her head so he could see. Her radiant, singsong voice proclaimed, "Teddee likee Oshokki-kon!"

No doubt it was the Okinawan word for "Hibiscus," for it was a bright red hibiscus flower blossom she wore in her hair. The first adornment Ted had ever seen anywhere upon her lovely body.

Her hands and voice were ever so tender as she methodically dipped up water and washed his body. When she had finished he did the same for her. Her soft supple body yielded to his hands as he washed away the dirt, and cleaned the scratches on her tender skin.

Somehow the river had become their link to each other, and their strength to blot out the Dark Evil Thing that had overwhelmed their souls.

He took her in his arms and they rocked back-and-forth, holding each other close, feeling the love flow between them. She hummed a cheery little ditty as they clung tightly to each other.

Her voice rang clear and danced upon the stream, and her voice smiled, even though her face could not do so.

They lingered longer at the stream than usual. It was as though each wanted to prolong the moment as long as possible, to savor the joys of just being together.

She was not afraid, but she clung to him in a way she had never clung before. It was as though each one wanted to cherish their last moments together. Each was indelibly stamping the profile and form of the other on their minds, "Bonding."

All at once Ted realized she knew what his plans for this day were. She was accepting and welcoming them, just as he had accepted this final eventuality. It was the only course left if they were to be together forever more.

How had he thought to keep this thing from her? Her, who knew the inner most working of his mind, even better than even he knew it himself. It shocked him no small amount to know that she knew this would be their last morning together. This would be their last moment together in the

"River of Life." The little stream gurgled as if it knew also, and who is to say it didn't; and was holding them in it's grasp as long as possible.

Though her body trembled imperceptibly, she showed no fear of what was to come. It was as though she knew, and understood that this was not the end, but a blessed release, to where they would be together forever, and forever. It was to be a new "beginning," not an ending. As warped as her precious mind was, she had comprehended this, indeed it seemed she invited it.

Their minds had become so intertwined that she could discern his innermost intentions. It was he who should have been her guardian, not the other way around. And yet it was always her that wielded the magic wand. It was Her that soothed the mind and pushed away the dark clouds that were ever hovering near. It was Her love that made him "almost" whole again.

Leaving the water they clung to each other as they made their way to the cave. It would be their last stroll here on this vile earth, for now they had found a way of conquering its wrath, a way to cheat it of it's prize.

Once inside the cave she smoothed the quilts upon the sleeping mats, then she removed the bright red hibiscus blossom from her hair. Plucking tiny bits from it, she scattered them around on the quilts. She sang a catchy little tune and continued anointing their sleeping mats until the hibiscus blossom was all gone.

She then stretched forth herself on the mats, opened her arms wide, and invited him to lie by her side. In her complete trust, and still in their total innocence, their souls consummated a love that their bodies never knew. There, on the anointed mats, two souls became one, a marriage without question, a marriage of souls. Without dishonor or shame, she had given "herself" to him, a love so perfect, so true. Could anyone ever ask for more?

Full of love and warmth; Ted lay perfectly content and at ease. He knew what he must do, had to do. As soon as she slept he would pick up the rifle, place it against her temple and have done with it. Then he would do the same to himself. He had no fear now, for he knew he could, and would do it.

So at ease was Ted that he dozed off to sleep before she did. Lying there in her arms was such a soft, wonderful, peaceful place. If only, if only, if only, it could have lasted forever.

Evidently, her soul was as satisfied as Ted's. Curled up close in his arms, she also fell asleep, two troubled minds in such perfect harmony.

Probably they both heard it at the same instant, and their blood ran cold. A footstep had sounded at the entrance to their cave. Why had he slept? This question would torment Ted for the rest of his days.

Three Okinawan men, peasants, came charging through the entrance. The lead one with an old sword or sugar cane knife raised high. In a flash Li Kim shoved Ted back from the onrushing men. She charged right into the midst of them with a fury such as Ted had never seen. She would protect her own.

Ted groped for the rifle that had been lying by his side, but before he could bring it up, the sword slashed down and twisted around. It had cleaved her asunder, and she fell to the ground, faithful to her very last gasp.

Ted would swear that as she was falling, mortally wounded, she turned her head to him; and a faint smile radiated from her lovely face. A smile she had never been able to issue before. A smile for the one to whom she had given her love. A love like few, if any, mortal beings have ever been given.

In death she had gained the release she had not been able to find in life. She was "Free" at last.

Ted brought the rifle up and fired three times and at such close range the three Okinawans were blasted back against the wall of the cave where they fell in a pile. With malice in his heart Ted bounded over to them and sent another bullet through each of their heads, just to make sure they were truly dead.

He knelt by Kim Li's side and grasped her hand, but she had already departed to that other side. Her soul was at rest.

Surrendering again, in a blind fury, Ted put the rifle barrel in his mouth. Placing his toe in the trigger guard, for one's arm is too short to reach it, he pressed the trigger. A deathly silence, there was nothing. He had forgotten to save a round for himself. Seven rounds was all the M-1 had contained. If only he had the round he so uselessly wasted last night in front of the cave.

This time Ted lost it all. The little red ball whirled off into the vast universe, screaming, "You can't catch me, you can't catch me, you can't catch me." The deep dark maws of the Pits of Hell opened wide to receive him. He staggered outside and fell to the ground. He laughed, he cried, he screamed, he pounded on the ground, but no relief would ever come to his poor tortured mind.

After surrendering to death once more, he had again been robbed and he would not be able to go with Her. God only, and God won't ever tell, knew if he would be able to get up the courage to try it again. How many times can one person be compelled to die?

Later that morning a platoon of Marines who had been reconnoitering the area, and had heard the shot last night, came up the streamside. The Marines found him lying there in front of the cave, still crying and retching and too weak to stand.

Going inside they discovered the grisly sight. Placing a satchel charge of explosives in the entrance of the cave they blew little Kim Li into dust, and sealed her tomb.

They took Ted back to their bivouac and nursed his body back to life, but they left an empty soul.

When he returned to his unit he found that he had never been listed as missing or dead. Indeed he had hardly been missed by the powers that be, so accustomed were they to his not reporting in.

Back at camp, his friends rejoiced, they laughed, they cried, they said what ere did happen. But still, they, had never sent, relief to guard post seven.

Some days later, as Ted lay on his cot, back at the cemetery, recuperating, there was a Chaplain holding a memorial service for some of the dead Marines who were being buried.

The all too familiar service proceeded with the Chaplain proclaiming. "Ashes to Ashes. Dust to Dust."

He then continued with, "The Lord giveth, and the Lord taketh away; blessed be the name of the Lord."

Only the Lord God, and I, Ted Alexander, would ever know how much "He" had given, and how much "He" had taken away, in that beautiful, lonely little glade, by the "River Of Life," their "Garden of Eden."

THE SOLDIER

During the time of Ted's "healing" this event took place. It was early July 1944 and the day was a very warm one. Chuck and Ted for some reason had nothing official to do this day so decided to try to find a little stream of which Ted knew. With canteens, rifles, and helmets they set off across country to explore. They left the cultivated fields of the flat land and meandered up through the foothills. Everything was lush and green from all the tropical storms which had come this way earlier.

Now they were several miles from camp and still ascending the low hills and traversing the valleys. They came up over another hill and out of the pines. The hill was barren of trees and looked much like Ted's homeland in the spring. It was covered with tall grass and no small amount of flowers.

The strenuous hike and the warm day were working wonders on Ted's "sickness." They had a healing effect far above any medication or therapy that could have been offered.

Cresting a rise, there was a dip in the terrain and more hills rising beyond. A few more yards and they could see there was a small lake or entrapment of water in the bottom of the depression. It looked clear cool and inviting.

A dozen or so steps closer and they noticed a man on the edge of the tiny lake. He was bent over washing his face and hair and he was naked except for a loincloth that looked to be quite soiled from age and wear. As he straightened up Ted could see that he was a Japanese man of an age that precluded his being a civilian. He looked to be in his mid twenties, not much older than Ted himself.

His eyes came up and they spotted Chuck and Ted there not more than a hundred steps from him. His eyes were filled with amazement (not fear) that anyone had been able to walk upon him so close while he was having a bath. He was most vulnerable; he was dead, no doubt about it.

What was he doing in that place? Was he a soldier spying out the land? Ted doubted this, as soldiers would have been with others. Was he lost from his company and trying to get back? Ted also doubted this as the Japanese armies were farther away now. Was he a young man who had been in Hell and could take no more? Ted would guess this was the case.

Ted raised his rifle but something unseen stilled his trigger finger. He just stood looking at the young Japanese for several minutes and the young Japanese soldier just stood looking back at him, waiting for the bullet to strike him down. There was no sign of surrender and no sign of any change of expression on his face. He only seemed resigned to his fate. "He was going to meet his ancestors."

Chuck said, "go ahead, bust him." Ordinarily no one would have to of said anything. Ted would have shot him and left him lying there beside or in the water and never have given it a second thought. Ted said, "no, not today" and they turned and walked away.

Possibly a hundred yards on up the hill and they turned to look back. The young Japanese soldier, for such he was, (he now had on his uniform and held a rifle in his hands) had turned and was starting to walk away, up the other side of the hill.

Chuck and Ted would have been such easy targets for him just as he had been for them, but he had chosen to walk away also. Sometimes Ted can still see him going over the crest of the hill, walking slowly.

What could it have been on that day that had spared the young man's life?

Possibly God had a duty for this young Japanese to fulfill just as Christ had a mission to fulfill. Ted would always realize that something had preserved him.

GOING HOME

The head Navy man in Ted's outfit was Chief Pharmacist Mate Eugene VanHorn. He was an old duffer of about thirty-eight. He had been with the First Marine Division since the days of Guadalcanal, and refused to go home after every campaign. The Chief had grown a little psycho, or at least "Asiatic," a term used for persons who had been too long in the Pacific, and who had became a little strange in their outlook on home and life. Who had the five hundred yard stare, if not the thousand-yard stare? While everyone else was counting the days until their relief would come, he was actually begging the Brass to let him stay over, for his name always topped the list to go home when new replacements arrived.

Chief VanHorn was a real nice person and never really gave any orders, so he had very little control over all the Corpsmen serving under him. They all did their jobs and somewhat more, so during combat campaigns they really needed very little, if any, supervision. They were Veterans, they knew what their jobs were, and what had to be done-and did it.

A section of the First Marine Division's cemetery on Okinawa

Somewhere, VanHorn had got the scoop that the Division was going to China after the Okinawa campaign was over. He had convinced Chuck and Ted they should sign over, and go to China with him, as their time overseas was almost up, and they were due for rotation. Going to China sounded like a great idea, so it didn't take too much talking to get them to say they would stay over when their time came.

It seems they had all become somewhat "Asiatic." One day, not too long before they were relieved a group of the Corpsmen and the Chief was in a dugout cave near their camp. The Chief was wanting something done; Ted couldn't remember just exactly what it was. At any rate, they didn't like the idea and probably said so in no few words, and them no doubt pretty profane. The final outcome was, he ordered Ted to stay and help him build whatever it was he wanted, and let the other fellows leave. It was something like shelves, or built in storage, which seemed very stupid, since they would only be there a few more weeks. Anyway, after two years of sloping around in the mud, dodging bullets, shells, bombs, and bayonets, it must not have appealed to Ted's imagination.

Ted has no recollection, and indeed, never had, an hour after the incident, of the slightest bit of anger, bitterness, or any thought whatsoever of what he was doing. The first recollection he had was of his carbine coming off his shoulder, and being leveled at the Chief. The next thing he recalls is the Chief begging him not to shoot, and telling him, "It is all right, we don't need to do that job anyway." Now the Chief was pleading for his life, (in retrospect, Ted believed he was probably pleading more for Ted's life than for his own) but Ted wasn't really hearing anything he said. By this period, a life meant almost nothing to him.

Before anything further happened one of the other Corpsmen, Cooley, returned and talked Ted into leaving the place. He said, as they left, that as he turned to go, he had seen something in Ted's eyes. Something that worried him, and he thought he better come back and check on him before he got into trouble.

Ted would always be glad he noticed whatever it was in his eyes that had tipped him off, and that he came back: for he had no doubt what so ever, that Chief VanHorn, his friend, would have died that day, for no reason at all.

As an example of the comradeship they enjoyed; this incident was never mentioned again by either VanHorn or any one of the other fellows and they remained friends to the very last.

Chief VanHorn, or Van, as he was commonly called, continued to talk to Chuck and Ted about staying over, and they continued to indicate that this was what they were going to do. Van had a good camera and spent a goodly portion of his income on film and processing. He promised Chuck and Ted that while they were in China he would get duplicates of all of his Great War pictures for them, and they were looking forward to getting them.

Promises are one thing, but reality is something different all together. During the last few weeks on Okinawa things were cooling down somewhat, and they found some extra time for things besides work. Each day one of the Corpsmen would go with the mail detail to headquarters, to check on their mail. A round trip of some sixty to eighty miles and that usually took all of a long day. In reality, they were trying to see if their orders to go home had arrived, for they had heard their replacements were on the way, day after long day, one of them made this trip to no avail.

It was about this time that they got word of the first Atomic Bomb being dropped on Japan, but they knew very little of its devastation. Rumors were always rampant, and the fact that this was going to end the war wasn't considered very seriously. All who had fought the Japs throughout the Pacific had no doubt it would be necessary to kill every last man, woman and child in Japan itself, before the war was over.

August 7, 1945

Ted never remembered the day of the week, but he would never forget the event. He had made the long hard mail run that day, and they got home (back to camp) just at dusk. The first words Ted heard as they pulled into camp were, "Ted, get your things together, we have just twenty minutes to catch the truck, that will take us to the ship to start home."

He could very well have given them back nineteen of those minutes, for even though their sea bags and personal item had been brought up, he had nothing what so ever on Okinawa that would delay his departure by one second, much less twenty minutes.

He grabbed his combat pack, (which was ever packed and handy) and his sea bag, and threw them aboard the truck. His Rifle, the most valuable piece of equipment a Marine ever owned, his blankets, and much personal gear were left where they lay. He was through with "war" forever.

They made such a hasty exit that Ted remembered only one "good bye." A great big Marine was lying on his cot crying like a baby. He said, "I have seen them come, and I see them go, but I am still here." The Corpsmen were replaced about every two years, but the Marines were still on a three-year rotation basis.

They got aboard the truck and it took them to a beach area, where they were to board ship the next morning. It seemed that all night long they were under air attack from the Jap planes. Seven raids, if memory served Ted right, and they had no shelters or holes to crawl into. Tracers flew around like the Fourth of July fire works, and shrapnel from the big guns fell like rain. Had they came this far only to die "going home?" Ted and two or three others finally found a culvert to huddle under. They spent the rest of the night there, lying in the mud, a fitting end to Okinawa.

August 8, 1945 Boarded the USS Bracken

Ted never remembered how he got aboard ship. The ships seemed to hardly move in the water. The L.S.T.s in the convoy could only travel from five to eight knots (a knot is slightly over a mile) per hour, and they hardly left a wake as they bob along on the water. They had been aboard almost a week when the ship pulled into the harbor at Saipan.

1200 August 14, 1945 Arrived Saipan
August 15,1945 V.J. Day

While sitting in this harbor they heard ship's guns being fired and whistles blowing. They were told that the war was over. They were let go ashore for a party and given two cans of beer per person, and Ted couldn't stand beer.

The next day they took the ship to haul occupation troops to Japan. Ted was left stranded on Saipan.

They had no more than got ashore when Ted came down with the worst case of malaria he had ever taken. All the fellows wanted him to check into the hospital, but he was afraid he would miss a ship for home and refused to do so.

The very first day on Saipan they had a very rude awakening. They were not war heroes, or veteran Marines. They were now back in the Navy, and not in the Marines. Whereas, in the Marines, the Corpsmen were treated as "Little Gods," and were never expected to do any physical labor, the Navy had no respect for they're rank or rate. Ratings come fast and easy in the Navy. But in the Marine Corps, a rating was earned the hard way, years of service, a lot of devotion to duty, and an occasional battlefield promotion for outstanding leadership or heroism. In the Marines the Privates and the Privates First Class did the work. A Corporal was in charge of work parties, and from Sergeant on up, one only gave orders or passed them on from higher up.

Since all of the Corpsmen were equal to, or above the rank of Sergeant, it was frowned upon when they would attempt to help with labor tasks. They were let know that "ranking people" just didn't do such things.

Quite often it was a little embarrassing. Though there was very little good to be had in the Pacific, the Corpsmen got theirs first and usually got the best of what ever there was to be had.

It was no wonder the Corpsmen learned to love and respect the Marines, for they were always good to them. Of course, the Corpsmen did their best to take care of their own Companies, and would crawl out of a foxhole, or off a cot to get a pain pill, or other medication for them when they really needed it.

There was a saying, "The Marines do the fighting, the Navy gets the pay, and the Army gets the credit."

The first day in the transient center on Saipan they were loaded in open trucks that hauled them out to some kind of a lumberyard, to stack lumber in a pouring rain. Of course, Ted could hardly remember a day in the South Pacific when it wasn't raining. The fellows tried covering Ted with Ponchos because he was sick and shivering with the Malaria shakes so bad. They finally stacked lumber over a small opening and made him crawl inside where it was somewhat drier than out in the downpour. They took off their shirts and most everything removable to wrap him in, and they worked in the nude, which wasn't really that, unusual. One or the other would take turns ducking in to see how he was, and someone was almost constantly by his side. If anyone in charge at the base had of found out about his condition he would have been sent to a hospital immediately.

Needless to say, "working" didn't appeal to any of the fellows, and they made almost a total disaster of that lumberyard, always "accidental," of course.

The next day they took them to the Officers Club to unload whiskey. The fellows took out a few cartons of whiskey and made Ted a snug little cave inside, then stacked the cartons back on top.

Needless to say, this detail was under very close observation, but it was only minutes before there were open bottles, and every time a person came by they would grab a swig. Most of the "Men" were not old enough to legally drink, even after two years overseas. There had been only a very rare can of beer in all that time, so it only took a couple of sniffs of the cork, and everyone was drunker than a skunk.

First they started dropping the cartons from the top of the stack to the cement floor. Then a big mock fight broke out, with everyone hurling bottles against the walls and ceilings. In no time at all the place was a shambles and they were hustled back to camp, in no time at all.

The best part of this was that Ted got to spend the next few days in a dry bed, with blankets a foot thick piled on top of him, in the tropical heat. They never attempted to send this bunch out on another detail, for two wrecked places was enough, some of the guys still had their rifles and Ted is sure there would have been much spilled blood had the work parties continued. No rear echelon people were going to do such things to troops who had served in the combat zones. Their eyes would tell you so.

Ted was still managing to stand muster each morning, and was beginning to get over the malaria attack, since they had literally been stuffing quinine down him. Orders finally came to board a ship again, but the only thing Ted could remember was trying to get up the gangplank with his sea bag. It was a good thing they didn't have to go up cargo nets for some of them would never have made it.

0650 Aug. 31, 1945 Left Saipan aboard the USS Wharton

Ted left his sea bag on deck at the top of the gangway, and staggered down into a hold and fell on a bunk. Here he spent another week flat on his back. It was over a week before he remembered his sea bag and was able to go topside to check on it. Sure enough, or miraculously, it was still there, where someone had shoved it back out of the way.

Most of the fellows had been bringing Ted food and making him eat. He started gaining some strength back and was able to make it to the head, and to the mess hall for the two meals a day that were served.

It was astonishing what a shave, a saltwater shower, and clean clothes can do for a person, after three or four weeks without either one. Ted's recovery was fast, even if the ship taking them home wasn't.

1030 Sept 15, 1945 Arrived San Pedro, Ca. USA

They pulled into the San Pedro, (Los Angeles) harbor on a Friday or Saturday afternoon. There was no welcoming flags or sheets waving from the windows. There was no welcoming band on the docks. No one wanted them ashore, for there would be lots of paperwork to process.

God Bless the skipper of the Wharton, for after several hours, tied up at the dock, he came on the ships P.A. and said. "You MEN have been gone too long, and have done too much for your country to be kept aboard ship until the first of the week. I am going to grant all of you weekend passes, as soon as we can get Out of Uniform Passes ready for you." The Out of Uniform Passes were necessary as none of the troops had anything but dungarees, and khakis, with no ties, dress shoes, or any of the usual clothes worn ashore.

It was almost night when Ted procured his pass and made his way out the front gate. He started to hitch hike down, or up, the Pacific Coast Highway. He had always been an excellent hitchhiker, or just plain lucky, he didn't know which, but during war-time, travelers weren't too plentiful. He got several short rides and finally ended up at Malibu.

He was stranded there for quite some time, and it was there that he became frightened of "going home." Was home still there? Were the folks still the same? Would they want him after the things he had did, and the lives he had taken. When one had left home a small boy of seventeen and returned a "hardened" veteran of the wars, a man, many things cross their frightened minds. It was surprising how many barricades one could build up in his mind.

From Malibu Ted got a ride up to Point Mugu, and again there seemed to be a long, long wait, before anyone came by.

There is no way that Ted could describe the emotions that flooded his soul. He cried, there in the dark that night, for the first time in his life, for no reason at all, and He is crying great tears now, as he tries to bring those memories back. How can one describe the joy, the fear, the pain, the trauma, of being whisked from the jaws of Hell. Back into a world they could hardly remember, and may be only a figment of their imagination, not real at all? It seemed so many lifetimes since Ted had seen this "make believe" world. Could it possibly be real? Would he be welcome?

An Old Fellow picked Ted up at Pt. Mugu, and they started across country towards Camarillo, and Saticoy. It is impossible for one who has not experienced it to know the thrill of settling down in a soft seat, and to feel the power and exhilaration when those cars started picking up speed. At fifteen, he gripped the seats, at twenty-five he wanted to bail out, at forty-five it was like the down hill side of a roller coaster ride. Having rode only trucks, and Jeeps, where it took hours slopping through the mud and muck to go a mile to going miles per hour. It was almost too much to bear after all that time.

The Old Fellow was very nice, and he wanted to talk to Ted. Ted has often, wondered if the Old Man had a son coming home, or, possibly, he had one that was not coming home, like so many others. But Ted only wanted to be alone, with the hurt, the fear. Wanted to be back in a sloppy wet dug out or fox hole, or on a lonely beach with mortars raining down death and destruction. To be back in a world he knew, and understood, with buddies who were closer than brothers. Fellows he had slept in foxholes with, who had shared their last drop of water with him. Ones he had stood by ship's rails with for endless hours, pouring out their very souls. Fellows he had laughed and joked with, who had shared the joys and the fears, the good and the bad.

320

The tension mounted as they neared Santa Paula. The Old Fellow wanted to know what part of town Ted wanted to go to. Ted told him to just drop him off up on Main Street. He insisted on taking Ted home, so Ted told him to let him off on the corner of twelfth and main streets. Again he insisted on taking Ted home. Maybe, he too had seen something in Ted's eyes. Something that said, in spite of all the love and devotion of the wonderful family Ted had; he was about to run away. That he was afraid of "going home."

"Come Ye Back A Hero, Or Come Ye Not Back Home." These words Ted had not thought of for centuries it seemed, now came to his mind. What was one to do when in the pit of their stomach was the memory of the Coward? The deep dark Pits of Hell were yawning wide, and the little red ball was beckoning Ted's Soul.

The Old Man turned down the street and just kept wanting to know which house Ted lived in, and Ted just kept saying, a little farther. At the corner of Harvard and Riverside Drive Ted told The Old Man to let him out, that he lived right over there, but he drove right on across, made a U turn, and parked in front of the house. Ted don't even remember if he even said "Thank You" but he knows the Old Man never left until after he was inside the house.

The thrill of those last few steps to the porch, Ted's hair stood on end and crawled up the back of his neck. Like the time a Jap had dropped down from a loft in front of him, and he had been so scared he had wet his pants, without even knowing it.

He knocked on the door, why, he didn't know, for it was never locked. His sister Vera answered the knock, and Ted didn't even recognize her. He must have been expecting his Mom or Dad. His sis screamed out something like, "It's Ted, He's Home" and the welcome was on. Ted was sure the Old Fellow waiting in the car had received his just reward.

Such a welcome you could never dream, and the fears melted away like hot butter. "Returned was the conquering Hero." "Not the Coward," and as human nature dictates, it was necessary to play the part. (The small boy, waiting for two strong arms to clasp him to a soft warm breast, and say, "It's all right, nothing can ever hurt you again" would never again be able to surface.)

They came back changed men

Oh the joy, the elation, as everyone welcomed Ted as one returned from the dead. Everyone wanted to talk at once.

His brother Evert went to the theater to bring the kids who were not at home when he arrived, for no one had the faintest idea Ted was on his way home, or when he would arrive.

Ted was placed on a chair, or stool, in the kitchen, with everyone gathered around, trying to talk to him, or touch him. How wonderful to be with family, in a warm house, with chairs to sit on, and food placed on a table, after two years of sitting on coconut logs, and eating slop from a mess kit, in the rain.

His two younger brothers, Doran and Wayne and his little sister Wanda came in from the movies. How they had changed. Almost grown up now were the boys, and little sister was a real young lady.

Ted remembered many things about that night, but his most vivid memory was the smell of a woman or girl, the sweet, soft scent of powder, perfume, and cleanliness. After the years of smelling sweat, and blood, and death and destruction. His eyes never missed the slightest movement in the room, but darted from one person to the other, like something wild.

It was late that night when they retired, and Ted's anticipation of crawling between two clean white sheets quickly dampened. The bed, his bed, in his room, with his things, left exactly as he had left them, two years before, was so soft it seemed to swallow him. He was so uncomfortable he could not go to sleep, and started several times to crawl out and lay on the floor, which was more to what he was accustomed.

Sometime before morning he must have dozed off from pure exhaustion, for the next thing he remembered was sitting bolt upright, with a cold sweat popping out, fear, and he had no rifle. His darling mother, anxious to see if her baby was really home and all right, had gotten out of bed, and was trying to tiptoe up to Ted's door to take a peak in. At that time and for a long time thereafter, nobody, but nobody, could sneak up on him. They could walk up normal and nothing would happen. Ted supposed the Marines had nearly reverted to animals after the years in the jungles.

Ted was "BACK," but it would be some time, before he was "HOME."

CONCLUSION

Dakeshi, Sugar Loaf and Shuri ridges would break the Japs backbone, but there was still another ridge. In the final battle for Okinawa, at Kunishi Ridge, the First Marine Division had suffered more than One thousand one hundred and fifty casualties. They had twenty-seven tanks knocked out in this one battle alone.

General Bolivar Buckner, the Sixth Army Commander had been killed by a long-range artillery shell from the Japanese big guns. General Ushijimi, the Japs Commanding Officer, committed Hari Kiri in front of the Marines lines. The Army Brass moved in to accept the Japs surrender on Okinawa.

The First Marine Division was the first American troops to take the offensive against the Japanese, at Guadalcanal. They spent more days in combat than any other Division. They suffered more casualties than any other Division. They fought the final battle of the war. The Division received three Presidential Unit Citations. Should they not have been the one's to lead the way into Tokyo Bay, and march down the streets of Tokyo? If not the First, at least some of the Six Marine Divisions that spearheaded the drive to Japan itself should have been represented.

As usual, "The Glory Hog," McArthur, got the Honor of accepting the Japs surrender. The Army's First Cavalry Division led the Parade down Tokyo's streets.

The First Marine Division was shipped to the remote regions of China to patrol the railroads and streets of Tientsin and Peiping. Again, they drew the short straw, but as one old Sergeant proclaimed, "If the S.O.B.'s can dish it out, I guess I can take it." Of such were the "Men" of the First Marine Division.

Ted was proud to have served with such a distinguished outfit.

UNIT CITATIONS

THE SECRETARY OF THE NAVY
WASHINGTON
4 February 1943
Cited in the Name of
The President of the United States
THE FIRST MARINE DIVISION, REINFORCED
Under command of
Major General Alexander A. Vandegrift, U.S.M.C.

CITATION:

"The officers and enlisted men of the First Marine Division, Reinforced, on August 7 to 9, 1942, demonstrated outstanding gallantry and determination in successfully executing forced landing assaults against a number of strongly defended Japanese positions on Tulagi, Gavutu, Tanambogo, Florida and Guadalcanal, British Solomon Islands, completely routing all the enemy forces and seizing a most valuable base and airfield within the enemy zone of operations in the South Pacific Ocean. From the above period until 9 December, 1942, this Reinforced Division not only held their important strategic positions despite determined and repeated Japanese naval, air and land attacks, but by a series of offensive operations against strong enemy resistance drove the Japanese from the proximity of the airfield and inflicted great losses on them by land and air attacks. The courage and determination displayed in these operations were of an inspiring order."

For the President,
Frank Knox
Secretary of the Navy

THE SECRETARY OF THE NAVY
WASHINGTON
The President of the United States takes pleasure in presenting the
PRESIDENTIAL UNIT CITATION to the
FIRST MARINE DIVISION (REINFORCED)

Consisting of FIRST Marine Division; First Amphibian Tractor Battalion, FMF; U. S. Navy Flame Thrower Unit Attached; Sixth Amphibian Tractor Battalion (Provisional), FMF; Third Armored Amphibian Battalion (Provisional), FMF; Detachment Eighth Amphibian Tractor Battalion, FMF; 454th Amphibian Truck Company, U. S. Army; Fourth Joint Assault Signal Company, FMF; Fifth Separate Wire Platoon, FMF; Sixth Separate Wire Platoon, FMF,

for service as set forth in the following

CITATION:
"For extraordinary heroism in action against enemy Japanese forces at Peleliu and Ngesebus from September 15 to 29, 1944. Landing over a treacherous coral reef against hostile mortar and artillery fire, the FIRST Marine Division, Reinforced, seized a narrow, heavily mined beachhead and advanced foot by foot in the face of relentless enfilade fire through rainforests and mangrove swamps toward the air strip, the key to the enemy defenses of the southern Palaus. Opposed all the way by thoroughly disciplined, veteran Japanese troops heavily entrenched in caves and in reinforced concrete pillboxes which honeycombed the high ground throughout the island, the officers and men of the Division fought with undiminished spirit and courage despite heavy losses, exhausting heat and difficult terrain, seizing and holding a highly strategic air and land base for future operations in the Western Pacific. By their individual acts of heroism, their aggressiveness and their fortitude, the men of the FIRST Marine Division, Reinforced, upheld the highest traditions of the United States Naval Service."

For the President
Frank Knox
Secretary of the Navy

THE SECRETARY OF THE NAVY
WASHINGTON
The President of the United States takes pleasure in presenting the
PRESIDENTIAL UNIT CITATION to the
FIRST MARINE DIVISION, REINFORCED

consisting of: The FIRST Marine Division; Fourth Marine War Dog Platoon; Fourth Provisional Rocket Detachment; Fourth joint Assault Signal Company; Third Amphibian Truck Company; Third Provisional Armored Amphibian Battalion; First Amphibian Tractor Battalion; Eighth Amphibian Tractor Battalion; Detachment, First Platoon, First Bomb Disposal Company; Second Platoon, First Bomb Disposal Company (less First Section); Battery "B," 88th Independent Chemical Mortar Battalion, U. S. Army; Company "B" (less First Platoon), 713th Armored Flame Thrower Battalion, U S. Army,

for service as set forth in the following

CITATION:

"For extraordinary heroism in action against enemy Japanese forces during the invasion and capture of Okinawa Shima, Ryukyu Islands, from April 1 to June 21, 1945. Securing its assigned area in the north of Okinawa by a series of lightning advances against stiffening resistance, the FIRST Marine Division, Reinforced, turned southward to drive steadily forward through a formidable system of natural and man-made defenses protecting the main enemy bastion at Shuri Castle. Laying bitter siege to the enemy until the defending garrison was reduced and the elaborate fortifications at Shuri destroyed, these intrepid Marines continued to wage fierce battle as they advanced relentlessly, cutting off the Japanese on Oroku Peninsula and smashing through a series of heavily fortified, mutually supporting ridges extending to the southernmost tip of the island to split the remaining hostile force into two pockets where they annihilated and trapped the savagely resisting enemy. By their valor and tenacity, the officers and men of the FIRST Marine Division, Reinforced, contributed materially to the conquest of Okinawa, and their gallantry in overcoming a fanatic enemy in the face of extraordinary danger and difficulty adds new luster to Marine Corps History and to the traditions of the United States Naval Services."

For the President,
John L. Sullivan
Secretary of the Navy

THE SECRETARY OF THE NAVY
WASHINGTON

June 22, 1946

My Dear Mr. Alexander:

I have addressed this letter to reach you after all the formalities of your separation from active service are completed. I have done so because, without formality but as clearly as I know how to say it, I want the Navy's pride in you, which it is my privilege to express, to reach into your civil life and to remain with you always.

You have served in the greatest Navy in the world.

It crushed two enemy fleets at once, receiving their surrenders only four months apart.

It brought our land-based air power within bombing range of the enemy, and set our ground armies on the beachheads of final victory.

It performed the multitude of tasks necessary to support these military operations.

No other Navy at any time has done so much. For your part in these achievements you deserve to be proud as long as you live. The Nation which you served at a time of crisis will remember you with gratitude.

The best wishes of the Navy go with you into civilian life. Good luck.

Sincerely yours,
James Forrestal

Mr. Ted Alexander
317 Riverside Dr.
Santa Paula, California

POSTLUDE

I have heard it said many, many times that time heals all things and I know to a certain degree that this is true. I also know that no matter how much time elapses, there are some things that will not heal. The memory may dim, the events may not come to mind quite so often; but the old festering wounds that are rooted in ones soul just keep on festering. When one least expects it, they will break out onto the surface of memory, and there is not one thing he can do about it.

How many times have I been told, and have heard some "commentator" proclaim, "The war is over, it is time to forget about it, and get on with life." Well, to a certain degree this is also true, but I have serious doubts that anyone saying these things has ever experienced "real war."

Like external wounds, internal wounds will heal in time and like external wounds, internal wounds will also leave scars. Scars that no amount of surgery or cosmetics can erase. They can be covered up and glossed over but they will never be erased from the minds of the ones experiencing them. These scars will more or less alter ones life from now to eternity.

There is no possible way to measure the amount of grief suffered by anyone in time of war? We count only the dead and the wounded or missing, but for every one of these there is probably hundreds or thousands that are "wounded" without visible scars to show for it. How would you measure the grief of a mother who had lost her every child, or the grief of children who have lost their parents? There is no way to measure the grief of those going through life maimed and suffering the loss of sight or limbs. There is no way to measure the pain and grief suffered by young wives, and the children of those who have been through the rigors of war, and have survived with "the wounds that don't show."

I know not where or how to produce this episode about a young man who experienced some very minor events in his life during World War Two. As with most events in life, one wants others to know a little of what it was like, but they don't want sympathy, they only want understanding. My great desire would not be that anyone knows of Ted's experiences. But that they might have an understanding and appreciate the great sacrifices that have been, and will be made. By the myriad's of persons from time immortal, to time everlasting, that they might have the freedom with which we are blessed today.

THE WOUNDS THAT DON'T SHOW

It is a lovely soft warm day, and there is not a care in the whole wide world. One is at peace with themselves, and every thing around them, when from out of no where comes the swish, swish, swish of mortar shells, coming in. It is hard to keep the wave of panic down.

The sound of an airplane diving can still make one want to dive for cover, even more than fifty years after the events.

Something wakes you in the night, and the cold sweat pops out all over. Was it the thump of a grenade, or possibly the imperceptible sound of a Jap footfall? From where did it come?

It is a gay party and everyone, including ones self, is having a grand time when the high pitched, shrieking voices proclaim; "Amellicans you die, Amellicans you die, Amellicans you die." The gaiety of the party is gone forever.

How many, many nights does one awake with the picture of the little kids, wounded and shivering, stamped on their minds. Sleep will not come while such images remain, and some nights they remain long, and one wakes weary in the mornings.

Have you ever awoke in the night and seen an old man clutching his chest where he has been shot, or felt the red hot entrails of an enemy entwine your feet, or seen the fear on the faces of civilians trying to save themselves, and their families from death? Have you ever seen the anguish on the face of a mother that has just hurled her child over a cliff to be dashed on the rocks below? In the night the call of Mama, Mama, Mama, from a blind youth, will shatter ones tranquillity.

As one stands naked before a mirror, the tiny remnants of a bayonet scar in the chest will draw the eyes to the hands, to see if they are still red.

The whiff of anything dead and decaying can bring back such vivid memories of the battlefields, the sight's of bloated bodies wriggling and squirming from the maggots within.

There is a taste of fear, for fear does have a distinct taste. It may come at any time, day or night, and there is no mistaking it. It will overwhelm all else and make a place for itself within your very being.

Hundreds and thousands of wounded and dead, happy and amusing thoughts of friends, and of times gone by, of stinking wet jungles and of burning hot sand, and of Kim Li.

"Forget it," the Man said, "the war is over." For whom?

Kim Li, Li Kim, Where are you tonight. Come guide my weary troubled soul to light.

Semper Fi Until I Die

The End

POST SCRIPT

PELELIU – 56 YEARS LATER
July 20, 2001

A very dear acquaintance, Don Brizzolara recently returned from a trip to Peleliu. He kindly sent me a bottle of sand in which I see a tiny drop of blood remaining (even though I know it is only a speck of red coral)from Beach White 1, and many picturesof which I include three.

Don states that the jungles have completely re-claimed the whole island. They had to hack their way through much of it with machetties.

It looks so peaceful now, but hundreds of Marines gave their lives on this beach, "The Point" - there are still machine guns in the rocksemplacements. Ordinance and signs of battle abound, wrecked amtracs, tanks and other equipment.

Giant trees cover the island and conceal the caves. There is bones and
Jap skeletons everywhere throughout the jungles and caves. There is
still un-exploded ammunition - American and Japanese laying
around. Untold numbers of Jap hand grenades litter the area. The
Japanese "Boat Guns" are still in place-rusting. Old forties Coke
bottles litter Beach White and Saki bottles litter the cave floors.

The jungle overgrown island looks almost level. The supersticious Natives will not visit the inland and because of the inhumane treatment will not let the Japanese recover their dead.

ABOUT THE AUTHOR

ISLANDS OF DEATH — ISLANDS OF VICTORY is a true-life account of military life by John W. Bailey Jr. as depicted through his character Ted Alexander.

John is a 76 year-old World War II veteran, who spent four years in the United States Navy (two and a half of them with the Marines).

He was attached to the 1st Marine Division as a Navy Hospital Corpsman and saw action with the Marine's while fighting the Japanese on New Guinea, New Britain, Peleliu and Okinawa.

His novel is based primarily on personal knowledge, recollection and experience. As far as he knows, it is the only work that gives the story of troops "in" and "out" of action. It deals mostly with seventeen and eighteen-year-olds who thought war would be a "great adventure". Instead, the war turned out to be a "never-ending nightmare" —a struggle for survival.

The tenacious Japanese took a tremendous toll; but; so did the incessant rain, mud, sweltering heat, and jungle diseases (such as typhus fever, malaria, dysentery and jungle rot.)

There was elation and there was boredom as the emaciated, exhausted men recovered from combat and prepared for the next invasion. Mail call, sick call, rats and land crabs all played a major roll in the daily life of troops.

John, like most veterans, feels frustration when trying to tell younger generations of his desperate battle plights in parts of the world they never heard of. It seems absolutely no one, who was not directly involved, has any knowledge of, or knows the names of the islands invaded in the South Pacific during World War II. Mention an island, and their first question is, "Where is that?" Not one history book gives a hint of the fierce battles fought and the hundreds of thousands of lives lost in the Pacific war with the Japanese.

Being only seventeen when he volunteered for service, John's formal education was put on hold. His high school education was garnered at Santa Paula Union High, Santa Paula, California. After the war, he attended Ventura College, in Ventura, California. However, most of his knowledge came from the "University of Hard Knocks!" Growing up during the depression years, John, (like many others) accepted whatever fate brought his way.

Mr. Bailey, along with his wife Naomi, owned and managed their own business for many years in Ventura. They were able to retire earlier than most. He has spent a great deal of time and effort completing his book:

ISLANDS OF DEATH — ISLANDS OF VICTORY.

It is with mixed emotions, after almost fifty-five years in the making, his manuscript has been published.

John and Naomi travel widely but most of all, they enjoy camping, fishing, hiking and skiing with their family. They have four children, (two daughters and two sons) four grandchildren and seven great grandchildren.

He has always had a passion for writing, and, as a youth, he would dream complete "western novels" while sleeping. Although this is his first full-length novel, John has written extensively in several genres, and is a long-time member of the *Ventura County Writers Club*.

The author was compelled to complete his work...desiring to leave a written account of his life during World War II for his family, fellow veterans and future generations.

Message from the author: "I sincerely hope this narrative will give readers a deeper knowledge and appreciation for the men and women who fought and served in the South Pacific during World War II. It is a book about real people, life and love—not just a factual account of military statistics and battles."

Semper Fi Until I Die!!!